RETRO-

KM

LORD OF THE LANDLORDS

- TO PRAISE A MILLION TIMES -

First and foremost I must give praise to the creator of all things; the great consciousness that goes by as many names as there are things in existence.

- DEDICATED TO -

I give this book to the world by way of my mother, Marie Randle, and my father, Edward H. Uzzle. To my three sisters, Brenda, Dovie, and Pamela, I have nothing but love and respect. To my four nephews: Roger, Chaud, David, and Gyasi, I send love and protection. To my three nieces, Adrienne, Antoinette, and Vanessa, I send a double portion of love and protection. And to my Great nieces; whom shall remain hidden, I send a triple dose of love and protection. To my Brothers and Sisters in arms, I say htp (peace). You know who you are. And naturally, to my beautiful wife Tonya Uzzle, and our three reflections, Anthony, Ari, and Asa, without your patience and support, I would not have been able to finish this book.

RETRO-

KM

LORD OF THE LANDLORDS

A Novel By

Edward Uzzle

Daathrekh Publishing
P.O. Box 292685
Sacramento, CA 95829

Copyright © 1997 by Edward Uzzle
For more cifer-Ra (High-Science-Entertainment) visit: www.daathrekh.com
ISBN 13: 978-0-9664568-4-4
ISBN 10: 0-966568-4-X
Cover design Edward Uzzle

Printed in the U.S.A

"Behold, something new. Daathrekh Publishing. The birthplace of cifer-RA. What is cifer-RA do you ask? It is a style or genre of fiction, that is speculative, African Centered, and Metaphysical in scope, as it relates to the idea of harmony or disharmony, between the biological, technological, and spiritual. It comes from that space where the subjective realm meets the phenomenal plain. It is cosmology, spun in a new way, striving for a new day. Conscious and thought provoking, Daathrekh Publishing is dedicated to bringing you *High-Science-Entertainment.*"

Edward Uzzle, author

CHAPTER 1

This is the worst time for a reconnaissance action. Aten (the sun) won't be up for an hour, and we've been 'tracking' all night. I guess I shouldn't worry though. I've got four of the best Warrior-Soldiers with me on this assignment. N'krumah and Tefnut shadow my right. Shu and Anpu cover my left. I'm on point as usual; delta formation. This place was once a thriving Metropolis. Now it's a Wasted City. Wasted Cities are abandoned urban centers that surround Nation States. They had to be abandoned. What with the Great Ethnic Clashes of 2013, the cities were the last place you wanted to live.

"Our intelligence reported the presence of Cold Wind activity in this vicinity. And the only reason Cold Wind would be in a place like this is for looting. And looting usually means slaves," Tefnut relayed calmly.

"We know, we know," Shu responded sarcastically. "Slaves are used by the racist government of Valhalla to scavenge the Wasted Cities. They are the descendants of brothers and sisters who refused to abandon their homes, and were captured by the enemy before the Relocation Act of 2017. How often do you have to remind us, Tefnut?"

"As many times as it takes, dumbass."

Our hearts racing, our weapons poised at the ready; we stealthily penetrated deeper into the Wasted City. Its horribly misshapen buildings mocked us. Huge scorched slabs of concrete lay everywhere. I couldn't image anyone wanting to live here, even when it was at its best.

"Kashta!"

"What?"

"About 20 het-meters ahead, Cold Wi- "

We had been made. They hit hard and fast. We scattered like black mist. In the blink of an eye, we had lost our edge.

"Over there! " We heard them shout.

"It's as if they knew we were coming," Anpu blurted between breaths.

Scrambling, we dipped behind a row of burned-out cars. Fat lot of good that did us. Their lasers easily penetrated the rusted steel.

"All right, people! On my mark, we exit this scenario." Scanning the immediate perimeter, I noticed a large grayish building several het-meters east of our location. "Move!" I shouted.

We made a mad dash towards the lonely complex. It's once dark and menacing windows now looked more like temple doors. Cold Wind. They were brutal and unrelenting. They are the special-ops military of Valhalla. They fell upon us like a winter storm. There were no words between us. Only centuries of combat. Then, in a dazzling display of precision guided hate, two of my best operatives were struck down.

"Kashta! They got N'krumah... and Shu-"

"I know, Tefnut... lets keep the same thing from happening to us!"

I've fought this war for a long time. I've seen a lot of people die. Over the years, I've learned to put the grieving process on hold.

"Damn it! It's locked!" Anpu bellowed.

"Then make a door... just get us inside!" I snapped back.

Without looking up, Anpu twisted then pressed the plastic spheres on his Ra-Canon. A slight humming sound began to emit from the powerful gun. "Stand back," he said, lifting his weapon.

Showing no hesitation, he aimed, then fired upon the thick rings. They hung from a series of small metal locks that secured two large steel-framed doors. Seconds later, the rings, the locks, and all its steel casings were reduced to a runny stream of liquid ore. Moving in unison, we kicked the heavy doors open and rushed inside.

Frantically, Anpu and I pushed the large doors closed.

"Lock it," I said pointing.

"No problem, Kashta." In a clap of light and energy, he welded the steel support structures in the center of each door.

Cautiously, we crept into the interior of the structure. The sound of cracking tile beneath our feet echoed throughout its seemingly empty chambers. I needed air. Real air. I lifted my right hand and made a fist. Tefnut and Anpu acknowledged my actions then did the same. We squeezed our palms. This caused the leather-like texture of our daath-Geb system to soften. The scaly ridges that covered our face-plates began to fold outward. Warm damp air rushed our nostrils. Forcing my fingers underneath the blue-black scales that hugged and protected my face, I lifted and pulled its reptilian visage up and over my head. It made a rubbery flapping sound when it snapped against the back of my neck.

Without the aid of our audio-dampers, the sounds came crashing in on us. As usual, Tefnut was first to speak.

"Okay, heroes, we're being rocked! So what's the plan?"

The sound of Cold Wind vehicles and the static noise from their communications equipment pierced the sagging walls of our crumbling sanctuary.

My eyes slowly adjusted to the dim. Mold spores and dust assaulted the senses. Despite my coughs and runny eyes, the interior of the building shimmered into focus. A large office... a long hallway, and a series of rooms. Next to a pile of overturned filling cabinets stood a wide fiberglass staircase. Its shiny steps ascended into darkness.

"Now what?" Tefnut asked nervously.

"We do what we always do," I answered stoically. "We live. Anpu, cover the second floor. Tefnut, snag us a sky-hopper. It's time we went home."

Anpu cautiously ascended the stairway. His daath-Geb boots glided silently across the rubber mats that lay across each step. Tefnut quickly adjusted the frequency of her wave-jumper, then reattached it to the small housing bays on her neck. Pressing both dark grayish buttons on either side, she began signaling for a pickup.

I began securing the first floor of the building. Instinctively, I began transmitting across our wave-jumpers, "Most of the rooms appear to be medical examination suites. A closet or storage bin faces the entrance of each door." *Strange.*

Cold Wind continued to pummel the entire complex. The structure was holding, but for how long?

I stumbled across an old-style computer in one of the examination suites. Several disks lay around the crusty machine.

"Tefnut, did you make contact?"

"Yes. I've got a hopper with an e.t.a. of six minutes."

"Good. Now come over here and see whether you can access this ter-"

It felt like an earthquake. The disks that sat on and around the CPU fell to the mossy floor.

"Kashta... Tefnut. Get up here!"

Grabbing as many disks as we could, we turned and raced up stairs. We found Anpu squatting next to a single large window. Its outer edges were scorched with ash and heat burns.

"What's up, are you hurt?" Tefnut asked.

"Not hardly. Look over there. Those file cabinets, computers, storage bins. Didn't you notice anything odd about the first floor?"

"Just get to the point!"

Smiling, Anpu pointed to the single window. "There's only one window in the entire building. None on the first floor. This is a Zero-Complex."

Zero Complexes were located all over the continental United States. They were found mostly in the Inner Cities. They were research facilities used by Project Harmony in the late 20th century. Their doctors of death routinely experimented on the surrounding populations.

"Okay, thanks for the news flash. Now who were you engaging?" I asked.

"Look over there," he said pointing. "We've got a heavy stream of Cold Wind soldiers pressing in on us. I'd say about fifty."

"This is bigger than any Aft-Patrol I've seen," Tefnut added. "Aft-Patrols usually group-up in units of twenty five. They specialize in capturing escaped slaves. Normally, they wouldn't deploy this many soldiers. This is something else?"

"Let's earn our money then, K'huti. We get airborne, rig a screen, and, if there are slaves in the vicinity, let's find 'em and take 'em home."

The orange flash came first, followed by a deafening thunder clap. We were blown clear across the room. The small rectangular window was now a gaping hole. The damage was extensive. The loud moans of failing support beams signaled the near end of a building that should have died hundreds of years ago.

We jumped to our feet and retreated to the wall that lay adjacent to the room's entrance. I thanked Amen-Ra that none of us were hurt. Pulling our face-plates up and over our heads, we squeezed our palms. The soft leather of our face-plates hardened into organic steel. We didn't have long to ponder our situation.

"They're trying to burn us out!" Anpu shouted.

Another explosion. This time the reinforced metal beams which until moments ago protected us, gave way to the continued onslaught. Everything started moving in slow motion. Pillows of black smoke drifted past the craggy hole that once sat as a window. Orange and yellow flames began to creep up the disintegrating stairway behind us.

"What's the e.t.a. on that sky-hopper?!"

"About another minute, Kashta," persists Tefnut. She was bent over, stuffing her side pouch full of floppies.

"That's not good enough!"

"We have you surrounded," a raspy voice bellowed from below. I stood in the direction of the smoke. Hidden behind it's noxious clouds, I watched several Cold Wind soldiers standing next to an attack-jeep. One of them had a long blond pony tail. He stood a little further ahead than the others. He held his *barker* close to his mouth and spoke again.

"Come out of the building. We have you surrounded. Our people will be here in three minutes. You are in violation of the Third Intra-Continental Treaty."

"Kashta, over there!"

Tefnut was the first to spot them. Anpu and I opened up on them. Almost immediately, the entire second floor was bombarded with plasma fire. Huge crimson streaks of super heated air smashed through and liquefied entire sections of the floor.

Anpu and Tefnut were firing wildly at the Cold Wind soldiers. We were running out of time. The heat from the greedy flames was becoming unbearable.

"Alright, people. I guess this is it. We live or die tonight," I shouted. Bathed in black, we stood our ground. For what seemed like an eternity, we engaged the enemy. The natural adaptability of our daath-Geb strained to keep pace with our ever shifting backdrop. We were winning the battle, but the war was still in doubt. Flames tickled at the lower edge of the damaged wall.

"Where's that sky-hopper!" I demanded.

"Never mind that, Kashta, I've found a way out!" Anpu shouted.

The building began burning and collapsing on top of us.

"Arraah!" Shouting and foaming at the mouth, two Cold Wind soldiers angrily rushed us. They appeared out of the smoke like ghosts, their swords unsheathed.

Anpu engaged a giant of a man. His red hair hung like limp flames. A large black Swastika laser-printed on his forehead. All K'huti soldiers are required by Ta-Amentan law to master the fighting science, 'N-gala'. Anpu took his opponent apart in a matter of seconds.

"Tefnut, where are you?" The smoke from the fire turned the air into a thick gray-green soup, and the heat from its flames began to interfere with the infrared augmentation granted by our daath-Geb peepers.

"Over here, Kashta! Look out... behind you, they're coming..."

Our wave-jumpers were useless. The smoke was too thick; it was nearly impossible to see. I had to rely on my senses. I craned and turned my head towards the sound of Tefnut's outcry. That's when I felt it. A sudden and sharp pain pricked its way up my side.

"That's right, boy. Come get some of this," he snarled. "I'm gonna carve yo black ass up like a holiday sewer hog!" He swung his sword wildly. I ducked and gave him the hardest right-hook I had. He coughed and slobbered. I pressed the attack.

"You should have killed me when you had the chance, Satan." I taunted. I was hurt, my back and side felt as though they had been set on fire.

"What ever you say, nigger," he snapped. He ran towards me with his sword raised. It's gleaming steel sparkled in the smoke.

"Humph, Humph." The air escaped my lungs as I spun and executed two swift spin kicks to his head and neck. He dropped like a sack of rocks. Anpu glanced at me with that, *'you're letting your feelings cloud your judgment look'*. He was right.

"K'huti... to... west... flyer-3...."

"We've been Lost-Found," Anpu sang. He then raised his Racanon and pointed at the wall. In two quick bursts of light, he blew a second hole through the dusty enclosure, then jumped out. Tefnut followed. No time to think. I hurled myself from the fading structure. I landed hard. There was smoke everywhere. My side hurt, yet I beheld an angel.

Whoever was flying that sky-hopper was one hell of a pilot. Engines roaring, lights flashing, it swung in midair. Like a darkly clad neter (angel), it raced towards us. We stood transfixed as it's sleek cylindrical form skimmed past the ragged rooftops.

The pilot's voice boomed across our wave-jumpers. *"K'huti to Wes F-3. Do you read... K'huti to Wes F-3. Do you read?"*

"Affirm," I returned. "What took you so long?"

"You're in 'heavy ground' Pod Leader. What's your status?"

"Three up, two down."

"Affirm. There's a clearing between those buildings to your left. I think I can set her down there," the pilot returned.

Falling debris, sporadic fires, and the occasional hollowed explosion put a definite edge on things. With a new sense of hope, we pressed on. We moved through the gray silence. Smoke... if you've seen it as often as I have, you learn to appreciate its beauty. Within its ethereal embrace, one can find shelter, protection.

"What are we doing? We can't just leave. What if there are slaves here? We can't just leave them here; we have to do something. That's our job. We retrieve the Lost-Found," Tefnut demanded.

"Anpu, you and Tefnut keep going. I'm going to divert their attention. Once you're in the air, get that screen up."

"But..."

"That's an order, Tefnut."

With a slight slump of her shoulders, she raised her weapon and signaled Anpu to follow.

"You two need help," he said jokingly, shaking his head as he walked behind her.

In the distance, I could vaguely see the faint outline of the sky-hopper. It's light absorbing hull caused it to melt into the surrounding ruin.

Cold Wind was getting closer. I jumped over a wall of blocks that had been set in a jagged fence of cinder, then decided to circle back.

I lowered my head and dashed down an alley. It's narrowness nearly caused me to collide with a Cold Wind soldier who had remained behind to take a shit.

"What the..."

"...fuck," I finished. I kicked his Plasma rifle into an oily stream that bubbled from a half buried sewer pipe. Without missing a beat, I struck the surprised soldier in the head with the butt of my cobalt pistol.

He was a tough one. Pants down between his legs, he was still full of fight. He angrily squirmed to retrieve his weapon. I raised my cobalt and let go with a series of violent discharges. The sound of contained energy filled the alley. Chunks of flesh splattered against its crusty walls.

His comrades were enraged. "We see you, nigger! Just wait right there... pay back is a son-of-a-bitch!"

"I'm gonna get me a spook tonight!"

Five Cold Wind soldiers were ripping through the cracked streets in a combat-jeep. Its obscene rubber tires screeched and howled as it's maniacal driver spun the vehicle, then steered it towards me. *"Target in sight,"* he yelled into his walkie-talkie.

"Don't worry, nigger. We'll make this as painless as possible," the unusually large soldier who barely fit in the passenger seat barked.

I managed to slip between two immense husks of what were once fairly large office buildings. Several windows were broken, and piles of glass lay sparkling at each base. Grabbing hold of a thin metal sheet that extended from a housing inside the window seal, I pulled myself inside. Stumbling over several file cabinets, it took a moment before my optic peepers adjusted to the darkness. I pressed the two thin columns of fiber alloy that sat snugly within the housing bays around my neck... activating my wave-jumper.

"Wes F-3 to Pod Leader. Do you read?" I whispered, straining to hear a reply. Wes F-3, to Pod leader, do you-"

"Affirm, Kashta. We read you loud and clear."

I knew that voice.

"You'd better get the hell out of there. That mess you made back there has really got them pissed off!"

"Where the hell are you?"

"Not far," Anpu answered. *"After we lifted, we swooped past you and landed near the plaza. It's about-"*

"Never mind that," I interrupted. "I've been made." Cold Wind They were gathered on other side of the wall...

"Hold it!" One of them yelled. "Not yet!"

"What the hell are we waiting for? That bastard just killed Pete. I'm going in after his black ass!"

"I know what the fuck he did!" His partner barked. "But it's dark in there, and he's probably in there waiting for us."

"Then what the fuck are we gonna do?" A third soldier asked angrily.

"We'll pull the whole fucking thing!"

Frantically, I raced towards the rear of the building. That's when I heard a tremendous *Whomp*. It came from the roof.

"The sky-hopper?" I whispered.

I ran as fast as I could from the building. It was dark. The smoke was thick, but my daath-Geb had already begun to recalibrate it's outer texture to resemble the surrounding environment. I ducked behind a row of dumpsters that lay elephant-like in the middle of the street.

"Wes F-3, to Pod Leader, do you read?" Nothing. *Were they...*

"Kashta to Wes F-3... we read you loud and clear," I heard over my wave-jumper.

"What's your status?"

"We're fine, Kashta. They took a shot at us, but we can fly circles around their UAV's (urban assault vehicles)," Anpu returned.

He's probably right. All sky-hoppers, or NARS; their official name, are some of the most maneuverable aviation vehicles in the world. Their sleek elongated shapes make them ideal for close range urban combat. Triple twin micro-lifts allow for vertical takeoffs. They were designed after the ancient flying crafts sketched on the temple walls in KMT (Egypt). They were depicted as having been used by Heru in his epic battles against Set.

Still keeping an eye out for Cold Wind, I asked, "Did you get anything on screen? Do we have Lost-Found?"

"Affirm. Two buildings from where you're standing... we've got four Lost-Found."

CRRAASSH!

The explosions were getting closer. I had to brace myself up against two of the dumpsters just to keep my balance. "North, south, where do I go?"

"Go south... to that old liquor store with the snake sign on top of it... we'll meet you there."

KRAH-KRAKUM!

Huge pillows of gray-black ash billowed skyward. Towers of orange, white, and red flames engulfed what was left of most of the old buildings I was using as cover.

Cautiously, I approached the burned-out liquor store. It was a strange place. I couldn't understand why it was so popular among our people in the late 20th and early 21st centuries. Surely, it was a place of evil. Overlooking its dark interior hung a huge plastic serpent. Its bright yellow eyes watched me as I entered its lair. Broken glass, heaps of charred wood, and a thick coat of fungus coated the floor. Silvery spider webs blanketed the corners. *Strange,* I mused. I could still feel the hallowed chill of death.

There were no signs of life. Perhaps Anpu was wrong. Maybe... "Oh, here we go," I said aloud. In the rear of the cramped building, behind a tattered row of glass refrigerators, stood a narrow, wooden staircase. Its decaying steps reached up and disappeared into a dark attic. I raised my cobalt, setting its controls for stun. I walked about halfway up the creaky stairs.

"Hey, is anyone here...." I shouted rhetorically. "My name's Kashta. I've got exactly 30 seconds to evacuate this building. I think you; whoever you are, already know that. I think you've been watching what's been going on since it started." I waited. The sound of screeching vehicles, and the dance of artillery fire broke the silence. Cold Wind was getting closer. I was torn. *Do I stay.*

"We're here," a small voice cried out.

"All of you, meet me at the stairway immediately!" I demanded. Before I took another breath, four small bodies appeared at the top of the archway. They stood transfixed, staring, frozen in fear. "Come on!" I yelled. But they wouldn't move. "What's wrong?" I snapped. There were three boys and a little girl. Not one over 12 years old. They were the most beautiful thing I'd seen all day. "It's all right. You're safe now."

The little girl stepped forward. Her tiny fingers pointing," But... but... your face," she said in a raspy whisper.

I forgot about my daath-Geb. I must look like a scaly monster to them. I squeezed both palms. The dynamic matrix of my D-Gear began to soften. Ignoring the shouts from outside, I slid my fingers underneath my face plate, and pushed it's now flexible contour up and over my head and face. The air stank of heat and mold.

They stood wide-eyed and smiling. "Come on!" I shouted. This time they complied. I grabbed the smallest, a little boy about six, and raced down the noisy stairs with the others. "This way," I said pointing. In unison, we moved towards the rear of the store.

BA-THOOOM!

"They're practically on top of us. Move!" I shouted. Adjusting the weight of little boy who held unto my side, I kicked the back door open. "Wes F-3, to Pod Leader, do you read?" No response. "Wes F-3-"

"We read you, Kashta ... heavy ground."

"I've got them... do you have our location?" I interrupted.

"Affirm."

"We need a clearing. Fast!"

FARROSSH! A huge fireball burned and scorched the weeds and garbage behind the liquor store, turning it into a flat sticky 'runway'.

"How's that," sang from my wave-jumper.

"Beautiful," I replied sarcastically.

The sky-hopper landed in a cloud of silver-brown dust. The loud whine of its triple twin engines settled to a low hum. The sweet sound of astonishment escaped from the mouths of the four children. They'd probably never seen a NAR before. At least not this close. As we crept from the shadows, we watched as a vertical sliver of light, morphed into a rectangular door on the side of the shimmering fuselage.

Anpu was the first to emerge. "We've only got seconds, Kashta. We've spotted two; count them, two UAV's about six blocks south. This place is claimed."

"Go," I said, pushing the children ahead. They darted towards the NAR. Running up its small ramp, Tefnut greeted them with open arms and smiles. Anpu and I stood near the liquor store, our cobalts raised at the ready.

"Come on, people. They'll be here in seconds," the pilot shouted.

First Anpu, then I rushed inside the black steel walls of the NAR. On board, Tefnut was seated in the first row. It's shiny melcron-seats provided comfort as well as safety. The children were seated snuggly behind Tefnut. Their faces showed years of hard labor. Anpu joined the pilot. From what I could see, he was a short, brown-skinned man with a kinky mass of hair. The broadness of his body nearly blocked the aero-control panel from view. *Pure pilot*, I mused. No Warrior-Soldier could grow as fat as he.

An ergonomically correct, silver wall of lights and buttons practically grew out of the forward wall. Stopping in front of the pilot's triangular shaped chair, it curled back onto itself... looking like the back of a cobra's hood. Three thick black throttles sprout from the top of the aero-control panel. They govern the speed, direction, as well as the lift and descent of the NAR.

Gripping the two outer control sticks, the pilot pulled them towards his body. First, there was a dull hum. Then there was silence. Only the soft vibration of the NAR itself betrayed its movement.

"We've got two UAV's headed our way," Anpu lamented.

"Have you calculated their range?" I asked.

"Yes sir. Let's just say we won't be safe until we get home," the pilot answered.

He's a practical man.

"Brace yourselves," he said. He then pushed the center throttle forward. This caused the nose of the NAR to lift and point skyward. The vibrations ceased. Suddenly, in a flash of light and energy, we escaped the clutches of Ta-earth's gravity. I held my breath as we soared past the jagged skyline. Like twisted concrete birds, the craggy peaks of human folly danced past our windows. Fast changes. I watched the colorless backdrop of the Wasted City grow smaller... fading.

Tefnut had somehow gotten the children to relax. And, judging from our trajectory, we were speeding towards the Southern States.

"Thank you, sir," I heard Anpu say. "We've been cleared to enter Aztlan air space."

The pilot's name is Oshun. He's a good-natured brother, and very efficient. He's seen a lot of lifts and drops. Knowing that he's piloting us home, I began to relax.

Moving at incredible speeds, we effortlessly broke the soft barrier of soot-stained clouds that lay just north of Aztlan. Reaching high above the malay, we were greeted by the ever present rays of Aten (the sun). In a brilliant glow of golden sparks, it illuminated the entire left hull of the NAR. We sky-hopped for a full ten minutes before we reached the outskirts of Aztlan.

A series of alarms sounded off throughout the NAR.

"We have just entered Aztlan air space. We should be safer. There's no way Cold Wind would follow us here. We're heading home!" Oshun announced with a grin.

Having heard that, I leaned back in my chair and looked out the window. The gleaming towers of Aztlan were a welcomed sight. Aztlan is the homeland of Native and Mexican American descendants. They are strong and trusted allies... for the most part. Ignoring the wanting stares from the children, I got up and moved towards the rear of the sky-hopper. I needed privacy. Painfully, I pulled my daath-Geb from my tired body. Folding it gently, I placed it on the seat and plopped down on top of it. I was tired. I was sad.

"Are you okay, Kashta?" Tefnut asked.

I pretended not to hear her. I leaned back in my chair and closed my eyes. Breathing in rhythmic tones, images of N'krumah and Shu colored the darkness in my mind. It was time for the grieving process.

CHAPTER 2

Ta-Amenta. Homeland of the descendants of Blacks who elected to separate during the Relocation Act of 2017. An independent nation that spans the length of what used to be the southeastern United States. Our enemies refer to it as 'The Black Lands.' *Works for me.* Our civilization is a merger of 22nd Century Vudoun technologies, African Spiritual Cultivation systems, and a grafting of mundane cultural elements fashioned by our Mystic scientists. We've been accused of trying to recreate a dream.

Huge gleaming pyramids bedeck the southern landscapes. Giant bio-engineered buildings built from the wood of genetically altered trees, twist into cyclopean towers. Environmentally friendly homes and factories house both our population and our industry. Using homeopathic remedies, the life expectancy for the average Ta-Amentan is well over 110 years.

"Kashta... Kashta..."

It's Tefnut. She wakes me up every Monday morning by screaming and hollering... banging on my forward entrance without any regard for anyone else who lives in my village (apartment complex). Villages are large beautifully sculptured spherichles that house as many as fifty K'huti. We live off-base; each in our own cube, complete with all the amenities a young brotha needs. I pulled myself out of bed and quickly wrapped myself in my favorite gold and purple tunic. "What?" I answered, walking towards the entrance of my het (house).

"What's this?"

"You know, you really shouldn't touch things that don't belong to you."

We both laughed.

"I just came from Kawa hospital. The children we found last week are in good shape. There's no indication of gen-mental tampering."

"That's good. I hate when we find people who have been 'negroized' and transformed," I responded somberly.

"I do too. Remember when we found that group near the Canadian border," she asked rhetorically. "They were so tapped out. They begged us to let them stay. I mean, freedom scared them worse than being slaves."

Tefnut has always been a sensitive woman. Even now, she struggled to hold back the tears. She stood at the edge of my living quarters, staring out the main window that overlooked the village plaza. I couldn't help noticing how beautiful she was. Huge almond shaped eyes dominated her round face. Her full lips formed a kind of subtle yet perpetual smile. Her red-brown skin sparkled of gold under tones. Medium length locks draped her perfectly sculptured head, where a graceful neck led to a shapely athletic frame.

"We better get going, we're due at the Ka-Ba-Ra Chamber in an hour," she interjected.

"Let me catch a shower. I'll be ready in 20 minutes."

It was one of those bright blue-yellow days. Simply breathtaking. The air was crisp and tasty. Our air is continually recycled by huge Air-filters. Like immense conical shaped lungs, they both ionize and 'wash' the air for us.

VWOOSSH!

A Menmen raced past us. Menmens are very much like what used to be called trains. But, unlike trains, Menmens travel on pure sound.

"Come on, Kash, we're already running late." Tefnut said with her usual display of urgency.

I couldn't resist teasing her, "Lets not go and say we did."

"Kashta, Warrior-King Senwosret, has ordered that all K'huti agents be evaluated by their superiors, and-"

A sleek silver and blue Menmen silently stopped along side us. We boarded, finding empty seats near the rear of its rectangular interior. These vehicles are truly amazing. A system of collapsing metal-forks lay 13 feet below the surface of our streets. When the rays of the morning sun strike the surface of the ensemble of solar powered Monoliths in the south, vibrations surge towards a catch-plate in the center of Ta-Amenta. Sound is then conducted on 35 foot metal slabs that cover the city streets. This gives the Menmens their power of movement, as well as their incredible speeds.

I watched the other brothas and sistahs strutting up and down the walkways, boarding Menmens, and just conducting their day to day business. They were magnificent. The sun reflected upon their beautiful black, brown, red, and yellow faces. Their eyes were clear and alert. Independence has transformed our people.

"Kashta, what are you thinking about? You have that 'far away look' in your eyes."

"I was thinking about the beautiful culture we have created. You know, kind of saturating my spirit with the strides we've made since the old days."

"I know what you mean. I can't imagine what it must have been like 300 years ago," Tefnut said. She leaned back in her seat and closed her eyes.

I joined her. Menmens are a major source of transportation in our country. The N'tiu Tut (High Elders) wanted to make sure our people would not become isolated and antisocial. Menmens were created as a means for establishing a social bond.

"We're here," Tefnut said, perking up in her seat.

Waset. One of six Prime Cities in Ta-Amenta. Location of the Ka-Ba-Ra Chamber. An immense Intelligence facility, the Ka-Ba-Ra Chamber houses the principle Spiritual, Scientific, Engineering, Social, Military, and Agricultural agencies, used by the Mystic scientist of this region of Ta-Amenta. Every four months, the military commanders of the Mesniu, summon all members of the K'huti; the highly specialized division within the Mesniu, to the Ka-Ba-Ra Chamber. The K'huti division is responsible for the retrieval of all Lost-Found.

"Warrior-King Senwosret is going to attend," I mentioned with a slight sense of dread. "This must be a serious meeting."

"They're all serious, Kashta. I don't understand how the greatest Warrior-Soldier ever to have served in the Mesniu army can have such a 'laid back' attitude towards his work."

"It's not that I'm not serious about my work, Tefnut, but we can't allow our emotions to dictate our behavior. That wouldn't be the HERU thing to do."

"You're right, Kashta. But sometimes it seems that you don't have any emotions to ignore," Tefnut returned with a smirk.

Managing a phony look of concern, I looked at Tefnut and said, "Wait, hold up, somehow I don't think we're talking about work anymore."

"Yeah that's right, get evasive and pretend that you don't know what I'm talking about-"

"Kashta, Tefnut..."

Anpu. He's my best friend. We've seen a lot of action together. From the deserts of East Asia, to the jungle swamps of South America, we've fought side by side for the covert interests of Ta-Amenta. I wouldn't have it any other way. He's one of the baddest brothas on the planet. Black as midnight, tall as a mountain, all muscle, and definitely a genius. Wiping the sweat from his bald head, a slight smile streamed across his face.

"You need to talk to your friend," Tefnut said in passing, catching up with a group of female K'huti.

"That's a beautiful sister, Kashta. What's up with you two?"

"Well, right now we're pretty close. I consider her one of my closet friends," I returned.

"Ah, c'mon, Black man. This is me you talking to."

I started laughing; realizing how phony I must have sounded.

"That's your problem, Kashta: you're too tight. You're always on guard. You only let go when it's time to fight. It's alright to be vulnerable sometimes."

"You're right. It's just that I don't know if I can. I haven't worked out all of my hang-ups, and I just don't want to look stupid."

"Yeah ... I know what you mean. Until we complete the rest of our Spiritual Initiation, we're still slaves to our emotions ... our conditioning."

The walk-way leading from the Menmen dock to the Ka-Ba-Ra Chamber, is a soft mosaic of concrete littered with golden specks. The bright purple light from its reflective surface bounced and scattered across its rich textures. Golden flecks give way to brown, as polished stone steps yawned from the mouth of the mighty structure. The Ka-Ba-Ra Chamber. Only a handful of people have been inside every room. Great is its girth, mysterious are its contents. Purple and black, smooth and shiny, it's a gigantic truncated pyramidal complex. One of three such buildings in all of Ta-Amenta.

Twenty foot tall marble doors mark its entrance. On either side stood two huge and armed dread-locked guards. Like ebony statues, they remained motionless. They see everything.

With a burst of energy we entered the Great Hall. It's beautiful Alabaster walls leading to the Military chamber. Images of past battles etched across its surfaces. Within the Military chamber sits the Grand Gallery. This is where the Warrior-Kings brief the different divisions of the Mesniu. There's Shango and Ogun; two of the fiercest Warrior-Soldiers around. I wouldn't mind having those two brothas on my Pod. And there is Nzinga and Shabazz. And over there is Anut and Anlamani. The Ka-Ba-Ra chamber is pregnant with Warrior-Soldiers, K'huti, and Military scientists of all kinds. It's good to see so many brothas and sistahs devoted to Black survival.

Just as I was about to enter the Military chamber; Grand Gallery in sight, a powerful and commanding voice stopped me in mid stride-

"Kashta, come here."

It was Shekem Muntu. A N'tiu Tut. The N'tiu Tut are the most venerated members within Ta-Amentan society. Through life long study and sacrifice, they have achieved a state of consciousness which allows them direct communication with Tehuti; pure wisdom. I turned to greet him in the proper manner.

"Anetch Hrak, Shekem Muntu," I said, while bending at the waist, and clapping the backside of my right hand into the palm of my left hand three times.

"Hetepu," he returned.

"What can I do for you, Shekem Muntu?" I asked humbly.

"You can start by identifying with your true self," he said smiling. N'tiu Tut always spoke with double meaning. It would be awhile before I truly understood what he was saying to me this day.

"Don't worry about the military conference today, Khasta. We have other plans for you." He waived Anpu on, then took me by the arm and led me towards a shiny wall of mist and steel. A green alabaster surface blended perfectly with smooth marble streaks. That's when I noticed the long diagonal fissure that stretched from one corner of the wall to the next. The closer we got, the wider and more violent the fissure became. A luminous white light shown from behind its mottled green and white design.

"Wait... what's happening?"

Shekem Muntu responded unemotionally. "Relax, warrior. Don't allow the sensation of fear to halt your progress into higher realms."

As we entered the warm glow of the pulsating light, soft sensations of movement wafted across my skin. We were moving without walking. I was being taken to another chamber, a hidden room. Shekem Muntu was no longer at my side. Instead, swirling balls of light carried me through the white nothingness. Sound returned first.

"I am not afraid," I said to myself, repeating one of the 'Declarations of Innocence' my father taught me when I was a child.

"Are you man or God, Kashta?" A deep penetrating voice resonated above my head; more double talk. Haze and light slowly gave way to ghostly images. Walls. No windows. Ascending rows of chairs. Emotionless faces. N'tiu Tut. A thousand eyes met my own. The weight of their penetrating stare was almost unbearable. I'm on point, as usual. I stood on a hard square floor in the center of what looked like an indoor plaza. Just thirty feet away, calmly seated in rows of chairs arranged in ascending tiers that reached up to an undetermined distance, sat the most N'tiu Tut I'd ever seen. It's an awesome sight. A room filled with the spiritual elite of Ta-Amentan society.

"One day, Kashta, you too will be seated here among the Elect," one of them said in an expressionless tone.

"Why me? I'm a Warrior-Soldier. I don't have the discipline for Spiritual endeavors."

"No, not now, Kashta. But you will. Even now you are very insightful. You do not allow your emotions to dictate your behavior," said another.

I counted at least 30 N'tiu Tut. I recognized only three. They are the Elect. Spiritual Elders who represent this region of Ta-Amenta. Like magnificent bronze statues, they sat emotionless. Almost dream-like. Their faces shown the timeless wisdom of lifelong study of the Honored and Sacred wisdom of Old Kush. They are men and women who represented the pinnacle of African spiritual achievement.

"Question, Warrior: what is the cultural foundation of Ta-Amenta?" a female N'tiu Tut asked, her gray locks sat like silver ropes about her shoulders. I'd never seen her before.

I knew the drill ... no hesitation, "It is composed of three distinct layers that overlap and function as one. Like the human body, each system is specialized to perform a certain function, yet without its sisters systems it would cease to exist."

"That's good, now go on," she countered.

"The first layer, or system, is the domain of the N'tiu Tut. They are responsible for guiding the civilization spiritually, culturally, and socially. They are men and women who are at least 45 years of age, and have achieved an advanced state of Spiritual Cultivation. The N'tiu Tut spend enormous amounts energy and time accessing the inner reaches of the human spirit. They live in the many Edfu Temples which stand in and around the cities. Many believe that they have the power to read minds, traverse time and space, control the weather, etc. Whatever the case, they represent the will of God here on earth."

"And how is Ta-Amenta shown to the world?" asked Shekem Muntu.

"From among the ranks of the N'tiu Tut, a King and Queen are chosen. The King and Queen represent our nation and culture to other countries. Like the N'tiu Tut, they must be at least 45 years of age. They are subjected to the most rigorous of spiritual training. They are always wed and are expected to behave as such. We believe that our leaders should be well-versed in the laws of God. This includes matters of warfare. They are known to the outside world as Shekem Amen Ur Shekem Ament. Their given names are never revealed. They serve until they are called by the ancestors, resignation, or the unthinkable; they lose their Men Ab (will power)," I answered with pride.

"And..."

"The second layer of Ta-Amentan society is called the Divine Waters. The Divine Waters consist of men and women whom are on the pathway to becoming N'tiu Tut. They are assigned specific regions in Ta-Amenta, and administer spiritually and culturally to the people. Within the Divine Waters are found the Mystic Scientists. They are the most advanced teachers, inventors, agriculturist, artists, and technicians in the world. These brothas and sistahs have successfully combined the spiritual and natural sciences. Led by divine intuition, they continue to make vast technological advancements. They invented the Menmen, NAR, as well as the Homeopathic complex, which keeps our bodies healthy and disease free," I continued. The N'tiu Tut nodded in agreement.

"What else are the Divine Waters responsible for, Warrior?"

"Like spores of dandelion, the Divine Waters reach out to each member of our society. Through them, everyone is guided to becoming a productive citizen. All dormant capabilities are nurtured within each individual, and every young person is placed under the tutorship of a Mentor or Clan group. A Clan or Mentor group leader must be at least 25 years of age and a graduate of their childhood Rites of Passage. Clan leaders are responsible for children who are born under the same Incarnation Objective, or destiny, as they. As a consequence, large 'peer groups' have been established. Each peer group acts as a moral, psychological, and spiritual catalyst for success within the age group striving for distinction and unity within Ta-Amentan society. Upon graduation from the first level of education, there are individuals from the various groups that begin to branch off into different spheres in our society. Since every person is a unique expression of Amen (God), various attributes, gifts, etc., are developed and used to further the advancement of Ta-Amentan culture and civilization."

"And to which layer do you belong, Warrior?"

"Distinct from the first two layers of Ta-Amentan society, but every bit as important, are the Mesniu. The Warrior class. The Mesniu is nearly a society or nation onto itself. The Mesniu are responsible only to the N'tiu Tut. Even Shekem Amen Ur Shekem Ament must get clearance from the N'tiu Tut before giving an executive command to the Mesniu. Following the Law of Correspondence, the Mesniu are organized in much the same way as Ta-Amenta itself. This organization is not based on layers, but established as adjacent pillars. On one side are the Warrior-Kings. They are men who have served with distinction and honor. These brothas are at least 45 years of age, have mastered the basics in the science of war, and have reached a very high state of spiritual cultivation. On the opposite pillar are the Warrior-Queens. They are women who have served with distinction and honor within the Mesniu. They, like the Warrior-Kings, must be at least 45 years old, have mastered the basics in the science of war, and have achieved a high degree of spiritual cultivation. The Warrior-Queens, an evolutionary offshoot of Queen-Mothers, give spiritual counsel and aid in the formation of military directives and objectives of Warrior-Kings."

"Excellent... excellent, but you didn't answer my question."

"The third pillar of the Mesniu are the Warrior-Soldiers. They are men and women whom currently serve within the Mesniu and are dedicated to the survival of the Ta-Amentan way of life. Each Warrior-Soldier must be at least 21 years of age and have completed their childhood Rites of Passage. Military science is practiced daily. The Art of War is woven into the hearts and minds of the Warrior-Soldier. Anything less than excellence is unacceptable," I responded, then continued on, "The sharpest brothas and sistahs are selected to serve in a highly specialized division of Warrior-Soldier. The K'huti. The K'huti engage in the most dangerous operations and maneuvers, most of which are behind enemy lines. I'm a member of the K'huti. We are known as the 'Bringers of Swift Justice to some'... and 'The Apostles of Death' to others."

"Kashta. Tehuti has revealed to us through the Oracles that your future flies high like Heru," Shekhem Muntu returned. He was seated with several other N'tiu Tut in a row of golden chairs.

"You must begin to prepare your person for a greater service," said another. I'd never seen her before.

"We have watched your progress, Kashta. It seems that your great potential is in danger of being consumed by the blood of your enemies," Shekhem Muntu added.

"What do you mean?"

"We are informed by Tehuti through the Oracles that you are in danger of upsetting the balance of Maat. None may upset Divine Order. You are beginning to forsake your spiritual cultivation. Spiritual cultivation is the most important aspect of human life. There is no greater responsibility in existence, then the endeavor to awaken the *Ausar* in man. You are responsible for your own Spiritual development, Kashta. No one is going to magically release you from your responsibilities. Stop watching the clouds. None are the excuses. Our society is rich in Cosmology. Everything we do, speak, feel, breath, is saturated with the Principles of the Creator of the Heavens and the Earth."

Anpu and I were just talking about this. "Everything you have said is true and just. I accept, understand, and submit to your right guidance." I was trying to maintain a little dignity. Mistake.

"We anticipated your acceptance of the truth, Kashta. However, that does not always translate into right action, now does it?" Shekem Muntu submitted with a slight smile.

"The Oracles have revealed to us that the K'huti division within the Mesniu must and will evolve into the 'Uatchet-Nekhebet' phase," Shekem Khufu added.

"N'tiu Tut. I understand that it was through Uatchet and Nekhebet, and not through brute force alone (Heru), that our people were allowed to endure for hundreds of thousands of years...."

"Then why do you not listen?!" another Shekem interrupted.

"Kashta, you will leave us now. But before you go, know this: you and others like you are destined to lead the K'huti into a higher sphere of activity. Ta-Amenta must and will evolve beyond this 'one-up-men-ship' with Valhalla."

Before I had a chance to respond, Shekem't Ti, one of the most beautiful women on the planet, appeared in a veil of mist, took me by the arm, and led me through the pulsating fissure of light. Just as my eyes adjusted to its brilliance, I was standing in the Grand Gallery. The other K'huti, apparently having completed their quarterly meeting, were standing outside of the Great Hall, socializing and trading war stories.

CHAPTER 3

The ride home was awkward. We just sat there, not talking. What could I say? How would I tell Tefnut about my experience at the Chamber? She'd think I was crazy. Lamenting, I leaned into the soft blue cushion of my chair, trying to put as much material between us as possible. It didn't work. Her angry glare bored a hole through my ineffective shield. She knew me too well. At least well enough to know that something wasn't right. Luckily, we reached her stop first. Frowning, she stood, huffed-and-puffed, then abruptly marched off the Menmen. She was upset, and rightly so. I should have opened up to her. Told her something... anything. From the crystal clear lens of the crescent shaped window, I watched Tefnut disappear into the crowd. She didn't even bother to look back.

What happened today? I asked myself. *Was it real? It had to be.* Still frame clips of today's events were etched in my memory. I began to think about what Tefnut said earlier. About Ta-Amenta, the K'huti, Valhalla, everything. My breathing became deeper, slower. Rhythmic. My lungs filled to their capacity. All thoughts ceased as I chanted the sacred words of Old Kush. Emptiness. Enlightenment. Everything. Nothing. My consciousness gave way to infinite black. I was no longer myself, but a microcosm of the dramas of times past...

* * * * *

... mired in the stench of a thousand carcasses, the descendants of Gog and MaGog pushed through the gates of Babylon. With untold impunity, they broke divine law and closed the mighty circle. Having obtained the secrets of 360 degrees, death and destruction followed. The world was forced to live upside down, as the Red Clouds perished, and the Dog Star fell from heaven...

* * * * *

"Kashta... Kashta."

A voice like that of the softest of music penetrated my self-inflicted darkness. When I opened my eyes, I was both pleased and nauseous at the same time. It was Kenya. Physically, she's one of the most beautiful sistahs on the planet. She and I were once involved in a serious relationship. It didn't work.

"Hetepu."

"Hetepu," she returned, a slight smile on her face. "I haven't seen you in so long," she added. She leaned next to me and kissed me on the cheek. Her full red-brown lips smelled of peaches.

"Yeah. It's been a while, Kenya."

She was definitely as beautiful as ever. In fact, few women can compare with Kenya in terms of sheer physical beauty. It's her mind that's the problem, or *my* problem, I should say. Like too many of our brothas and sistahs, Kenya is an example of the millions of Black people who refuse to give up the religious and philosophical doctrines of our enemies. The cultural ideology of our beloved country is Kushite in origin. Yet within our great nation, there are those who are the descendants of they, who have given themselves over to the gods of Gog and MaGog. They want nothing to do with our original spiritual concepts. Instead, they hide behind a mountain of complex arguments to support their adopted belief systems.

"What were you doing? I called your name a hundred times."

"I was walking with the ancestors," I returned, wishing almost immediately that I hadn't said what I said.

"Are you still into that *black spiritual stuff?*" she asked in her usual condescending way.

She still has no respect for our culture, I said to myself.

"Well, if you put it that way, I guess so," I responded. "I mean let's remember, it was this *black stuff* that allowed our people to erect Kush, Kmt (Egypt), Songhoy, Mali, and other advanced African civilizations and high cultures-"

"Look, you don't have to get an attitude. I just asked you a question," she said teasingly.

"You're right," I returned. "I wont get an attitude. How have you been?" I asked; wholeheartedly endorsing the subject change.

"I've been fine. I just got back from New America. My husband and I are thinking about moving there."

"Oh, so you're wed?"

"Yes. I've been married for almost two years. He's a dentist and he's been offered a job in New America."

"That's good." Her excitement was contagious. "So, what part of New America are you moving to?"

"We were thinking about moving to the Central-D region," she said with a big grin on her face. The Central-D area of New America has a large African population. Most Black people live there. It's totally European in culture and tastes. Kenya will fit in good there. But still, I'm happy for her anyway.

"I've been keeping up with you," she said to my amazement. "I've seen you on the monitors several times. You're quite the mighty Warrior-Soldier aren't you?" she finished, a twinkle in her eye.

"Tua (Thank you; pronounced Twau). I didn't know you cared."

"Of course I care, fat head," she said jokingly.

We both laughed, which was followed by one of those mutually intense moments of silence. There's that *look*, that look she used to give me when everything was alright. It's almost as if we were still together, still in love. The feelings, the memories, and the plain truth of the moment made us both turn away, embarrassed.

"Well, here's my stop," she said standing. Her curvy body naturally striking one of those dynamic 'sistah' poses.

"Alright then, sis. I hope everything works out for you and your mate."

"Why thank you," she said cheerfully. "Hopefully it wont be another three years before I see you again," she finished. She gracefully picked up her belongings and walked off the Menmen as only a Black woman could.

It was good seeing her again. I nearly blew it. I thought it would be painful, but it was just the opposite. We both have done a lot of growing since the last time we've seen each other. I remember Shekem't Ti once told me, *It's useless to try and run from one's past; it always catches up with you...*

* * * * *

... heralded by a cloud of noxious dust, the Pale Rider descended upon the land of the Perfect Black. Wars and Revelation. With newfound knowledge and blood in his throat, he left the burning sands and crossed the great waters. Wars and Revelations. Cities were uprooted. Lives were lost. None could with stand the intoxicating evil of the eldest child of Gog and MaGog. Wars and Revelations...

* * * * *

I awoke from a most haunting, yet familiar dream. A vision filled with metaphors and allegories. I was sweating wildly, and judging from the way the other brothas and sistahs were looking at me, I was probably talking in my sleep as well. Calming myself, I was gladdened to find that we were traveling through Napata. Napata is the leading financial districts in all of Ta-Amenta. In fact, it's the economic capital in the western hemisphere. Here can be found dignitaries from all over the world. They come from near and far to partake in the money game. Many of our Mystic scientists are continually working on developing a 'fairer' system for dividing the resources of the world. At this time however, our techniques are a mixture of the 'trading formulas' once used by ancient Ghana, Songhoy, and the exploitative traps of old America. Ta-Amenta is Great, but it's not utopia.

Ever since I was a boy, I've always loved traveling through Napata. I often enjoyed watching the people run back and forth, from building to building, from quarter to quarter. Today was no different. I sat mesmerized, staring out the window like a child.

The familiar weight of slow-down came, then, in a gut wrenching turn, we entered the center of Napata.

Sebek Way. A huge twisted avenue of tortured souls. Rows of beautifully sculptured green and yellow buildings festoon an endless avenue of commerce. Behind these brightly colored walls are the visiting chambers for men and women who engage in trade and commerce. They're some of the most ruthless people on the planet.

Like a wooden Ninja, the Watanabe building sits brooding on the east corner. The business warriors from Japan are housed there. To its right is the Red Soil building. That's where China does her trade. A few years ago, we had to force the Red Army out of the entire complex. China felt she could dictate the coming and going of anyone within the building. It took us two days to teach China... and the rest of the world for that matter, that any and all entities within

Ta-Amentan boundaries, are under Black rule. Next to the Red Soil building is the Oceanic Community Institute. It houses the rest of the progressive nations of the Pacific Rim.

Sitting directly across from the visiting Asian countries, and taking-up almost the entire block, is the United European Embassy. That's where the United States of Europe tries to cheat and bully its way into capturing the lion's share of the earth's resources. It's amazing. They still want to relate to the rest of the world as if we're still living in the 20th century. On several occasions, we nearly had to shut them down as well.

"Wait a minute," I said aloud, startling the other passengers. *I couldn't believe my eyes!* In front of the United European Embassy, were two white males; military types. Crew-cuts, square jaws, cold glaring eyes, and all. *Those two don't look like bankers to me!* I immediately signaled the controller of the Menmen to slow down. As we neared the station's 'off ramp,' I quickly forced the doors open, then leapt out.

Strange, in situations like this my heart actually slows down. I find myself entering a more peaceful state of consciousness. It's quite deceiving because this is when I'm most dangerous.

I unassumingly approached the two men standing in front of the Embassy. They were definitely trained soldiers; their body language and the way they readied themselves as I got closer spoke volumes.

"What's up?" I asked, quickly flashing my Mesniu badge. "You two are a long ways from home; let's see your identification."

"What the fuck is this shit? You just want to see our identification because we're white," the shorter man answered sarcastically.

"Yeah, don't tell me this is a white thang," the larger man said with a stupid smirk.

"Check this out, man. I'm not in the mood to play games, so I'll ask the both of you one more-"

"Hey, fuck you!" the larger man blurted. He casually extended his arm in efforts to push me away. Before he got close enough to touch me, I grabbed his left wrist. What happened next was due to years of training and living the life of the K'huti. I twisted his wrist, spun him around, then shoved his arm into his back. Without thinking, I gave his wrist a final wrench. The dull sound of snapping bone followed.

Tearing himself from my grasp, he screamed, "Arrarah! You crazy spook! I'm gonna break your fucking neck!"

In one fluid motion, I turned and completed a left-spin-kick to his throat. He dropped like a rock. I sensed his partner tensing. I turned to greet him like a 'warrior born'. Just then, the doors of the United European Embassy burst open. Several white men in 'played out' Italian suits rushed out. *There was going to be blood on the streets tonight.* Several of them reached for concealed weapons. *It was on.* But before Ta-Amentan and European relations were damaged any further, ghosts of blue and white strobe danced across the embassy walls. Ta-Amentan security units were surrounding the building. Things were starting to get messy.

"What's going on here?" one of the embassy members asked. I decided to play along.

"This crazy 'son of a bitch' attacked us for no reason," the still conscious man lied. It took all of my will power (Heru) to keep from smacking him.

"Pick up Mr. McIntyre and take him inside," one of the embassy members commanded. He looked to be in charge. He was about fifty, had short white hair, and the palest blue eyes. He was standing in the corner of the entrance.

"Wait a minute," countered the lead security officer. "Nobody move!"

I was wondering when he was going to say something.

"Hey, that's Kashta," one of his security officers shouted. "He's one of the baddest Warrior-Soldiers around," she finished.

I gave my identification to the lead officer. He slid it through his mobile tapper (computer); scanning it's tiny black glyphs. It came back *Classified with an X.* The lead officer immediately recognized my authority.

"I'm sorry, sir. We got a call about someone breaking into the Euro-Embassy."

"This is all very touching. May we be excused, or do I have to contact your superiors?" the head embassy member interrupted. He was arrogant, and he held a look of contempt on his face.

He's right though. I'll need clearance before I can get a team down here to ID anyone. And I definitely wanted to get inside that embassy. Cold Wind Soldiers on Ta-Amentan soil! That's never been done before.

"NUT SENNI HURH, EURO-EMBASSI." Using a revised dialect of the kamitic language, I order the security unit to 'stand down' but keep watch over the European Embassy. I didn't want its membership to know my suspicions. Nor did I want to alarm the security unit. I'll report the infiltration to Warrior-King Senwosret tomorrow.

It was a strange gray-still of a scene; almost like a dream. Lights were flashing, people yelling, while disembodied voices streamed from unseen audio amps. *Here we go again.*

CHAPTER 4

I've been up for hours... hunched over my multi-viewer, and desperately trying to catch a trace on the Cold Wind soldiers I tangled with last night. *How did they get past the Mafdet...and what is their connection to the United European Embassy?* I rubbed my tired eyes, and lamented over last night's fiasco. *I allowed things to get way out of control. So much for Men Ab En Aunghk En Maat (will power).*

My search within the 'Sia' was going nowhere. Sia is an old Kamitic (Egyptian) term that back in day meant 'exceptional insight.' Today it's used to describe the most advanced virtual network in the world. It was created by several Black computer engineers in the early twenty-first century. After it's first few years in service, it both out performed and out distanced the leading Internet competitors soundly.

I fell upon the myriad of buttons that grew tooth-like from my key-pad. My fingers danced across its glossy black surface. The pop of fiber-plastic clicks, created a kind of rhythmic chorus. Pages of information flashed across the pale gray of my multi-viewer screen. Instinctively, I linked into the 'war pages.'

Okay... nothing. Let's check the general population files... nothing! I don't understand...

"Wait a minute," I said aloud. *I'm going about this all wrong. I'm looking for soldiers, known thugs, assassins. I should be looking for politicians...or maybe even businessmen.*

Within a few minutes, I had a complete listing of every political and business person who entered the country in the last five days. Narrowing my search to Valhalla and The United States of Europe, I struck gold. A '3D holo' of a middle aged white man named Dawik Hiemer jumped from the center of my screen, then rested in the upper right hand corner. I immediately recognized him as the arrogant jerk that was calling the shots at the Euro-Embassy. His file, which I'm sure is fake, says he's here on business. Apparently he and...

My heart froze. Standing next to Dawik Hiemer are the two Cold Wind soldiers I fought last night. They're in at least six holo's with Him. Hiemer's bio doesn't mention either of them by name. It simply states that they're his personal body guards. As far I'm concerned, they're Cold Wind soldiers. Assassins. And they're in the heart of the economic district of Ta-Amenta!

Before I completed my next thought, my multi-viewer began to whistle an incoming message.

"Hetepu (eternal peace)," I said into the tiny set of speakers that grew like deformed flowers from the top of my viewer's flat screen.

"Hetepu," I heard in that familiar baritone voice. It was Warrior-King Senwosret.

"Heru Nefer (good morning), I hope this glorious day finds you in good spirits," I said, trying to soften the impending reprimand. The look on his face said otherwise.

"Let's just say that this morning finds *some* in better spirits than others," he responded.

"I know what you mean-"

"That's enough, Kashta," he interrupted. "Last night was unacceptable. Not only did you violate Intra-Continental protocol, but you lost your Men Ab," he added. "I am beginning to wonder if the responsibility of being a Leader of a K'huti Pod, is too much for you." He paused, then started up again. "Tell me something, Kashta, don't you have enough to do?"

"Tu (yes), Senwosret. I was riding the Menmen last night -"

"I understand that part, but are you working with your spirit?" he asked, eyebrows raised in anticipation...

"Tem (no). Not as much as I should."

"Obviously. Unfortunately for you, there is a file detailing your lack of spiritual growth. In Sino (China), you instructed your Pod to outright kill 20 Cold Wind soldiers and 50 Red Infantrymen without provocation. In Den- Europe (Germany), you took out 15 Cold Wind Soldiers and 25 Elite German ground troops. In North Alkebulan (Africa), you decimated several Bedouin villages, killed three Arab gunmen, and took out two elite Arab ground troops. Granted, the North Alkebulan assignment was for the recapture of African soil, but once it was established that the battle had been won, you had your troops 'Shock Wave' their way through Algeria and Libya; straight through to old Kam (Egypt). Now it seems that you want to bring your aggressions home. I hope you don't plan on declaring War against Valhalla without consulting the N'tiu Tut (High Elders)."

He hit hard this time. Senwosret was not one to mince words. He was always hard and straight. "If I may respond, Atef (Sir). On each of those occasions except North Alkebulan, I was following orders-"

"Were you, Kashta? Although you were not technically in command, your natural leadership...and your raw charisma could have swayed the Pod as well it's commander to 'stop the killing,'" he answered.

"Tu, Senwosret."

We quickly reached that point in the conversation where I thought it better not to try and justify what happened last night. Besides, it wouldn't do me any good to get into an argument with Warrior-King Senwosret. I respected him too much for that.

"Kashta. Intelligence has detected Cold Wind movement in the Fourth Quadrant. You've got 36 hours to assemble a team of five. I want your Pod in there, and I want to know what's going on. It's dangerous, but I trust you can handle it. I want a presentation of how deep you plan on penetrating the Wasted Cities adjacent to Quadrant 4. Also, I know Tefnut is the best '3D fractal Imager' we've got, but she's not going with you. I've got another assignment for her. Get back to me in 36 hours," he finished, cutting his transmission.

Quadrant 4 is definitely High Risk. It borders on what used to be known as the 'Bay Area'. From Old Oakland up through Old Sacramento. It's mostly Wasted City know. And it's just about impossible to predict what we'll run into out there. I've lost some good friends in that stretch of land. I don't know what Cold Wind is doing, but it can't be good.

I decided I had better contact Tefnut. If I'm not mistaken, she did several in-depth surveys of northern California. During the early morning hours, Tefnut is usually accessing the Nun. Nun is the huge expanse of electronic images, information, and complex data files that most of the Alkebulan (African), South American, and some

Asian countries use to communicate and exchange information. It's used in conjunction with Sia. Nun is the body of water of information, electronic images, archives, and so on, while Sia is the ship which navigates its virtual surface. The brothas and sistahs in the early twenty-first century who created this wonder of old style science did not re-invent the wheel; they simply made it better.

Stretching my tired body, I pushed away from my multi-viewer, then walked across the cold floor and into the food-space. I made a hot-round of tea and tore a few pieces of sweat bread from a loaf which sat on its wooden seal. Looking out the window, I watched as the yellow-blue rays of Ra cracked, chasing the darkness across the heavens; it was going to be a beautiful day. I plopped back into my chair, stuffed my last piece of bread into my mouth, then sent an electronic impulse to Tefnut's personal avenue...

"Brrrazip.zip, brrrazip.zip," sang my multi-viewer. Connecting electronically, a small window opened in the upper left corner of my flat-screen. It quickly expanded and filled the entire view.

"Hetepu, my sistah," I said into my audio-port while re-adjusting the glare on my flat screen. *I needed a new one.*

"Hetepu, Kashta. What's up?" Tefnut returned smiling.

"I've got orders; Quadrant 4. Apparently Cold Wind has stepped up their activities in that region. Senwosret wants me to assemble a Pod...do some snooping."

"Hmmnn...Quadrant 4 is extremely dangerous, Kashta. Why would he send you there when he knows that I have an assignment in the Northeast?"

"I'm not sure. Anyway, who would you recommend I get to do my frags, and do you still have that layout you did of northern California?"

"Get Sa'Ra. He's young, but from what I hear, he's highly skilled. And yes, I'll send those files to you immediately. Still got some dark areas...just never had time to follow up on them."

"Good. I'm sending Anpu a message as we speak... informing him to assemble the rest of the K'huti."

"When it's all said and done, you should have yourself a pretty good team. It'd be even better if I were going, but you can't have everything," she teased.

"I hope this won't interfere with your assignment, Tefnut."

"No, no. I've already gotten a survey team together. We're generating fractals of what appears to be a very large slave complex.

It's tucked away... in-between the southeast border of Valhalla; right outside of New America."

"Now how did we find out about that? The last time we directed one of our astro-peeps towards that part of the western hemisphere, both New America and Valhalla accused us of spying." I had to bang on my multi-viewer; the picture was starting to fade...

"Believe it or not, we received most of the information from Cuba," she said smiling.

"Cuba?"

"Yeah, Cuba. From what I understand, we've gotten a lot of tips from Cuba in the last few months. I guess we'll take what we can get. Sometimes Cuba looks to be on our side, sometimes she sides with New America or the United States of Europe. It's all a game," she finished.

"I know what you mean. For obvious reasons, Cuba despite its substantial Black and Brown populations, isn't quite in step with what Ta-Amenta and the rest of the Caribbean is doing."

"That's because Cuba has been strongly influenced by Eastern European concepts and philosophies. And its ruling class is, and always has been, largely white," she returned. "Anyway, may Heru K'huti protect you on your assignment," she ended.

"And may the Neteru bless your person on its journey also," I returned; watching her picture fade from view. It was still early, so I pushed what few pieces of furniture I had aside, then walked over to the large hanging wooden closet that slopped insect-like in my main living quarter. I pulled out a thick soft blue cotton rug, then laid it across the floor. I grabbed two fat black pillows and threw them on top of the rug. I lay down on top of one, then concentrated on relaxing my body mind and spirit. It didn't take long. First the tingling came. Then the trembling. I was used to this; it was always like this before one my dreams came. Tefnut said they were visions...

* * * * *

... a thousand, thousand years ago, on a spinning carcass in the blackest of voids, a wave of maggots overcame a swarm of flies. They plucked their wings and stole their dreams and caused the flies to crawl on their knees like them. A sick twisted mass were they. A mockery of their former selves. So bad off were they that the memory of flight escaped them. These things pleased the maggots. It gave them peace and happiness, for the maggots understood a great truth that the flies had forgotten. The maggots would one day be flies, having the ability to fly when there would be no more flies... or so they thought...

* * * * *

Later that day, my presentation with Warrior-King Senwosret went good. We covered a lot of ground, making adjustments as needed. As soon as we finished, he left as abruptly as he came. It didn't matter, though. I could tell by the look on his face that he was quite pleased with how it looked on papyrus. If you do it right, recon-assignments always look good on papyrus. And, if it looks good, you can justify sending people into hostile situations. That's just how it works.

I gathered the remaining plasto-charts, then folded them into their containers. I wrote today's date across each flexible label and handed them over to the clerk, who sat statue-like behind the rectangular marble-encased window. Leaving the Ka-Ba-Ra Chamber, I heard its huge doors slam shut behind me. The streets were crowded. The soft constant murmur of voices, mingled freely with the sweet aroma of incense. The night air was ripe with electricity.

"Kashta... over here," a voice shouted from across the pavement. It was Anpu.

"Hetepu, Atef," I welcomed; patting my left breast with my right hand, thumb in palm, fingers extended yet together.

"Hetepu, Atef," he returned, using the same gestures and postures.

"What's up... you ready for the 4th Quadrant?"

"Of course, Black man," he answered stoically. Anpu is one of the most capable people I know. He's extremely detail oriented and has a lot of pride in what he does. "Check your multi-viewer when you get home - that is, if it still works. I sent the files about an hour ago," he added. "Listen, there's someone I want you to meet," he began, a mischievous look shown on his face. "This brother is a 'trip.' He moved to New America from Alkebulan (Africa) a few years ago. He's a media-doll. I mean, they really love him there! He's a philosopher... of sorts. And he's singing that same tired old song, you know... how we should love all human beings as one."

Anpu always does this. He knows how irritated I get from people like that. He introduces me to them, then he starts the conversation going, I attack, he starts it up again, I attack. I always look like the bad guy. He never gets blamed for anything. I guess that's why it's so much fun.

"He's currently on tour in the Southern District. He's hot. People by the thousands flock to hear his lectures."

"And I'm sure he has the full backing of the American government," I added sarcastically.

"Absolutely, my brother. He's their answer to Ta-Amenta. He's one of those Black people who bashes other Black people."

"Okay, well yeah, then I'm sure he's paid."

"Hell yeah, he's paid," Anpu retorted...laughing. "When I first saw Mr. Mogu, Shango and I were on leave in New America, you know, over in that huge Plaza where most of the so-called progressive American Blacks hangout; right across the border..."

I nodded.

"Anyway, he was talking about how we as Black people never should have created Ta-Amenta; how we should love all races, etc. It was obvious to me that this brother was a Rain Head."

Rain Heads are what we call Black people who have undergone special conditioning. They are created by the military to subvert other Black people into thinking that everything black is negative or evil. Through drugs and virtual media, they are convinced that only white or European concepts are natural, good, and should be defended at all costs. After they reach a certain age, it's almost impossible to treat them.

Anpu continued in rare form, "He damn near started a riot in the middle of the Plaza. Military police were everywhere. He had the crowd under a spell! But what really got me, was when he said that Ta-Amenta was a ghetto of Black Supremacists, and that it needed to be destroyed. And check it: he then called for its citizens, us Ta-Amentans, to rejoin the American Republic. I damn near took a shot at him right there," Anpu announce, shaking his head in renewed disbelief.

"Wow, now that's amazing. Why do people automatically assume that when Black people move towards unity, independence, and the reclamation of culture and identity that we are actually wasting our time sitting around hating the rest of the human family?" I asked rhetorically. "We want... hell, we need what they have. Power! And not this mind numbing bullshit that this Mogu guy is pushing!"

"Well, you know what time it is, Atef," Anpu started in. "Populations that have been oppressed, and thus educated by that same oppressing group, have been psychologically implanted with a type of self-destruct program. This program surfaces, then forces the 'unconscious' victim to subvert or stop any and all progressive attempts to overthrow the oppressive community. I mean what else is a Rain Head supposed to do?"

"It's too bad none of these brothas and sistahs have ever taken the time to seriously question where in fact they learned their belief systems from," I responded. "Maybe if they took a real inventory of where their ideas about themselves, about God, and about the very nature of reality came from, I think *that* in itself would initiate some really powerful growth."

"Tu (yes)," Anpu said in agreement. "I mean, I'm feeling you. One of the major problems I see with brothers and sisters who continue to think that way is that they fail to understand the destructive results of allowing another people to define reality for them. It's mostly out of fear... I mean it has to be a terrible thing for some, to actually push beyond what they've been taught all their lives. They don't know anything else."

"Yeah, I feel you and all, but that's not an excuse. Just imagine...millions of African people. Born in a hostile world. Held hostage by a dysfunctional and alien culture. Never really knowing the simple pleasure of loving themselves. Think about it. Trapped in an illusion, a world of make believe. A place that is nothing more than an agreement between The Keep and their enslaved. What can be worse than sleepwalking through a life, wishing you were something else... someone else."

"Better to be dead than to live a lie," Anpu responded somberly.

"Tu. So, when do I get to meet this so-called brotha?"

"Hopefully after this assignment. He's scheduled to be in the Southern District next cycle (month). We could take leave, go into New America, and..."

"... and do an unauthorized hit," I interjected jokingly.

Anpu started laughing. Real hard. While holding his stomach, he suggested, "Kash, Lets go to the Het Nefer, you need some relaxation."

"Lets go."

The Het Nefer is an amazing, Audio-Visual-Virtual-Concert. There are several of them throughout Ta-Amenta. Huge buildings, three stories; the first two are under ground. We're talking State-of-the-Art technology here. Within it's pulsating walls of micro circuitry, the population of Ta-Amenta is offered a simulated cultural festival. The Het Nefer is electronically linked to several similar complexes throughout the free world. It's incredible. People from all over the globe simultaneously partake in the enjoyments of world citizenship. Folks in Alkebulan (Africa) can talk and laugh with people in Ta-Amenta or Asia, and vice versa. Latin America, too.

"Did they ever make a connection in the United States of Europe?" I asked, knowing if anyone knew, it would be Anpu.

"Not that I know of, something about there not being that much of a demand or response to the idea of 'Intercontinental virtual concerts.' But you know just like I do that the United States of Europe doesn't, and still don't for that matter, want anything to do with Ta-Amenta. Besides, they haven't up dated their *virtual-barriers* yet."

The United States of Europe and a large part of East Asia are still using the original Internet technology. Most other nations are using both SIA/NUN and the Newly created VirtualRA. It's superior in terms of speed and stability. And it also has an impregnable Plasma Wall, as opposed to the old standard Fire Wall technology. Despite its name, the Plasma wall freezes or locks all known cyber viruses, taps, and hacks.

"You would think that after the Cyber Wars, The United States of Europe would have switched over to the leading technology of the day, regardless of the color of the people who created it. Even New America has opened a few Virtual-Parks."

"Well, some people never learn, Atef. Besides, the longer they use their outdated techniques, the longer The Mesniu are able to access their archives," Anpu retorted.

This is the time of year when the streets remain crowded. Even up through the early morning hours, it's not uncommon to have to work really hard to avoid stepping on toes. The warm humid air is awash with consciousness and anticipation. We press on, the unyielding call of the virtual concert beckoning us onward.

As we approached the Het Nefer, it's huge green and yellow doors swung open. Inside, the eerie outline of black bodies bathed in the iridescent orange glow of technology, contrasted sharply with the surrounding architecture. Brothas and sistahs crowded the outer steps, standing around talking and greeting each other near the entrance way. Warrior-Soldier and civilian alike, there were no caste systems here. Even ethnicity faded behind these walls.

"Listen. I met some people from Togo last week. Hopefully they'll be using the Audio Visual Environment (A.V.E.). One of them was a Senegalese sistah. She's a student at the chemical institute in Togo."

"Who is she, what's her ren (name)?" Anpu asked.

"Her name is Inki. She's working on her credentials in Chemistry. She's conscious and absolutely beautiful. She's one of those Sudanese-looking sistahs; probably about six-three," I answered.

"You need to let me talk to her," Anpu interjected. "Besides, you've already got Tefnut," he finished sarcastically.

"I wish I *did* have Tefnut like that. I mean...we just never got around to making things happen."

"Yeah okay...what you really mean is that you haven't handled your business yet," Anpu blasted.

I ignored him.

As we entered the Het Nefer, we were immediately cascaded in rows of colors, shaken by vibrations, and startled by images of people moving towards us, around us, and through us. It takes getting used to. One minute you're walking towards a group of people, they acknowledge your presence; some may even greet you. Then, without warning, they past right through you. Many are dressed in their traditional attire. Some are from different regions of Alkebulan. Others are from different Latin American, Asian, and South Pacific countries. Even Aztlan joins the world community. It's a cultural feast of music, sights, artistic expressions, languages, and virtual entertainment.

I can remember back in the day, when Cold Wind soldiers would access our virtual environments from Valhalla, or sometimes from inside New America. We would be in the middle of VI (Virtual Interaction), catch a glimpse of a Cold Wind soldier, then start shooting; no questions asked. People would be diving under tables and behind speakers. It was crazy back then.

My reminiscing is put on hold as a hush falls over the crowd. The gaseous lights dim then flicker. A steady pulse fills the A.V.E. When the artificial world returns, we have been transported to a picturesque lake scene. A soft breeze swims past our faces. Birds fly over head. Even the ripples on the water seem real. Then, without warning, a column of golden light erupts from the center of the lake, stabbing the perfectly simulated sky. An Afro-Caribbean band materializes from the candescent beam of energy. It's one of my favorite groups: The Rubber People.

I was excited. Turning towards Anpu, I asked, "Have you checked this group out?"

"Of course, this me you talking to," Anpu retorted.

"Yeah, they are definitely the next phase. They always dropping some conscious lyrics, too"

"Yeah, they are, that's why they've been banned in India, " Anpu added.

"Yeah, but since they're over a billion strong, we're-"

Our rant is immediately hushed. The Rubber People began their melodic assault on the senses. It's a slow hypnotic beat, full of bass...sprinkled with African horns. The master drummer sets the pace. The horns burst in, followed by three beautiful brown women; combination of African, European, and Native South American, began chanting in the ancient languages.

Here it comes; that feeling I get before an assignment. Electric anticipation. My mind races like a multi-viewer. It's on auto, conceiving then solving as many mission scenarios as possible. It's an old K'huti technique. We go into trance and 'see' ourselves successfully completing our objectives. It just seems to happen for me all too often. The combination of the music and my self-induced trance is causing my body to sweat and tremble.

Laughing, Anpu said, "Kashta, you can't even relax in a Het Nefer."

"I know, I got it bad," I returned. "I can feel the ancestors pulling at me. I'm going home. I need to initiate a ritual for tomorrow's objectives."

"Alright then, my brother," Anpu said, patting his left breast with his right hand; thumb in palm, fingers extended, yet together. "Kheru Nefer (good night)," he finished.

"Kheru Nefer," I said standing, using the same gestures and postures. I wished I had more time. Inki is probably in here somewhere.

Ignoring the masterful music and the rhythmic bounce of the international crowd, I pressed through their bodies. Some real, some virtual. For an instant, I thought I heard my ren (name). Turning, I scanned the crowd for Inki... Tefnut...

When I got outside, the cool air rested my nerves, calming me. I reached into my side-pouch, and pulled out my C.P.C.I. (Computerized Pocket City Itinerary). Mesniu issued. Its sleek black form sparkled in the night's sky. No bigger than a man's hand, it held over ten Rads of data. *"Okay, let me see,"* I whispered. Pressing a sequence of keys, a tiny screen began to flicker. City schedule.

Tomorrow's assignment was going to be dangerous. Total High End endeavor. The bad part is we'll have to cross through New America to reach our objective. If we get caught, they'll let the whole world know *before* they throw us in jail. And with all that unwanted Media coverage; and the usual American distortion of facts, Ta-Amenta will be made to look bad in the eyes of the world community. And, of course, Valhallan authorities will be made aware of the presence of Warrior-Soldiers in New America; a total violation of the 3rd Intra-continental treaty of 2150. A series of schedules flashed across the tiny screen of my CPCI. I had an hour to get to market.

As soon as I looked up, a short, light-skinned, narrow featured brother came walking out of the 'Table of the Sun' electronics store. "Ra-Anu," I said, directing my call at his person.

"Heyyy... hetepu, my brotha," he returned.

Ra-Anu and I go way back. We were both in the same 'Rites of Passage'. We crossed over to adulthood together. His natural proclivities were more inclined with science and technology. Mine were geared towards philosophy and Warfare. After graduation, he went on to pursue a career in the technological fields. I became a Warrior-Soldier.

"How's your person?" I asked.

"Fine, fine," he returned. "It's been a long time. How's your person? I mean, traveling across the hemisphere, fighting to save the sovereignty and integrity of Ta-Amenta must be hard work," he added with a broad smile.

"Well, it's getting easier, thanks to brothas and sistahs like you. The technical innovations coming out of the Sebek-Sebek-Sebek Institute are phenomenal."

Responding with pride, he retorts, "We gotta do what we gotta do. Anyway, I saw your mother and father at the Garvey Institute last week. Your mother said that she hasn't heard from you in two weeks."

"I know. It's a shame. I'll have to call them tomorrow morning. It seems that I get so caught up in my work that I neglect to pay homage to my ancestors; the ones that are still here. What have you brothas and sistahs come up with in those tech-labs?" I asked, changing the subject.

"Oh, Atef," he said excitedly. "We've got a new 'Phase Rocket engine' in development. This means that soon we'll be able to begin exploring the heavens...the moon and beyond!"

"Damn," I responded in shock.

"Well, what's important about our Phase Engine is that it's based on Solar Magnetic Technology, not chemical reactions."

"That's great, my brotha. Listen, I'm headed to the market. I want to hear all about this new technology, and about what you've been doing for the past few years," I said smiling, motioning him to walk with me.

CHAPTER 5

I've got my orders. In 32 hours, I'll have a Pod of five of the best K'huti under my command. In the heart of Quadrant 4. I subconsciously reached for the stack of 'draks' that grew mound-like on the floor next to me. Grabbing the top one, I inserted its smooth oval shape into the side of my aging terminal, then punched in my code. Windows within windows gave birth to a brightly colored column of data. I found what I was looking for. A large red glyph sat blinking in the center of the viewer.

I created this program several years ago. It's a simple script that I use to set up combat-profiles. If one of us doesn't make it home, it'll be used to notifying the next-of-kin. This is the only part of the job I hate. It's almost ghoulish. *I mean how do you prepare for the death of a Mesniu, a K'huti?* Almost holding my breath, I cracked my file first.

Most of the information I have stored about myself is current. A few minor adjustments should bring me up to date. My new resistance training program has increased my muscle mass considerably. I've gone from 174 to 190 pounds. I've got a new scar on my right shoulder; plasma rifle burn. And I now have all of my wisdom teeth. The rest of the data should be current: 5'10", dark red-brown pigmentation, right handed, shaved head...

"Brrra.zip.zip, brrra.zip.zip," hummed the familiar song of my multi-viewer. Hmmnn, I lamented. Now was not a good time.

"Hetepu," I answered; switching the dusty screen on at the same time.

"Heru Nefer (good morning)," I got back. Shimmering into focus was a face that I had not seen in years. It was Damuzi. He and I became friends about ten years ago, in New America. I was on one of my first assignments there. He has since resigned from the Mesniu. I never asked why.

"I don't believe it. Damuzi of the Sebek Clan. What's up, beloved?"

Smiling, he returned, "The same as it ever was, Black man. Peace love and war. How's your person?"

"Protected by the Most High," I answered. He and I always spoke to one another like this. It was what *made* our friendship. I guess it was a kind of a mutual respect for self and culture. "So, what have you been up to?"

"Well, I've been living in New America mostly. Existing contract to contract, you know how *Building* is," he answered stoically. Damuzi is a Builder. An engineer of Sebek proportions. Mathematics has always been his first love, bringing numbers to life in the shape of buildings, machines; you name it, he can do it.

"Well you look great, brotha. I'd say the world has been good to you."

Frowning, he stood, reaching out of view. He reappeared with a stack of papers. "You see this, Kashta? This is 18 months of hard labor," he said, shaking the disheveled mass as he spoke. "I had a team, my own team at that. We were on the West Coast working on a new facility for the Americans. Don't ask me why, or for what for, but-"

"The West Coast! Why would they build anything on the West Coast? I mean isn't that where they nearly went to war with Aztlan; over who owns the geography next to the Pacific?" I interrupted. *Something's not right. Valhalla has a troop of Cold Wind Soldiers permanently stationed in that region. The Americans have got themselves a brand new facility, and now Warrior-King Senwosret wants to put the K'huti in the mix.*

"I've been out of the loop for a while now, Kash. I don't know anything about a war. But what I *can* tell you is that the Pacific region is hot. The Americans are contracting out to the lowest team..." *Damuzi was unusually animated.* "They allow each team to work for about six months, then that's it. They use some bullshit excuse to let you go."

"Sorry to hear that, Damuzi. You did get credited, right?"

"Not yet. And if it weren't for the odd jobs I've been getting in the Central D Region, I'd be starving."

"You can always come back home."

"No thanks, too many bad memories."

Yeah, Damuzi has history in Ta-Amenta. A long story. A fable fit for another day.

A half smile slowly slid across his golden-brown face. "Listen, Kash. Didn't mean to take up too much of your time. I just wanted to check in, see how you were doing. I'll send you a link. I'm staying in the Central D; for now, until I get another job." And that was it. He turned his multi viewer off almost before he finished his sentence. *Typical Damuzi*, I thought.

My fingers became a soft blur. Moving wildly, they jigged across the narrow row of keys. Code danced and flashed, on and off, in a series of colors. Bleeps and chaotic images of light caught rhythm and joined in the dance.

The Bay Area. A stretch of land along the coast of what used to be California. Oil, gold, and a huge expanse of Red Woods.

Like shimmering green ants, columns of files rolled across my multi-viewer's screen. Each one spilling rads of data, most of it useless. Basic geography, ecology, and so on. Yeah, the West Coast is heating up. And the K'huti are being sent in to cool things off.

I managed to complete the rest of the com-files by mid-afternoon. I then saved them to a virtual flex-file, and electronically sent them to a classified location somewhere deep within the Ka-Ba-Ra Chamber. They'll be kept there until after our assignment. Hopefully they'll be deleted without any changes. Tomorrow will be a day of discovery; or at least that's what I like to tell myself before missions like this.

Stretching my aching fingers, I turned my system off. The screen instantly went gray, brilliant colors giving way to smooth black. The color of peace.

Lazily, I lifted myself up and away from my multi-viewer and walked over to the entrance of my het (house). When I opened the door, I was startled to find Tefnut standing there.

"Hetepu, my sista," I said, displaying the appropriate posture and gestures.

"Hetepu, Kashta," she returned.

"Oh, so you're calling me by my full ren (name)?" I returned jokingly.

"You know what's wrong, Kashta. I'm a little worried about you going into Q.4. Every time we send someone to that region, nothing good comes of it. Don't get me wrong, I know you're very capable, it's just... never mind," she finished, shaking her head as she started for the door.

Jumping in front of her, I asked, "What's the problem, Tefnut? I've been on many assignments before; not as many as you, but hundreds. Besides, you know as well I do that we must always be careful on how we *think* about things... listen. I've meditated and prayed over this thing all night. I'm very healthy, and I haven't transgressed against too many Divine Laws. I know Amen (God) will watch over me."

"You're right, I'm just being silly," she returned, tears running down her face. "You're my best friend, I just don't want anything to happen to you, okay?"

Best friends... great. Managing a fake smile, I proclaimed, "I'm protected by the most high."

Recognizing my discomfort, she closed her huge brown eyes, then kissed me on the cheek. "Alright, Kashta. I'm already late for my assignment. I just wanted to see you before you left. Warrior-King Senwosret is going to be displeased, but I don't care," she said defiantly. "Just take care of yourself, and get back in one piece."

"I plan on it."

We embraced. She felt so good. I didn't want to let her go. I then slipped on a pair of soles and walked with her outside. We held hands. I wanted to tell her how I've felt about her since the first day we met. I didn't. When we reached the Sekert Menmen station, I barely looked at her when she boarded. I couldn't. It hurt too much. Before long, she disappeared among the black, red, yellow, and brown tones moving in and out of the waiting Menmen. In a cloud of silver dust, it rose on a column of inaudible sound and streaked off, it's elongated shape blending with the horizon. I blew it. And the wild thing is, I couldn't help but wonder if I'd ever get a second chance.

I closed my eyes and raised my face towards Aten (the sun), it's brilliance revealing itself in the blood of my eyelids. Deep red. War colors. I still had a few hours before I needed to leave for the Ka-Ba-Ra Chamber, though. The K'huti would be there. A Pod of five of the best. And sometime tomorrow, we'd be deep in heavy ground; Quadrant Four. Heart pounding, I marshaled a burst of energy and jogged back to my Het; thinking about tomorrow's mission, and already missing Tefnut.

It's late. This is my favorite time to be in the Ka-Ba-Ra Chamber. You don't have the mad dash of civilians, bureaucrats, and guests, moving in and out of its many rooms. Only the Mesniu and Mystic scientists are on post. I laughed to myself as I visualized a half asleep Senwosret peaking from one of the Chamber doors. "Pure fantasy," I said aloud. Warrior-King Senwosret never sleeps. Most of us go as far as to even govern the way we think in his presence. I'd swear sometimes it seems that man can read our minds. One day, if I'm lucky, I'll be as evolved as he is.

I reserved Chamber Zero. It's large and it has a nice info-system. We can go over our objectives, and use the multi fractals to familiarize ourselves with the terrain and current weather patterns of Quadrant four.

As I approached its outer door, I could hear the K'huti inside. I recognized a few voices; close friends. The others were unknown to me. But that'll change in the field.

By the time I opened the door, they had stopped talking. Like ebony statues, they were standing at attention. I was reassured by who I saw. Once again, I was indebted to Anpu. This was good company.

Feeling relaxed and well rested, I greeted the K'huti; the baddest set of brothers this side of the Atlantic Ocean, "Hetepu, Kheru Nefer!"

After the formal and informal greetings, the clasping of hands, and some loud obnoxious laughter, I walked to the front of the Chamber room. I lowered the info-system window from its housing, then activated the multi-fract imager. A perfect halo of Quadrant Four shimmered into focus.

"Alright, K'huti, listen up. In about 12 hours we'll be in the heart of Quadrant Four. I'm sure I don't have to tell you how dangerous that region is. We've all lost family and friends in that part of the world." Their heads nodded in agreement. "Each of you has been selected because of your expertise in a given field. Frankly, we're all Special Forces; The K'huti. We work behind Enemy Lines. We're the best at what we do." I pulled a drak from a heap of papers that sat haphazardly next to the multi-fract. I plugged it into its housing, then stretched the large orange icon in the center of the screen. A short list of names formed a neat column.

"First, I'll go through the rostrum; see who's here. I'll then give a brief description of what we're up against. Keep in mind this is on a need-to-know basis. As soon as I learn something, you'll hear about it. I'll be happy to answer anything that I can about tomorrow's assignment, provided-"

"Hetepu, Kashta," a tall light skinned brotha blurted. "You probably don't have me on the rostrum yet. I was referred to you by Tefnut," he finished.

"Oh yes, hetepu, my brotha. It's good to have you with us. Okay, let's see who else is here..."

"Anpu, weapons specialist..."

"Hetepu, my brother," he responded.

"Sa-Ra, computer fractal surveyor..."

"Present and accounted for," he said, looking at, and acknowledging the others.

"Enlil. Information specialist..."

"Right here, Atef. Pleasure working with you again," he finished.

"Tanakamani, communications..."

"Hotep (peace), my brother."

"Oshun, navigator. This brotha gon' get us home," I said jokingly.

"Hetepu," he answered.

"First of all, I appreciate you brothas for being here. Like I said earlier, this is a 'High Risk' situation. Were moving on Heavy ground. Our objectives are simple-"

"That's the worst kind," Tanakamani interjected.

Although he's right, I can't have him interrupting me. All it takes is a look.

"Anyway, Atefs, none the less, we're going to make it work," I continued. "We get in by 0500 hours. We stay low and close to the water. If we stay on a South-East 'trek,' we'll reach one of several objectives. Remember, Warrior-King Senwosret is basically calling this a covert Information-Counter-Information exercise. Keep that in mind in case you're captured. If you've all read your reports, you know about the heightened activity in and around Quadrant Four. We need to know why. We don't want Valhalla, New America, Den-Canada, or for that matter, Aztlan, discovering our presence in their backyard...business as usual. Also, we'll explore and generate a complete fract-map of 'Wasted City V-4'. No one has successfully been able to do that. We will. Independent sources have confirmed high levels of slave activity in close proximity to V-4. And that, Atefs (black men), is why the K'huti were created. The rest is history."

"Hold up, Atef. We've been getting reports about slave activity in V-4 for nearly eight months. Why is it so important to go in now?" Enlil asked.

"Good question," I returned. "If you'll remember, those reports were tentative at best. I mean we're talking five, sometimes seven slaves. The records just aren't clear. Propaganda maybe. I don't know. Anyway, the Ntiu Tut would never authorize a motion on those kinds of figures. The number of slaves was too small for the risk."

"One slave is one slave too many," Enlil returned.

"I agree, Atef, but for now, let's just get beyond this mission. I hate the fact that hundreds and thousands of our people are being held in bondage as much as the next brotha. I mean, that's why I busted my ass to become a member of the K'huti."

"Tu (yes), I understand, Kashta. It's just that I've been through this before. I don't know if you're aware of operation 'Quicken,' but we lost 14 Warrior-Soldiers; five of whom were K'huti. I was there," Enlil returned.

"Wait a minute, Atef. Are you saying that the Ntiu Tut have already authorized a Pod of K'huti into Quadrant Four?" I asked, glancing at Anpu; the shock and irritation showing on both our faces.

"Tu (yes). That's heavy ground, blood (Black man). Hell, while I was recovering at Kawa hospital, I overheard other K'huti talking about the dangers they faced in V-4...and, based on what they were saying, they were there two months before the Pod I went in with," he added.

"Did you get any Fractals generated?" Sa-Ra asked. I was beginning to like this kid. He couldn't have been more than 23 years old, but he had heart. He wasn't afraid to jump right in there with the rest of us.

"Tem (no), wait a minute, we did. It's just that all of our non-essential equipment was discarded," Enlil answered.

"So you just left what may have been our only chance of putting together a frag of V-4. Just what the hell did you guys run into...exactly?" I asked.

"Well, my brotha, when we entered Q.4., we didn't take the route you just suggested. Maybe if we did, things would have turned out for the better. Anyway, we were being fought hard. Factions from Cold Wind and New America had us pressed up against the Aztlann border. Maybe it would have been different if we weren't K'huti. Everything was hush-hush. You know, there's no record of our existence anywhere. Once we're in, we're on our own. And that night, we had a real blood bath on our hands," he continued. "Oh yeah, and I'll tell you something else. There were Blacks there, too. I didn't recognize them. They didn't belong to any military faction; or for that matter, country that I'd ever seen," he finished.

"What do you mean, 'Blacks?'" Sa-Ra interjected.

"Just what I said. Black people. Don't get me wrong, they weren't part of what was going on. They seemed more interested in just staying out of our way. They kind of watched us from the shadows," Enlil answered. "As soon as we trekked our way through Quadrant four and entered V-4, you could feel them. I mean, throughout the mission we would often catch glimpses of them. They were like ghosts or something. They may have been escaped slaves; I don't know," he ended.

"I've heard about these 'Blacks' living in the Wasted-Cities. I thought they were supposed to be a myth or something," Sa-Ra said innocently.

"No. They're real. I've seen them. They're all over the place. Mostly in the Wasted-Cities bordering Valhalla's southwestern regions," Oshun responded. "The more missions you take, the more likely you'll see them, too."

"He's right. I've been on more assignments then I can count. I didn't see them at first. But after awhile, as if they were ready to reveal themselves, they would allow me to see a shadow; or out of the corner-of-my-eye, I would catch one of them watching me. They never made themselves fully available. They just watched," I added.

"Tu (yes). They're out there, mostly concentrated on the southwest coastal regions of Q.4. They've always been there. When I was a child, I heard the older K'huti talk about them," Anpu added.

"Did you ever feel threatened?" Sa-Ra asked, his young face scanning the room; looking for anyone to respond.

"When I'm not in my own country, behind enemy lines, or under another man's jurisdiction, I always feel threatened," I responded.

CHAPTER 6

Under the cover of darkness, streaking towards the outer fringes of Valhalla, are three NARS. Gliding effortlessly across the heavens, their special coating of synthetic melanin polymers makes them invisible to enemy detection. Riding the electromagnetic currents generated by the earth's rotation, the NARS complete a parabola-jump over and across New America. Reaching a crescendo of five miles, they begin their descent towards the largest and most dangerous cluster of Wasted-Cities south of Valhalla. Quadrant Four. On board the highly specialized aircraft, we hardly notice the difference. Their triangular-wedged bodies and their superior energy welding capabilities make for a smooth and comfortable ride.

Vreeet.vreeet, Vreeet.vreeet. The landing protocols sound-off. Instinctively, we began to pull ourselves from our passive meditative states and shifted to a highly 'awakened' trance.

"We're here," Oshun transmitted across our wave-jumpers. Almost immediately, the perpetual gloom of Q-4 began to stain the chemically treated win-frames of the NAR. It's a frightening sight. A composite of metal, concrete, and jungle, twisted in a grotesque mockery of unholy copulation.

It's just as I remembered. The buildings were the first to die, lying on top of one another like broken titans. The streets are covered with everything from wrecked vehicles to weapons waste. And the remains of the dead are everywhere. Trees and other foliage have managed to reclaim lost terrain, hungrily reaching into man's ruin. I motioned to Oshun to drop us on the shore of the polluted bay that bubbled under what appeared to have once been a medium sized bridge.

A 3D holo of the surrounding terrain shimmered into focus. It shifted and hovered in front of Oshun like a tiny spirit. He pointed and reached at the floating image, "Okay, that's where I'm going to drop you guys off...over there," he said pointing at the nearly translucent map. The holo faded as the drop-off filled the view screen. It was an oily beachhead. Several pieces of mangled steel burst thorn-like from a small sandy hillside.

"Get us on the east bank. It's a little too early for a swim."

"No problem, Kash."

This is when we're most vulnerable. Laser snipers, air mines, anything could be waiting for us. That's why we travel in threes. The lead NAR stays at an altitude of half way between our highest point and our landing point. The second NAR remains half way between the Lead NAR, and the Birth NAR. We're in the Birth NAR.

On the ground, we moved with blurred and hurried motions. Like wild men, we snatched and pulled our supplies from the safety of the Birth NAR.

"I've got a good feeling about this one, Oshun," I said, trying to lighten the mood.

"Tu. I'm sure you do, Kashta," he returned, a slight smirk on his face.

After Anpu and the others had gotten the rest of the equipment off ship, I patted my chest, thumb in palm, fingers extended. Oshun nodded in acknowledgement. Taking a final and cautious look around, he turned and guided the shadowy NAR up and away from our location, it's blue-yellow exhaust disappearing into the mist above.

Eventually, all three will escape the dangers of the Wasted-City and 'lean' in mid-air towards Ta-Amenta. Maintaining equal distances apart, the Birth-NAR remains the closes to the drop-off, while the Lead NAR will be the furthest away.

Tanakamani began tracking their movements almost immediately. He's one of the best communications officers I know.

"They've already achieved stationary orbits," he announced. "Amazing. For all the Valhallans know, they might as well be natural gases, or simple anomalies on their radar," he finished.

Sa-Ra was busy unpacking and setting up his modular fract-imager. With it, he's going to reflect and bounce light off of the clouds, the ground, the water, the city; V-4, and using a sideways-digi-cam, he's going to generate a virtual map of Quadrant Four.

Anpu is setting up our armament. All things have their proper place. Accessibility is the prime objective. Lives depend on his expertise.

Our wave-jumpers have been properly configured for our mission. Compliments of Tanakamani. All of us are on the same secret channel. It's a highly classified band, a frequency discovered by one of our Mystic scientists. She found it while experimenting with new forms of sound. We call it the Zero Width. So far, Cold Wind have yet to decipher it. Many of the Ntiu Tut; as well as the Mystic scientists, maintain that it's our melanin that allows us to utilize its 'wave form.'

Enlil began feeding information into his mobile-comp. Programming it with bits and pieces of fragmented information and human memories, they'll be used to generate probable-maps.

"Alright, people, let's make it happen. We've got 81 hours to advance on heavy ground. We'll stay close to the water for as long as we can and continue on a southeast trek. By this time tomorrow, we should be well within range of V-4. It's a small Wasted-City, but no less dangerous. Intelligence reports high Cold Wind activity. Don't be surprised if we run into Aztlann and New American forces either."

"Okay, Kashta. I've set the coordinates to our fract-cams. They should be recording as we speak," Sa-Ra said smiling.

"Good. Tanakamani -"

"Everything's fine, Kashta. All channels are open, I mean as far as the Birth NAR goes," he answered.

"These should help us get as far as the outer perimeter of V-4," Enlil said, handing out the nearly transparent probable maps. We folded the micro thin plastic like squares, and placed them within the housings of our skin tight gloves.

Glancing over at Anpu, he gave me that familiar look. A look I've seen on many assignments; I don't even have to ask.

"Enlil, how far is the first point of contact?"

"About 20 nilo-meters southeast of here. They're all over the place, Kash."

"I'm placing us on zero-width. All it takes is a whisper, and everything we say will come across loud and clear," Tanakamani said, tapping three red buttons on his wave-jumper.

Every K'huti carries at least five standard pieces. All of it lightly built and sturdy as hell. The most important is the daath-Geb. It's made from a highly flexible plant material. It was dreamt up by one of our Warrior-Kings. I once heard a Cold Wind soldier refer to it as 'the dry suit from hell.' It covers everything from the neck down; I mean, our feet and everything. It has a flexi-helm which when not in use, sits attached in tiny rows across the nape of the head and neck. Using both hands, we reach back over our shoulders, and pull it up, over, and around our heads and faces, causing it to divide and separate into micro-sectioned plates. We then press and mold it against our faces. Having done that, we squeeze our palms together, causing the daath plates located in the cell walls of the plantlike 'dermis' to absorb as much air as possible. This causes the armor to harden around our bodies. It also gives us a frightening 'Reptilian Hawk-like' appearance.

It's simply an amazing piece of equipment. It can withstand most hand-held concussive weapons, up to and including small explosions. The thing changes colors to suit the environment, hardens or softens at the push of a button (located in our palms), and disposes of bodily wastes. It regulates our body temperature. And if we run out of food, we can actually eat it. It tastes like shit.

The mobile-comp is an improvement on the old lap-tops of the late 20th century. Today, they fit in the palm of our hands. And, when not in use, we 'clamp' them to a depression in the right shoulder plate of our daath-Geb. We each carry a Colbot Rifle. This is Anpu's favorite weapon. It generates vast amounts of heat...capable of melting reinforced titanium in minutes. Basically, it speeds up the atoms of its target, causing it to 'splatter' like water. We all have wave-jumpers. They're our means of communication. They fit securely within housings located in the front center of the neck, protected for the most part by the daath plates that hang over our faces. Each of us carries 'hand-held projectiles.' They're the next evolutionary jump on pistols. They have that old-school look about them. Glocks. And they are capable of generating a concussive force of 6000 feet per second. If it were not for the 'exoskeleton like' qualities of our daath-Geb, we wouldn't be able to shoot the things...

* * * * *

February 22 – 20th Century

The Keep, the most ancient of the secret orders of Gog and MaGog, ordered their minions to prevent the rise of a Black Messiah.

The entire African Diaspora had been designated as food. And so using a system of light-code transmissions, they confused the time and preformed arcane rituals to feed on the faith, fear, and genius of Black people. The progressive Blacks who would emerge from the community were assassinated and replaced with chippers - mind-controlled slaves. Those who did not fall victim to the social-religious engineering of the schools, churches, and movies, were deemed enemies of the state and hunted like animals.

"Why?" she whispered. "It was as if those in power needed Black people in some sick twisted way," she resigned.

It was an idea that was crossing her mind more and more these days. And what of her brothas and sistahs in struggle? They only wanted to help Black people become productive citizens in American society. Her husband, and the bulk of the Black United Front out of Oakland, California, were missing. The past five days had been pure hell. Scattered images of police cars, helicopters, and the sound of gunfire were her constant companions.

Kandace was a brown-skinned black woman. She felt quite privileged at having been born during these times. With the awakening 'Black Consciousness,' sisters her complexion and darker were suddenly deemed quite beautiful. She didn't have to trip off of the short kinks that grew tangled and hard from her head. And her 'fat round booty' didn't hurt matters either. Maybe it was the politics of the time, but like a lot of young African American women her age, she chose to be with the darkest brotha she could find. The brothas and sistahs in struggle called him Tarharka. His mother and father called him Calvin. Kandace and Tarharka had been together for three years. They were strong, full of fire, and they were in love. This is what hurt Kandace the most. It took so long to find a brotha she could trust, a brotha who was real.

"*God please let him be alright*, she whispered. She should have been more concerned about her own well being.

She had been up all night, running, hiding, crying. Her dress was soiled, and her body had not been washed in days. She was alone, she was afraid, and she was in labor. The dark alley on 14th street in East Oakland that had comforted her for the past few days would be the first of many homes to her unborn child. She didn't care; she was a trained 'Urban Soldier'. She was also a pragmatic sister. She was already thinking of ways to beat the system out of food-stamps and medical. She didn't give a fuck, *they did it to everyone else, why couldn't she do it to them?* she thought.

To the untrained eye, this was a death hole. But to Kandace, this alley was a special place. There are two huge garbage cans that are always full. You can find anything from 'day old' vegetables, to fresh breads and fruits. The steam from the china-shops supplied warmth to the transits, prostitutes, and various street peoples that matriculated this place. And the moss covered cement gives its tenants a kind of natural carpeting. Food, heat, a place to lie down, all the comforts of home.

The pains were getting sharper and lasting longer. She desperately needed a soft place to rest. Realizing this, Kandace pulled herself up and braced herself against a muck encrusted wall. Slowly and carefully, she guided herself towards the far end of the alley. Exhausted, she collapsed in a pile of newspapers and boxes of old cloths. Minutes passed, then it happened. In a flash of light bathed in an indescribable surge of pain, she let out a yell. Grunting and snorting, bodily fluids running, she pushed new life into the world. Wrapping herself in her already filthy dress, she cut the umbilical cord with a pair of scissors she was holding for protection. Wiping the blood, and pulling the soft lumpy stuff from her baby's mouth, she was relieved to hear its cry. Pushing its fat legs apart, she was doubly happy to discover it was a boy. Not knowing if she would ever see her beloved Tarharka again, she followed through on his ultimate wish. She named their son, SKAH...

* * * * *

CHAPTER 7

... aung, hang, kashang... aung, hang, kashang. We chanted the hekau of protection. Moving in unison, we splashed through thick green slime, jogged across fog covered marshes, and crawled over hills of mud and granite, all at a terrific pace. Our reward: a smoldering ghostly skyline. We called it V-4. The most dangerous vicinity in Northern California. With what little information we've been able to gather, Northern California has been divided into equal regions; hence the name 'Quadrant Four.' The first block is considered permissive. It rests along the lifeless Bay of brown water where we were dropped.

The fourth block is deep inland. Heavy Ground. The fourth vicinity, or V-4 for short. Great are the number of K'huti who have fallen in this wasted plain.

"I can't believe I'm actually here," Sa-Ra whispered. "And don't forget to make sure your micro-cams are recording."

"Wow. You're a crazy man. I don't think I've ever met anyone happy to be in this place," Anpu remarked half jokingly.

"Enlil, what's up?" Tanakamani whispered, his voice sliding across our wave-jumpers.

"I don't know. Something just doesn't feel right."

He's good. I got the same impression a few miles back.

"Hey, do you think it's Cold Wind?" Sa-Ra asked, the excitement booming in his voice.

"Don't be so enthusiastic to get into a fight, young blood. The wise man seeks to avoid confrontation if he can," Tanakamani replied.

There was a time when I - no we - were just like him. It wasn't until I smelled the rancid breath of death before I changed my mind.

"Sa-Ra, I need you to maintain your Men-Ab (stability). I can't have you risking the lives of this Pod just to satisfy your bloodlust," I barked, pulling the daath-Geb plates up and away from my face.

"Tu (yes), Kashta, I understand. I hope I haven't caused you or the brothers to doubt my abilities. I'm quite capable of behaving as an adult-"

"Hetepu (peace), my brotha. We were all like you once upon a time," Enlil chimed in.

Ten minutes later, we reached a small embankment and began laying camp. It was High ground. An excellent location in which to begin our descent into the heart of V-4. I could smell the burnt asphalt from here. Nerve-wracking. Seemed like every few minutes, the sound of breaking glass had us jumping; weapons drawn, ready to engage. As the sun began to slip into the underworld (west), our daath-Geb began to darken. Looking more like a shadow than a man, Anpu walked to the edge of the camp. He positioned himself next to a pile of scattered asphalt and began first watch. Tanakamani was busy sending and receiving coded messages to and from the NARS which hovered somewhere above us. Enlil and Sa-Ra had successfully managed to generate a pretty decent fract-map of the outer fringes of V-4, and almost a third of Quadrant Four respectfully. Things were going well. Too well.

"Enlil, show Sa-Ra how to upload a stream to Oshun. Then let him pair up with Anpu. I want him to learn how to POST-UP. You and Tanakamani get some rest, you'll both be on POST tomorrow evening."

"Tu," he responded. Enlil was a true soldier. It took him less than 5 minutes to get Sa-Ra situated. On 'down time', K'huti cause their gear to 'harden' next to trees, rocks, or in water. The melanin crystals within the daath-Geb constantly adjusts it's frequency to match that of the surrounding environment. This causes the gear to change it's outer coloring. The K'huti are trained to sleep standing up. My Pod is a little more innovative. Enlil took a kneeling stance next to a patch of shrubs. Four minutes later, he was nearly invisible. I preferred to lie on my back. Flat across the ground; sort of a hide-in-plain-sight method. Over the years, Anpu and I have worked out a very basic sign language. I held up 3 fingers. Three fingers meant three hours on-post, three hours off-post. We would followed this procedure for the next two days...

* * * * *

October 17, late twentieth-century

One day after the Million Man March, Skah and his father Tarharka, were feeling quite ecstatic. Having missed his son's birth, Tarharka thanked the 'Creator of the Heavens and Earth', for granting him such a wonderful opportunity to create still another great memory with his beloved son. They were very close, these two. Skah was lucky. He had two loving parents, two attentive parents, and more importantly, two conscious parents. On the plane ride home, they both leaned back in their chairs, savoring the glorious experience of having joined with over a Million members of the *Original Brotherhood*; Black men, all poised and standing alert, on and at the Capital of the most powerful country on the face of the earth.

Walking through the Airport stations was such an exhilarating experience for Skah. He noticed how the white folks were looking at him. They seemed drawn to look. Brief eye contact was made, then they would lower their eyes. Skah felt powerful. He felt that on that day, the black race scored a victory. *Now it was the Black race 1, the white race 400,* he laughed to himself.

Noticing everything about Skah since he was a week old, Tarharka couldn't help but ask, "So...what's on your mind, how do you feel about what we just did?"

Looking at his father, Skah proudly said, "I feel that our people are beginning to stir from their sleep. I figure that we have... maybe... another 50 to 100 years of sleepy-time left. Then we'll become totally aware of what Time-It-Is."

Tarharka, having served in several Black, Nationalistic, and Africentric armies, was pleased with his son's answer. *I taught him well,* he said to himself. "And, after waking from this supposed sleepy-time, what's next?" he asked, becoming excited at what his son would possibly say. You see, Skah was a gifted child. He saw things beyond his years - hell, beyond his generation. At 15, he organized all of the athletes at his High school to stop playing football, basketball, and running track, until the school hired more Black Faculty. He did the same thing in College.

"I see a time when our people will be self sufficient. They, or we, won't rely on anyone else. We will develop our own institutions, economies, relationships with other peoples and countries, it's all going to happen," he said forcefully.

"Wait a minute now, Black man. Just calm down. Remember, never allow your feelings to dictate your behavior," Tarharka said, smiling at the passion in his son's voice.

"Yeah, I know, Atef (father, Black man), it's just that we're running out of time. Even destiny can be averted. If the people aren't ready to fill the void that destiny brings, those people get past over."

"That's right. You know, son, you're starting to sound more and more like your mother. You look like me. You have my fire and strength, but you have your mother's connection to reality," Tarharka said. Skah's mother; a beautiful and powerful sister, was totally devoted to the resurrection of the Black race. She was named after the Great Queens of ancient Kush: Kandace.

"Well, actually I think I have a perfect combination. I couldn't have asked for a better mother and father. And yesterday," Skah continued, "yesterday was the greatest day of my life. I thank God everyday for having been blessed with conscious people in my life," Skah added. "If you and mother were not conscious, I probably would be out buying chicken, or playing hoops somewhere!"

They both laughed loud and hard. The people on the plane; having watched the news coverage of the 'Million Man March,' just figured that every loud and obnoxious Black man had just come from the event; *better to leave them alone today*, they whispered among themselves.

"I can't wait to get home to Kandace," Tarharka said to his son. "I know she's very proud of all of the brothers who joined us, but I'm the lucky one. I'm the one who is going to be loved by a 'Down Sistah,'" he ended, leaning further back in his chair, and intentionally annoying the white man seated behind him.

"So, what's it like to have a conscious Black woman loving you?" Skah asked his father.

"Why are you asking me, son? With all those beautiful sistahs you used to bring around the house...I know one of them was conscious," he replied. "When are you going to give me some 'Granbabies' anyway?"

"When I find a conscious Black woman," Skah answered. "I mean, wouldn't it be hard to create a family with a woman who didn't know who or what she was?"

"That depends on the man or woman who was supposed to be conscious," his father returned. Tarharka always answered his son in that manner. He felt it made his son think. Kandace thought it unnecessary. "Listen son, don't always assume 'the grass is greener on the other side of the fence.' Sometimes you may not need a conscious sister. Maybe you need to pair up with an unconscious Black woman and wake her up," Tarharka replied.

"Ah, c'mon, Pop. You know just like I do that no matter how much knowledge, wisdom, and understanding you 'drop' on an unconscious sistah, she'll reject everything you tell her. The both of you will argue for two or three years over what to do on Christmas and Easter, and then you'll break-up. Then a couple of years will pass, and you'll run into her at some rally, or at some lecture or something, and she'll have an 'African name,' three or four little beautiful Black babies, and a lucky-ass brother benefiting from all the work you put in," Skah answered sarcastically.

"BWHA, HA, HAR, HA... HEH, HEH... HAR, HA, HA," Tarharka laughed hard. He enjoyed his conversations with his son. Skah chuckled to himself.

Suddenly, the plane made a sharp dip, then vibrated and shivered. A few minutes later, it let out a loud groaning noise.

"Oh shit! That's it. We get back from the Million Man March, and we're going to crash before we fucking get home!" Tarharka said out loud. Tarharka always hated planes. If he could walk to Africa, he would have. "Anything but fly on a damn plane," he often said.

"Calm down, dad. We're just landing, we're home; in Oakland. I can't believe a serious warrior like you is afraid of flying."

"Hey, look, I've still got a lot of work to do. I ain't got time to be crashing on some plane," Tarharka answered. They both started laughing. This was one of the best weeks they've had together; hanging out in D.C., attending the Million Man March, and going to the various lectures in Washington. It was priceless.

Tarharka didn't waste time retrieving his belongings. He pushed past several waiting passengers, then bumrushed the lobby. He knew Kandace would be there waiting for him. He couldn't wait to see her. After almost 30 years of marriage, they still loved one another like school kids. Scanning the lobbies one by one, he finally saw her. She was standing with Freida, a friend of Skah's. Tarharka began grinning like a kid in an arcade with $50 in tokens. Upon seeing him, Kandace started laughing and running towards him. They found each other in a tight embrace. They stood there, holding each other for what seemed like an eternity. It wasn't until Skah walked up behind them that they realized that they were in public. They didn't care; they knew they had something special. Skah, moving in his usual slow and deliberate manner, finally managed to walk over to Freida. He kissed her. She loved him more than he loved her. He tolerated her because she was fine; she had beautiful skin, was well educated, and had a big ass.

"So, how is my Mr. One in a million Black man?" Freida asked smiling, showing rows of pearly white teeth.

"I'm doing fine, baby, how're you?"

"Great, honey. I'm so proud of you. I cried when I saw you all on television. The Minister pulled it off. I just hope he don't sell-out and go 'mainstream' after this," Freida responded.

Skah was taken aback. He began to realize how far Freida had come since they first met. She suddenly became more attractive to him.

"Naahhh. That brotha will never give up his post," Skah replied.

CHAPTER 8

We were ghosts. Haunting ruined and abandoned buildings. My mind was set adrift, dwelling on the countless lives that toiled and died in places like this. Over the years, I've come to realize why V-4 was more dangerous in comparison to most Wasted-cities. It's a sea of torn concrete and glass. Jungle and vacant lots crashing into collapsed ten and twenty story buildings. A hideous tapestry of broken highways and derelict suburbs. Now it sits like an unwanted child...full of despair and contempt. I bet in the late 20th century, communities like this lulled millions of middle class Black folk to sleep. Now it's just a boil.

"Kashta-," Anpu's voice burst from my wave-jumper.

"What do you think they've found, Kashta?" Tanakamani asked, pulling his flexi-helm over and around his head and face.

"Don't know. But what ever it is, we'll deal with it straight and proper."

Our daath-Geb automatically began *listening* to our bodies. Regulating our temperatures and monitoring our pulse; its internal nano-mechs synched with our involuntary nervous systems.

"Anpu, location-"

"We're south of your position. Maybe 150 het-meters-"

The three of us turned in unison. We were greeted by rows of rubble and scorched asphalt.

"There. He's in there. Let's go. Tanakamani, cover us."

"No problem, Kashta, you know how we do it."

I went first, then Enlil. We darted towards a large domed building. It was burned up pretty bad. A series of faded pictures ran across its outer walls. The entrance was a hole with a pile of rocks for a door. I looked back at Tanakamani. He stood motionless, bent in a crouched position, his portable-comp clamped to his right shoulder. His armor was beginning to blend with its surroundings. Before Enlil and I reached the other side of the rocky street, Tanakamani was nearly indistinguishable from the heap of granite which lay behind him. I walked past the makeshift door. Enlil ran through the gaping hole that was probably once a window. We were met by a green haze. Colbot rifles raised, we scanned its spacious interior.

"Alright, Tanakamani. Let's make it happen-" I was growing restless.

When he stood, he shimmered into focus. Barely a shadow, he methodically crept his way across the rock littered streets. This is when we're most vulnerable. If we remain motionless, eventually our armor will make an attempt to re-adjust its outer skin to match that of its surroundings. But when we move, it flickers. And if we keep moving, it'll eventually assume it's neutral bark-like coloring. By the time Tanakamani pushed past the thick haze on the lower level, Enlil and I were half way up the dingy stairs. We found Anpu and Sa-Ra on the second floor, their daath-Geb desperately trying to match the ridiculously red colored carpet.

"Okay, Anpu. Report," I said, motioning the others to *Post-up*. Like phantoms, they quietly complied.

"Look over there," he said pointing. "Towards those old dwellings. Over there, next to the entrance to that large subway hole. Cold Wind," he answered, handing me his peepers. I held them up to the long V-shaped visor that barely pierced the hard reptilian-like folds of my flexi-helm.

"Tanakamani. Notify Oshun. Inform him that we've made contact with a team of Cold Wind Soldiers at 1600 hours-"

"Sa-Ra, how are your f-maps coming?"

"Going great, Kashta."

"Our objectives at this point are only to observe and report. I'll make the determination if and when we go *live*."

"What the hell are we waiting for? Let's just go in there and blow their pink asses away!"

I glanced at Enlil. He shook his head in disagreement. Anpu and Tanakamani just ignored Sa-Ra. I couldn't. I've served with the others before. They knew how and when to voice their opinions. Sa-Ra was young and inexperienced, and that was the only thing that kept me from 'dropping' him where he stood.

"I don't have time to go through this with you again, Sa-Ra. All I need from you is cooperation. I thought we took care of this problem the other night," I asked rhetorically.

"Kashta, they're moving. Shut the kid up, and let's go," Anpu interrupted. He's right. I'll have to settle my concerns with Sa-Ra another time. Pulling myself together, I motioned to the others to group-up and follow the Cold Wind unit. Without hesitation, the three of them scattered down the wide birth of stairs and disappeared into the courtyard.

Maintaining my Men-Ab (stability), I turned to Sa-Ra...

"Listen up. In order to be a successful Warrior-Soldier; let alone, K'huti, you've got to learn to follow direction. I'm At least 10 seasons your senior, and I've seen a whole lot of fights. I think it would be of service to you if you'd try to remember that. You came highly recommended. I'd hate to think that Tefnut misjudged you."

Pulling himself upright, Sa-Ra pulled his flexi-Helm over and around his head and face. Squeezing his palms, I heard the harsh whisper of air filling the cells of his daath-Geb. Yanking his Colbot rifle from his shoulder harness, he looked at me and replied, "You're right, Kashta. Sometimes I tend to get over zealous about things. I definitely want to do the right thing. You won't have any more problems out of me."

"I hope not, now lets get the hell out here." Changing subjects, "This particular Cold Wind unit was a large one. Usually they travel in groups of 10. This company looked to be around 25 or 30."

"Do you think they're an Aft-Patrol?"

He's smart. I hope his discipline will match his intellect one day.

"Not sure. At any rate, we've got to be extra careful. A company this size is definitely combat-ready." We scrambled through mist, rocks, and shrubbery, before we finally caught up with the others. They were practically invisible, except for the occasional flicker of grey-brown armor. They were crouched behind an ancient water fountain.

"Anpu... how many-"

"Over 20. Five on point, six lagging behind. The rest are casing the buildings. My guess is that they're looking for escaped slaves. Or maybe just a perimeter drop-"

"I don't like it. Something's not right. Tanakamani. Advise Oshun to signal the chain (Nars). We'll need a pick-up in 15 minutes. Looks like we've got ourselves a MOR (mission over-ride)," I said stoically.

"I can't get through. It's the weather. It's changing up on them. It'll take at least 20... 25 minutes before they can break orbit. Whatever you've got planned, we had better get started," Tanakamani said urgently.

"I suppose you'll get your wish today, young-blood. Your first taste of battle. Just remember, though, it's not as romantic as you might think."

I signaled Anpu and Enlil to take-up 'east and west' positions; covering the only natural escape routes available to the Cold Wind unit.

Anpu was first to get situated. A few seconds later, Enlil had posted up just opposite his location. They'd managed to get right along side the Cold Wind unit. Perhaps a few het-meters behind, but close enough. I showed Tanakamani five fingers. He shook his head and remained behind; hulled-up behind the cracked fountain which sat near the center of the abandoned plaza.

Sa-Ra and I followed directly behind the Cold Wind Team. Like ghosts, we dogged their every step. They're not far, 20, maybe 30 het-meters ahead of us. *There was something about the way they moved...*

"Sa-Ra, what is the primary objective of the K'huti?"

"Our first and most important Oath as a K'huti, is to secure the Lost-Found. Free the slaves. That's it. That's why we become K'huti. No matter what our original orders are, if we suspect that Lost-Found are within 100 het-meters of our location, we fight."

The kid has a good memory for sure. But he has no idea of what he's about to experience. Maybe that was for the best.

"Enlil, how many-"

"I've got four soldiers in plan sight. They're moving away from the main pack. I can't believe this; they're making this too easy."

"Anpu-"

"I've got three in plan sight. The other two are casing the buildings. What about you and 'greeny' back there," he returned.

"Heh, heh...I count six stragglers. They're moving in five het-meter spreads, aft-speed," I answered. "Me and the kid can take them. How about you and Enlil?"

"We're clear, just waiting for you and Greeny to get situated."

As I glanced at Sa-Ra, I couldn't help but wonder if he passed his 'Rites of Passage'. *Nah, what am I thinking?*

CHAPTER 9

Anpu and Enlil struck in unison. The kid and I were 20 meters lagging, but there was no mistaking the rapid echo of artillery discharge or the damnable squawk of Cold Wind com-units. We rushed to join the fray and took them on in unconscious fashion. That's how we've been taught. Just keep it on the subconscious level...you just do it, and you do it for keeps.

"Sa-Ra...watch your back! You need to be more flexible." He's better than I'd imagined. He's holding his own, a little wild, but holding his own. "Anpu, Enlil, report-"

Cold Wind. It didn't take them long to regroup. Like wild men, they took up positions in and around the scorched and dusty buildings that dominated the landscape like rotten teeth in a dead man's mouth. Their Mercury based rifles spit streams of orange death. Over the years, Valhallan scientists have been able to take advantage of three major holes in our ground defense. The first and probably most serious is that every time we discharge our weapons, the carbon based atoms in our daath-Geb reflects a shadow. For an instant, they're able to see through our camouflage. Secondly, they train their bio-enhanced soldiers to automatically direct their attention at the source of our discharge. They've gotten pretty good at it. And third, there's the whole motion factor. If we move, we can more readily be seen.

"Enlil, watch your back. They're closing-" Anpu's shouts went unanswered.

"Enlil, Enlil, where the hell are you!" I interrupted.

"Maybe he's -" Sa-Ra interjected.

"That's enough damn it! Enlil, report-"

"I'm stuck! These crackers have got me 'hemmed in.' I don't know where I'm at-"

"Tanakamani, are you picking this up?!"

"Everything, Kashta. I'm simultaneously transmitting to Oshun. They're breaking orbit *on the now!*"

Cold Wind had managed to split the four of us, and we had no idea were Enlil was. This assignment was going to hell.

"Hey look. More of them," one of them barked. He and three others began firing wildly from behind a pile of half melted PVC pipes. Blue eyes flashing, their braided hair swung like fat golden ropes. They were possessed. Their mechanical accuracy, countered only by our disciplined improvisation.

Two more stepped from inside a square shaped building of white stone. Even in the midst of battle, I couldn't help noticing a large bronze statue of an eagle. It sat stoically across the building's crumbling entrance.

"I guess it's our lucky day," another one shouted from across the plaza. He and a tall lanky red haired man darted from behind a fallen balcony. Their green and brown uniforms made them look like giant moss rats. Cold Wind soldiers are bionic. Not in the mechanical sense. Their natural organic musculature and skeletal systems have been genetically enhanced. Valhallan scientists have isolated the alleles which hold the genes responsible for muscle and bone growth.

Ta-Amentans have managed to keep pace by augmenting our hearts and minds spiritually. By becoming spiritual soldiers; K'huti. We *think* our bodies into becoming as perfect as possible.

Our sword welding adversaries were relentless. A short stocky man with a blond crew-cut activated a loud shrieking alarm. And within minutes, a bunch of his cohorts sprang from the countless crevices that grew vine-like all around us.

"Pod-4, do you read... Pod-4, do you read... this is Oshun. What's your location-?"

Finding respite, I managed to blurt out, "We're southeast of the delta drop off. We ran out of options and had to go inland. Quadrant Four...v-4. We look to be in a large outdoor Plaza or Mall of some sort-"

"Yeah, mother fuckers," Sa-Ra screamed. He frantically fired at every green, brown, and beige uniform in sight. He sent them scrambling.

Colbot Rifle in hand, I followed up with a wide burst of blue discharge. I heard the familiar cracking of bone, final screams, and the hollow thud of felled bodies. I didn't stick around to take note though. Battle was never glamorous. It was quick, brutal, and never personal. I dropped to my belly and swam through the dirt and rocks. I scrambled like a lizard until I reached several recently blown holes in the side of a large wall. I crawled through the darkness. Moments later, I found myself in a large room. Its floors were made of blue marble. I was alone. Ignoring the deadly exchanges outside, and trying to avoid bringing any attention to my newly found hiding place, I reached for my neck and pinched the slender coils of plastic steel, which fit snugly within the folds of my daath-Geb. "Enlil, what's your status?... Enlil-"

"I'm okay. When in the hell are you brothers going to get here? I can hear that idiot Sa-Ra from-"

Turning with the grace and speed of years of combat experience, I twisted and leapt to my feet, rifle in front, palm on trigger.

"Wait a minute, Kashta," I heard from the shadows. Anpu was huddled up against the corner on the far wall. His breathing was labored, and he was holding his side. "I think I've been shot enough for today," He said.

"Sorry about that, my brotha, but you know how it is..."

Anpu peeled his flexi-helm from over his face.

"Just need some real air...even if it's polluted."

"Yeah, Satan. Take that," We heard Sa-Ra shout from the other side of the dew stained walls. The good part was that he was managing to hold his own, the bad part was that he was basically alone...

"Enlil is close by. He says he can hear Sa-Ra's antics outside," I advised Anpu. "Tanakamani, what's going on in your part of the world-"

"Kashta, I've got all NARS online. They can hear everything that's going on," He responded.

"Anpu, I'm going out to help the kid. You find Enlil and establish contact with Oshun and the others. Let's end this shit!" I ordered.

"Bet. I'm on my way," he answered, disappearing into the smoke filled room.

As soon as Anpu faded into the darkened catacombs, I stopped, dropped, and wriggled through the same space I crawled in from. It's a mess out here. Small concussive explosions could be heard in the distance. The occasional streak of mercury laser, and the cold hollowed moans of the dying was our background music. No signs of Sa-Ra.

Dammit, how could I have left him out here alone? Did I do it on purpose? I asked myself. Remaining flat on my stomach, I continued to crawl over and through the hard rubble.

"Kashta...over here," a low raspy voice uttered from my above right. "Look up," it said again. Squinting my eyes, and turning my head in slow motion, I noticed a shadowy figure standing five meters above me. It was Sa-Ra. He was okay, a little shaken, but alive. He was crouched behind a slab of what used to be the rear balcony of an old Town house or something. His daath-Geb barely blending with it's matrix of grays and browns.

Pulling myself up, and standing under and against the same balcony, I looked up and asked, "How many are left?"

"About seven. They're held-up in that building across the second Plaza," he finished, the exhaustion shown in his voice. *He's a fighter.*

"Where the hell is Tanakamani? I spoke to him over six minutes ago-"

"Didn't you hear? He's got an e.t.a. of two minutes. Oshun and the others are maintaining their positions until further orders. It turns out this area is Heavy Ground. Tanakamani said something about there being interference or something. Oshun can't get a fix on us."

Instinctively, I reached for my wave-jumper. It was gone.

Helping him down and off the edge of the balcony, I ordered, "Get Tanakamani on the horn, we need a pick up!"

Sa-Ra complied. I wished I could hear what he was saying. Without my wave-jumper, I felt cut-off from the world.

"This way, Kashta." I followed Sa-Ra through the haze and smoke. Without my wave-jumper, it was difficult to keep up with him. It's our wave-jumpers that allow us to physically 'know' where the other K'huti are. Something to do with the melanin in our nervous systems, and the Zero frequency we use. At least that's how the Mystic-Scientists explained it. Otherwise, we'd have to wait until a K'huti moved. That's when his daath-Geb flickers, hence making him temporarily visible.

Swerving around an endless maze of darkened corners, rifle in hand, I was relieved to see Anpu and Enlil. Anpu was supporting

Enlil by his left side, while he himself leaned up against a granite column. They looked like hell. "We're ready when you are, Kashta," Enlil said smiling. His flexi-helm, a shredded mass of tree bark, lay around his neck.

Making too much noise for one man, Tanakamani came crashing through the dust and smoke. He stood wide-eyed, looking amazed that we had actually scattered the Cold Wind unit.

"Alright, Atefs. Lets go home. Single file, five het-meter spread. We got a date with a sky-hopper," I said, pointing northwest.

Un-strapping his Colbot rifle, Tanakamani re-attached his portable-comp to his right shoulder. Pointing first to Anpu, then to Sa-Ra, I motioned for them to take the point. I'd bring up the rear, with Enlil and Tanakamani five and ten het-meters ahead of me.

Stealthily, we began our trek across the remains of one of the most dangerous Wasted-Cities in this region. We each alternately scanned left and right, occasionally making 360 degree turns, not wanting to take any chances with a Cold Wind ambush. We wouldn't survive it. We were too close to Valhalla.

This is a drawn out process. Whenever we'd reached a building, or any fallen structure for that matter, we had to time our departure. One at a time, we bounced over and across the rocks and gravel. We looked like scampering insects in need of shelter. Time seemed to move in slow motion. It was all surreal. Call it an altered state of consciousness, or deep concentration; whatever it was, we were caught totally unawares by the intrusion of Oshun's voice emanating from Tanakamani's mobile-comp-

"Oshun, to Pod-4... do you read," we heard over its tiny audiocrom speakers. "Pod-4, do you read...come in!"

"Shut that thing off, Tanakamani. Everyone switch to zero-frequency."

From out of nowhere, pencil thin streaks of crimson death recklessly flashed passed us.

"Kashta, over there next to that slag heap! Cold Wind! The bastards followed us!" Anpu shouted.

"Tanakamani, break right, head for that temple. Get Oshun on the horn, tell him we need a Flash Maneuver," I shouted. "Enlil, take the kid and cover Tanakamani. Anpu, let's do this."

In this highly variable and artificial environment, our armor was providing little to no camouflage. We'd have to rely on its actual sturdiness for protection. So long as we didn't take a direct hit, we'd survive the mercury. Problem is, it'll only be a matter of time before Cold Wind reinforcements arrive.

Tanakamani rushed ahead, crisscrossing over and between a pile of telephone poles. Shadow-like, he tucked himself behind them and yanked off his mobile-comp. Seconds later, his daath-Geb readjusted and he was nearly invisible.

Enlil grabbed Sa-Ra by the arm, and proceeded to follow Tanakamani through a litter of busted pipes and tangles of thick black wires. Another surreal moment. I mean, despite the constant streams of enemy fire, the sound of exploding concrete and rupturing steel, I couldn't help laughing out loud. Sa-Ra was amazing. Here we are in the heat of battle, death everywhere you turned, and the kid still refused to just follow Enlil to safety.

"We can't keep this up forever, Anpu," I shouted, peeking from behind a huge marble statue. It was covered in bird droppings and scorch marks.

Anpu rushed to join me. Cold Wind soldiers were taking up positions in and around the outer buildings. We were surrounded. Breathing heavily, Anpu leaned against the crusty statue.

"Agreed. We need a miracle...something to keep them busy so we can catch our ride home. Besides, I definitely don't want to be around for the post-burn," Anpu said, pointing towards the southern skies.

I looked up. My heart skipped. Above the tattered buildings and smoky haze, I could see the unmistakable signatures of the NARS. From this distance, they looked like three black dots surrounded by blue-yellow circles.

"Yeah... the post-burn." A flash-maneuver is a devastating flyby. It's as dangerous for us as it is for its intended target. The Birth NAR takes root, while the second and third NAR burst from the clouds and streaks over head to deliver a 'Contained Colbot Bomb.' It's a weapon that was designed by a Warrior-Queen named Sekmet. She arranged the molecular structure of the free radicals within the bomb's nuclear matrix, such that once it is detonates, it destroys all organic materials within a 200 het-meter radius. It then feeds on itself, disappearing without a trace. The effects of the flash-maneuver are commonly referred to as the Post-Burn.

I didn't have long to lament our current situation.

"Kashta, it's the kid. He got away from me. He's headed your way!" Without my wave-jumper, I was using my mobile-comp as a means for communication; at least that's how the K'huti kept me appraised of what was going on. The only problem was, that I couldn't use it to communicate with them.

Sa-Ra's lack of discipline is going to get us killed. If not by Cold Wind, then our atoms would be scattered by the flash-maneuver.

I worked my way closer to the far east end of the colossal figure of stone. Catching Anpu's attention, I yelled, "Raise the kid on your wave-jumper, find out where the hell he is." I continued to fire at our tormentors. This was definitely becoming a 'white situation'.

A loud obnoxious voice emanated from my mobile-comp. "I'm over here, Kashta. I'm coming to save you and Anpu's butts."

Crazy ass, Sa-Ra.

Anpu just shook his head. "I guess that answers our question."

"What the hell is he doing? At this range he'll be dead meat before he reaches us," I responded. "And why isn't he wearing his flexi-helm?"

"Kashta... Anpu, this is Tanakamani, do you read. Kashta... Anpu..."

I pointed at Anpu. He knew immediately that from this point on, he was the contact man. I was making myself totally responsible for Sa-Ra. Leaping up and over a chunk of statue, I rushed towards Sa-Ra. He just stood there, transfixed. I dared not avert my eyes from his; an old Mesniu trick. Sometimes it works, sometimes it doesn't. His eyes began to get bigger and bigger. *Now this is working too good*, I thought. Usually it only freezes a person up, but Sa-Ra...

"What the hell is wrong with you? Why are you trying to get us all killed?!" No answer. He just stood there, slowly raising his arms and pointing. His mouth was wide opened, and he stared right through me.

I grabbed him with one arm, then violently pulled and twisted him to the hard gravel. As our armor re-adjusted it's outer skin, I turned, rifle in hand, poised and ready for anything. Or so I thought. Storming from behind a wall of raised buildings and rusted out ground vehicles were at least 20 Cold Wind Soldiers with heavy artillery! I mean these guys had weapons I'd never seen before. They must have laid low; followed us. *But why, why not just take us out?*

Pulling Sa-Ra up by his rifle strap, I managed to discharge a few rounds of Colbot. "Alright kid, it doesn't get any worse than this. Maybe next time you'll be more careful about what you wish for."

Blinking his eyes and looking a little ashamed, he raised his fire arm. "I'm... I'm with you, Kashta," he said; starting to get his color back.

Almost simultaneously, Both Enlil and Tanakamani fell in behind us and started kicking off round after round of Colbot juice. Sa-Ra and I joined them in action.

"Did you make contact with Oshun?"

Tanakamani nodded, "Tu (yes). He'll be here in two minutes. Get yourselves together!"

"It's about time you brothers got here!" Anpu shouted from behind a pair of pine trees. He was hit. Luckily he had his daath-Geb on maximum density. At that level of hardness, it slows the reflexes, but it protects you from the burn.

"Look, I'm all for doing things the conventional way, but let's get that flash-maneuver going!" I said sarcastically.

Tanakamani shook his head, "It's no good, Kashta. We couldn't get clearance. We've been ordered not to-"

"Why the fuck not?!" I yelled, losing a degree of Men-Ab (stability) in the process.

"Warrior-King Senwosret," Tanakamani responded somberly.

"Here we go again," Enlil said under his breath. "*Hmmnn.* Obviously they don't want to risk destroying any chances at recovering whatever it is that they really want in this place. I'd wish they just came out and say what the hell it is that we're supposed to retrieve. It ain't Lost-Found."

I felt nauseous. This is the one thing I hate about being K'huti.

"The Ntui-Tut just used us. They don't care about us," Sa-Ra blurted.

It was time to re-evaluate. I had three of the best K'huti any man could hope to serve with on this exercise. But no matter how good they were, this was a no-win situation. We were forced out of the centers of Quadrant-four before we were able to get a visual of a Looting-team, let alone slaves. And Anpu was starting to stiffen up. There was a hole torn straight through his bark. His arm looked broken. Tanankamani and Enlil were no worse for wear. And Sa-Ra was as dangerous and unpredictable as the Cold Wind unit that leapt at us from this hell hole.

"Okay, Atef's. Lets bounce."

Too late. Sa-Ra jumped and dashed towards the approaching Cold Wind unit. His timing couldn't be worse. The NARS were slicing and dipping through the murky clouds, cutting a wobbly path right for us. Half of the Cold Wind unit engaged the NARS; the other half concentrated their weapons on us. Sa-Ra didn't stand a chance! This is the nature of battle. In an instant, everything that can go wrong does.

I crawled up and over a trail of fallen girders. I rolled past a wet bed of grass and got behind a pile of tires. I got Tanakamani's attention by waving my arms, and pointed to where my wave-jumper used to be.

"Contact Oshun, advise him to land in that clearing over there," I shouted, pointing to an unobstructed section of street. It lay beyond a small heap of sand and brick. It was probably 20 square meters of dirt and gravel.

Pulling his portable-comp from his right shoulder, Tanakamani began dialing instructions to Oshun. If he hadn't moved, I wouldn't have noticed him. I gave Anpu a 'raised fist' gesture. He and Enlil immediately jumped to their feet and began spraying waves of Colbot at our assailants. Cold Wind soldiers were dropping like Mist dogs at an electric fence.

"Anpu, Enlil, catch up with Tanakamani. Don't look back, and don't hesitate to board that hopper! Give me three minutes. If it gets too hot, get the hell out of here-"

"Wait, Kashta! We can't just leave you here! We all go home together. That's the way it's always been, that's the way it stays!" Anpu returned.

"Tem (no). Not this time, Black man. Not today. If something happens to me, get back home, come back to fight another day. Avenge me."

Picking up what was left of his supplies, Anpu turned. Shaking his head, he looked at me then said, "He's not worth it, Atef." He then joined Enlil in a stealthily approach to the *stairway to heaven.*

Sa-Ra was like a mad man. He was shooting at everything that moved. I had to be careful in my approach. *Why was I risking my life for his? Did I feel guilty about leaving him alone earlier?* I looked back at my three brothas and felt torn when I saw the Birth NAR landing quietly in the shadowy streets. It looked like a great Black Neter descending silently in the night. For a moment, I started to run across the cement fields and join them in the safety of the *Birth.* I immediately closed my eyes and turned my head to face my objective: bringing a lost brotha home.

"Yeah, mother fuckers, yeah! You can't stop me, you can't stop me!"

Sa-Ra's shouts were sounding less and less coherent. He was possessed by the Blood-Lust. I've heard about it many times. It's when a Mesniu is consumed by the hatred heaped upon our ancestors. He or she is actually re-living the past. There's usually nothing we can do for them. Convincing myself this time was different, I started in towards Sa-Ra. The entire scene was almost dream-like. A background of desolation and ruin; a foreground of humanity steeped in hatred for the original man. And in the middle stood two lost and tormented souls. I rushed for Sa-Ra as fast as I could. He was young, and had managed to put a lot of space between himself and me. *Even if I could catch and subdue him, would I have enough time to reach the NAR?*

When I finally reached him, he turned towards me, the glazed shown in his eyes. His pupils looked like tiny black specks in a sea of white. Tears streamed down his face, as a bottomless stare returned my on. He didn't recognize me. He raised his Colbot rifle and prepared to shoot. I shot first.

Catching his limp body on my left shoulder, I turned to race towards the NAR. I was too slow. Even in the shadowy night; distorted by the smoke and flames of battle, I could see my ride home silently float effortlessly off the ground. Within seconds, it joined its two companions hundreds of het-meters in the sky and quickly vanished southeast. I was dead meat. Feeling a lot more sure of themselves, what was left of the Cold Wind unit began to advance. My daath was providing some degree of camouflage; allowing me to fade into the darkness, but it wouldn't be enough.

"Hell yes!" I said out loud, my spirits beginning to lift. A wave-jumper sat alter-like on a pile of rocks.

Adjusting my weight, I shifted my body forward and reached down to pick up the silvery-green instrument. That's when it hit. A huge explosion rocked the entire east end of the plaza. Everything around me was red and glowing. Thick black smoke billowed, and large pieces of brick and mortar dropped from the sky. Losing Sa-Ra and indescribable pain struck at the same time. I couldn't see. I couldn't breathe. I didn't have the strength to keep the chunks of falling debris from clubbing me. I was being buried alive. The warm Black-Nothing began to dull my senses. I felt a sinking sensation.

Everything seemed so far away. It was as if a small light was on one minute, and the next moment, it was out...

CHAPTER 10

May 1 - Late 20th Century

Skah leaned back in his chair. Every Thursday night, after the brothas and sistahs left for the evening, he managed to repeat the same old routine. Punching the names of potential members into the data files, laughing at the so-called stories in the Newspapers, and racking his brain on trying to come-up with a name for the gathering of men and women who had managed to assemble on a monthly bases. Even without a name, they were well known throughout several African American communities in California.

"That's enough for tonight," Skah whispered to himself, pushing away from his computer terminal. Walking down the dark hallway of the once abandoned dental clinic, now refurbished 'African Directive Center,' Skah placed this month's receipts into the steel blue-colored safe that was located in the rear of the building.

As he approached the front entrance of the African Directive Center, or ADC, he always stopped and visually studied the immediate parking facilities, adjacent street corners, and neighboring buildings. He learned a long time ago, that the enemy was afraid of people like him. They spared no expense at striking from the darkness, ending all that he; and others like him, had worked so hard for. A small room near the back office served as a security booth. There were several digital cameras in and around the building, each feeding 'real-time' images into the five large monitors that sat on three desks in the cramped room. Video tapes littered the cabinet shelves, and thick cables ran wild along its plastered walls. Skah studied the film every night; looking for abnormalities.

Nothing out of the ordinary, he said to himself. A few minutes later, he had managed to 'hook-up' with a pre-arranged ride and was safely on his way home.

"What's on your mind, Skah?" the dark skinned brotha with locks asked, turning the vehicle with one hand and gulping down a half pint of orange juice with the other.

"Same old thang, Amani. Just trying to create a way to bring the original family together," Skah answered. He rubbed his brow and closed his eyes. "If we could just figure out a way to squash the petty differences and unite our people-"

"Try not to worry about it too much, Black man. You know niggas ain't ready," Amani responded. He and Skah had been best friends since college. In fact, it was he and Amani who sat in Skah's father's living room, and hammered out a plan to create a 'front' organization and use it to recruit a more militant and conscious set of brothers and sisters from within it's fictitious gathering.

"I wish I could stop, my brotha. But every time I let my guard down, the images of our people... they haunt me."

"When was the last time you meditated? I mean, *really* meditated. You know what I'm saying? I mean, slap in one of them Auset tapes and get busy," Amani asked laughing. He knew it would only be a matter of time before he cheered Skah up. "So, what did you think of those brothas and sistahs who came by tonight? The sistah with the red hair looked familiar to me," Amani added, deliberately trying to change the subject. Besides, he was in charge of security and he trusted Skah's judgment.

"I don't know yet. We'll have to invite them to a few more meetings; feed them a bunch of African Directive bullshit. Then I'll know. Even if they turn out to be chipers, we can use them to spread disinformation to the so-called authorities. Anyway, make sure you separate the brothas. Pair them up with the old-timers. I'll have to talk with Nefertari to find out what's to be done with the sistahs," Skah answered.

"Alright then, Black man. I'll schedule a voter's registration class the Thursday after next, after which I'll assign a couple of Vets to tag our knew recruits."

"Good. You know, it surprises me how many conscious brothas and sistahs turn out for those things. You would have thought by now that they would have figured out a long time ago that this political process shit is just that... shit. Our folks still believe power is in voting. They have not realized or asked themselves how they got the power to vote in the first place. I mean they didn't *vote* to give themselves the right to vote."

"Yeah, exactly. Power is not in voting, it's in strategies, coalitions, and planned execution. I mean, I had to keep myself from smacking a crazy ass preacher I ran into the other day. This silly motherfucker was going on about how the President and the government were going to save black people. How the Black race was cursed because of Ham; he was just a sick motherfucker who needed to be shot right there on the spot," Amani added, the disgust showing in his voice.

"Damn, I'm glad I wasn't there. I probably would have gone off on his cloud-watching ass." Both Skah and Amani had a very low tolerance for non-progressive Black men and women. It was rumored on the streets that they burned down more black churches than the Skins.

"Hey, take me over Freida's house. I haven't seen her in two weeks. I think I've pretty much blown it with her, but if I kiss her ass long enough, maybe she'll give me some," Skah said, not breaking a smile.

Most folks didn't know how to read Skah. He often said outrageous things...things that would often shock and surprise people who really didn't know him. He didn't care. He simply said what was on his mind, and his desert-dry sense of humor only added to their confusion. Amani knew Skah too well to be fazed by what he said and did. He understood that like all conscious brothers and sisters, himself included, Skah was a walking dichotomy. These two knew the difference between right and wrong; more so than most people, but they also understood and accepted the fact that they were slaves to their conditionings...

* * * * *

I'm alive. My entire body ached. Even my eyelids hurt. Confused, I was relieved to find myself above ground. *How. What happened? Where was my crew*, I asked myself. Pain was my only answer. Lying still, I stared into the night sky. I felt languid, almost hypnotized by the billions of stars that danced their eternal dance against an immense backdrop of indigo. Ignoring the anguished protests of my battered person, I strained against gravity and sat myself upright. I quickly ran short of breath and decided I had better lay back down. I tried to focus, remember. My mind searched, reaching back, back before the Great Nothing.

No answers came to rescue me from the uncertainty of missing time; of gone experience. I closed my eyes and began to listen to the wisdom of my person. Moments, or maybe hours passed, I don't know. My person...my body, spoke to me in a natural way, a way that goes back to the beginning of life itself. Lightning fast currents of electricity informed my mind of the degree of injury my body suffered.

Ribs were broken. Bones were bruised, and flesh was torn. But I was whole. I would live on. Moving was not an option. I decided to allow my natural recuperative powers to affect repairs upon my person. I still didn't trust just turning my body over to my daath-Geb. I was totally vulnerable, but I dared not disobey the Spirit. Our Mystic-scientists have taught us that it is the spirit (subconscious) part of our being, if properly trained, that can do wondrous things. Mine was telling me to stay put, don't move for a while. I obeyed, closed my eyes, and stopped all thoughts.

I awoke to greet the full midday sun, Aten. My dark red-brown skin drank the energy of its life-giving rays like a hungry plant. It wasn't until I felt almost completely satiated that I realized I was not wearing my geb. Sitting up with a start, I quickly scanned the area around me. At first, all I saw were small yellow shrubs, rust colored rocks, and the ever present ruins of Quadrant-Four. I slowed my breathing down and decided to look more closely...and with a calmer mind. Turning my head in slow rhythmic motions, I found my geb. I couldn't decide if I should be relieved or slip into battle mode.

What was left of my daath-Geb lay next to a green and brown shrub, neatly folded, with my Colbot rifle, projectile, and what looked like a wooden bowl of fruit lying next to it. Sa-Ra was no where to be found. Like a rush of cold water, memories flooded my mind's eye. Sa-Ra...I shot him! Oshun, Anpu, gone. They probably saw the explosion and assumed I died in it. *Perhaps I should have*, I said to myself. *This was a sloppy job, and I was responsible for it-*

I was being watched! My thoughts quickly turned lethal. I leapt to my feet, then ran towards my geb and weapons. I could hear them in the bush, whispers, feet trying not to make too much noise as they stepped from cement to soil. And worst of all, the silent yet deafening sound of eyes peering from the shadows.

Trying not to show how rattled I was, I calmly picked up what was left of my belongings, then slowly walked away from the thick foliage. Whoever was watching me stayed at an acceptable distance. *Fine by me.*

They were good. They knew I was aware of their presence, - they wanted me to know. They definitely weren't Cold Wind. I'd be dead by now if they were.

Hours passed. I was still being followed. They remained behind me, keeping an even pace. When I stopped, they stopped. This went on for several miles and several more hours. My tolerance began to wear thin. I was starting to hate the idea of someone, or something, watching me, stalking me. Keeping track of time by noting the position of Aten, I decided that I would end this game at dusk.

It was getting dark, and my strength was returning. It would be awhile before my ribs were back to full capacity, but I'm sure that wouldn't prevent me from inflicting some serious damage on any would-be attackers. I needed coverage, a place to gather my thoughts, put together a plan to get home. I immediately slipped into an abandoned building that was several stories tall. Its entrance was marked by two huge wooden doors. There were paintings and sculptures of battle scenes across its outer walls. Two warrior figures were carved into the walls on either side of its entrance; they faced one another. First pushing. then pulling, I managed to slip inside. Pacing myself just right, I knew exactly when my followers would enter the building behind me. I had managed to get five minutes ahead of them.

I entered slowly, Colbot rifle in hand. I had it set for wide bursts. Its Colbot energy would liquify any living thing. It was dark. It smelled. But it was empty. Nothing but swirling dust and the occasional darting of rust rats. I walked over to a large berth, which spread into a row of stairs. They were covered in a purple velvety material. Halfway up, I paused, expecting to catch a glimpse at who or what was following me. Minutes passed, but nothing came. I continued on.

On the second floor, I began to encounter strangely decorated rooms. Religious scenes. Pictures of monstrous animals and so on. My curiosity peaked. When I reached the end of a dark hallway, I noticed a series of lights. They were arranged in a semi circle and hung arch-like across a heavy double layered door. I pried the door open, then realized it was an old lift of some type. It was extremely cramped inside, and it smelled of dust and urine. A small metal panel bedecked the interior left wall, showing a tiny row of numbers. I counted them.

"Thirteen stories," I said aloud.

I stepped inside the tiny box, then pressed the first button I saw. *Well, there was no need in going up to the 13th floor, the 4th floor would do nicely*, I said to myself.

To my amazement, the lift was still operational. It probably would have been faster to just use the stairs, but I couldn't resist the urge to take a ride in the rectangular space. When I reached the fourth floor (I knew this because the number four on the panel began to glow), the lift stopped. It was slow but fairly smooth. The doors refused to open completely. Using the back-end of my rifle, I pried and tugged until they finally flung from their hinges.

The opening led to a small narrow hallway, which, in turn, led to a single room. Two huge oak doors stood like giant brown and purple sentinels. Not caring if I were still being followed, I aimed and shot. I struck dead center, the echo from the discharge was almost deafening. *Now that was stupid.*

As I got closer, I instantly forgave myself; the three steel serpentine locks that held the doors in place were blown clean off. I calmly walked over, and pushed. Ignoring the loud crashing sound of solid oak doors slamming onto marble floors, I was almost mesmerized by the room's interior.

The design of the room was definitely old world. Rows of marble columns gave it an almost temple feel. Book shelves and desks, populated the entire space. Most amazing of all were the images. Behind swirling clouds of dust were pictures of idyllic scenes of ancient Kush, KMT, and other African nations. They were painted in the most brilliant hues.

It wasn't until my excitement passed that I noticed the statues and pictures of white men in uniforms. They were carrying swords, guns, and wearing strange ritualistic garbs. Placing my rifle back onto its shoulder harness, I penetrated deeper into the gloom. Pushing over a small desk, I stumbled across a strange brightly colored journal or diary. Thinking that I would amuse myself until I fell asleep - or until my followers found me - I began thumbing through its yellowed pages.

The book contained a historical synopsis of the ruling class of people in Old America. It was an actual account of a class of white men who secretly mimicked my people and played a major role in the genocidal programs directed at undesirables, as the book stated, in the 20th century.

Feeling a renewed sense of passion, I began feverishly searching through every book that clung to the dusty shelves. Walls and walls of volumes littered the entire fourth floor. *This is a library of mischief-makers.* These writs contained truths, half truths, and outright lies. They were organized and written in such a way as to cause confusion. They began to cry out to me, begging me to rescue them from their unfit mother. I decided to start at the western end of the complex, and I was quickly rewarded. My prize was a thick and heavy work.

Flipping through its pages like a mad man, I stumbled across a most startling revelation: these people charted the destiny of the world. More than that, they actually played a part in shaping the history of entire nations. What surprised me most was that the very principles they used for their evil machinations were developed from a twisted bastardized mockery of the ancient High Sciences of KMT (Egypt).

Now it was beginning to make sense to me: these people practiced the sciences of Old Africa. They met annually, and they met in secret. They performed strange rituals to maintain their power. These powerful white men believed themselves to be the successors to the ancient Kamites (Egyptians).

"Wow, they actually believed themselves not only to be 'our' successors, but they felt that their only insurance was to remove the Black race from the planet. They actually practiced this," I said aloud, mesmerized at the huge picture of the black hand of God reaching out of the clouds. In grand splendor, it extended to a landscape populated by White folk. I had found their manifesto.

Falling back into a stylized Egyptian chair, I placed the book on the edge of the large round table sitting silently to my right. That's when I noticed the oddly shaped symbol hidden on the lower part of the wall.

"That's our Crest!" I shouted, my mouth wide open in shock. It was the symbol used by the Ntiu Tut! "How in the hell did our Country's 'Sacred Seal' find it's way here?" Leaping from the 'counterfeit' chair, I hurried to examine the symbol. It was carved into the wall. It was very crude, and looked like its maker fashioned it centuries ago. *It looked as though someone had done this in a hurry.* "It was probably K'huti," I said, shaking my head. "Yeah, K'huti."

With the book tightly clutched in my left hand, I stood and looked for a place to rest...a place to sleep. Realizing that I had furniture to work with, I quickly fashioned myself a large bed. I then folded my tattered daath-Geb under my neck, and used it as a pillow. I placed my weapons to my right side, respectively. Looking out of the large rectangular shaped window, my thoughts were on Tefnut. She would be so excited at having a chance at exploring a place like this. My breathing became deep. My eyes began to keep pace with the setting sun. Ten minutes later, they, like Aten (the sun), sank into the West.

CHAPTER 11

The rays of Aten energized me. And, despite my circumstances, this was a beautiful morning. I left everything as it was; well, minus the thousand page volume I decided to cop. As I walked through the shrubbery, I looked back at the strange building. I made a mental note of where it was and how it looked.

I was out of food and would have to use my daath-Geb for nourishment. Kneeling in front of a large bush that burst from a row of concrete, I pressed the large flexible silver disks in the palms of the geb. First, the remaining air rushed out, making a hissing noise in the process. Then the suit began to soften and liquefy. Pulling at the few remaining solid areas, I tore off ten large leathery strips.

Incredible. A few hours ago, this was the only thing between me and the super heated mercury that leapt from the rifles of my enemies. It provided protection from their hateful eyes, regulated the temperature of my body, and could double its density at the touch of a button. Now it would be my food. I twisted each strand, making thick black eatable ropes. I then grabbed my rifle, rescuing it from the sticky mass of chlorophyll and fiber.

They were back. Several of them this time. They must have waited for me. Ignoring them, I continued on my southern trek. Stopping every three hours, I rested and ate small crunchy pieces of my former geb. It tasted of dried seaweed, but it provided long lasting energy. I watched Aten rise and sink twice. The nights were cold, but the thoughts of Ta-Amenta; of Tefnut, were what kept me going. I traveled through several small cities. Each as derelict as the first, rust rats and scaly mist-dogs their only inhabitants.

Pushing over and around the dense underbrush, I could hear the cold hollow sounds of machinery. I was getting close, but to what? Crouching low to the red earth, then laying flat on my stomach, I wriggled through a field of thick vegetation. The smell of oil and petroleum was in the air. I continued to pull myself along the ground, beyond the dirt-hills and thick shrubbery.

Peering from underneath a row of matted shrubs, I found myself about 100 het-meters away from a Cold Wind facility. It was rectangular and about as large as a city block. The roof was covered in a greenish brown mesh. Its outer walls were blotted with foliage, white cement showing at its foundation. There were easily a dozen urban tanks parked in and around the immense structure. All terrain attack-jeeps rolled back and forth across the base perimeter. I could see at least five short range 'Gull stinger' missiles.

Installations this size always housed hundreds of slaves. My heart starting pumping, the controlled adrenalin-rush surged through my body. "This is what I live for," I said to myself, scanning every corner of the base.

The easiest way in would also take the longest. I was situated on the south end of the base. As a general rule, Valhallan facilities were always least secure on the side that faced their country, the north side. Reaching over my shoulder, I tore off a small piece of my leathery snack. I placed all of it in my mouth and squinted as the foul taste assaulted my tongue. Slowing my breathing to three breaths per minute, I slowly crawled towards my destination.

* * * * *

December 6 - Late 20th Century

Josh Hollis wasn't happy about the situation going on in his prison. The White and Mexican inmates were forming huge and powerful gangs. The Blacks were busy killing each other off. Josh complained openly to the Warden but always got a racist joke in return. Warden Franks was just that, a racist. He hated most people, especially Blacks. He and his assistant, Carl Bowers, ran their prison like a science experiment gone wild. Spewing forth 'Darwinian' concepts daily, Warden Franks openly suggested that the Black inmates were biologically unfit and would soon do everybody a favor and kill themselves off. Josh hated Warden Franks for his ideals, and because he feared the Warden was right.

It was nearing the end of the century, when Josh and many other well-to-do Blacks started noticing a change in *White attitudes* on the job. Josh and his friend of six years, Hector Reeves, were snooping around the Warden's office when they discovered that they were going to be fired at the end of the next quarter. Warden Franks said that there was no need for a *Black Counselor* in his prison any more. He continued by saying that he "Just wanted a Counselor for everybody, not just for black people."

Hector started kissing ass as soon as he found out he was going to be terminated. He was a good-natured, fun loving brother, but he was totally unconscious as to who he was and what the hell was going on.

Josh was well read and hung-out with this militant sistah from up north. Her name was Lakishia, but everybody called her Nefertari. Josh was really impressed by the way she carried herself and by the company she kept. Her intellect was prodigious, and her physical beauty was enough to make a brotha *act right* for the rest of his life. She had those huge almond shaped eyes, high cheek bones, nappy locks, and golden brown skin. She told him about a couple of *bad* brothas named Skah and Amani, and how these brothas were both culturally and politically aware of the reality of things around us. She continued by suggesting that he invite Skah up to speak to the brothas in prison, and that maybe it would do the brothas on *lock down* some good. Josh agreed. He felt that since he was going to be fired anyway, fuck it. He might as well go out with a bang.

———

Doing close to 80 miles per hour, Skah was *flying* down Interstate-5. He was running late, and he wanted to get to the prison on time. *Damn*, he thought. "I'm spreading myself too thin. I hope this brotha is worth the effort," he said to himself, gulping down his last drop of spring water. He threw the plastic bottle in the back seat, and began Looking through his rear-view mirror.

Skah was a busy man. He and Amani, Nefertari, and others had managed to organize a fairly consistent number of serious minded conscious black men and women. With supreme arrogance, each felt qualified to rescue and rebuild the entire African world community.

They carefully selected their inner membership by a sophisticated process. Skah chuckled to himself. He thought it funny how he and Amani created a 'front organization' solely in order to recruit from among its ranks a more militant membership.

The African Path Center. The ultimate smoke-screen. It was dreamt up by Amani. It was erected as a means for attracting progressive Blacks without scaring them off. Skah and Amani, and eventually Nefertari and Nola, would ask certain questions and present certain scenarios to the members. Observing their reactions, the stronger, more militant members were then recruited into the 'hidden' organization within the African Path Center.

"I'm approaching my exit. I'll call you when I get to the prison yard," Skah said, clicking off the small black cellular phone.

Freida didn't have time to tell Skah she loved him. He always hung-up too quick.

"One day he'll wish I was around," she said, placing her cordless phone on top of her dresser.

The prison was huge. Giant bricks formed its outer walls. Thick black barbed wire rings flowered over and around the top of its immense cement barriers. The entrance was basically two giant iron girders. It was connected by a system of steel beams that grew out of the ground. On either side of the entrance stood two gigantic towers, both of which housed two menacing and well armed guards. They stared while Skah parked his overheating car in the visitors parking area. Gathering his pass, and scrapping up most of his notes, Skah rushed passed six rows of gray buses and hurried to the pedestrian entrance.

A large heavy-set man checked everybody's pass as they entered the facilities. He held his rifle in his left hand so tight that the blood could be seen through the pink flesh of his fingers. Waving each person in, he seemed almost indifferent at the amount of people gathered about him. Skah was next. His instincts told him something wasn't right. Holding up his pass, Skah deliberately tried to conceal his face. He didn't want to take any chances at his picture being taken by the sleek cameras stationed over the prison entrance.

"How do you pronounce this name, boy?" the hulking figure asked.

"It sure in the fuck ain't boy!"

Before any more words were exchanged, Josh Hollis came running through the crowd. He knew how the guards were, especially about Black visitors. Glaring at the guard, Josh motioned at Skah to enter through the gates. The guard said nothing. He just continued to wave people in.

"Business as usual?" Skah asked, extending his hand to Josh.

Smiling, Josh shook Skah's hand. "You know how it is, my brotha. They can't help it. They're afraid of us."

"That's what my father always says. I just wish someone would tell them that, maybe then they'd stop kicking our ass," Skah responded. Both men laughed as they walked toward the open grounds of the yard.

Walking through the main court, the walls of the interior of the prison seemed to go on for blocks. Endless rows of towers topped with guards separated one section of the cement city from the next. Skah didn't much notice the guards at first. What immediately caught his eye were the near limitless sea of "Black Heads" that dotted the immense prison grounds. Black men by the thousands were everywhere. Where ever Skah rested his eye, there stood another 10 brothas.

"This is fucking amazing. I've never seen so many brothas outside the Million Man March in one place."

Smiling, Josh placed his hand on Skah's shoulder. "This is the early shift. Wait until you see the 1:00 pm crowd."

Frowning, Skah turned and looked at Josh. "You mean, there are even *more* brothas than this on lock-down?"

"Absolutely," Josh answered.

"This shit is breaking my heart," Shah said, shaking his head in disbelief. "I mean, it really hurts to see this many Black men in here. Can I get pictures of this?"

The two men walked into the main check-in area and were immediately greeted by Hector Reeves. Hector methodically looked over Skah and his belongings, winked at Josh, and allowed the men to pass. They walked through the main hall that connected the courtyard to the main quarters. The stale air, damp floors, and thick steel bars, continued to remind Skah that he was in a different world. A world with a different set of rules. A world ruled by a different type of man.

"Over here, Skah," Josh said, motioning Skah to follow him to a large lightly colored room.

Upon entering the room, a familiar smell greeted Skah's nostrils. It was the smell of books. The room was much more than just a mere room, it was a library. Rows of chairs were arranged in need rows, all facing front. Seated in them were some of the hardest looking brothas Skah had ever seen. He immediately felt at home.

Josh noticed the ease at which Skah walked around the library, ignoring the inmates, while taking the time to look through as many books as he so pleased. The rest of the brothas noticed this also. They were annoyed at Skah's indifference, but they sensed that he meant no disrespect. Working his way around the library, Skah satisfied his love-urge for books and walked to the center of the gathering of black men. There were probably in the neighborhood of 50 to 60 men seated in the tightly fixed rows of chairs. Looking first at Josh, then at the brothas, Skah balled-up his notes and tossed them in the trash next to the tiny podium.

"Alright, brothas. I didn't come here to waste your time. Let's talk." A low murmur sounded-off across the room. Several heads nodded in agreement. Josh could sense that the brothas had; on the surface, accepted Skah. In the past, visitors who usually came to "help" were so intimidated that they never gained the respect of the hardened men who sat before them. Skah was different. He didn't try to pretend that he was as hard as they were. He simply stayed true to himself and true to the game. He hadn't earned their respect yet, but they appreciated his naturalness.

"I imagine that most of you have already read something or another about the fact that Black people were the original people of the earth. I'm also sure that most of you are aware that we as a people are at war, with you brothas being the prisoners of war," Skah said, causing some of the men to laugh. "Anyway, I didn't come here to read you a bedtime story. I came here to ask for your help."

"How can we help you from here, Black man?"

"It's simple... we need you. Most of you represent the Warrior-Class of Black men back on the street. Without you, we ain't got a fucking chance. The conditions on the outside today are worse than they were when most of you 'old-heads' came in. Those of you who will never leave this place, help the brothas who will. We need you to train them to build a Nation. They will be the Warrior-Class; highly regarded in the New Black Order."

Josh was taken aback by Skah's comments. He didn't think Skah was as hard as his words expressed. The gathering stared and continued to listen. Most of them sensed something different about this Skah.

"What's up with this New Black Order?" another man asked, while sitting up straight in his chair.

"From undifferentiation comes order. From order comes chaos, and ultimately, chaos must return to order. The African community the world over is in a state of chaos. We mean to return the original community to Order," Skah answered.

"We who? We always hear about black folks on the outside talking about changing shit and whatnot. But you mother fuckers never do," a huge brotha standing in the back of the library bellowed.

"Right now I'm not at liberty to give you or anybody else any specifics. Just know that we are here, and we need your help. If that's not good enough for you at this point, then fuck you in your ass then!" Skah returned.

Josh immediately jumped from his tiny chair and proceeded to interrupt the meeting. "Alright now, people, lets give the man-"

"Ah, come on, Josh. I think the man is doing just fine," one of the brothas yelled from the front of the library.

"That's right," a resounding return of approval erupted from the remaining brothas gathered in the library.

Skah, without missing his cue, continued. "You brothas don't know me, and I don't know you. As we develop a relationship, you'll find out more about me, and I'll learn more about many of you. But for now, let's just say that I didn't come here to give you a damn thing. I came here for your help..."

CHAPTER 12

Crawling through the cold mud caused my hands and feet to freeze and cramp-up. I hadn't counted on the underbrush being as damp as it was. *A crucial mistake. I should have known better.* Without my daath-Geb, my Mesniu-issued shorts were the only thing separating me from the elements.

I continued to trek past the small muddy ridge which overlooked the base. The lights from the Cold Wind facility were showing larger and brighter. I could feel the vibrations from their heavy machinery in the ground beneath me. My heart began to quicken. Pulling myself up from the thick foliage, I leaned against a mossy tree and smiled.

Discarding what was left of my foodstuff, I stealthily began my final decent onto the outer perimeter of the huge facility. Luckily, the shrubs and bushes hadn't been trimmed in quite some time. They almost grew as far back as 20 het-meters, nearly reaching the electric fence that surrounded the large complex. Staying low and close to the ground, I timed my movements to the rhythms of my heart. I followed its dictates to the letter. Two, maybe three minutes later, I had managed to slip through the wet grass and was standing 10 het-meters from the gate. I dropped to my belly, then crawled the rest of the way. The soft hum from the electric fence reminded me of the warm security of the NARS. That's the strange thing about technology; it spoils us, making the unnatural more desirous than the natural. "Where do I go from here?" I asked myself, looking at what appeared to be an endless mesh of tangled death.

Heart racing, rifle in hand, I glided across the soft wet dirt. I easily avoided their cumbersome motion detectors. But I was tired. I slipped and stumbled, nearly slamming into the electric fence!

Things were starting to get messy. I remained still, staring at the sticky mud on my Colbot rifle.

"Damn, where's the door?" I said aloud, not caring if anyone heard me. A silver-gray fence stood mockingly in silence. I rose, took a deep breath, then boldly walked the length of the base.

––––––––

When I reached the northeast corner of the gated building, I was relieved to find a large and expansive entrance. Attack-jeeps were coming and going with impunity. And so would I. I walked as fast I could towards the open and unlocked fence. Stopping directly in front of the inviting gate, I slipped into the base yard. I ran as fast I could from the electric gate to the steel sliding doors of the huge cement building. I could hear their voices, the voices of my enemies. I wanted to unleash as much destruction and terror on them as I possibly could. Visions of death swam through my mind. The deep purple-red colors of revenge nearly stole my sense of self and purpose. For what seemed like forever, I stood directly at the front entrance, under the brightest lights; standing there with my rifle raised and poised for the killing. And no one saw me.

"I'm Protected by The Most High," I whispered.

I dashed and ducked behind a huge stash of artillery. They were stored in large boxes: each stacked on top of the other. Armor piercing shells, all-terrain tires, Eagle-730 urban missiles, and rows and rows of fuel littered the entire east wing of the building. Whatever they were preparing for, it was big. I decided to execute a detailed account of everything in here, or at least as much as I could. I couldn't help myself. I'm K'huti. The suspense alone was enough to make me drunk, almost high. I appreciated this feeling. Knowing I could die at any moment always made life that much more tasty. Warrior-King Senwosret said he used to be the same way. *I wonder what made him change?* Then I thought of Sa-Ra.

I counted more weapons than I cared to. Attack-jeeps, urban-tanks, vice-copters, and missiles were everywhere. I had seen enough. I needed to find some food, some clothing, and a vehicle. I'd report my findings to the Ntiu Tut when I got home. I slowly made my way towards the interior of the facility. The further I went in, the more activity I noticed. Jeeps, cranes, soldiers, all rushing back and forth, in and out as if their lives depended on it.

It didn't take long to stumble across several cans of processed food. I hated it. I never understood how these people lived off synthetic, hormonally laced, and artificially flavored meats. Ignoring the inevitable stomach cramps, I continued to quietly rummage through the small green and black boxes. With the speed and efficiency of years of experience, I managed to discard my filthy garments, fill a back-pack full of what they called food, and clothed myself in a well padded uniform. Turning to exit the building, I smiled as I beheld rows of all-terrain attack-jeeps, or ATAJ's. They formed a neat half circle near the walkway.

I returned to the shadows that permeated the facility. Avoiding the lit areas of the complex, I walked silently along side some of Valhalla's best. I was a ghost. Grabbing three large cans of fuel, I awkwardly walked towards the Attack-jeep closest to the main entrance. Working from the shadows, I loaded the Attack-jeep until it started to lean on its right side. "This is too much shit," I whispered, pulling two of the large canisters of fuel back off the jeep. The feeling of urgency and the nerve racking impatience that comes when an objective is almost met was making me careless.

Having secured all that I needed, I pulled the remaining Colbot capsules from my rifle. Slowly and methodically, I dropped the large grey pellets into the fuel tanks of the rest of the vehicles. A sly smile slid across my face. Purple and yellow residue glistened on my finger tips. When the charge-light on my weapon went dark, I made my move.

Minutes felt more like hours as I waited for the chance to escape. The walls were beginning to close in on me. The pounding of my heart was almost audible. I took a deep breath, and rushed behind a large stack of dried fish. Minutes later, I had managed to ease my way towards the entrance of the building. Peering out of its wide mouth-like entrance, I nearly froze when I saw a second group of Cold Wind soldiers walking up the granite bay. I turned and bolted towards the third row of Attack-jeeps. When I got close enough to touch one, I tripped on a hard cylindrical object. Biting my tongue, I knelt down next to one of the jeep's huge rubber tires.

As my eyes adjusted, I noticed that the jeeps were secured by a single 'railing' device. It was about 12 het-meters long and held each vehicle in place. Luckily, there were no locks. *I guess they never imagined someone would actually steal one.* I quietly began unclasping the metal slabs from each rear tire. Balancing the rectangular silver and blue rods in my hands, I gently placed them to the side. Pushing the jeep slowly away from the remaining vehicles, I returned to the shadows and waited for the next team of Cold Wind Soldiers to enter the facility.

It didn't take long. The rumble from their urban-tanks, the harsh wine of their attack-jeeps, and the sporadic laughter of men returning from a day's work filled the air. I counted five vehicles, holding two men each as they entered the entrance of the complex. I remained hidden, like Amen. Fighting the urge to strike, I was able to determine that they came and went in intervals of 200 heartbeats.

I was beginning to lose my Men-Ab (stability, composure). I had to do something before they locked the facility down for the night. Checking and then re-checking the vehicle, I slowly started to push it towards the left corner of the gaping doors. The cool fresh breeze of the night air greeted my nostrils. I took in a deep breath, and with one last push I found myself outside of the immense cement structure. The ramp, which stretched from the entrance of the storage facility to the marshy ground, looked like a 1000 foot bridge. I gently put the jeep in neutral and allowed it to roll down the ramp and into the nearby bushes. That's when everything went wrong. About half way down the ramp, I heard their voices. They came from the thick wooded area just east of me. I scrambled off the jeep, pulled the supplies from the rear storage container, and jumped into the thickest section of shrubbery.

My heart sank as I watched well over 10 Cold Wind Soldiers emerge from the surrounding bush. There were no vehicles with them, but they were well armed. Rolling my eyes, all I could think of was how I'd just emptied my Colbot rifle. The Lead Officer was the first to notice the Attack-jeep sitting at the base of the ramp. He held up his right hand. His team stopped immediately.

"What the hell is this thing doing here?" one of the officers in the back asked, looking at the empty entrance of the building. His commanding officer said nothing. He just suspiciously looked up the ramp, eyeing the entrance, and then the surrounding foliage.

"What should we do, sir?" another asked. The lead officer continued to scan the surrounding area. He was good, an old veteran. Walking around the jeep, he just stood there, staring at his troops. My heart was pounding; if he decided to put in some overtime, I was dead meat.

"McCormick, stay here and keep watch. The rest of you turn in." Watching his men rush up the ramp, he turned toward his remaining soldier. "I'll try to find out what's going on and why this thing was left here. It shouldn't take long, Private," He said, winking and patting McCormick on the back. Taking one last look, he slowly walked up the ramp and into the building. I smiled as I watched him disappear into the glow of its yellow-orange entrance. I then began to concentrate on McCormick. I'd only have one chance. If I didn't do it right, he'd have time to warn the others. Lifting myself from the damp thickets, I silently walked towards the solitary figure. He stood there, smoking a cigar and counting the stars. I remained in a crouched position. My body was concealed by the tall blades of grass that grew wild and unkempt around the base perimeter. Then, for whatever reason, I felt him. I watched him puff on his cigar and talk to himself. He was no doubt cursing his Commanding Officer for placing him on watch. How similar we seemed in that brief instance. Looking up at the entrance to the storage facility, I turned and methodically crept towards a man who probably had a family...a man who was just following orders...a man who would never see the morning sun.

It would take them hours to find the dead officer's body. I stashed it pretty good. But it didn't matter, because if and when they did, I'd be several miles away. I was covering a lot of territory, and the high pitched wine of the attack-jeep's engines were swallowed by the thick natural barrier of the surrounding forest. I had to be extra careful on the open stretches though. They were usually flat lands of dirt and bushes. Without the aid of trees to provide coverage, I kept the jeep on full throttle. Glancing down at the Compass built into the plastic dashboard, I remained on a southeast trek. I figured in about two days I'd either enter New American territory or Aztlann borders. Either way... I was going home.

———

I've been traveling for almost two days, and still no sign of civilization. *I should have entered New American territory by now.* Grumbling, I steered the jeep along side a small stream. It was little more than a lumpy depression surrounded by red clay. The water was bright, and it sparkled like a bed of crystals. Looking into its shallow depths, I noticed the absence of fish, frogs, and moss, which usually inhabit these tiny banks and shorelines. There were no birds present, nor did I hear any.

"This is a dead stream," I whispered.

Cautiously, I slid from the smooth plastic seat of the attack-jeep. Two huge coils immediately re-adjusted themselves, causing the buggy to bounce and wiggle. I walked to the back of the vehicle and started digging through its fairly spacious rear compartment. It took a few minutes, but I found what I was looking for. I removed a large silvery gray canister from a set of metal clamps that lay alongside the interior of the rear rack. I shook the smooth cylindrical object and was pleased to hear its liquid contents slush around inside. Fresh water.

Twisting the hard lid from the top, I took two gulps, then twisted the metal cap back in place. Leaning up against the Attack-jeep, I marveled at its simple design. *One thing is for sure, the Valhallans are great engineers*. This thing was a work of art. A light titanium alloy mesh, shaped into a well defined body. A flexible rear spoiler, capable of holding missiles and other instruments of destruction, wrapped around twin octane engines. Four huge steel-rubber tires held the sleek engine of death in place. It looked like an obscene toy.

I returned the water holder to its housing and pushed the deceptively light vehicle across the stale creek. Grunting, I then managed to push it up and over a small rocky embankment. I looked at the position and dip of Aten (the sun), and watched the clouds drift across the blue gray sky. I guessed that it was early evening.

I pushed the jeep to the low hump on the south side of the stream, then jumped on the synthetic seat. I kept it in neutral as I coasted down the bumpy hillside. It wasn't until I was well within the safety of the dense wooded area that I cranked the engine. Moments later, I was ripping through one of the most beautiful forests in the western hemisphere.

The extremes found in the natural environment of the northwest continued to amaze me. One moment I was traveling through dense forest, trees as tall as skyscrapers; the next, I'm rolling across vast hilly sections of golden brown mounds. Even the occasional abandoned structure only added to the beauty of this composite scenery. This was one of those rare moments... when time stood still. Everything was perfect. I was definitely *In The Now*.

———

I'm probably about 35 nilometers into Quadrant Three. This puts me even further away from both Quadrant Four...and Valhalla.

The jeep began to jerk and buckle. It was running out of fuel. Choosing a medium sized summit located under a clump of trees, I steered the jeep up and onto a grassy hill. In a final surge of acceleration, I reached the top of the hill in a puff of pale blue smoke.

This was good ground. I've got a spot to hide my vehicle, and a place to rest my tired bones. I hid the jeep under a pile of lush vegetation. I then gathered the remaining supplies from its rear storage rack and walked wearily to a thicket of inviting trees. Tired and sore, I slumped in a pile of thick foliage. I went through my rations. I was doing well on fresh water, processed food, and clothing. I had two sets of thermos and a liter of octane for my jeep. Smiling, I returned the items - except the water and fuel - to the flexible leather crate that housed them. From my new vantage point, I could survey most of the landscape, up to 20 nilometers without any real hindrance. *If only it were daylight*, I mused...

* * * * *

April 24 - End of the 20th Century

Driving south on 14th street in east Oakland, Skah and Amani were joined by Nefertari, Nola, and Jerome. They were enjoying a lively talk on 'Afrocentrism' versus 'Pan-Africanism'. Laughing hard and loud, they were totally oblivious to the 'unconscious masses' around them.

"Fuck Pan-Africanism. The only thing African about that shit is the fucking name!" Skah shouted, reaching back over his head and slapping hands with Nefertari.

"Man, I don't believe you said that shit. Pan-Africanism is the ultimate objective of all African people, my brotha!" Amani returned, glaring at Skah. Despite the fact that these two men were closer than most biological brothers, they continued to debate on many issues.

"That's right, my brotha, help the nigga out!" Jerome interjected. Jerome was new, and still a little raw. He still used words like 'nigga' and 'bitch,' but having done a lot of reading and independent study, there was still hope for him. He used to be a member of a dying Pan-Africanist organization up north. Having moved to the Bay Area, he met Amani in one of the more progressive Black Book stores in Oakland. Amani invited him to an 'African Directive' meeting, and the rest is history.

"What did we tell you about using that term, Black man?" Nefertari asked, the venom showing in her voice.

"Oh, oh, you right sister, you right," Jerome responded humbly. They liked him because he struggled with himself and was genuinely embarrassed about using slave terms and concepts.

"Listen, my brotha. Pan-Africanism has no pure African systems governing any of its tenants. I mean, don't give me no bullshit about how Communism, dialectical opposites, and the rest of that shit has it's origins in Africa. Granted, most of the founders of the philosophies that permeate Pan-Africanism were well read in ancient African Spiritual, economic, and political systems, but they failed in truly releasing the people from mental bondage when they neglected to incorporate our philosophies into the struggle," Skah bellowed, looking quite arrogant and pompous behind the steering wheel. Skah didn't respect any tradition that did not originate 'first hand' on African soil. He concentrated all of his energies on learning African belief systems, from the beginning of human history to just before European and Asian influences.

"How the fuck you brothas and sistahs digest that maggot-laced shit from China - what, the Red Book or something - but refuse to study the Metu Neter, is way the fuck beyond me!" Skah added.

"OOkaaay," Nefertari interjected. She too, was an Africentrist. And as quiet as it was kept, most believed that she was even more vicious than Skah, especially when it came to dismantling people and their belief systems. "What African languages do you use? What's your African Spiritual Foundation? I mean what the fuck is African about Pan-Africanism." she asked rhetorically.

"And don't give us no general, non-specific 'flowery' crap either," Skah interrupted. Both he and Nefertari howled with laughter. They knew that their brothas in struggle never had a real answer to that question. That's why they always saved it for last.

"That's hard. Don't be doing that shit to them," Nola added. She was a good sistah. Besides, she liked Jerome. He had no idea.

"It's like my dad always says," Skah started in again, "African people ultimately need a purely African culture and frame of reference. Nothing else will truly resurrect our people."

Amani and Jerome didn't respond, they just frowned and looked at one another. Trying to make a come back, Amani made one last thrust for Pan-Africanism. "What I'm tired of, is seeing all of these brothas and sistahs wearing the African garbs, the hats, Kente cloth, etc., and when you need them to do something, they don't do shit. I mean the other day, I saw a brother wearing dreads, and he had a white woman on his arm."

"So what! You mean to tell me that you brothas and sistahs who don't know 'jack-shit' about anything African don't do the same kinds of things?" Nefertari slammed back, knowing full well that she had just dealt the death blow.

"That's true, my sistah. I guess there are 'reactionary' types in all movements," Amani responded, trying to hold in his laughter.

"Skah, that's the cheapest gas station on this side of Oakland. Pull in over there," Nola said pointing, intentionally brushing her arm up against Jerome.

Looking at Nola and Jerome through the rear-view mirror, Skah turned and winked at Nefertari and Amani. Then, avoiding the oncoming traffic, he steered his piece of shit ford through a yellow light and darted across the hot tar. Seconds later, the five of them came to a screeching halt in the main lot of a small shack-like gas station on the opposite side of the street. They had been clowning all day. It was hard to believe that they were in their late twenties and early thirties. But their clean living, day-long meditation sessions, and diet, sustained their youth.

Skah was a fireman. Or at least on paper. He's been out of work for months. He is currently on administrative leave, and is in the process of suing the San Francisco Fire Department on charges of racism. *The price to pay for being a conscious Black man in America, is the lack of tolerance for both cultural and political racism*, he often told himself. None of the White firefighters liked him. They felt he was a trouble maker and was always looking for any sign of discrimination in the Department.

Amani was a Substitute Teacher. He got most of his jobs in the Oakland Unified School District. Almost all of the students, Black and White, loved him while nearly all of the White faculty hated him. Some of the White parents complained that Amani was teaching hate in the schools. But with the newfound strength and vigor of the mostly Black faculty in the Oakland Unified School District, Amani was relatively secure. Besides, he and Skah were in the process of re-creating the 'Mystery Systems.' They'd planned to use it to foster the development of Black Youth. These days, he really didn't care what the school district had in store for him. "There is a higher agenda," he would often tell his parents.

Nefertari was a social worker for the County of Oakland. She was just past her 12 months probation and already raising hell. She didn't care; she knew if she stuck to policy, it would take an act of Congress to fire her. She routinely gave the young brothas and sistahs who came to see her break after break after break. She showed them how to go to school while receiving Government and County checks. She loved her job. She felt that she was actually making a difference. Up until recently, work was the only way; she felt, that she could strike at the system. That was, until she met Skah and Amani at a lecture at the Oakland Convention Center.

Nola was the proud parent to a four year-old son named Tomac. He was brilliant, energetic, and a handful. His father left a long time ago and was only heard from twice in three years. Nola worked at the Oakland Airport; in the Customer Service Department. She helped people collect their bags, showed them which Terminal to stand in, and tried to collect as much overtime as possible. She loved meeting Black people from different parts of the country, and especially from all over the world. She completed two years of community college and could debate with the best of them. She read more than most college Professors and was considered a genius by anyone who talked with her for more than 20 minutes. She started hanging out with Skah and the others almost two years ago. It's done her and her son a world of good.

Jerome was a tall, good looking brotha from Sacramento. He was semi-conscious. He was Brilliant. He was well read. And he was unemployed. He couldn't keep a job for six months if his life depended on it. He didn't care. Jerome knew way too many conscious Black men and women to live on the streets or go hungry. They loved him because he, like Skah, was a true Warrior. In fact, the two of them often kept the other brothas and sistahs on pins and needles, wondering what they would do next.

These men and women felt themselves to be the beginning-end process. The Holy Initiatory Agents of Gods Great Plan. They would be the final spark to ignite the fire of resurrection of the Black communities throughout the world. They were the 'off-spring' of all the prayers, struggles, and sacrifices of the countless Black men and women who served and died before them. "All for the glory of the Black Race," they would often say.

CHAPTER 13

I awoke to a most glorious morning. My nostrils were greeted by a sweet summer's breeze. I stood on the small hilltop and surveyed its many mounds, peaks, and small valleys. *I bet Africa must have looked like this a long time ago.* I was amazed by the herd of wild horses that ran across the patch work of brown and tan savannahs. Leaning over and picking up my supplies, I couldn't help thinking about how beautiful a country this once must have been. If it weren't for the Wasted Cities...

I turned and walked towards my jeep. It sat motionless, hidden behind a mound of branches, vines, and damp leaves.

Pulling the foliage away from its engines, I secured the leathery pouch on the rear storage rack. I then took the large flat canister of fuel from its housing, and emptied its remaining contents into its nearly dry tank. I then casually tossed the canister onto the storage rack and examined the irregular shaped dials that spread across the face of the small dashboard. Reading the compass, I determined which way was southeast and pointed the vehicle thusly. Pushing as hard as I could, I mounted the jeep as it began to roll. Smiling, I sailed down hill, the wind howling as it whizzed passed me. It wasn't until I nearly reached the bottom of the small impression when I cranked the engine and sped off into the forest. *I wonder if a search party is looking for me.*

I was engulfed by an organic city. Redwoods. Living skyscrapers. They stood untouched, perhaps for hundreds of years. This was virgin territory. Surprisingly, neither the Valhallans nor the New Americans have altered this region. Usually the Valhallans engage in a campaign of 'resource-rape' on any and all environments they come in contact with. They carry on as if they are the only people on earth. Slashing and burning, exploiting and consuming everything in their path.

The Valhallans labor under the misconception that they are the chosen people of God. And that when their forefathers broke away from twenty-first century America, it was because the White race was being exploited by a government gone mad. Well, that's only half true. The Keep, those who serve unearthly powers, simply needed an army willing to die for its causes. Nameless, faceless trailer trash mobs were manipulated. Enemies were manufactured, agendas were set, and wars were big money.

We believe that the Valhallans are continuing the unholy agenda of their ancient masters. The destruction of the original people, Blacks, and our advanced spiritual cultivation system. But we as Ta-Amentans stand ready to defend the principles of Maat and to establish the kingdom of God here on earth.

Ours is not an easy task. The Valhallans have joined with various factions in Den-Europe and have since emerged as technological wizards. They have forsaken the development of their Spirituality and have chosen instead the Materialist path. Rockets of all shapes and manner scream towards the heavens in search of more territories to exploit and ruin. Their cities are no better. Cold gleaming buildings populate its landscapes. Like gigantic ice sheets, they shelter its people in shimmering towers of stone. Our Intelligence reports that entire city blocks are allocated towards warehousing millions of children. All are reared and indoctrinated by a wicked media driven Totalitarian Government. I have been within the boundaries of Valhalla on so many Covert-Assignments that I've simply stopped counting. I can remember observing how strange and artificial the people seemed. They were more like mindless robots or puppets. They kept their homes and yards so pristine and manicured that not even a single blade of grass stood out of place. I hated it, and I hated the people who lived in such an unnatural world. I felt great satisfaction in infiltrating and de-stabilizing its government. I declared everything within Valhallan boundaries my enemy. I still feel that way today.

The ruling government within the Valhallan Nation-State is known as 'The House of Harmony.' They are the descendants of the Elitist Social Engineers of Old America. Under the direction of The House of Harmony is the Paramilitary army known as Cold Wind.

They are genocidal in practice and have sworn allegiance to their inhuman masters. The Cold Wind army stands ready to defend what the Valhallans term 'The Final Solution': the systematic annihilation of all nonwhite populations. It is a great sore in the eyes of Amen (God).

The masses of people who live as citizens of Valhalla are beyond reason. I remember on several occasions how we would take them as hostages and try to interrogate them. It almost never worked. They were totally convinced that Black people were the cursed offspring of Cain and that we were only useful as slaves. This is a major component of their culture, a part of their belief system, and one of the many reasons why they are our sworn enemies.

New America is different in terms of mannerisms, but identical in its appetites. She is ruled by the same Secret Orders that fashioned her in the beginning. Gog and Magog are the throne of power in that land. They use arcane rituals and light-code transmissions to keeps its people locked in a dream-like web. A media-culture purposefully distracts its populace from higher endeavors. Few are aware of their spiritual, economic, and political enslavement.

———

The skies were changing. Blue tapestry gave way to gray film. Even the ground seemed different. I chucked the attack-jeep next to a pile of yellowed boulders and pulled my supplies from the rear storage rack. I gathered the remaining water canisters, changed uniforms, and began to walk in a Southeast direction.

* * * * *

August 10 - End of the 20th Century

Freida had been waiting for Skah for almost an hour. She was tired of him always being late and was pretty much fed-up with his overall attitude. She hated standing in front of the small Records Keeping Office she worked at. The women inside always watched her from behind its dusty windows. They were miserable bitches and took great pleasure in needling Freida whenever Skah was late. She was young, beautiful, and had a man in her life. Most of them didn't, and for that they hated her. Pacing up and down the sidewalk, Freida was beginning to question her relationship with Skah. She felt that he resented the fact that she wasn't Africentric, and therefore was not really interested in maintaining their relationship. She herself was beginning to contemplate going out with Ron.

Ron was handsome, educated, and paid. He was a flashy dresser and had a light and jovial way about himself. He wasn't moody like Skah. *He wasn't an impatient, brooding, militant asshole.* She and Ron got along well. Ron really didn't care about political issues, he just wanted to get paid, dress in the latest fashions, and stay-up on the latest trends. When they went to lunch, they never talked about the condition of Black people. Television and music, gossip and people. That's as heavy as it went.

Freida turned and started heading back towards the entrance to the building. She figured she'd call Skah's house again and find out what was taking him so long. Before she could open the door and enter, she was greeted by Ron. He had just clocked out and was leaving the front office. She watched his tall lean figure walk towards her. "He sure is good looking," she said to herself, watching his broad shoulders sway back and forth.

"What's up, gorgeous," he said, rows of white teeth bursting from behind his full lips.

"Oh nothing, just waiting for my ride," she answered. She was visibly upset. Ron, who was no dummy, picked up on this immediately.

"Well, why don't you let me take you home. Besides, your man is probably off saving the world or something."

"I don't know, Ron. If Skah came by and I wasn't here, he'd be really pissed off."

"Look Freida, if Skah actually gave a damn, he'd be here," Ron responded. He never liked Skah. He thought Skah was a pain in the ass. He still resented the political bashing Skah gave him a year ago. He took every opportunity to speak ill of Skah. This was one of the things Freida didn't like about Ron. She thought it strange how Ron would laugh and smile in Skah's face, but then talk bad about him behind his back.

Looking down both sides of the street, Freida stood there like a child not knowing what to do next. She knew Skah would be there, but the way their relationship had been going for the past few weeks-

"Come on, Freida. It's hot out here. Lets go," Ron said impatiently. He took Freida by the hand, and gently pulled her towards the parking lot. Five minutes later, the two of them were in Ron's used orange Mercedes, speeding down Broadway.

———

Skah came rolling up in his faded blue Ford and hurriedly parked the noisy vehicle in the guest lot. He jumped out of the car and marched to the front end of the building. Looking into the rectangular shaped windows, he was greeted with several smiles from the multitude of sisters within. They often whispered about how attractive they thought he was, and, whenever Freida wasn't around, they made sure that they spoke to him. Lisa was the boldest of the bunch. There were several occasions when she actually brushed up against Skah, causing her extremely large butt to bounce and rub against Skah's thigh. Freida hated Lisa.

"Damn, where the hell is she?" Skah said, raising his hands in the air. He decided to enter the building. He did this hesitantly because he knew Freida didn't trust the women inside. Opening the double doors, he immediately walked to Freida's desk. Her computer was turned off. Skah placed his hands on top of the monitor. *It's cold; she must have been gone for a while now*, he guessed.

"She left with Ron," a soft voice uttered from behind him.

Skah immediately recognized the voice. It was Lisa. She was wearing a tight fitting jacket and skirt. Skah noticed her ample thighs spreading from beneath the cut of her dark blue jacket.

Catching himself, Skah looked into Lisa's face and asked about his woman. "When did she leave with him?"

"About 30 minutes ago, I think. It looked like they had a date or something. Did she know you were coming?" Lisa was a master. She sensed a long time ago that there was trouble in paradise. Lisa had a friend, but she wanted Skah in a big way. She thought he was the best thing since sliced bread and took every opportunity to flirt.

Resisting the temptation of Lisa's inviting gestures, Skah thanked her, then excused himself. While walking out of the small office, Skah felt dozens of almond shaped eyes watching his every stride.

He was angry. He couldn't figure out how Freida could leave with Ron. *He was an unconscious jerk.* "Had the relationship been that bad?" he asked himself. Speeding down Broadway, Skah decided to pull over into a nearby liquor store to buy some bottled water. Still upset, and not paying attention to where he was walking, Skah bumped into several young brothas loitering in front of the store.

"Man, what the fuck is wrong with you?" a short bald brotha with sagging paints groaned, his hands and arms gesturing.

"Look, boss, why you wanna walk all over us and shit?" another brotha wearing shades protested.

Skah had accidentally walked into several young 'Bloods.' They had been hanging out in front of 'RG's Liquor' all day. They were smoking weed, gambling, and intimidating customers to amuse themselves.

Still upset, Skah was in no mood to be messed with. Ordinarily, he would have apologized and walked on about his business. Today, he was feeling betrayed and had an all around foul disposition. Glaring at the six young men, Skah's body language communicated to them that he was not afraid and possibly dangerous.

Finally, Skah spoke to the nearest young Blood. "Listen, Black man, I meant no disrespect. It's just been one of them days, you know what I'm saying?"

"Hell nah, nigga. Why the fuck you wanna be in our space? You better fix yo self," the largest brother said. He was probably about 21 years old, looked hard as hell, and was most likely carrying a weapon.

Skah was unmoved. With one eyebrow raised, Skah decided to go for broke. "Well, lets play it like this: anybody carrying a weapon is a punk bitch." The six Bloods stood there. They were slightly shocked, but amused at the same time. They didn't expect Skah to react the way he did. Looking at one another, they then looked at Skah and tilted their heads. They were giving him a chance to talk...to explain himself.

"Which one of you brothas is carrying a weapon? Come on now, which one?" Skah asked, not feeling really angry anymore. He was automatically slipping into brotha-to-brotha mode.

"We all packing," several of them said simultaneously. They reached into their pants and pulled out an assortment of pistols. They were well kept. Polished with pride.

"So basically, you brothas would actually shoot and kill another brotha over who can stand in another man's parking lot." Skah was a master at getting his point across. He learned a long time ago that the brothas and sistahs who made their living hustling and bustling on the streets had a kind of genius about them. They were masters at recognizing who really had something to say, and, more importantly, who was not afraid to say it.

"Man, I don't want to hear no damn speech. I just wanna be wit ma partners," the first Blood said, his mouth twisted in a downward frown.

"I'm just asking a fucking question. Why the fuck you young brothas always blowing each others faces off over stupid shit? I know you brothas are in pain. I know you brothas are hurting, but why take that shit out on each other? Why not take on the muthafuckas who got you in this situation in the first place?" Skah was doing what he does best, making Black people think.

"Man, I don't know what the hell you talking about. All I know is that if I got muthafuckas trying to smoke me, I'ma smoke them first!" a tall skinny brother of 17 said. He was arrogant. He waved his gun as he spoke. He probably wouldn't live to see 25. Skah was just warming up.

"Yeah, yeah, I think you brothas kill each other because you don't want to fuck with the 'Number One' Gangster. You all scared of him, huh?" Skah asked. He knew he was starting to penetrate their defenses, starting to wear them down.

"What do you mean, Number One Gangsta? We the number one gangstas," an overweight brotha said. He was totally sloppy, his shirt was filthy, and his pistol didn't quit fit in his pants.

"Nah... you brothas ain't the Number One Gangster. I'm afraid there's another Gangster out there, and he's the baddest muthafucka on the planet. He's the one who controls our minds...got us acting the way we do," Skah retorted. The initial reason for these men speaking in the first place is no longer an issue. These brothas were now more interested in knowing who it was that was supposedly badder than they were. They needed to know him, to understand him, to destroy him. Skah understood this. He had them where he wanted them.

"What's your name, man?" the tall dark skinned brotha asked, his entire demeanor beginning to soften. He was obviously the leader. The others began to adopt the same posture as he.

"The ancient ones call me Skah."

"Man what you smoking? You trippin'," the same brotha retorted. "Anyway, they call me 'Country.'" He was smiling. The Bloods had long since put their guns away.

"I'm serious. My name is Skah. I'm named after an attribute of God. My name has meaning, purpose. It makes me live up to that purpose. It keeps me on the right track, my brotha," Skah returned. "Maybe someday I'll tell you about the Number One Gangster, that is, if you youngsters are ready," he said, knowing full well he was piquing their interest.

"Ah, c'mon, man...I mean, Skah. What's up with the Number One Gangsta?" they asked. They started to look like the children they were. Hungry, eager, wanting to learn.

"Who is it, where is he-" they continued.

"I don't know if I can trust you brothas. I mean this is really important information and shit. I can't just tell anybody. Some people can't handle this type of knowledge, you know what I'm saying?" It was killing them. They were like babies on Christmas Eve. They wanted it at any cost. Skah knew this. "I tell you what. Lets make a trade. I just can't give you this kind of stuff without a price. You brothas will have to qualify for this type of blessing. I'll choose the day and time. But I'm gonna need your word on something first."

"What do you need from us, Skah?" the tall skinny brotha asked. "Oh yeah, my name's Zoe," he added.

"This is what I need. When I give the call, I need you brothas to bring as many 'Blood Leaders' as possible."

"Oh man that ain't shit. I got hook-up," Country responded.

"I know you do, that's why you'll have to go a step further. You also need to bring as many 'Crips' as possible too. And, you brothas must respect each other while in our presence."

"Who's presence, Skah?"

"You'll find out about that later. What I need to know now is, are you brothas strong enough to pay the price. If not, I understand. Everybody can't be an Original God," Skah finished. He used the language of the streets. They all immediately recognized where he was coming from. They used the same terminology in their Gang Initiations; their Secret Teachings.

"Alright then, Skah. When you give the call, we'll do our part to make it happen. Word is Bond," Country said, the others nodding in agreement.

By then, a small crowd had gathered around the entrance to the liquor store. Even the owner was peeking from behind the double glass doors. He was too afraid of the young men to tell them to leave.

Skah stood there looking at the young men. He liked what he saw. They had strength, power, and a certain amount of respect on the streets. He and Amani had being talking for several months about how they would approach the Gangs. They knew a long time ago, that they would eventually need these young men. They were serious warriors, while most of the Black masses of men and women were too afraid of their own shadows to really engage the enemy.

"Alright brothas, here's my cell number. I'll leave it up to you. I'll let you decide where and when to do this," Skah said, handing Country a small black card.

Country complied. He wasn't the kind to promise something and then not follow through. Skah knew this. "Here you go, Skah," Country said, handing Skah a dirty piece of paper with his cell number on it.

"Alright then, Black men. Why don't you brothas get started? Oh yeah, stop hanging out in front of this man's store," Skah said.

Walking through the small crowd of stunned onlookers, Skah made his way into the store. A slight smirk shown on his face as he watched the young men get inside their red van, slam its rusted doors, then drive recklessly up the street.

CHAPTER 14

I watched calmly as a shimmering Aten sank beneath a beautiful purple-orange horizon. It slipped from view, looking like a giant red tear drop. Even from this distance, the strange neon borders of New America illuminated the desert. Sirens blaring, horns barking, the American Border patrol was racing back and forth on their dune lifts. As the blue sky gave way to the black of night, the search lights automatically kicked in.

I was anxious to get home. A feeling of excitement welled up inside. *It won't be long now*, I thought. I recognized this section of the New American borders. It was the area adjacent to the northwest region of the Aztlan territories. In fact, Aztlan was probably about 10 to 15 nilometers south of this place. I trusted the Aztlans more than I trusted the Americans. Although there were several issues that still needed to be worked out between our countries, I'd stand a better chance at getting home safely, and quietly, from within Aztlan boundaries.

In terms of computer technology and environmental resource management, the Aztlans are second to none. They successfully dispose of their waste products and are enjoying an Oil Rich Based Economy. In many respects, she shares many cultural similarities with our homeland. Like Ta-Amenta, Aztlan's landscape is littered with Pyramids. A powerful irrigation system cuts across its cities, and an advanced degree of astronomical knowledge makes it one of the leading countries in the field. In fact, our Mystic Scientists often compare and exchange information with the 'Plumbed Scientists' of Aztlan. Aside from what seems like perpetual border skirmishes, they are considered allies.

Small scavenging communities stand like blades of yellow weeds between America and Aztlan. They are populated by Miners. Miners are an interesting lot. They basically loot Wasted-Cities and abandoned towns in search of valuables. They then trade these items with Patrol men and Metal Smiths who live in the cities that sit huddled near the borders. If I get lucky, I'd be able to trade my remaining water, or maybe even this uniform, for a ride home.

––––––––––

The night air felt good. It was warm and comforting. I knew from past experience that the Americans always trained their search lights on Aztlan. *Due south.* I followed the blue yellow beams for as far as they would reach. I walked until they shone no more than an opaque shadow across the night sky. That's when I heard the voices drifting across the sandy dunes which lay like a vast inland beach. I instinctively froze.

"They definitely aren't Miners," I said to myself.

I considered disappearing into the shadows, fading into the liquid night. But as their voices grew louder, so did my interest. Squinting, I sniffed at the sweet night air. The familiar scent of burning wood greeted my nostrils. The sound of laughter teased at my ears. Crouching low to a soft curve of sand, I peered over the smooth sparse lump of earth.

About fifteen men and women were singing and dancing around a small camp fire. They were Americans. It was easy to spot Americans. They usually came in several different colors. If they were all Black, I'd assumed that they were Ta-Amentans. If they were all Mexicans or Native, they'd most likely be Aztlans. All White; Valhallans. The most difficult thing about Americans was that you never knew what frame of mind they'd be in. That's the problem with chippers.

I quietly watched for signs of American authorities. I saw none. What I did spot were two large vehicles. They looked like vans. Discarding what was left of my supplies, I scrambled towards the waiting vehicles. With all the shrubbery and sand dunes, I had plenty of coverage. The unsuspecting group continued to sing and dance. Silver cans and wooden boxes were scattered throughout their camp. They were totally oblivious to my encroachment. They appeared to be in a kind of trance.

"I guess Black folks are still providing entertainment for the American public," I whispered.

These people were no real threat. They were too intoxicated. I could probably take a vehicle without them even knowing it. Hopefully, they'll have a passport of some sort. Without one, I won't get past the Border Patrol.

I watched in awe as the small group worked themselves into a frenzy. They began chanting a mixture of old-world spiritual recipes, further altering their state of consciousness. That was the funny thing about Americans. They had a tendency to borrow from different cultures, never properly researching the meaning and purpose of the things they took. The Ntiu Tut teach us, that in order to spiritually gain from a set of principles, one must fully understand every aspect of the society from which they come.

When I reached the first van, I wiped the thick coating of dust from the passenger side window. The keys were still in the ignition. I quietly crawled inside the dirty vehicle and started rambling through the compartments. No passport. I then began searching under the seats; hoping to find a weapon of some kind.

"Empty," I whispered. Easing myself from the drivers side door, I crept over to the dark purple van that sat next to what looked like a row of palm trees. Both the driver and passenger doors were locked. In my haste, I lost my edge. I felt it first. Then I saw him. Someone... a male, was glaring at me from inside the dirt-encrusted window. Startled, I stepped back and hid myself behind the nearest tree. I heard the loud clang of rusty locks snap and pop. The large sliding door, which sat on the passenger's side, began to slide open.

A rancid cloud of smoke floated from the van's interior. Then a low harsh voice called out, "Hey, Jude. Is that you? Jude... quit goofing."

I just stood there, motionless. I didn't want to walk over to the van and then have this 'Jude' guy pop-up out of nowhere.

"I'm over here," I said, deciding to take advantage of the situation.

"Where are you, man? I can't see you. It's too dark out here," He returned laughing. "Alright, man. I'm coming."

He pulled himself from the van. He was a fairly large Asian man. Mid-to-late twenties. He was carrying keys. Wiping his eyes, his mouth fell open when he saw me. That's all I needed. Before he could get off another word, I had already slammed him to the ground, snatched the keys, and was positioned to respond to anyone who may have heard the short skirmish.

I lifted him from the dirt, and held him in an arm-lock. Leaning close to his ear, I spoke in a low menacing tone, "Where are the passports?"

"I... I have them in the glove compartment," he answered.

I pushed and shoved him back into the vehicle. A loud thumping noise arose from its rusty metal walls.

"What are you going to do to me?"

"That depends on you." I stared at him for about 10 seconds. I wanted the fear to sink in... to touch his very bones. "What's your name?"

"My name is Bako. Thomas Bako," he returned.

"Bako, I know I was a little rough on you and everything, but I'm desperate. I'm just trying to get home, man. I need your help," I said, loosening my grip on him.

"What do you want me to do? I ain't got no money-"

"My name is Kashta."

"Yeah, right. Mr. Kashta. How can I help you?" he continued. He was becoming more at ease. He dropped his shoulders and managed a slight smile.

"How far are we from Aztlan?" I asked, studying his every action.

"We're not far, maybe seven or eight miles... I don't know."

Before I could utter another word, a tall Black man and a short shapely white woman came from behind the van. They were just as startled to see me, as I was to see them. The Black man was carrying a shiny silver revolver. It was securely embedded in a cheap leather holster. He looked first at Bako, then he looked at me. Frowning, he spoke in quick nervous bursts-

"What, what's going on here?"

I'd already judged that he was three steps to my left. Bako was in arm's reach, and the female had more curves than fight. If the brotha went for his weapon, it would be the last thing he'd ever do.

"I'm just trying to get a ride to Aztlan. I've been traveling on foot for days. I could really use some help."

"Who the hell are you, man? I mean, we don't know you from Adam," he retorted. I was beginning to tense up. I counted about ten to fifteen people in all. If I were to get a hold of his weapon, it wouldn't be too much effort to dispatch all of them. "No," I said to myself. *There has to be another way.*

"What difference does it make who I am, my brotha? Listen, I wasn't looking for any trouble, just thought-"

"Look man, I'm not your brother!" he responded. "Anyway, there's a killer on the loose in the northern regions. Somebody 'offed' a Valhallan Soldier," he said, looking me up and down.

"Ah come on, Jude. Let's help the guy out. Besides, that soldier was over 60 miles north of here," Bako interjected.

"Yeah, Jude, let's give him whatever he wants. He's so beautiful. My name's Helen by the way," she said with a sly grin.

Jude stared at Helen. Without lifting his head, he motioned to Bako, "Go tell the others. Helen, you stay here while we take this gentleman to the Aztlann Borders."

I was relieved. For a moment, I thought I was going to have to kill another Black man. I stared at Jude's gun. Yeah, he was helping me alright, but I still didn't like the fact that he had a weapon and I didn't. *Sometime during the night, I was going to have to take it from him.*

CHAPTER 15

October 5 - End of the 20th Century

On the 4th floor of the Master Grip Lodge, which rose majestically in the heart of Downtown Oakland California, a panel of distinguished Blacks sat calmly in their seats. They watched impatiently as the crowd of people poured into the spacious library room. It had been rented out weeks ago; by whom, they weren't sure. This made them uncomfortable. They were privileged Blacks. They had money, power, prestige. They were used to calling the shots.

Every year around this time, just before the big holidays, they were instructed to organize a 'community dialogue.' It wasn't their idea; the orders came from higher up. All that was told to them was that they were being challenged as 'Pillars' of the Black Community, and that the 'natives were getting restless.' They had to obey; they sold their souls a long time ago.

The audience quickly swelled to capacity. They were members of the church. They were concerned citizens who believed in the political process. They were hard working middle-class African American men and women. And, of course, the ever present sympathetic whites, Jews and Gentiles alike, who always seemed compelled to sit in on African American affairs. Most of the Blacks in the audience looked up to the people sitting on the stage. They were mesmerized by their fancy cars, big homes, and 'proper English.' Among the excited men and women who acted like children at the movies, sat a brooding and calculating Skah. Amani sat to his left, a tape recorder hidden under his chair. Nefertari and Nola would be there later. They both were busy processing the new members who recently 'passed over' from the ranks of the African Directive into the Secret Order hidden within its membership.

The man seated at the left end of the rectangular table was Dr. Wilbur Todd, a practicing physician in the Oakland area. Sitting next to him was Mr. Avery Jefferson, a local business man. He owned three large car lots. Pulling up a chair next to Mr. Jefferson was a Dr. Cortiny Wright. She holds a Doctorate in Education and is the Director of the Bay Area 'Educational Agency.' She is also being groomed to run for Mayor. Her ex-husband, Dr. Gatling Price, was seated beside her. He was a tenured History Professor at the local Community College. And finally, Pastor Bill Hardley. He was the Pastor for one of the largest Black churches in the Bay Area.

Every year, these individuals and others like them, called their 'assigned' communities together, in efforts to participate in a cultural exchange of ideas and to determine which way the Black Community should be moving. It was all a farce. The local newspapers were paid by an unknown source to 'drum-up' the event. Amani and Skah found the free publicity to be both a blessing and a wake up call. They debated amongst themselves as to who made the payment and why. They would later conclude that individuals in positions of power, real power, were becoming aware of their activities in northern California.

Skah and Amani were recognized by most of the men and women in the audience. They had managed to accomplish over the past few years what the panelists promised to do decades ago. The people didn't fully understand what these young men were all about, but they knew that Black people were at the top of their list. The people saw how the 'African Directive' seemed to straighten young folk out. The people remembered how money was raised by the AD and channeled into predominantly Black schools. They watched and secretly appreciated how this group of 'radicals' was actually doing something in the community.

The Moderator stepped to the microphone. She was a tall, dark-skinned sister with a long weave. She wore a lot of jewelry and smiled too much. Clearing her throat, she pulled the thin microphone from its stand and began addressing the crowd.

"Hello everybody. My name is Joyce Martin. I hope this evening finds you in good spirits. I guess most of you are aware that we are here to conduct our annual Community Dialogue. Today, I am pleased to introduce a panel of distinguished guests."

She walked back and forth across the room like she was on the 'cat-walk.' Her dress was especially tight, and she could barely keep her balance in her 8 inch heels. She thought she was the shit.

After clearing her throat, she introduced the panelists. She then explained the format of the proceedings and told a corny joke to loosen-up the audience.

"Well... let's start with Dr. Cortiny Wright. As many of you already know, Dr. Wright is the Director of the Bay Area Educational Agency. She's responsible for most of the curriculum found in our schools. Dr. Wright, the floor is yours," she said smiling. She then placed the microphone into the housing on its stand and walked to the rear of the stage.

Dr. Wright pulled and prodded at the microphone placed in front of her, then straightened her thin black glasses. She scooted her chair closer to the long flat table and shuffled her notes.

"Hello," she said in a dry tone. She sounded like one of those mean teachers who never smiled. "African Americans have made tremendous strides in education, but we still have a long way to go. Our test scores are the lowest of all ethnic groups in the country, and violence permeates our class rooms-"

Dr. Wright was an eloquent speaker. Years of talking before crowds had trained her to effectively say in 15 minutes, what would take the average person an hour. She used her time well. She quoted various sources, told more horror stories, and generally painted a picture of gloom and doom. By the time she had completed her speech, the audience members were stunned into submission. One lady even started crying.

From out of the corner of his eye, Skah noticed Nefertari, Nola, and two other sistahs he'd only recently met walk into the conference room. Nola had a huge smile on her face. Leaning over towards Amani, Skah whispered, "I guess she and Jerome must be getting on pretty good." Amani laughed. The four women pushed and squirmed their way through the rows of seats and sat behind the two men.

"Where's Freida? How come you never bring her with you anymore?" Nefertari asked, popping Skah on the back of the head.

Skah was visibly annoyed. He and Freida have not been keeping company in months. She felt he didn't appreciate her. He often complained about the fact that she wasn't as culturally aware as he would like. Skah thought that he was being constructive. Freida felt he was being a big pain in the ass. They both decided to spend some time apart. The last Skah had heard, Freida had stopped straightening her hair, and was wearing Kente cloth. Amani saw her on the University campus at Berkeley and was amazed that she could carry on a conversation about the 'molecular dynamics' of African Spirituality. As quiet as it was kept, she was influenced far more by Skah than either of them cared to admit. In the end, they both missed out.

"I don't know where the sistah is," Skah answered.

"Anyway, this is Tracy, and this is Donna," Nefertari explained. "Nola and I just finished processing them."

They were both beautiful. Their eyes were bright and youthful. The smell of expensive perfume danced around the brothas nostrils.

"How are you?" Amani asked, extending his hand.

"Hello," the woman identified as Tracy returned, placing her hand in Amani's. She was one of those 'super gorgeous' sistahs. She had a short Afro and full round lips. She wore a dark blue silk dress. Its intense blue dye reflected off her incredible skin tone. Amani was always quick to make his interests known.

"After the meeting, we have to talk," he said, winking at Tracy before he turned his head to continue listening to the speakers. Skah said nothing, he simply acknowledged both women with a nod of his head and turned his attention towards the moderator.

Joyce Martin was totally unaware of the conversation taking shape between Amani and the others. She had a job to do.

"Okay, ladies and gentlemen, if you could keep your questions until after the meeting, that would be greatly appreciated. Next we have Mr. Avery Jefferson. Many of your children have received scholarships or grants from Mr. Jefferson, so I'm sure most of you know him," she said gleefully. It was becoming more and more apparent to Skah that she was possibly not just a journalist 'hard up' for a job, but probably under the same direction as the panelists she so proudly introduced.

Mr. Jefferson was a large man, nearly six and a half feet tall and close to 250 pounds. His voice rang like a thunder clap. His suits were the best that money could buy, and he was a player to the bone. He smiled at the audience members as he scooted his chair closer to the table. Pulling the microphone up, then down, he spoke into its metallic face.

"Alright people, we all know why we're here. We need to do better than what we've been doing," he said. "I mean if we expect to have respect from other people, people outside of our community, then we need to respect ourselves." Mr. Jefferson was a business man. His mannerisms were cold and sharp. For almost 30 minutes, he went on about how important it was to support Black businesses, while offering no real explanation as to why and how the ramifications of not supporting Black businesses actually affected the community.

Mr. Jefferson finished his speech as abruptly as it began. He had no tact or style. He was simple and to the point. Skah was a student of the human condition. He noticed how most of the people in the audience clapped after Mr. Jefferson and Dr. Wright finished their speeches. All but four.

Leaning closer to Amani, Skah pointed them out, "Looks like I've located the 'watchers,'" he whispered, pointing at four white men who sat near the back of the conference room. They each wore dark glasses, suits, and one of them looked like the Mayor's son. "Watch their reactions, Amani. They probably work for The Department on Human Affairs or The Department of Race Relations or some other County or state-financed Spy Operation," Skah whispered.

"Damn, I must be slipping. I didn't even notice them," Amani responded.

"That's alright, my brotha. I got your back," Skah returned, smiling and winking his eye.

"Now, this is the muthafucka I've been waiting to hear. He's the asshole that tried to get me kicked out of the school district. I mean this Negro actually sided with the white faculty. He said I was teaching hate," Amani said angrily.

The Moderator had introduced Dr. Gatling Price. He was the only black history Professor who was tenured at a community college. For whatever reason, he never questioned his superiors, never tried to get on board with a *good* university. He just pushed his weight around at the Jr. College level. Amani referred to him as a 'gate keeper.'

Dr. Gatling did something the other two speakers did not do. He stood up and walked over to the dusty podium that was leaning against the wooden chalk holder. He seemed different from the other panelists. He had a kind of awareness in his eyes that both Skah and Amani recognized immediately. Nefertari and Nola sensed it, too. The four of them sat attentively in their chairs.

"I greet you all in peace. I'm not here to tell you how bad everything is. I'm here to tell you what's been improving for the last few years," Dr. Gatling said. Amani was in shock. He was sure this man was a 'sell out', a Negro. Tracy noticed Amani's reaction from where she was sitting. A slight smile shown on her delicate face.

"I'm at a point in my life now when I don't think telling you how bad everything is, is what's needed," Dr. Gatling continued. "You need solutions that work. You need positive reinforcement. And some of you need a swift kick in the ass." The crowd roared with laughter. Skah, Nefertari, and Nola laughed the loudest. Amani was in shock. He thought he knew what Dr. Gatling was all about. The confusion passing from his brow, Amani leaned back in his chair, a slight smile creeping across his face. Tracy and Donna watched Amani's reactions with amusement.

Dr. Gatling delivered a passionate speech. He covered everything from the 'Eurocentric' school curriculum to the abundance of drugs in the community. He even offered several suggestions on how to combat these plagues. Amani sat in amazement.

Skah was refreshed. He thought he was about to have to sit through several hours of controlled speech, then muster up enough strength and passion to intellectually crush these people at the end of the day. As Dr. Gatling finished his talk, and the people began to clap, he hit Amani on the knee, then pointed to the silent observers strategically located in the back of the room. Amani nodded in agreement.

The Moderator smiled as Dr. Gatling sat down. She shook her long weave while she waited for the crowd to stop clapping.

"Alright, that was good," she said. The people continued to talk and clap. They were excited about what Dr. Gatling had to say.

"I like him, we need to hook-up with him, find out what he's doing," Nefertari said, patting Skah on the back. She wrote his name down on a small piece of scrap paper. "I'm calling that brotha."

"Damn, I'm in shock. I still don't trust him though. I'll have to check him out myself."

"We can put the brothas on him, have them follow him around, find out who his friends are," Skah interjected.

The four of them started talking amongst themselves. It wasn't until they were 10 minutes into their conversation that they noticed the new speaker. It was Pastor Hardley.

Pastor Hardley spoke long and hard about the coming of Jesus Christ and how everyone needed to pray and wait on the savior. He basically conducted a sermon. His approach and solution to the problems infesting the Black community was for everyone to pray, watch the clouds, and, in the next few years or so, someone would come floating out of the sky and save everybody. He said all of this while holding a picture of a blond haired, blue eyed Jesus.

Nola leaned over to Nefertari and whispered, "Is he going to pass a tray around and try to get our money?" They both giggled. Amani was still tripping off Dr. Gatling. He couldn't wait to talk to him after the meeting. Tracy and Donna said nothing. They just watched the four young revolutionaries talk and laugh amongst themselves.

Joyce Martin was an efficient Moderator. She quickly quieted the fairly large sized crowd, and introduced Dr. Wilbur Todd before the claps had completely faded. As Dr. Todd adjusted the microphone, Joyce was already in the back of the room, talking with the four individuals who never saw fit to clap for the various speakers.

Dr. Todd speech was uneventful. He basically talked about problems that were pretty much understood by the community. He covered such topics as AIDS, drug abuse, breast and prostate cancer, and sickle cell anemia. He painted a grim picture for the future of African Americans and offered no solutions. Skah was well aware of how this format would proceed. He'd been to too many such discussions and found them to be staged mechanisms designed to give the uninitiated a sense of power. They were controlled and contrived by people who never set foot in the community. This was just one of many ways in which the ruling classes pacified the poor teeming masses of Blacks; standard procedures for the populations of Urban America. This was a hard lesson for Skah to learn. He had to forget the color of the skin these people lived in and pay more attention to the culture and philosophy they lived by.

Skah sat and reminisced about the many nights he and his mother and father would stay up late and discuss the nature of the enemies of Black people. Skah was too young at that time to realize that not all Black people were working for the betterment of the Black race. He had to be taught that some Black people had accepted the ways of the enemy and were in service to the powers of anti-life.

As the Community Dialogue began to close, a thick crowd of audience members began to converge around the microphones. They were placed three per aisle. As they gathered themselves, Skah noticed the excitement in their faces. *They actually fell for this shit*, he thought, as he hurriedly walked through them, racing for the nearest elevator. He decided halfway through the 'meeting' that he would personally gather the license plates of the white men who sat stone-like during the meeting. He wouldn't have to do this alone, because throughout the strangely decorated library room were several members of the Secret Order within the ranks of the African Directive. Skah had made eye contact with them as he left the room and motioned for them to follow him outside. Three men followed him. They were Kafra, Kesu'kt, and Muwangi. They were some of the first brothas to 'cross-over' to the Secret Order. They were long and trusted friends. They proved their worth a long time ago.

"I guess you noticed them crackers sitting in the audience, too," Kafra said, winking at Skah. Kafra was a serious warrior. He and Skah found themselves members of many of the same Black organizations. They both had the same kind of temperament; it probably explained why they got along so well.

"Of course, Black man. They stood out like beacons."

"Yes, they did, my brothas," Muwangi interjected. He was a seasoned soldier; been around a long time.

"Kesu'kt, did you pick up on which way they exited the room?" Kafra asked.

"Yes. They left behind the stage. But check it, before they left, they handed each speaker, except for the history teacher, a package. They moved fast; if you weren't paying attention, you would have missed it."

The elevator came to a gravity-straining halt. The four Black men exited the small box in a hurry. The crowd that was waiting for the elevator on the first floor had to jump out of the way of the fast walking, angular young men striding through its opened doors.

"Let's go through the kitchen," Skah said pointing. The four men immediately rushed through the lobby, then the dinning room, and finally the kitchen. They walked with strength and purpose. The kitchen hands, who were mostly foreigners, left them alone. Pushing the cold steel doors open, the four Black men walked to the far side of the parking lot. Kesu'kt pointed to each corner of the parking facility, and motioned for the men to separate and take up positions.

It didn't take long. Four white men in business suits walked out of a side exit. It was almost indistinguishable from the surrounding wall. It sat on the east end of the building.

"They look like politicians, or maybe high-ranking corporate heads. They got juice, but they look more like *operators* as opposed to *owners*," Skah said under his breath.

Skah motioned to his four partners to move in closer. Each of them found and targeted a particular man to follow. Oddly, the shadowy white men separated without talking. Skah and Kesu'kt followed their respective prey to the lower parking lot, section G. They were silent, stealthy. The men in question had no idea they were being followed. They just routinely walked to their vehicles and looked straight ahead. Skah moved in as close as he could, then pulled out a small note pad and pen from his jacket pocket. Crouching behind a large jeep, he was able to get three car rows away from his target. From behind the stationary rows of steel, he observed his quarry. He was not a large man, about average. He wore his hair neatly cropped and brushed to the back. He was probably about 45 years old. His suit was loosely cut and expensive. That's when Skah noticed the other peculiarities.

The man wore a thick gold and silver ring on his right hand. It had some type of design on it, but Skah couldn't make it out. He also noticed three large emblems attached to the back of the gentlemen's vehicle. They were brightly colored, and were fashioned into geometric symbols. Skah wrote the man's license plate number on the note pad, and tried to sketch-out the details of the symbols on the back of the vehicle. Oblivious to the fact that he had been tagged and followed, the middle-aged White man started his vehicle, lit a cigarette, and, without missing a beat, sped out of the lower level parking lot.

Skah jumped from behind the Jeep Rover and ran toward the east end of the parking facility. He found Kesu'kt hiding behind a faded blue trash bender. He was busy jotting down the license plate number of a large black van. From where he stood, Skah could see that the van also had the strange decals plastered on its rear window. His heart skipped a beat. A broad smile spread across his face.

Kesu'kt noticed Skah approaching and motioned for him to duck down. Skah obliged. Kesu'kt then pointed past several rows of automobiles. Turning his head, Skah noticed Muwangi crouching behind a red Volkswagen. Upon seeing Skah, Muwangi let out a huge grin, then pointed to his left. There was Kafra. He was leaning behind a large dumpster.

Within the span of a few minutes, each vehicle was out of its parking stall and accelerating from the dusty garage. Their four pursuers watched as the vehicles disappeared into the Oakland traffic. Skah was excited. He knew that they stumbled on something big. He always knew that the enemy was well organized, but he had no idea that they would be so blatant in their mannerisms.

He thought he recognized one of the symbols as that belonging to the Fraternal Order his uncle belonged to. *Was his uncle in on it?* he asked himself. He always assumed that groups like the ones his uncle held membership in were basically harmless. *Is there a connection?* he thought. He never could understand why his father often scoffed at his uncle. He never understood the rift. He began to reflect on how his father and uncle would argue into the night, his father calling his uncle a 'sell-out.' He even told Skah that one day he would have to confront Black men like his uncle. He informed Skah that these Black men were well organized and had the backing of a powerful inner circle of whites, whom they concealed from the African community.

The four men met in the center of the parking facility and exchanged notes. They each had the license plate numbers from the vehicles they observed, and each expressed interest in the fact that there were symbolic emblems on the vehicles in question.

"Okay, so you brothas noticed them, too?" Skah asked rhetorically.

CHAPTER 16

It was a bumpy ride home. We passed a handful of New American border stations along the way. There were several occasions when I thought Jude was going to turn me in. I mean, each time we passed an Out-Post, I felt him hesitate. I wondered what he'd do if he knew I lifted his pistol while he slept. Bako was a lot more agreeable. I actually kind of liked the guy. Helen was a different story.

Units of New American Soldiers passed us as we traveled south. Their shiny rifles glistened under the moonlit sky. Angry glares peered into our van as we continued on our journey. Jude said nothing. He just drove, listening to the audio as we skipped and toggled over the uneven terrain.

"So where you from, Kashta?" Bako asked, smiling extra hard.

"I'm from the Southern States," I returned. Jude glared at me through the rear-view mirror.

"What part of the Southern States? The Central D section in New America, or that nigga country across the border?" Jude popped off.

"Why are we always at each other's throat, Jude?" I asked, trying to avoid a confrontation with the brotha. He didn't answer. He just exhaled and shook his head. Helen was looking me up and down. Her interests peeked.

"Wow... are you from there? You know, the Black Lands?" she asked. Yawning, she reached for the small refrigerator huddled in the dirty corner of the misshapen van. Her large breasts brushed against me. Her thin lips formed a sly smile. Leaning on me for what seemed a little too long, she reached into the tiny ice-box and pulled a small container of water from its filthy compartment.

"How do you pronounce your name again?"

"Kashta."

"Wow, that's a beautiful name. Where is it from?"

"It's an old Kushite name. My father gave it to me," I returned. Jude managed a slight smile. Looking through the rear-view mirror, he interrupted-

"Are you sure you're not from that nigga country? Those are the kinds of names they have."

Bako was watching everything. He was a lot more level-headed than Jude. I was relieved when he entered the conversation.

"Oh come on Jude. I mean you're Black, right? Why do you always talk bad about their country?"

"Yeah, what's wrong with their country?" I added, hoping to pit Bako against Jude.

"From the books I've read and the micro-libraries I've visited, back in the twentieth century, Blacks were treated like shit." Bako said.

"Well, it ain't the twentieth century anymore, man. Things are different now," Jude replied. "Besides, who would want to live next to all them niggas-"

"Jude, you're a Black man. Listen to yourself. If you have that type of attitude, just imagine the types of ideas swimming around in the minds of white-" Helen had grabbed my crotch.

"I love Black people. Especially Black men," Helen mentioned, pressing up against me.

"I'm sure you do, Helen" I retorted, moving her hand away.

"Look, man. I don't have to answer to you. If it weren't for me, your Black ass would be footing it back to Aztlan. Oh yeah, what in the hell is a nigga, I mean black man, doing going to Aztlan anyway?"

"First of all, Jude, I appreciate the ride. But tell me something, my brotha - oops, wait, you're not my brother. But anyway, are you giving me a ride to Aztlan because you're afraid of a little competition?" Jude was fuming. Bako and Helen were enjoying every moment.

Looking out of the mud-stained windshield, my spirits were lifted as I saw the red and green searchlights from the Aztlan Borders. Three medium-sized Eagles left their hangers and rocketed toward us. They were on top of us in seconds.

Leaning from one of its oval shaped windows, an Aztlan Soldier motioned for us to pull over. A grumbling Jude obliged.

"You see the type of shit you putting us through, man? I care, I give a damn," he bellowed, the engines from the approaching jeeps nearly drowning out his voice.

I just looked at him and smiled. Jude was a brotha in pain. Maybe one day he'd see the light. I opened the shaky door and slowly got out. I stood in a whirling cloud of dust. Above me, I watched as the dark green Eagle slowly began its descent. I raised my left arm and placed my right hand over my chest. The Aztlan Soldiers immediately recognized my actions.

"One moment, sir. Our Border Police will be here shortly," we heard blaring over the vehicle's barker. Jude, Bako, and Helen sat motionless in their seats. They just looked at me. Jude was more surprised than anyone.

Two green and brown jeeps rolled noisily passed me. They stopped in front of the van. Five Aztlan soldiers got out of the lead jeep and walked over toward the van. They peered inside, then asked to see Jude's passport. He complied.

"Do you have identification, sir?"

Turning, I was greeted by a beautiful female officer. She had dark brown slanted eyes, high cheekbones, and shiny jet black hair. *Pure Aztlan*. She held her weapon in a half-raised position. She was lowering her guard, but she was still capable of dealing instant death.

"I do," I answered. Moving slow and deliberate, I reached into my jacket pocket, and retrieved my metal alloy identification badge. She took the small card from me and examined it. A smirk crept across her face.

"Nice uniform. Since when did Valhalla start enlisting brothers in its ranks?"

* * * * *

April 6 - Early 21rst Century

It's been years since the Million Man March. Hundreds of Black organizations have come and gone in its wake. Many were destroyed by inside fighting. Some were defeated by lack of preparation. Government operatives gutted still others. These were desperate times. America was at war. Chippers, mind controlled puppets, were creating havoc, and the borders between the nations were dissolving.

Basic Civil Rights continued to take a beating. The people voted, but it seemed as if the choices really didn't matter. The common voice of the nation was ignored. The American people were fed a constant stream of fear, becoming more and more paranoid as stories of weapons of mass destruction blared twenty four-seven. Every nut promising a bigger, better, and brighter tomorrow was able to fleece an already panic-stricken populace.

The African American community was in a strange state of flux. The Latino or Mexican populations were gaining serious power in the southern states. And the white majority population was becoming increasing aware of the fact that its status as White people didn't have the same meaning it did in the previous century. Skah would often reflect on how he overheard Muwangi and Kafra talking...

"White people are in a 'pre-nigga' state. Getting over simply because you white is over," Muwangi said.

"These are interesting times indeed, my brotha. It's a great time to be alive," Kafra returned. "You see that chipper at the library? I mean, that brotha took out six white folks."

"The key and salvation to the rebirth of the Black race lay in the chaotic condition of the White nations. As long as they are in a state of panic, paranoia, and disorganization, most of which is inside family fighting, there's hope for us."

Like a cancerous tumor, world-wide terrorism continued to spread. Airports, State and Federal buildings, and other public government facilities were under increasing threat. The Mid-Eastern Nations were rising in power and influence. After the hit they pulled off in the Big Apple, every rouge nation on the planet was anxious at taking a swing at the States.

The African Directive was one of many Black Organizations that survived the transition from twentieth to twenty-first century America. It's membership swelled to a consistent 288, half of which were members of the hidden order within its own ranks. Brothas and sistahs have come and gone. Some were scared away, some weren't really serious, while others have lost their lives in the struggle. The conscious members of the African American community were in full support of the African Directive. Money was raised to establish Black Owned private educational institutions. Black businesses of all manners increased and proliferated under the zone of influence of the invisible army of Black men and women, who operated under the front.

Coalitions were established between the African Directive and other Black Organizations. Infiltration of these organizations by the 'double-members' within the AD was enacted. The most courageous, militant, and Africentric individuals were recruited into the silent Brotherhood, which lay just below the surface of the African Directive. Even the Church would turn out to be a major source of membership and finance. Skah made certain that any and all individuals who qualified to pass into the double echelon of the AD remained in their respective groups, committees, and organizations. Skah, Amani, and Nefertari, agreed that if the recruited members of different organizations continued their membership in said groups, etc., then what better way could they themselves keep abreast of what was going on in the African American community? The unseen hand of the double-members of the AD had its eyes and ears everywhere.

Skah, as an individual, as a man, and as a Spiritual being was undergoing tremendous growth. He stepped up his meditative sessions from 10 minutes a day to an hour and a half a day. His dietary habits, sexual habits, and conditional reflexes were either being eliminated altogether, or controlled and harnessed for the betterment of himself and his community. Nefertari and Amani were experiencing similar rewards, but not to the extent that Skah was. They often teased him; said he was born into this role. Skah's Husia (authoritative insight) was becoming clearer. His studying was no longer a chore or a necessity, but a way of life. His consciousness was at such a state that he could remember a lecture, a book, or recall anything from memory almost instantaneously. "Such are the rewards for following the laws of God. Such is the birthright of all human beings," Skah would often say.

There were disturbing insights into the true nature of the enemy, including who and what the enemy was. These were the things Skah shared only with double-members. They were the most conscious, and therefore the strongest.

"The common membership of the African Directive would have to wait," Skah would often say. "The enemy was no longer an abstract thing, but actual men and women in positions of power. They have names and faces. They are flesh and blood."

* * * * *

I'm going home. Calling from the Informational Center of the Aztlan Northwest Military facility, I was able to make contact with the Ka-Ba-Ra Chamber. Punching my secret code into the fiber-glass computer terminal, I made sure to utilize one of our Zero-frequencies. It took less than 10 minutes to establish contact, when an excited Warrior-King Senwosret answered my call. I watched his smile materializing on the electronic view screen, even before his complete image shimmered into focus. *I don't think I've ever seen that man smile.*

"Hetepu (eternal peace), Kashta. It's good to see you. It'll be good to have you home again, Atef," he said, looking at the Director of Security for the Aztlan Military Base.

"You'll have him back, friend," the Director responded. They both nodded their heads.

"It'll be good to be home, Atef. I've seen some of the most beautiful terrain a man could ever dream to behold, but I'd pick Ta-Amenta over Heaven itself."

"What's the difference?" Senwosret responded. We both laughed.

"I've secured permission from the Aztlan border authorities, Kashta. I've dispatched an Emergency Escort Unit, or EEU, to your location. It shouldn't take more than an hour for pick-up. Until then, stay out of trouble," he said smiling.

"Tu (yes)," I responded. The electronic screen went blank. Turning, I acknowledged the Director of Securities and walked towards what appeared to be a large cafeteria. My belly was empty, and I knew that the Aztlans followed a natural diet. The smells were incredible. The green leafy salads, the bright colors of tropical plants, and the scent of fruit flavored spring water beckoned for me to partake in its delicacies.

I seated myself next to one of the huge panoramic windows and anxiously watched for the EEU. That's when she came and sat down beside me. It was the same female officer who picked me up earlier. I was stunned by her natural beauty. She reminded me of the women back home.

I missed Tefnut.

"Hello, soldier," she said grinning, showing rows of white teeth. She was wearing a type of red and white jump suit. she looked incredible. Ample thighs and a full posterior only added to my pain.

"Hetepu," I returned. She gave me a puzzled look.

"What does that mean?" she asked, deliberately staring into my eyes and smiling.

"It means 'eternal peace.' That's how people in my country greet one another," I answered. She shook her head and smiled.

"Oh, that's beautiful. It's so refreshing to see a Black man speak an African or Black language. I mean, all we see here are Black people from New America. They only speak one of the four American Dialects. We could never understand why they didn't use one of their own languages."

"Yeah, well, you won't find that problem in Ta-Amenta. We don't speak ill of another man's culture or language, but we sure as hell don't pretend that we aren't proud of our own."

"You see, I mean names like 'Ta... Ta-Amenta," she said. "That's a beautiful name for a country. Our 'Sun Priests' have taught us that it means Heavens Land... and hidden land."

"That's right. The name of a *thing* is very important. It gives meaning and life to whatever object it touches," I returned. She nodded her head in agreement. She sat there, drinking up everything I said. We must have talked for 45 minutes, laughing joking, just learning about one another.

"Oh, look, I think that's your ride home," she said pointing, the sadness showing in her large brown eyes. I had to admit, I was kind of disappointed myself. *Damn she was beautiful.*

I watched quietly, as two Black NARS slid unto the Aztlan airstrip. Dozens of Aztlan soldiers went running towards the shiny black crafts. They greeted the Mafdet as they emerged from the aero-ships. Standing, I thanked my beautiful companion for her company and conversation.

"Oh, wait a minute. I don't know your name. What do they call you back home?" she asked.

"My name is Kashta."

"And my name is Tliloc."

CHAPTER 17

My head was ringing. I've been home for three days now, and I still haven't had time to rest. *They don't care*, I said to myself. The Ntiu Tut have summoned me to the Ka-Ba-Ra Chamber. As I sat in the huge circular enclosure, I waited impatiently as the Elect seated themselves in the immense tiered room. On the immaculate walls behind them, the Sacred Seal of Ta-Amenta, shown in its brilliant colors, casted a magnificent crimson glow around their baldheads. Those who had Locks looked as though they were sprouting purple snakes.

Shekem Muntu was the first to speak. He and I have developed a good relationship over the past four years. I hoped that friendship would present itself here.

"Hetepu, Kashta. It is by the grace of the Most High that you find yourself seated before us today. Tell us, young one. Tell us of your past week's journey. Tell us of the things you saw, while the all-seeing eye watched you," he asked. He, like most Ntiu Tut, spoke in a strange yet beautifully melodic language. It was a language descendant of the highly adaptive speech patterns used by Africans in the 19th, and 20th centuries. We called it the 'Time-less Dialect.'

"Hetepu," I returned, standing then bending at the waist, clapping the back of my right hand into the palm of my left. We Ta-Amentans always greet our Elders in this fashion. "I saw many things of great interest to our society. I beheld an open terrain, beautiful in scope and vast in size. I saw free animals running without care. I saw the landscape change before my eyes; this I did see. However, beloved, I also saw the folly and the ruin of man in Quadrant Four." The Ntiu Tut began to nod and shake their heads. "I saw the remains of a civilization that rose and perished before the dream of Ta-Amenta was realized. An old place, infested with the scourge of Valhallan shock troops."

Shekem Muntu smiled. I can only guess he was pleased that I honored the Ntiu Tut by speaking in the Time-less Dialect. It shows respect for the culture that sustained our ancestors, and gratitude to the languages we used before we remembered our original African mother tongues.

"We see your journey, Kashta. We are there," he responded. The rest of the Elect nodded in agreement.

"Oh, yes, we need to have our geb-scientists re-survey the entire area of Quadrant Four. It seems that there are many miscalculations in the understanding of that place. Whole areas that should be further north are far south, while entire regions that should be drawn south, are further north. The land is in pain," I added. The Ntiu Tut shook their heads and spoke in low tones amongst themselves. They were preoccupied for several minutes before Shekem Muntu spoke again.

"Yes. We will look into this. What else did you see?"

"We found no slaves in that region, only buildings-"

"What else did you find there? Was there anything worth saving?" he asked.

Worth saving, I thought. *What kind of question was that?*

"In one of the buildings, I saw a most interesting thing." They began to perk up. "In this building, on the 4th floor, I saw what appeared to be the Sacred Seal, or Symbol of Ta-Amenta. It was carved into the wall of this structure. The puzzling thing however, was that it appeared to be an ancient engraving. Perhaps older then Ta-Amenta itself."

The Ntiu Tut were beginning to stir in their rounded seats. They started to talk among themselves. I felt so insignificant just sitting there. It must have been 15 minutes before they remembered I was still in the room. If it weren't for Shekem't Ari-an, I probably would have fallen asleep. I liked her; she was always nice to me when I was a child. She was Shekem't Ti's sister. Standing from her small circular stool, she hushed the mumbling gathering of Elders and turned towards me.

"Hetepu, Kashta. This seal you speak of, are you sure it was that which represents Ta-Amenta?" Her question caught me off guard, but I was sure in what I saw.

"Tu (yes) Shekem't Ari-an," I answered. "The Seal of our beloved land was carved into the walls of a building that stood in the heart of Quadrant Four. It was as if I were looking at a smaller version of the mighty glyph that sparkles from behind all of you." They continued their rumblings. "Also, beloved, Ntiu Tut, I observed a most curious thing. I felt a presence in that land. A presence unlike that of Valhalla, New America, or Aztlan."

"What do you mean, Kashta?" a powerful voice commanded. It was Shekem Amenhotep. He is one of the most powerful Ntiu Tut in Ta-Amenta. When he speaks, all Ntiu Tut take heed.

After giving Shekem Amenhotep the proper greeting, I proceeded to explain my last comment. "It's difficult to explain. It was as if I were being watched."

I don't know what set them off, but, whatever it was, they said nothing. They simply stood from their small cotton padded stools and began to walk out of the purple mist-filled room. I called out to them, but they didn't answer. In total silence, I stood there confused. And, like a small child, I watched as the mysterious Ntiu Tut slowly streamed out of the conference Chamber.

* * * * *

August 10 - Early 21rst Century

It was just after 9 pm, and another Thursday night meeting was over. The membership of the African Directive had swelled to a steady 407 persons. All were upstanding citizens in the African American community. Laughing and going over tonight's proceedings, they filed out of the double glass doors of the main entrance. Several of the men and women stood in front of the medium sized complex and exchanged numbers. They almost hated to go home. It was during such gatherings when they as Black people were able to acknowledge, as well as provide validation to and for one another. They needed these meetings. It was the only 'fix' capable of countering the 'soul numbing' effects of a society gone mad.

Amani watched them from the long rectangular shaped window at the north end of the building. He waited patiently as the crowd of brothas and sistahs exchanged hugs, walked down the street, and entered their automobiles. *Tonight was just the beginning*, he thought.

"Are they gone yet?" a low calm voice asked from the shadowy hallway. It was Skah. He was carrying a brief case and waved to several other brothas and sistahs as they left the building.

Shaking his head in the affirmative, Amani continued to look through the cold glass. "For the most part, you'll probably want to get the others on their way," he answered.

"Tu (yes)," Skah responded. He was beginning to use African words more and more these days. His understanding of the 'Metu Neter' was becoming profound, and he felt it appropriate for the Hidden Order within the ranks of the AD to utilize the Kamitic language as much as possible.

As the last of the AD Membership drove off into the night, a second wave of men and women exited the premises. They were the Elect or double-members. It was they who actually controlled the direction of the African Directive, as well as several other Black organizations. Amani, Nefertari, Nola, and Skah hand-picked them from out of the ranks of various Black societies and organizations throughout California. They were the most Spiritual, Africentric, Courageous, Militant, Industrious, Politically savvy, and Culturally aware Black men and women around. "These are the people who would engineer the rebirth of the Kushite Nation," Skah would often say to his friends.

Skah locked the double glass doors with an Ankh shaped key and quickly got into Amani's small blue sedan. Amani, not wasting any time, pressed on the acceleration and followed the other vehicles around the corner, up the street, and unto the freeway. There were six cars ahead of them: all going to the same location. Tracy's house. She and Amani were pretty close these days, especially after she earned her 'Double-membership.'

"Kafra says that he's gotten a hold of some pretty conclusive evidence, something to do with 'biological agents' being tested on the general population," Skah said, looking over a small note pad.

"I'll bet it's the Department of Defense trying out another one of its monstrous pets," Amani said jokingly. Over the years, he and Skah have learned never to be surprised by the actions of the enemy. They both came to the mutual understanding that certain individuals in positions of power were basically Anti-Life. It was just that simple.

"I wouldn't doubt it, my brotha. It's amazing to think that so many of our people expect to be rescued by the government, while at the same time it's that very same government that's busy killing off its citizens," Skah responded.

"You got that right. I guess they can always keep watching the clouds and shit. Maybe someday, someone will come floating out of the sky and save them," Amani said, laughing as he put his car in park. "Don't get me wrong, my brotha. I understood the presence of God. And I also know that God has equipped every man woman and child, with the tools and abilities to change their condition. If the people really had faith in God, they would know this, and be free overnight."

A group of hard-looking brothas watched Skah and Amani walk up the drive-way and onto the narrow strip of concrete leading to Tracy's front door. They were Kafra, Kesu'kt, Muwangi, Jerome, and Charles X, to name a few. Several other brothas stood in front of the house, acknowledging the two men with a quick nod of the head, as only Black men do.

"Where are the sistahs?" Skah asked.

"They're inside, beloved, setting-up the big-screen. I think they were able to put together that piece on the various Black Fraternal organizations," Jerome answered.

Skah was feeling pretty good about the way things were going thus far. He and the others had successfully managed to create a powerful organization. It wasn't just a group of people getting together to complain. It was a seriously complex structure of progressives, with nothing less than African Independence as a final agenda. Smiling, Skah threw up one of the many 'signs' used by this group, and watched as they returned his gesture. Almost 20 Black men held their right hands in the air and offered four fingers; their thumb was kept folded against the palm. They turned their hands such that the back part of their hands faced one another. Then, in an incredible display of unison, they all put their hands to their sides and walked single file into the small house.

––––––––

The second meeting ended early the following morning. Amani, Muwangi, and Skah were sailing down an empty freeway. The fog had rolled in thick, blanketing the lanes in a beautiful white mist.

"That was a serious piece the sistahs put together on those Black Fraternal Orders, Skah. Where do you plan on going with it?" Muwangi asked.

"I'd like to put the information together in pamphlet form and distribute it to the people," Skah returned. "I think it's about time we cause some confusion within the ranks of these organizations. I want to see who, or what, comes up for air," he continued. "Anyway, it's up to the sistahs. They did the research. They put in the work. They get the final say."

"I can't wait. Oh, yeah, I'm pretty close to uncovering the various money Lending Groups in this part of the city. After watching that piece the sistahs put together, I wouldn't be surprised to discover that many of the individuals we saw on the tape are connected in some way to the various money Lending institutions, County and State Agencies, and other government funded entities. I bet it's a giant web of interdependencies," Amani added.

"So how are you and Tracy doing?"

"We're doing good. She's conscious. That's the most important thing," Amani answered.

"That's good, Amani. I'm happy for you. If I'm lucky, hopefully I'll find my Queen as well," Skah said somberly.

Amani didn't respond. Something caught his eye. He followed a car off the freeway, and steered up and around a bus on east 14th street. Pointing, he directed Skah's attention to a large white car.

"Look, on the rear window."

Turning, Skah saw what appeared to be a large circular symbol. It was placed on the outside rear window of the long white car. It was green, white, blue, and yellow. From the distance, it had what looked like a sword, moon, and star, enclosed in a pentagram of some sort.

"Now, that's what I'm talking about, my brotha," Skah exclaimed. Pulling a pencil from his briefcase. Skah wrote the license plate number of the bloated vehicle onto a tiny note pad.

"Okay. This time it's a white man driving the vehicle, but yesterday, we saw a Black man driving a car with what looked like the same kind of symbol," Amani added.

"Yes. That's what it's all about. With the various *feelers* we've got in the community, it'll only be a matter of months before we begin to put this thing together."

"Put what together?"

"A schematic of the actual rulers of this city. When we do that, using the Kamitic Axiom, 'As above, so below; as below, so above,' we'll be able to apply the same principles on a Macro level and uncover the Rulers of the World," Skah answered.

Amani was smiling. He knew his brotha in struggle had done his homework. If there was anyone on the planet he trusted, it was Skah. "I'm sure you're on the right path, Black man."

"If *I'm* on to something, then we're all onto something. I've put everything I've been studying on disks. There's no real excuse for you; or anyone else for that matter, not to know everything I know," Skah said.

* * * * *

Walking into the entrance of my het (house), I closed the door behind me, and dropped face down onto the soft lap of my ostrich-sofa. That's when it dawned on me to check my messages. Leaping to my feet, I rushed to my multi-viewer and punched in my access codes. Almost instantaneously, a series of brightly-colored icons danced across the slick display. A row of encrypted letters arranged themselves in a neat column on the right side of the steel blue viewer screen.

Clicking the pyramid shapes one at a time, steel blue gave way to a series of brilliantly colored windows. Ignoring the first set of cells, I was pleased to see several messages from my parents, Tefnut, and Anpu. *I had better call my mother and father first,* I said to myself. Punching the sankofa-button, I was patched into my parents' electronic in-box. I began typing in an 'I'm alright message' when my mother's face appeared across the shimmering display.

"Kashta! I'm so glad you're alright!" my mother screamed into the dim blue screen. She was all smiles. My father, grinning from ear to ear, was trying to squeeze into view behind her. Looking at them smiling and carrying on, I almost broke down in tears. *How precious life is,* I thought.

"Hey, son. When are you coming home? I think you've served our country long enough. I don't think I can take too much more of this," my father said. Hearing him say that caught me off guard. He was an old veteran himself. He was the one who convinced me to pursue a career in the Mesniu. He said I would be an asset to Ta-Amenta. Now he was asking me to quit.

"Ah come on, Atef (father). With all of the things I've been through, it should be obvious by now that I'm 'Protected by the Most High.' Besides, wasn't it you who decided that, since I had a double 'Incarnation Objective (destiny),' the creator had a master plan for my person?" I returned, trying to convince myself as well.

"Listen, I don't care about that stuff," my father responded. He had managed to push my mother out of view, and was beginning to lose his Men-Ab (stability). "Look, son, you've never been out of contact for that long before. Your mother and I thought you were gone this time. It's too hard on us to have to wait to find out if our child is alive or dead."

"This is what I do. You and mom know this. I've almost completed my Mesniu responsibilities to Ta-Amenta. I mean we've come too far as a people, our independence, the re-capturing of our culture, and the tremendous accomplishments our country has experienced...I just can't 'bail out' now. I love what I do. It gives me a certain satisfaction. I won't stop!"

I watched him through the view screen. He was saying something to my mother. He was very animated, his arms flailing. When my mother walked into focus, I saw the tracks of tears streaming down her face; they fell like liquid diamonds. Her eyes have always been huge and glassy. I tried not to look at them; they always made me weak.

"Kashta, maybe this time you should at least consider what your father is saying. We're getting old; who knows how much time we have left?"

Ouch! That hurt. Mothers really know how to pour on the guilt. Mine was no exception. She used it like a double edged sword; she took no prisoners.

"Mom. Lets not start with the guilt. I've got enough problems in my life as it is-"

"What kind of problems do you have? You're not the one sitting at home worrying about what you have to wear to your son's tombing," she countered. *She was good.*

Their minds were closed. I'd have better luck with them another day. "Okay, Ma. I'll talk to the both of you later. Mer-Tri (love always)."

"Don't try to rush us off. You always want to break contact when you don't like what we have to say. Stop being so selfish, and try to put yourself in our position. When you have your own children, you'll know what we're going through!"

"Alright, ma."

"Ah huh. You better come home and see us," she said; that mother look showing on her face. "Mer-Tri," she finished, breaking the connection.

I was seriously out matched. That's how they usually worked. They wore you down one at a time. Shaking my head, I closed out the channel then punched into Tefnut's electronic nome.

There was no answer. I tried again. Still no answer. *Where is she?* It's not like Tefnut not to at least call me after returning from a mission; especially one like this.

Several bleeps and whistles later, I was greeted by Tefnut's automated response service. I sat back in my chair and watched in dismay, as a hazy light blue screen featuring Tefnut's face shown on the metallic screen. Icons with instructions on how to navigate through her response service began to line up on the bottom of the screen. Before they completed their march, I closed out the channel. *Something's definitely wrong.*

Gathering my wits, I punched in Anpu's encrypted code, then sat back and waited for his response. He and I both created these codes in case of emergencies. I didn't have to wait long.

Brrrazip.zip, brrrazip.zip. The familiar song of an electronic call hummed over the speakers of my multi-viewer. I opened the channel, and in a flash of brilliance, Anpu's face materializes across the display.

"Hetepu Atef (peace black man). It's good to see your person in one piece. I knew you were okay, I knew it!" he shouted. His eyes were beaming.

"My brotha, when that explosion hit, everything went black. No memories, no feelings. Nothing but pain," I responded. Anpu and I often talked about our experiences in the field. We often went on for hours, laughing, crying, just trying to deal.

"Did your parents call?"

"Several times. You know I took a beating," I said jokingly. Anpu started laughing. He, Tefnut, and I often had wars with our parents after returning from our missions. Warrior-King Senwosret told us that it came with the territory.

"Well, my brotha, it was a blessing to hear that you were alright. My parents were the first to receive the message. They, in turn, told your mother and father."

"What's up?" I asked, noticing his sudden change in mood.

"It's Tefnut. I guess you didn't hear," he said somberly.

"Hear what?"

"Tefnut was really upset about you not coming back with us. She went off on Senwosret. The last we heard was that she took a leave of absence and was headed to New America. You and I both know that she went to Quadrant Four. That was four days ago, beloved."

"Wait a minute, Black man. You let her go?" I asked, my Men-Ab (stability, calmness) slipping away.

"That wasn't the idea, Kashta. When I informed Enlil and the others of my plan to go looking for her, word of your return spread throughout the ranks like wildfire," he answered. "Besides, have I ever let you down?" he returned.

"Senwosret has given me a rest period. How soon can you organize a team?"

Smiling, Anpu lifted a small sheet of paper and held it into view. "I already have a team of brothas ready and willing to do this."

"Then I'm ready when you are, Atef."

"Are you sure you've rested enough? I suggest taking another day. Besides, we wont be able to get any daath-Geb. This is supposed to be recreational-"

"I'm fine," I interrupted. "I'm sure you've got time off coming to you, make sure the others are clear to go as well," I finished.

"I'm way ahead of you, Kash. The day after sunrise, we go back to Quadrant Four. I've already secured tickets to New America. We'll spend twelve hours in the central D Section, and then catch a ride to Q.4," he said.

"Tu (yes). I'll get some rest. I'll give you a call sunrise-afternoon."

"Tu," he responded. "Just make sure you're well rested. I don't know what it is that's out there, but we're still getting reports of high concentrations of Cold Wind activity-"

"And if Tefnut is out there by herself..."

"Don't think like that, Kash. Just be ready to go. And get some rest." We broke connection at the same time. Looking out of my large southeast window, I quietly watched as two black birds sang to one another.

CHAPTER 18

November 7 - Early 21rst Century

"Someone in the lower ranks is a spy," Nola said, handing the wrinkled newspaper to Kafra. The Double-Members of the African Directive called an emergency meeting. The newspapers had been circulating, warning of the possible existence of a Black terrorist group in the Bay Area.

Kafra was visibly upset. He was head of security and prided himself on being very thorough.

"That's my fault, brothas and sistahs. I must have let one get past me," he said, handing the paper to Nefertari.

"Not necessarily, beloved," Skah interjected. "Someone may just have a big mouth, but that doesn't make them a spy," he continued. "Many may never qualify for 'Double Membership,' but I don't think they'll intentionally sell us out either."

"That's right, Kafra. I bet someone is probably running off at the mouth. You never know who's listening. I mean, one minute you're sitting at a hamburger stand, talking too much, and the next thing you know everything you said two days ago is 'front page' news," Jerome added.

Amani said nothing. In times like this, it was his job to observe how the others reacted. He watched for every little movement, how they moved their mouths, how they held their heads when they spoke, how they sounded; was their voice strong, or was it soft and weak. Amani didn't miss much, and he trusted few.

Nola was uneasy about the mention of a Black terrorist group in the newspapers. She was a true Black woman, tired of catching hell from a wickedly racist society and poised to replace that society with an Africentric reality. She wasn't about to let her chance at freedom slip away.

"Listen, we all pretty much know who the 'real' Black people in the African Directive are. I mean, we've all seen the brothas and sistahs who actually want to do something for the community. They may not want what *we* want, but they at least want to make the community safe. And then there are the 'Negroes'; they don't care about the Black Race at all, they just want to be apart of whatever's in. They dress in all the latest African fashions, but when it comes to really making a difference they always fall short."

Skah started laughing. "That's true, my sistah. They ain't worth a damn, but they usually have connections, so we use them. They're 'respectable pillars' in the eyes of the larger society, and they afford us a kind of legitimacy in the public. I wouldn't be surprised if one of them was in some restaurant somewhere, drinking, laughing, and talking too much."

"Why do you keep playing this down, Skah? I mean we've got ourselves a spy. They probably know all about us, not to mention the real agenda of the AD," Nzinga said, a look of concern shown on her face. She earned her Double Membership a month ago. She exemplified the perfect blend of grace, strength, and intellect. And she was fine as hell.

"I'm not playing this down, Nzinga. It's just that we can't let what's already happened upset us to the point where we can't function. Okay, so we may have a spy, now what? Do we stop everything we're doing, give up, go home? Do we attack the lower order, beat the hell out of everyone in the lower order, destroying what we've accomplished, confirming the rumors? Or do we simply continue what we've started, making a few adjustments of course, but moving forward in the process?" Skah countered.

"I think I understand, Skah. So what are we going to do, how do we fix it?" Nzinga asked. Everyone in the Inner Circle noticed how Nzinga pressed Skah on every issue. She never missed a chance at keeping him on his toes. They often smiled as she debated Skah across the board. Sometimes she won. Sometimes she lost. She earned their respect, especially Skah's. The women felt she was attracted to him. Skah just assumed she hated him.

"We all know that Black people, having been kicked in the ass for so long, are an attention-starved group. Any and every time something good happens to one of us, or we think we know something someone else doesn't know, we can't wait to run off at the mouth. We talk too damn much. And we'll use that to our advantage." Skah didn't wait for any feedback. "That's where you come in, Kafra. I want you to gather up the potential spies. Partner them up with the wannabe's and fakers. We'll feed them misinformation, then send them back to the enemy. Whatever the enemy 'knows' about us, it'll be what *we* want them to know. You feel me?"

"Tu (yes)," Kafra answered, using the ancient Kamitic language. More and more of the Inner Circle were beginning to use African or Alkebulanian words and phrases. They were evolving, growing in scope and power.

———

November 12 - Early 21rst Century

The 'After School Program' sponsored by the African Directive was becoming a huge success. More and more children had convinced their parents to let them join. Sometimes, even the parents would come and sit in the classrooms. They learned about African history and culture. They learned about the ancient religions and philosophies of Black people and how these systems shaped and influenced the rest of the world. At least 10 African words were learned each day. The children had to know where all of the African countries were, as well as which culture sprang from its soil. Black Pride was instilled in the hearts and minds of all who sat and learned of the ingenious people of old Alkebulan (Africa).

Nola had quit her job at the Airport and was teaching full-time at the After School Program. She loved it. Besides, Jerome was there to help her. He had finally gotten serious about the struggle and was working full time as a janitor at one of the nearby schools. He and Nola had moved in together over a month ago and were getting along great. Little Tomac liked Jerome. He knew Jerome wasn't his father, but he liked him anyway.

"Nola, look at this," Jerome said, pointing to a long white sheet of paper.

"What's up?" Nola asked.

"It looks like a picture of a white Jesus."

"Oh yeah," Nola said. "It's Earl's. His mother and father are Baptists. They go to Church out there on Martin Luther King Avenue. His mother brought him here because she said she was sick and tired of teaching Earl that God, Jesus, and everybody else in heaven are white."

"That's a brave sistah. I'd wish more parents were like her," Jerome said somberly. He continued to stare at the pale image on the sheet of paper. "Damn, I wonder whats it's like to want to go to a heaven where everyone of any importance is white? I mean, you're on earth, and everyone in a position of power is white. Then you die, and more white people are running shit, only this time it's for eternity."

"Well, that's why she brought him here, so we can help him."

"Wait a minute, I just thought of something," Jerome said, a frown showing on his face. "Is he still a member of that church? If she really wants to help the little brotha, she'd keep him away from that shit."

"I think they're still members," Nola responded.

"Then she's really not serious about helping little, Earl," Jerome said, placing the picture back onto the miniature table.

November 28 - Early 21rst Century

Kafra and Kesu'kt had been following the long white Buick all morning. It was shiny, well manicured, and had three large circular symbols stuck on its rear window. Between the two of them, they had managed to compile a very large database on individuals who had such symbols on their automobiles. Most of them were White men. But some, to their amazement, were Black men. They determined that the White men met every 3rd Sunday of each month. They would leave their homes at the same time every afternoon at around 4:00 pm and meet at the same location. Downtown at the Money Lenders Building.

The Blacks didn't meet on Sundays. They met every 2nd Saturday of each month. They left their homes at the same time every Saturday afternoon and would meet downtown at the United Way Office.

Kesu'kt had assigned for the members in the lower division of The African Directive to match the license plates of the vehicles in question with the names and faces in his data files. He told them it was for a project he was working on. Something about how many cars sold in Oakland, and how much of the money was being spent in the community.

He was amazed at who some of the people were and how they secretly met on those sunny Saturday and Sunday afternoons. They were Politicians, Clergy, Professors, Businessmen, Teachers, Entertainers (both Black and White), and they were all meeting in secret.

"This shit is incredible," Kafra said. He and Kesu'kt were hiding behind a row of shiny new cars that sat just across the street from the United Way building. "Look, there's that brotha who owns those two car lots Downtown. And look over there, isn't that the brotha who teaches Black politics at the University?" Kafra asked with excitement.

"The 'Cream of the Negro Crop', my brotha. Hell, they're all in on it," Kesu'kt responded. He didn't bother to look up, he was busy writing down the license plate numbers of the individuals who were new in the area. He then tapped a line of instructions into his laptop. A few seconds later, a grey block popped up on his screen. A smiley face appeared, reading, 'Mail.' It was Debra and Tracy. They had managed to put together a similar file of 'Well to do' Blacks months earlier.

"You see this shit, Kesu'kt?" Kafra asked, leaning into the tiny screen on Kesu'kt computer. "The sistahs are turning out the same kinds of shit. I'll bet the entire city is run by these motherfuckers. I mean, all of them - the niggas too. I guess the White man needs these Negroes to work the Black community. I wouldn't be surprised if they had operatives everywhere," Kafra whispered. The two men continued to take pictures and write down license plate numbers. They had a long but fruitful day.

———

December 18 - Early 21rst Century

Skah and Amani had rented several row boats from the small shop which sat at the edge of the lake in Oakland. They were in the middle of the greenish black pool, surrounded by boats filled with 'Bloods' and 'Crips.' They met with the young warriors on a regular basis and were finally making some progress. The 'Bangers' had learned to trust the two men and knew about their work in the African Directive. They respected Skah and Amani and listened to them every chance they got. Many lives were saved after these meetings. Lessons were learned, and mutual exchanges of information and ideas were routine.

"So, how you been, Country?" Skah asked the lean young man sitting beside him. He and Country had become friends over the past several months; both of them looked forward to their monthly meetings.

Country, in his usual arrogant way, answered his friend, "I'm alright, brotha. I haven't shot another Black man in over a year now. I mean, just look around you. When was the last time you seen Bloods and Crips kicking it like this?" he answered. Their relationship was real. They spoke to one another as if they've known each other for years. It was obvious to all who knew them that they had developed a genuine relationship. Through Country, Skah had access to the streets and to the untapped 'Warrior-Class' of Black men and women who ruled them. From Skah, Country was tapping into the knowledge of self, and to the nature of the beast.

"What about the rest of you brothas, how's life been treating you?" Skah asked, directing his attention at the crowd of red and blue scarves bobbing up and down across the silent waters.

"We alright, Skah. Just trying to get the word, that's all," a short dark skinned brotha answered. He was a Crip. Skah's relationship with the Crips was fairly new. In fact, it was only a couple months old. He met them through Country. It was shaky at first; several skirmishes broke out at different meetings. But things were finally beginning to smooth themselves out.

"I'm glad to hear that. And you all know Amani," Skah said, dipping his head towards his friend. I put my life in this brotha's hands everyday, and he puts his life in mine. Do you brothas have that kind of trust?" Skah asked, trying to stir up some serious dialogue.

"That's what our brotherhood is all about, Skah," Country responded. He was sharp and quick. Over the past few months, Skah had been grooming Country, grooming him for something great.

Amani was finally beginning to feel comfortable around these young killers. He was dying to get into the conversation. "I want to ride with you brothas, see what you all do at night. I want to see the places you brothas go."

"Why you want to hang with us, Amani? We want to hang with you brothas. Shit man, we want to change ourselves, and the world," a young black man responded. He was articulate, very well spoken. He dressed like a gangster, but he was something different. Both Amani and Skah saw a potential member of the African Directive.

"This is Frog," Country said. "Frog is a master mathematician. He keeps our money straight."

"Why you call him Frog?" Amani asked.

"Because he brings us good luck," another brother responded. He started to laugh after he said that. "I bet you two brothas didn't know we knew about that, huh?" He was a different kind of banger, kind of like Frog, a mixture of scholar and gangster...

December 19 - Early 21rst Century

Nefertari and Josh had managed to add all of the stolen prison notes to the data files of the African Directive. After sorting them in the main computer archives, they stored them according to subject, transferring them to an undisclosed location. Only five other members of the Inner Circle knew of this 'wellspring' of information. Even Josh didn't know where the notes he risked his life to steal would finally end up. He didn't care; he just wanted to be a part of the struggle.

"This is amazing; the prison system is big business. The final solution to America's perpetual quest for cheap labor," Nefertari said, the excitement in her voice.

"I know. It's good to finally have someone to share this with. When I tried to tell Hector, he got scared and begged me not tell anybody," Josh responded. For months now, he and Nefertari had been pillaging the file-cabinets in the Warden's office. They developed connections across the country. It was the same everywhere. Slavery was in full effect, and the prisons were the new plantation.

"Look at some of the Corporations and Industries funding this shit. Damn, I get my cable, telephone, and credit card services from some of these people," Nefertari said somberly. She was both frightened and exhilarated at the same time.

"Check this one out, Nefertari. Let's not forget about the medical research being carried out in prisons, too. Look at this," Josh said, handing Nefertari a printout. "It's about an experiment from back in the 1960's. It about research for creating a virus that destroys the immune system."

"Hell yes, give me that! I've been looking for this for the past two years. I've found mention of it over the Internet, but this actual documented survey details all of the needed procedures, costs, and target populations; this is just what we needed. This is some really good stuff, Josh." Nefertari could hardly contain herself.

———

January 15 - 21rst Century

Tracy and Raven were busy trying to figure out a symbol for the Double-Members of the African Directive. They had looked through several journals, books, and magazines of both ancient and modern African spiritual, cultural, and philosophical motifs. They weren't having any luck.

"Maybe we should just use the Ankh. I mean...it's been around for thousands of years. It's recognized as an African symbol throughout the world, and it's the symbol of life, electricity, and regeneration, to name a few," Tracy said, handing a beautiful picture of a golden Ankh to Raven.

"No. Although the Ankh is a standard in African symbolism, it's not what we want today. We need something modern, something that speaks to the future. We need to stop totally relying on the wisdom of our ancestors. It's time to build on that wisdom; it's time to create something new." Raven was one of those people who hardly ever came outside her home. The only place you'd find her was in the Black bookstores throughout the Bay Area, or in the libraries of universities. She was a short, thick, caramel-colored sistah with shiny black twists. Most of the brothas in the African Directive wanted her. That didn't matter; Raven swore a vow of celibacy. She was currently going on her fourth year.

"Alright, girlfriend. I guess it *is* time we actually start doing something with the knowledge," Tracy said, a frown on her face. Tracy was a light skinned black woman with hazel eyes. She almost always wore jeans, and kept her hair in a bushy ponytail. She was about six feet tall, and skinny but shapely. With her fair skin and model's body, she could have easily passed for one of those chicks in the fashion magazines. She and Raven have been best friends since Kindergarten.

Laughing, the two women continued to look through the volumes. They were quietly cutting the pictures from their brightly colored pages. "The library won't miss them," the ladies whispered as they stuffed the cut outs into their purses.

"Why don't we combine several images, see what type of shape it takes; create a sketch of it's outline," Tracy said.

"That's an idea," Raven said smiling. "We can create the image based on several symbols, and draw a multitude of meanings from it," she continued.

The sounds of tearing and cutting echoed across the library. Several people would peer from around the bookshelves, being nosy or trying to see what the women were doing. It wasn't until about an hour later that someone finally alerted the librarian. When the young man approached their table, they had managed to conceal all of the images they had snatched from the expensive journals.

"Are *we* alright?" the librarian asked. He was a tall white guy, about 25 years old. He wore his cloths in that wanna-be thug style. Guys like him were called 'wiggers.' The ladies struggled to keep from laughing out loud.

Without looking up, Raven responded in a low calm voice, "We're fine, sir." She was easing one of the bloated Egyptian volumes in her bookbag. Tracy, noticing what Raven was doing, decided to distract the young man.

"Hey, I've got a question. Um, let's see, how do I ask this. Oh, yeah, um, where does the Caucasian come from? I mean, everywhere you go, the Caucasian, or White, is not a native anywhere. They've invaded every square inch of the globe, spreading like a virus. What's up with that?" she asked, smiling as a frown appeared on the young man's face.

"Well, you're welcome to search the anthropology section, it's on the second floor," he responded. He was perplexed. He was taken totally off guard by Tracy's question; he'd completely forgotten why he'd approached the women.

"I did. It said that some people believe you evolved from Neanderthals. Others say that they came from Asia. Some even maintain that you, I mean Caucasians, evolved from Black people who migrated to Europe. You're white, what do you think?" Tracy asked. She was starting to have fun. The librarian wasn't.

"Never really thought about it. I think I read something about us all having the same mother, an African," he answered.

"That's funny, I always hear white people talking about us having the same mother. I guess that's acceptable. Why don't you people ever talk about the fact that in order for that African woman to produce children, there must have been an African man there with her?" Raven retorted. "I guess that's not acceptable... I mean the part about having a Black father, too," she added, winking at Tracy.

The poor librarian was wishing he'd never approached the two black women sitting before him. "Look, lady, I don't know or care about that racial stuff. I think we're all equal, what's the big deal about all this Black shit anyway?" he responded.

"What! I don't appreciate you swearing at us, where's your boss?" Tracy asked, finding just the loophole she was looking for.

"Um, um, what's the problem? I didn't mean anything. I was only-"

"That's it. We're never coming back to this place again," Raven said, gathering her things. Tracy followed her lead. The two women were up and walking down the stairs before the librarian could compose himself. He just watched, stupefied, as the women disappeared through the entrance doors.

February 13 - 21rst Century

It was late, and most of the members of the African Directive had already gone home. All but Skah and Nzinga. They stayed behind and processed the new applicants. The membership was strong; it attracted Black men and women from all walks of life. The upper echelons of the AD had managed to successfully infiltrate the churches, the school boards, and the local politics, and were now making serious gains into both the entertainment fields, and the athletic world. Things were looking up.

"This was a good meeting, huh, sis?" Skah asked. He didn't wait for an answer. He was busy punching the license plate numbers of the new applicants into the huge screen shaped computer. Both he and Amani always kept a complete data file on every member of the AD, including the Double-Members. Kafra had designed a program to automatically cross reference the information they entered, with files stored on various county and city databases that they hacked. They were always surprised at what they found.

"Hey, Nzinga, that brotha who plays ball for that weak team in southern California, he's almost 4 million dollars in debt."

"Well, you know those brothas were never allowed to learn how to manage their own money. I mean, their sense of responsibility is basically retarded while they're still in college. That's why I hate sports," she responded.

"You don't have to hate sports, just be aware of the deplorable conditions our brothas exist in; the money notwithstanding."

"Screw the money. Those brothers are old enough to know what the hell is going on, they just don't give a damn." Nzinga was a true Warrior-Queen. She pulled no punches, and she took no prisoners.

"Now wait a minute, sistah. Don't be so sure that these brothas, and sistahs for that matter, are fully aware of what's going on. It seems to me that they're basically overgrown and overpaid adolescents," Skah retorted.

"You've got a point there, Skah. Just think...what if we can seriously influence the black athletes, the young hardcore rappers? With all the money they've tapped into-" She didn't finish; she didn't have to. Skah was already on the same mental page.

"Baby, don't tease me like that. If we hook up with that crowd, our financial problems are over. You see what I'm saying? But how do we reach them?"

Nzinga was smiling. She had managed to work her way into having to stay late to process files with Skah. For the first time since she'd joined the AD, she was actually having a real conversation with the man. *This was a good meeting indeed,* she thought to herself.

Reaching over him, and intentionally brushing up against him in the process, Nzinga picked up the folder containing the names of all the professional athletes who had joined the AD. Showing a huge row of pearly white teeth, she teasingly held the folder up to Skah's face.

"This is how. I mean, even if this guy turns out to be a true puppet, we can still use him to reach the rest of the brothers and sisters who travel in his circles."

"Okay, I like that," Skah returned, reaching for the folder. "Let me see that." Skah examined the contents of the folder. Lifting his head, he smiled at the prospects. "This brotha is going to have to be trained. I want a team on him like yesterday. Assign Jerome and Mike to him immediately. Those two are 'down to earth' and non-threatening. I'll do the background check myself. I'm sure he has friends. So let's make the African Directive as attractive as possible to him."

"What do you want me to do?"

"You can assist me on reaching into the entertainment field. I can't stay on any one project for too long. I've got way too many responsibilities. I'll place you in charge of infiltrating the entertainment sphere. That's a great agenda, can you handle it?"

"I think I'll do fine. Don't tell me you don't have faith in the Black woman?" she retorted jokingly. She was just as excited as Skah. She took the yellow folder from him and placed it in her briefcase.

"Now wait a minute, Nzinga. I need that information to complete my background check."

"Ah, come on, Skah. Let me do it. It will be just as thorough as if you did it. Besides, I already know where you're headed."

"What are you talking about?" *This was an intriguing woman,* he thought to himself.

She closed her briefcase, then winked at him instead. "Come on, lets go," she said standing, her shapely body casting an equally curvy shadow on the far wall. This didn't go unnoticed.

Shaking his head, Skah turned the system terminal off, then piled his remaining notes into his book-bag. "Alright then, sis. You handle the project. I want to know how and with whom you've made contact with on a weekly basis. And I want results." It was times like this when he confused the people around him the most. One minute he was all smiles. The next, he was as serious as a heart attack. Nzinga found this trait very attractive. "Hey, before you go, what did you mean when you said that you knew where I was headed?"

"You probably haven't noticed, Mr. Skah, but I've been watching you. I know about the 'Web of Interdependence' you've stumbled across. The Secret Societies, the Fraternal Orders, and the

Bloodlines. I don't know exactly what you've got cooking in that brilliant mind of yours-"

"You're pretty sharp yourself, Nzinga. But right now, I'm not at liberty to discuss what I'm putting together at this time. Let's see how you do on *this* project, then perhaps I'll show you something really special." Skah was teasing her. He watched with great satisfaction at how she twisted her lips in a mocking frown.

"I don't think so, Skah. Maybe if you play *your* cards right, I'll show *you* something really special," she returned.

* * * * *

CHAPTER 19

New America. Fantasy capital of the world. Where virtual families, empty hearts, and stolen souls are the norm. The land of the sleepwalkers. It's all here. He who gathers the most things at the expense of his own humanity wins. Life here is a media driven event.

"It's noisy," Piankhi said.

"You'll get used it," I said, leaning up against an automated telenet booth. Piankhi and I were waiting for Anpu, Shango, and Ogun to come out of the transport-terminal. We had managed to enter New America via the Central D station.

"Look, there they are," said Piankhi.

"Okay, we've exchanged Ta-Amentan Stats for New American credit. This should be enough to get us through for the next few days," Oshun said, handing each of us a small metallic card.

Anpu turned his card over and pointed at the tiny row of icons on the bottom. "Look at this, Atefs. Is this the land of the lost or what?" The card was small and bluish silver in color. It had strange glyphs across the middle. It was heavier than it looked, and paper-thin. The most interesting feature however, were the icons.

"Look at this. The pictures are moving. They look like tiny people writhing in pain," Piankhi said, holding the card up to Aten (sun).

"Don't trip, Piankhi," Oshun responded. "Stick around, it gets better."

We were all holding our cards up so that we could see them more clearly. The icons were shaped like people. They were red and intertwined. We were fixated on the unholy currency when a beautiful black woman approached us.

"Where are you guys from? I don't think I've ever seen men with such beautiful skin," she said. She stood there marveling at us. Other people were doing it too, but they kept their distance.

"We're from Africa," Anpu responded. "We're trying to get to the Northwest county before Sekerts Day (Saturday)."

"That's the W-Quadrant, there's nothing up there. I mean hardly any Blacks. Besides, it's next to Valhalla. And it's notorious for slavers."

"We're on very important business. We work for the Government. We need to survey the Wasted Cities outside of the Northwest counties," I answered.

"I ain't never seen government officials with bodies like yours," she said, crossing her arms and tapping her foot on the dirty pavement. "Anyway, I'm going to meet some friends at the African Cafe. Why don't you and your *government* friends join me?"

Nodding my head, we followed her across the crowded streets.

Piankhi, being about the same age as our hostess, pushed past us and walked beside her. "What's your ren- I mean name?" he asked.

"It's about time one of you asked me that. I was beginning to think that we were going to have to address each other as, 'hey you,'" she said sarcastically. "Anyway, my name's Eboni."

"That's a nice name. It fits," Piankhi returned. Eboni was a beautiful woman. She had delicate bones and a kind of regal style about her. I found it quite strange, though, the chemicals she wore in her hair to make it straw-yellow. Millions of Black women in America tortured their hair like this. It made them look strange. Turning, she stood next to a huge transport-vehicle. She held the fiberglass doors of the shuttle opened and giggled as we rushed on board. Piankhi sat next to her. The rest of us took up strategic positions on the crowded bus.

New America really hadn't changed all that much. The people still lived in multi-storied dwellings and stuffed themselves in tiny foreign cars. A profusion of lights, images, and sounds created a perpetual environment of distractions. They never knew if they're coming or going. And the look on their faces....

That's what's wrong with the Americans, I thought. They're shell shocked, suffering from a constant bombardment of blips, media clips, and negative doctrines. Even Eboni, as beautiful as she was, displayed the tell-all signs of living in a war zone.

We're still being stared at, but not as much as before. I guess they're getting used to us. Tapping Oshun on the shoulder, I quietly pointed to a man sitting on a park bench. He was breast feeding.

"That's contrary to nature. Damn, how can people live this way?" Oshun whispered. We sat there on the Shuttle, staring out the window like kids looking at animals in a zoo. The people, the buildings, it all seemed unreal. Except for the neon lights and computer generated images on the advertisement signs, the city was an oily grey still, animated by the slaves who created it.

"I'm tripping off those kids, look at them," Shango said pointing.

The children looked old and tired. Their eyes shown wisdom beyond their years. Despite the obscene conditions of New American society, they still managed to play, darting in and out of traffic. We rode past parks with security guards and cameras mounted throughout their perimeter. The homeless filled the streets, sleeping under 'designer food stands' and laying in their own wastes. We saw bodies that had been dead for days. The people simply walked over them, unaffected, numb. The population was a teeming mass of humanity. A sea of cattle gorged upon by the Keep.

Piankhi was sitting next to Eboni. He was talking and flirting, when all of a sudden he stopped in mid-sentence and pointed to a group of men standing on a busy corner.

"Wait a minute, I've never seen so many twins before," Piankhi said pointing.

"They're not twins, Piankhi, they're clones. Probably third or fourth generation," Eboni responded. "Why are you so surprised, it's almost as if you never seen clones before? Wait a minute, you haven't, have you? You guys aren't from Africa, are you? I mean if you were, you'd know about the 'clone experiments' in Old Zaire. Hundreds, some say thousands of people were cloned in the forests of Zaire. They were tube-copied by the scientists of Project Harmony in the early part of the twenty-first century. If you and your partners were from Africa, you'd be used to seeing-"

"Eboni, could you lower your voice. Okay, so we're not from Africa. We're Ta-Amentans. Everything else we told you is true. We need to get to the Northwest County before Saturday," I interrupted. "And please don't cause a scene on this vehicle, we're perfectly capable of protecting ourselves if we have to," I added.

"Wait, I'm cool with Ta-Amentans. Not every brother and sister is against you guys. Some of us are conscious and recognize that we're all one people."

It just occurred to me how much she reminded me of Tefnut. The clear brown skin, the beautiful and full lips. And those huge almond shaped eyes. *Damn, except for the hair, they could be sisters.*

"Atefs (brothas, fathers, black men), look over there. I guess we've reached the privileged part of town," Shango said. Gone were the blocks of asphalt. The teeming masses that moved in hurried anticipation were suddenly somehow different as well. Glittering towers of plastic and steel penetrated the heavens.

"This is where we get off," Eboni said standing.

"Here? The African Cafe is in this part of town?" I asked in amazement.

"Hell no, we need to catch the number 4 Shuttle. It'll take us to the east end of the Central D."

"Wait a minute, sis, we need to go north." Shango barked. I couldn't blame him. Tefnut is his cousin.

"I know, Shango. I've got friends on the East end. They'll be able to take you guys up north," Eboni said smiling.

"What's in those towers?" I asked.

"Oh, that's the western Head Quarters for the New Atlantis Corporation. They own half of New America, and some say most of Valhalla." Oshun and Shango stopped talking and walked over to where we were standing.

"Do you have access to any of those buildings?" Oshun asked.

Lifting my hand, I motioned for him to back off. Out of the corner of my eye, I caught Anpu taking notes. "What's the Atlantis Corporation? What do they do?" I asked.

"They're responsible for the distribution of American Technologies. They have offices in Japan, Den Europe, and about 75 percent of the Pacific Rim," she answered.

"Where can we find the owner of the Corporation? Does he or she operate out of those buildings, or from somewhere in Den Europe?" Anpu asked.

"Wow, I don't really know. I've never really thought about it." That's typical of Americans. They almost always know about the industrial layout of a Corporation or Institution, but they almost never know who owns it or who runs it.

"Here comes the next Shuttle," she shouted. We pulled out our debit cards and waited for it to stop.

This time, I sat in the back. Anpu and Shango sat in the middle, while Oshun sat in the front of the shuttle, next to the driver. Piankhi was busy flirting.

I watched a lane of flying cars. They narrowly missed each other as they recklessly flew past the towering buildings. The sky itself was a polluted sea of activity, a perpetual blanket of exhaust fumes spewing into the atmosphere. We nearly went to war with New America over their disregard for nature. It wasn't until the signing of the Intra-Continental Environmental Treaty that both countries relaxed arms and pulled back. The Mesniu were poised and ready that day. I just wish I was old enough to fight.

It was a long ride. Huge, gleaming skyscrapers eventually gave way to moderately-sized buildings. They were nicely made and blended well with the environment. I was amazed to see so many stylized African motifs. They crowned just about every advertisement monitor.

"What part of town is this?"

"This is the East end. As you can see, it has a multi-cultural flare about it," Eboni said smiling. She was obviously proud of this section of New America.

"Who controls it?" Oshun asked, bursting Eboni's bubble in the process.

"Damn, I've never seen people so concerned with power before. What's up with that?" she responded. She was most comfortable with Piankhi. I decided to use this to our advantage. I subtlety nodded my head; he picked up on it immediately.

Tapping her on the shoulder, Piankhi said, "I'm sure you realize that in order to control ones destiny, one must have power. I'm not talking about currency; I'm talking about the ability to define, as well as determine, a particular version of reality that's conducive for survival. It really doesn't matter how many Black or African images you have on a building if the people who own the building are from outside the community. And if that's the case here, Eboni, then you might as well put a picture of a dog on the building."

They both started laughing. She laughed harder than he did; that was a good sign.

* * * * *

April 23 - 21rst Century

Skah had been up all night talking to his father. They were debating if he should continue trying to convince the Bangers to throw away their red and blue rags. He was hoping to replace them with black ones; a sign of unity. Skah was convinced that anti-Black organizations were on the rise across America.

"There is a very real need for hardened soldiers, and those brothas and sistahs are the only ones who qualify."

"Look, Skah, I know what you're saying. It's just that I don't know if the African Directive is ready for that kind of scrutiny. If too much attention is directed at you... the enemy is ruthless. If something happens, there goes everything you've worked for," Tarharka said calmly.

"Ah, c'mon, pop. You know just like I do that the Bangers are the Warrior-class from ancient Kamit... reincarnated. They're just waiting for someone to train them!" Skah exclaimed, slamming his hands on the wooden dinning room table. His father was not amused. "Hey, Mom, what do you think? I mean with the recent shootings those white boys did in those southern Californian schools, killing people in the name of 'White Rights.' Don't you think it's time we start preparing the brothas and sistas on the street for battle?" Skah was serious. In fact, he really didn't care what his parents thought. He and Kafra had already hooked up with hundreds of brothas who were discharged from the Armed services for refusing to take part in the takeover of the Middle East.

"I agree. It's about time Black men started standing up and protecting the community. If I were a young Black woman today, I'd tell any Black man trying to get with me that he ain't getting no pussy until he joined a Black organization and proved his manhood by serving the people," Kandace responded.

"Ah, hell, I knew you would agree with him. You always take his side," Tarharka bellowed. He was all smiles. He understood the special bond most Black mothers had with their male children. It was that same bond which provided the nurturing for his own conscious development.

———

July 11 - 21rst Century

News of the fantastic job Nola and Jerome were doing with the After School Program traveled fast. They were known throughout the Black community as great teachers. When the various News agencies came out to spy, Jerome and Nola made sure to give all credit to the African Directive. Over the past few years, the AD had gained a fair amount of credibility in the larger community. Famous people were known to be members of the AD, and several institutions gave grants to the Center on several occasions.

Funded by Black politicians looking for support, professional Black athletes, and the occasional anonymous Black entertainer, the After School Program had grown to a yearly course, complete with college prep courses, computers, and hundreds of eager black children, all clamoring to fill its classrooms. Black Culture was the main curriculum, but general education was also stressed.

The grade point average of the children attending the Program rose sharply. Their test scores continued to shock both their parents, as well as their teachers. This attracted the best and most conscious college students in the Bay Area. Once the progressive college students took hold of the After School Program, they spread and duplicated the *Program* throughout the various Black communities across the country. An African Centered mind-set was beginning to infest the Black community. Nola and Jerome had done their job well.

———

September 19 - 21rst Century

The propaganda prepared by Nefertari and Josh had been circulating throughout the community for years. As a result, the overall level of consciousness began to rise. Black people were beginning to understand the importance of non-traditional forms of information. Black bookstores, Black websites, and general membership in Black organizations were on the increase. Everything Black was all the rage. Both Nefertari and Josh managed to put together a fact-finding team that was second to none. In an instant, information from any part of the world could be accessed, then sent anywhere in the Diaspora. Again, the African Directive was given full credit for this huge endeavor.

"With the college students running the various programs, we really don't need to be here," Josh said. "I've got reports coming in from New York that the three teams we have out there are basically receiving information directly from Africa and Asia."

"You're right. The research teams are basically self-sufficient. I wonder what Skah has in mind. I mean, how many more clubs can we maintain before we start duplicating our findings?" Nefertari responded.

Nefertari was proud of the AD's huge data base. Not only could the membership of the AD pull up any and all information concerning African people, but a team of brothas and sistahs were busy developing a new kind of Internet Service. Totally African Centered in its style and scope. It was being developed to be in complete opposition to, as well as competition with, the existing Internet Service providers. They elected to call it the HUSIA.

October 7 - 21rst Century

The secret military wing of the African Directive was growing stronger with each meeting. Kafra was the director of security. He had managed to assemble a very capable group of men and women. Over the past few months, they had managed to gather enough information on the various Secret Societies, Fraternal Orders, and Aristocratic Bloodlines to fill a twenty volume set of encyclopedias.

"You see what I'm saying, man. These brothers and sisters are under the control of the enemy. I don't care how long this so-called Black organization has been in existence. It was created by white men, and it is under the control of their descendants. I say we expose these motherfuckers now!" Charles X shouted.

"Now wait a minute, X. I say we continue to infiltrate these groups and work on them from within," Kafra responded. The two of them went way back. They always started out on opposite sides of an argument, but, like true brothas in struggle, they almost always found middle ground.

"Kafra's right, brothers and sisters. We can't just outright destroy this organization. It has too much sentimental value. Besides, many of the men and women who work for them aren't really aware of who actually pulls the strings," Karamen interjected.

"Well, we'll have to be careful about how we address their organization. We've got some of their members attending our general Thursday night meetings," Muwangi said. He punched the names of the known members into a special data file.

"Wow, who would have thought that the country's oldest Black civil rights group was organized, directed, and maintained by some of the most dangerous racists on the planet?" Stacy was a reporter for the local 'Black' Newspaper. She had stumbled across an old story about a Secret Order of Black men, who fashioned their organization after the Secret Orders of Old Europe and America. To her dismay, she discovered that many prominent Black Leaders were members of this Secret Fraternity.

"You see, it's devils like that who keep the people ignorant of what's really going on. They want things to stay the same because if things change the traitors lose their special rights and privileges," Charles X exclaimed.

Pulling a stack of papers from a small brown briefcase, Kafra held them in his hands and shook them as he spoke, "Check this shit out, brothas and sistahs. Based on all of the research we've managed to piece together, the entire Police Department everywhere is one huge Fraternal Order. I'm telling you... we're really onto something. At first, I couldn't figure out why Skah was so excited about the different Fraternal segments of society; that is, until know. It's all connected."

"More than you realize, Kafra," Stacy said somberly. Years of working as a reporter, she'd seen many things, watched how stories - important stories - were buried by unknown authorities. She'd seen how life threatening incidents were covered up, not by the editors of the various news organizations she's worked for, but by people in places so high that they dared not be disobeyed.

"Ah, c'mon, sis. Don't get it twisted. I know what time it is. You're talking about the 'Owners.' The Soulless Ones who control everything. The Keep," Kafra said.

"I'll never forget the first time I felt it. As my consciousness rose, I began to notice, to comprehend, the presence of an invisible yet all encompassing and smothering hindrance. This force, this negative influence, is not that of the Creator. It belongs to a pretender to the throne. A sinister programmer, devoid of good, and a practitioner of the laws of Gog and MaGog," Charles X explained.

"It's all coming together. We've got pictures and addresses of Members of various Secret Societies, Fraternal, Masonic, Governmental, Religious, and Entertainment groups. When you look at them deeply, you start to see a pattern. This pattern can be traced from as high as the most lofty International Group or Committee down to the most local state scholarship fund," Muwangi said.

"So, I'm not crazy then?" Stacy asked smiling.

Pointing to a section on a huge map clustered with red tacks, Charles X was first to respond, "We got most of the information here, downtown. We checked places kin to 'The United Way', 'Savings and Loans'; we looked at all kinds of sources."

Bursting into the small gathering like a man possessed, Kesu'kt entered the room holding a sack of notes. "Brothas and sistahs. Skah wants an emergency meeting."

* * * * *

As I walked towards the African Cafe, I observed how the crowds of people were sitting and talking, shopping in the various stores, and dancing in the grass. The cultural Bazaar, the music, the exotic scents in the air created a most festive atmosphere.

"So, this is the African Cafe?" I asked, looking at the rows of security personnel who were lined up against the perimeter of the parkway.

"Yes, it is," Eboni said happily. "We come here every Wednesday to talk, to exchange ideas, and to people watch," she added. Anpu and I glanced at each other. It was obvious that she had no real clue as to her true condition. It was as if the guards lined up against the entire backdrop of the Cafe's parkway were invisible.

Pointing to a group of brightly dressed Black folks, Eboni let out a happy shout. "Look, there they are. Come on, I want to introduce you guys to my friends!" she said, pulling Piankhi by the arm. Anpu and I followed behind. I motioned to Shango and Oshun to look over the perimeter, to find out what they could.

By the time Anpu and I reached the group of young Africans, Eboni was already telling them that we were from Ta-Amenta, and that we had business in the W-Quadrant. There were four men and six women, all probably in their late twenties or early thirties.

167

"Look, Eboni, I thought we agreed to keep our intentions on a need-to-know basis," Piankhi interrupted.

—————

We had been sitting with the group of New American Blacks for about an hour. They were idealistic, fairly progressive, and about as conscious as one could be under the circumstances. Anpu, Piankhi, and myself made sure to position ourselves in such a way as to not allow the surveillance cameras to get a clear picture of our faces. This did not go unnoticed.

"Why do you brothers continue to move and shift your bodies in that manner?" the thin red-bone sister asked. Her name was Cynthia. She was a student at the local State College, and she worked for the transportation department.

"We're kind of camera shy," I returned. "Aren't you brothas and sistahs tired of being constantly watched and listened to?"

Before any of them could respond, I felt a slight tug on my left shoulder. I swung around. Oshun and Shango were standing there; both of them expressionless.

"Kashta, this place is one big zoo. There are cameras monitoring everything that goes on here; they even have audio-chips in the water fountains," Shango said.

"Well, I think that's enough for me," Anpu said standing.

"How about that ride to the W-Quadrant?" Piankhi asked, directing his question at Eboni. She sat motionless.

"Look, these guys need a ride to Hell City, don't ask me why. Anyway, how about you, Robert? Do you think you can take them there?"

CHAPTER 20

We've been traveling for hours, cutting a northwest trek across New America. It had become obvious to all that we were getting closer to the W-Quadrant. The number of people of non-European descent began to drop dramatically. Everywhere we looked, there was another white face staring back at us. They weren't used to seeing black people in these parts. We ignored their taunts and jeers.

"It won't be long now," Robert said, handing Oshun a wrinkled map.

"If you'll notice the color of the sky, that purple and red glow," he continued, "it's coming off their Power Plants," he finished.

"What do you mean, Power Plants?" Oshun asked.

"The Valhallans," Eboni squeezed in.

"Tell me something, why would the Valhallans need a functioning Power Plant on the border?" Oshun asked.

"Well, I mean it's no secret; at least not to us. The Valhallans have been supplying power to Old Canada. Especially since the last of the Native peoples have been shipped to Aztlan...or worse," Robert said somberly. Pausing, he then asked, "Now, answer this, why on earth would Ta-Amentans want to visit the W-Quadrant? The Valhallans are very active there. You might not get out alive."

"We can take care of ourselves. And remember to go back home after the drop off," I answered coldly.

"You see, Robert. I told you. Nobody talks like that. I mean, who says things like *drop off?* You guys are military," Eboni chimed in.

Our journey continued in relative silence. The houses were getting further and further apart. Civilization was slowly giving way to lush farmland, then eventually dense forest. The auto-response programming in Robert's rock-van kicked in: the three huge rubber spheres that carried us began to harden, adjusting themselves for 'off road' conditions. Alongside the narrow strip of gravel, I spotted a small outpost about 300 het-meters north. It was basically a granite wall, accompanied by two patrolmen and a jeep. *It seems the Americans aren't concerned about a Valhallan invasion.*

"It's time," I said, handing Anpu the pair of peepers I'd been using.

Without making a sound, he pulled five Colbot Rifles from the large brown duffle bag he'd been carrying. Oshun and Shango were quickly snatching off their civilian cloths, and started gathering their reconnaissance ware. We all had reconnaissance ware; that's all we could bring. If we tried to bring anything else, like daath-Geb, it would have been difficult for Senwosret to turn the other way.

"Wow, what are you brothers doing?" Eboni asked, a look of wonderment shown on her face. Robert didn't say a word; he just continued to take quick and uncertain peeks into his rear-view mirror. His eyes were as wide as comets.

Before we got within 100 het-meters of the outpost station, I told Robert to pull off the side of the road.

"Why are we pulling over?" he asked.

"You don't expect us to ask you two to put your lives in danger, do you?" My crew said nothing.

"I guess not, Kashta," he answered. Eboni said nothing; in fact, I got the feeling she wanted to join us.

It took us no more than seven minutes to completely change into our patented recon-ware. Our Colbot-rifles slung over our shoulders, our wave-jumpers attached to our belts, we stood outside Robert's vehicle. Impatiently, we watched as Aten made its initial dip towards the horizon. We stood transfixed, as we mentally prepared ourselves to enter the W-Quadrant.

"I still don't know why you guys would want to go into the W-Quadrant; it's dangerous in there, and you could get hurt," Eboni exclaimed, her eyes transfixed on Piankhi.

I motioned to the others, nodding; they silently slipped into the bush. "For reasons I need not go into, my companions and I are on important business. I'm very grateful for your help-"

"Why don't you guys just go to the New American authorities?" Robert asked. His voice full of trust... ignorance.

"Anyway, if anyone asks you about us, tell them you don't know anything. Tell them we forced you into the rear compartment of the vehicle-" The two of them just sat in their seats and nodded their heads. Wide eyed, they reminded me of Ta-Amentan children.

I couldn't say anymore. I didn't have to. Black Americans were so naïve; I just wanted them to go.

Turning, I darted off into the mat of green and yellow foliage. It spread from where the parked vehicle sat and reached well beyond the New American-Valhallan perimeter. At first it was dark, and without the benefit of my daath-Geb, it was difficult to hear. Millions of huge and moist leaves dampened the sounds. I quickly spotted a micro-trail. Micro trails are deliberate... almost indistinguishable markings left behind by Warrior-Soldiers. This one... nearly invisible, was fixed to every other patch of grass, which grew carpet-like from the soft earth.

It didn't take long before I caught up with the others. They were posted up next to a break in the yellowish granite wall that made-up the so-called border. It was no more than ten feet tall, peppered with scorch marks and littered with pot holes. "Some barrier," I said to myself.

"Good of you to join us, Black man," Anpu said from behind a hill of melted slag. A heap of it lay around a series of cracks so big that we could see the Valhallan patrolmen standing 50 het-meters away. It looked as if someone tried to patch the holes up with chalk.

Anpu kept watch over the Valhallan patrolmen, as Shango, Piankhi, and Oshun went over the reg-maps.

"So how we doing on time?"

"Not bad, Kashta. Thanks to Eboni and her friend, we've gotten ahead by more than a day's travel," Oshun answered, his eyes glued to the Map.

"Alright then, if we move that way," Oshun said pointing in a westerly direction, "We'll reach Quadrant-4 in less than 14 hours. We'll still have time to make camp, rest, and decide on how we should approach this situation."

"I say we just get in and out as quietly as possible. There's no need in alerting the Valhallans to our presence," Piankhi responded. He was young, but a hell of a lot more level headed than Sa-Ra.

"Then lets go, Atefs." I was getting impatient. My heart pounded as Aten continued its journey into the underworld. We moved in the twilight. First Anpu, then Piankhi. Then Oshun, and finally Shango. I brought up the rear. We entered the W-quadrant in a single line, three het-meters apart, and poised for battle.

* * * * *

October 7 - 21rst Century

"What's the emergency, Skah?" Kafra asked, slamming the door behind him. Nola and Jerome were there, Nefertari and Josh were sitting next to them; all of the Double Members were present, and most of the general membership was in attendance.

A grim faced Skah said nothing. He sat in his shiny oak chair, and watched as Michael-Ra pushed a huge black flat-screen onto the center of the conference room floor. The young man then pulled a micro-DVD from a worn case, and slid it into the embedded slot on the side of the huge monitor. Moving with the grace of an athlete, he snatched the remote from underneath the monitor base and leisurely tossed it to Skah. Without moving from his chair, Skah caught the slender dark object in mid flight. Pointing, then clicking several buttons on the face of the instrument, the screen of the flat-screen suddenly sparked, flickered, and sprang to life.

As the image cleared and straightened itself out, a panel of six White men and a light skinned, balding Black man, sat on a brightly lit stage. An audience of reporters littered the background.

"I've seen that brother before; he's the White man's favorite Negro. Every time you see that fool on television, you know we're about to get 'hit' with some shit. I wonder what the hell they've got him up to now?" Josh asked.

The reporters were addressing the panel. The Black man it turns out, is an Administrator for the Government, a puppet utilized by several right-wing administrations. The six White men who joined him were representatives of an until recently unknown scientific community known as 'Project Harmony.' As the cameras zoomed in, showing close-ups of the scientists from Project Harmony, a series of white letters moved across the bottom of the screen. It read, *Scientists for Project Harmony find evidence of a genetic component believed to be responsible for the propensity for extreme violence in Black people.* It continued by stating, *...Black on Black violence is not the result of racism, poverty, and the so-called self-hatred that stems from said conditions, but is directly attributable to a hyper sensitive nervous system. A genetically inferior condition stemming from a proposed violent gene, located somewhere within primitive African physiology.* The general membership of the African Directive gasped in shock. The Double Membership said nothing. In fact, Skah and Amani had a smirk of anticipation on their faces.

"As you can see, brothas and sistahs, it's on." Skah said coldly. These were the first words he'd spoken since he became aware of the report.

"What do we do? I mean we've done nothing but good things for the community. We never threatened the White Establishment," William said. William was an athlete. Since signing his multi-million dollar contract, he'd been a good boy. The only reason he joined the African Directive was that it was seen as an organization of 'good Blacks.'

In fact, Skah had managed to orchestrate for several members of the AD to denounce several more Militant Black organizations in public. He got the idea from Nzinga.

"We continue to do what we've always done...we build a strong Black Community," Skah answered calmly.

"I don't understand. Why do they keep saying that we're violent, animal-like?" Sheila asked. She trembled. She was more frightened then she'd ever been. "I don't think I can be a member anymore," she continued. Almost 75 percent of the general membership agreed; nodding their heads, grumbling. Several of them even got up and stormed out of the conference room, then out of the building itself.

"Look at them. Punks" Nzinga slammed. She had a look of total disgust on her face. She, like most conscious Black women, hated the sight of weakness. Especially from Black men. She watched from behind tinted windows as the sound of slamming doors and screeching automobiles resounded in the streets. When it was over, only the Double-Members of the African Directive remained.

"I guess it's time to get down to business," Nefertari said, pulling her chair closer to the mahogany table.

"Listen, I don't want anyone speaking ill of our former members. They served their purpose well. If it were not for them, *we* wouldn't be at the stage we're at now. It was *their* work that made the Black community feel comfortable enough to rally around us when the press began its negative campaigns. It was *they* who worked hard in establishing an image that was acceptable, safe. Remember, beloved brothas and sistahs, it is *they* who shall inherit the earth," Skah said stoically. He was subdued when he said it, but he meant every word.

"Skah's right. We've got to be careful. The New World that we create is more for them than it is for us," Raven said smiling.

"That's right. We all swore to sacrifice our own happiness for the sake of our descendants," Charles X squeezed in. "I'll see what I can do from my end. It's about time the Nation gets some new instructions," he finished.

"I'll see what I can do on my side also," Akanaton said. Akanaton was a member of the local 'Africentric Cultural Community'. He had been guiding the Community using instructions gleaned from instructions taken from the Double Membership of the AD.

Muwangi was very pleased about the recent events. He turned to Stacy, a Double Member, and asked, "What's up, Sis? Have you made contact with your people yet? The time to start planting the news of our *Next-Phase* is now."

"Oh, yes, my brother. It's already in the works," she answered.

"Good then," Skah commented. "Our next agenda will be to completely merge all African-Centric Organizations in the Diaspora. Starting here, now. The seeds have already been sown."

May 1 - 21rst Century

Birthed in a metallic storm of a million advertising blips, they came forth in a hideous display of living wires and cyber slick sound bites. Bathed in a cascade of obscene imagery. Like purple black clouds slamming in mid-air, the Operators proclaimed their presence to the world. All eyes turned north, as the descendants of Gog and MaGog, hidden behind their Global Fraternal Societies, and supported by powerful planetary institutions, publicly launched their insidious neo-religious, scientific organization, Project Harmony.

Until recently, its very existence was but a myth, an urban legend spoken of by the most hardened conspiracy theorists. Today, the world would learn otherwise. Following the dictates of an ancient worldwide agenda, this hidden brotherhood has moved behind the scenes for centuries. A burned out American public watched in placid submission, as the body of men and women who so stunned the nation less than a year ago, with its supposed findings on the so-called 'violent gene' in Black people, were greeted by the major politicians, scientists, and mainstream religious leaders of the day.

———

In the weeks that followed, the world became a blurry surreal landscape. Nearly every college campus in America would erupt in racial strife. Opposing groups of men and women clashed in the streets, on the job, and just about everywhere else. Yet despite the seemingly abrupt nature in which Project Harmony emerged onto the world stage, to the conscious ones, there was a kind of 'orchestrated feel' about the whole thing. As usual, the majority of Black people were caught off guard, in the dark, and totally unprepared. Like frightened rabbits, they buried their collective heads in the sand, and pretended that nothing was happening. It wasn't until one of the members of Project Harmony was elected as the Governor of California, before Black people finally openned their eyes and realize the seriousness of what was going on around them.

* * * * *

The W-Quadrant is a strange and dangerous place. The entire region zig zags and snakes around the northwest boundaries of New America, then bleeds into the southeast borders of Valhalla. Its vast topography is a mesh of artificial structures and natural environs. Urban swamps with concrete fields populated by steel girders masquerading as trees, make for a challenging and hostile place. The Americans own it outright, but the Valhallans come and go as they please. And despite the supposed racial tolerance of New America, white youth view this place as a National Treasure.

We had been traveling for over a day now...nonstop, when Shango appeared from the mist and haze that surrounded us. He was on point, about 20 het-meters ahead. A look of relief shown on his face.

"We're almost there. Quadrant-4 is just beyond that field. If we hurry, we'll be there before nightfall," Shango said pointing. A sea of scorched concrete met our gaze. Black smoke gently lifted from a series of rubble that lay across its surface.

————

Almighty Aten rose on a cloud of yellow-orange brilliance. The air was sweetened as it surfed the infinite blue on wings of liquid gold. We watched as it traversed along its eternal arch... then, finally slip into the soup of night. We had yet to reach Quadrant 4.

Beneath a sea of a million, million stars, I began to get anxious. Images of Tefnut haunted my every step. It was difficult, no, impossible to concentrate on anything else. If we were going to find Tefnut, alive that is, we needed to do so in a hurry. Besides, if she were captured, it would only be a matter of time before the Valhallans discovered that she was Ta-Amentan.

We marched, stepping across the crunchy rubble of hundreds of years of waste and neglect. Under the cover of darkness, we entered one of the largest regions adjacent to Quadrant-4. It had no name. It was simply a wall of toppled buildings that lay over warped and melted streets of tar. Huge sections of once traveled highways stood silently in the distance. Our breathing quickened as the sound of wild dogs fighting echoed from the hallowed out structures that once housed a mighty industry.

"Stay on post, brothas. I'm starting to get a bad feeling about this place."

"What's up, Kash?" Anpu asked.

"We've got company, don't know who or what, but it's a lot of them."

"Well, one thing's for sure, they're obviously not Cold Wind. If they were, they would have attacked us a long time ago," Oshun added.

"Lets tighten up the ranks, Atefs. Two het-meter spread... double time," I snapped.

Like thieves in the night, we stole into the darkness, throwing caution to the wind. We quickly entered a deep state of waking-trance. Our senses heightened, our blood boiling, we danced through the dust of a dead world. We became as ghosts.

In this highly acute state of mind, our intuition is as sharp as the most advanced recon-screens. We felt ready for anything... or so we thought.

At first it felt like someone was slowly turning down the lights. The stars dimmed as our pursuers closed in on us.

"Alright, K'huti... they're getting, bolder!" I shouted.

"I think I know what we're up against, Kashta. Those dogs we saw back in those shattered buildings. I say we just keep driving, keep our minds focused. If they want us, we take them out," Piankhi added, his Colbot-rifle gleaming under the moonlit sky.

"Just watch our backsides, kid," Shango returned.

"Over there," Anpu said pointing, "Open ground. This should even things up a bit."

"Go!" I shouted. I remained behind. I turned and watched for signs of movement. I was prepared to rain death on anything that moved.

"Alright, Kashta, come on!" Enlil shouted.

Turning, I ran as fast as I could toward the inviting hillside where my brothas waited. We stood motionless, poised and waiting, expecting our pursuers to appear from everywhere at once.

Lifting his rifle over his head, Anpu was first to move towards a small but lush oasis. "Cover me!" he shouted. With huge strides, Anpu nearly flew to the edge of the greenery. Almost before he started, he was already waving to us from the safety of the thick mat of trees that lay at the base of the grassy hill.

I pointed to Piankhi. Without a word, he went for broke. He was young, but he knew how to run. Seconds later, he stood by Anpu, smiling, and beckoning for us to join them.

"Oshun, Shango, you two go next, I'll cover."

When they were about halfway there, I began to follow them. I ran backwards, covering myself as best I could. The grass was wet. It made smacking noises as I ran across its shiny surface.

The five of us stood panting beneath a patch of tangled trees and shrubs. Amazingly, it felt as though our tormentors were there before us. I felt their prying eyes. They were everywhere.

"They're still with us," Piankhi said somberly. "Only animals could move that fast," he added.

I held my finger up to my mouth.

"Let's go. Enlil, what's our location?" Without waiting for an answer, I motioned for Shango to go on ahead us. "Stay within 10 het-meters...we don't want to lose you, Atef." I motioned to the others, "Come on then, lets go." We moved in swift unison.

Navigating through the thick green underbrush, we spread out in Delta formation. I've got the point.

"Kashta, listen up. Noticed how quiet it's gotten?" Anpu asked, pointing to his left ear.

"Keep moving," I returned, "Enlil, get a hold of Shango."

We moved west. The darkness of the forest slowly gave way to the brilliant yellow white glow of a full moon. It was like an invasion of light as shimmering silver cascaded down through the treetops. We emerged from the green and brown canopy. Like newborn babes, we basked in the starry night. Several het-meters ahead, Shango stood against the black sky, motionless; he looked like a buffed out statue.

"Look down there. A Temple," Shango said pointing.

We gathered ourselves and stood beside him. Total amazement. In a small mossy depression sat what appeared to be a modest temple. Images of black Gods were painted across its tiny marble walls. It looked like something I'd seen in history books when I was a child...

* * * * *

March 19 - 21rst Century

Things were going from bad to worse. Every time you switched on a tele-monitor, there was another 'respectable' scientist, complete with charts and graphs, explaining the genetic inferiority of the Black race. Computer animation, media distortions, and pseudo scientific double talk were woven into an incredible offensive strike against African people.

Media Evangelists, an evolutionary offshoot of the television evangelists of the 20th century, started talking about the 'Curse of Ham' and how Black people were divinely cursed and better off as slaves. Politicians began discussing laws that would enforce sterilization upon its urban populations.

In the community, agent provocateurs had all but successfully destroyed most Black Organizations. They were exposed to the local authorities, infiltrated, and scattered like dust in an urban storm. Not so with the more militant nationalistic groups however. These brothas and sistahs were Spiritually cleansed, culturally sound, politically astute, and economically independent. Some said it was like the Middle Passage all over again. Only the strong survived.

Skah stood gargoyle-like on the edge of an abandoned second story building. It sat like so many others, in the heart of East Oakland. He watched patiently as the long row of Police cars rolled slowly down 14th street. They were packed four deep; angry white cops, nursed on tele-monitor propaganda. Like most middle Americans, both Black and White, these cops hated the rebellious Blacks who lived in the inner cities. Their Black culture, music, dance, and speech were seen as an insult to what America stood for. "They needed to be eliminated," the African American Chief of Police would often say. He was new to Oakland; shipped in from back east. Some said he was a Rhodes Scholar.

"You see what I'm saying, if you don't allow your emotions to get the best of you, you can observe your enemies unafraid," Skah said, handing the tiny plastic binoculars to Country. Over the years, the two of them had become like brothers. In fact, most of the so-called 'Gang Bangers' across the country were seen as a very important component to the destiny of Black people. They were viewed as the warrior class... reborn.

Country didn't respond. He'd learned over the years that it wasn't always necessary to do so. He was the first of the so-called 'Bangers' to start attending the 'Original Klan' meetings on Thursday. Soon, he bought more and more of his fellow warriors with him, male and female. They were young, strong, hungry for information, fearless, and brilliant.

With his jet-black bandanna flowing in the wind, Country continued to observe the movements of the Police cars. In order to become members in the Original Klan, all so-called 'bangers' had to swear allegiance to the Race, throw away their colors in exchange for black bandannas, and defend the Laws of MAAT.

"They're becoming very predictable, Skah," Country remarked in a cold emotionless tone. "It won't be long now," he finished.

Skah said nothing.

Just then, Amani came running up the stairs to where the two men were standing.

"Atefs (Black men, etc.), word is that our good old Uncle Tom-ass police chief is a proud member of the 'Griffins.' Check this out... here's his picture. He was sworn in by that no-good history professor last year."

The three men stared at the tattered images.

"Damn, it seems like every Black man who don't catch hell in this country is a member of the Griffins. Just how large is this group of sellouts?" Country asked.

"Too big," Skah responded. "It doesn't matter though. We've pretty much gotten a handle on all West Coast members. We have their addresses, the names of their oldest children, and we know where to find them if we have to," he added, smirking in the process.

"Lets go, brothas. It's almost time for them to send their Gun ships. You know the routine," Amani said, motioning for them to follow.

The three soldiers walked confidently down the old stairs and into the back alley of the abandoned structure that once served as a County Administrative building. Before that, it was part of a medium sized department store. Their cars were parked in the rear, engines running. Four heavily armed Black men stood watch over them. One of them was Charles X.

"So did you brothas see anything different?" he asked.

"Not this time, X. It's like clock work. They roll up and down East 14th like they own it. Then they fly over head." Skah was short and to the point.

"The rats are gearing up for something," Charles X returned sarcastically. "We'll be ready, though." Both men laughed. It was good to hear Skah laugh. Lately, he rarely even smiled...

* * * * *

As we approached the small Temple, there were indications that it had been recently visited. Burned candles, freshly cut fruits and vegetables, and scattered incense lay in and around its marble floors. In the southwest corner of the beautifully carved structure sat several rows of what appeared to be tiny columns. As we got closer, we saw that they were in fact thick pieces of yellow paper, which had been carefully folded and meticulously placed at the foot of a large offering. Piankhi was the first to grab and pick up one of the tiny scrolls. Unraveling it, we were caught off guard at what we saw.

"Look at this, Atefs. What kind of words are these?" Piankhi asked, holding the yellowed paper up to the moonlight.

"Let me take a look," Enlil interjected. As a communications specialist, Enlil has learned over fifteen old world dialects, and has had a love affair with words for as long as he can remember. "This is an early version of the exact same language now spoken by the Ntiu Tut in their rituals. The Timeless Dialect!"

"Are you sure? I mean why would something like that be out here?" Piankhi asked.

"Try not to desecrate the Temple, brothas. Obviously, whomever built this place still uses it," I said.

"Listen up, Atefs. Let's not forget where we are. This *is* heavy ground," Shango interrupted.

"Just take some of the scrolls," Piankhi added.

"Um, Atefs," Anpu sounded startled, "I hate to interrupt you brothas, but we've got company."

We all stopped and whirled around, Colbot-rifles raised, attack positions on. That's when we saw them...

* * * * *

April 11 - 21rst Century

Black History Month was ended and replaced with Multi-Cultural month. Every other commercial on the tele-monitors had something to do with Project Harmony or one of its insidious government propositions. The negative press on Africans had gotten so bad that words like nigger, spook, coon, and jigaboo, were commonplace on the tele-monitors. It was totally acceptable for budding Politicians to use the most racist phrases they could think of in order to sell themselves to the public. Things really got out of hand when the Super Nazis filmed themselves burning down several Black churches. A month later, they turned themselves in. Two weeks after that, they got off. And in the midst of the unrest, the armies of La Raza were on the move.

"Did you read this shit?" Amani said, handing Skah the newspaper. "They're merging all Black or colored Civil Rights groups into one huge bullshit organization."

"Right on time. One thing about the White man, he runs a tight ship," Skah returned. "And did you notice? Look at the membership: Griffins."

"You've got a point there, handsome." Nzinga had entered the room in her usual flare and grace. She, Raven, Nola, and Nefertari had just returned from the East Coast. They were helping to setup an International trading company with three West African Nations. She and Skah had gotten close over the years. Except for the image-viewers on the HUSIA, they hadn't seen each other in over a month. She was conscious, spiritual, brilliant, and beautiful. She was Skah's lady. In fact, she was the only real source of happiness in Skah's revolutionary life.

Winking as she rushed past Amani, Nzinga jumped into Skah's arms, kissing him passionately. Whenever the two of them held each other, they were lost to this world. They were at the wellspring of the waters of Amenta. "You look tired, Skah. Amani, have you been working my man too hard?" Nzinga asked jokingly.

"Now c'mon, sis. You know how your he is."

"So, how have you been, lover? Did you miss me?" She was all smiles.

"Always," Skah answered, patting her on the butt. He took her by the hand, then walked her over to the reinforced window of their new Head Quarters. "Look over there, do you see that advertisement sign?"

"I noticed it before I walked in. Volunteered sterilization, huh?" Nzinga said, squeezing Skah's hand.

"Yeah. And you wouldn't believe how many sisters in this part of town have participated in that shit," Amani interjected. "Anyway, you two play catch-up, I'll talk to you later." Amani left without another word.

Skah and Nzinga said nothing. They just stood in the middle of the cold empty room and watched the flickering images of hate on the tele-monitors. Pure propaganda. Several members of Project Harmony who had recently been sworn into Congress were promising to end the scourge of the inner cities.

"Millions of people are watching this shit, Nz," Skah said, breaking the long silence. "Everybody we know and care about-"

"It'll be alright, Skah. I just know it will. Back on the East Coast, the brothers and sisters have managed to connect with several

African countries. We've even done some things to facilitate a relationship with the Blacks of Latin America as well."

Nzinga was the eternal optimist. She'd managed to keep her soul in this long war. Skah forgot he'd even had one. His heart was as cold and hard as stone. The horrible things he'd done in the name of Black people. Killing was second nature to him. He was a walking contradiction. On one hand, he'd managed to maintain strict dietary habits. He exercised daily. His studying was second to none, and he meditated for hours on end. For all intents and purposes, he'd lived the life of a priest while becoming the most deadly assassin. He lived in two worlds, and despite his desperate attempts at denying at what he was becoming, he was exactly what Black people needed in these times...

* * * * *

We stood there in total shock. This was something I definitely had not expected. Standing before us was a most amazing, yet beautiful sight. There must have been 30 or 40 of them. Black men. Black women. They wore the most beautiful and articulate clothing I'd ever seen. It appeared to be hand-sewn. The men wore brown and red Tunics, pants, and coveralls. The women were draped in the most splendid two- and three-piece wraps. Blue and yellow leather, hand stitched and flowing, the sistahs wore the same kinds of complicated patterns I'd seen in the history books on our ancestors in Old America.

We all stood motionless for what seemed liked hours, eyeing each other. The elders were in the back. The young men made up the first three rows, followed by the young women. They carried old style Plasma rifles, no doubt taken from the armories in the Wasted Cities.

An Elder walked from behind the wall of young male and female warriors. I swear he looked just like one of the Ntiu Tut from back home. His movements were slow, deliberate, and graceful. He was totally hairless, from top to bottom. His eyes shown a clarity and alertness, the likes of which I hadn't seen outside of Ta-Amenta.

Holding a staff carved of glistening black wood, he pointed to my person and motioned for me to step forward.

"Maintain your Men-Ab (stability) at all times, Kashta," Enlil whispered.

I found myself standing before a Grand Elder. He had a kind of power emanating from his person. I could feel his strength. It felt like waves. He held his long wooden staff so that it leaned from right to left across his body. He then asked, "What Isolate Klan are you from?" His voice was low and dry. "I've never seen gear such as yours before," he continued.

"I know no 'Isolate Klan', Elder." I kept my eyes slightly lower than his; it shows respect.

He noticed. "We are from Ta-Amenta," I continued.

His eyes widened. He then turned to the others. They all appeared to be excited and spoke in low, melodic whispers. Smiling, he approached my person, stopping just inches away. His dark brown eyes looked like bottomless pools of pure melanin.

"Amenta means, 'Heaven,' does it not? Are you and your men from Heaven?" he asked. His eyes sparkled as he verbally danced in the rhythms of the Timeless Dialect.

"Only the Heaven that we have made here on the Earth," I answered.

"How is it that you have come to use some of our sacred words? And yet your accent is unlike any I have ever heard?" the Elder asked, a puzzled look shown on his face.

I was thinking the very same thing. He used words like 'gear' for clothing. That is very similar to the highly adaptive languages spoken by our ancestors in the 20th century. "Perhaps we speak the same because we are the same," I returned.

He said nothing. He lifted his staff, then held it straight at his right side. A huge grin appeared on his face. The entire demeanor of the rest of the brothas and sistahs lightened as well. Smiling, he stood there looking me up and down, nodding his head.

Turning, he waived his hand; motioning for us to follow.

CHAPTER 21

We stayed with them for three days, and in that short time we learned perhaps as much about ourselves as we did about our most gracious hosts. My only hope is that they learned a thing or two from us as well. The five of us prided ourselves on being Ta-Amentans. We were Independent Blacks from one of the richest countries in the western hemisphere. Ours was a civilization born out of desperation, struggle, and divine intervention. Yet here we stood in the presence of a separate and distinct Black nation. *Were they, too, a divinely inspired people?*

In some respects, their civilization was similar to our own. They honored their Elders, divided their population into separate classes, based on needs and production, yet it was their religion that fascinated me the most. It was at times vaguely familiar, and yet utterly impossible. An incredible blend of ancient spiritual systems, occupied by deified historical figures. It was simply astonishing.

Enlil documented as much as he could about the various Isolate Klans. Their Kingship as it were and their incredible culture were recorded for the Ntiu Tut. Their fabulous history was relayed to us in a beautiful tale of grief, adventure, and triumph. It was rhythmically delivered in the Timeless Dialect by their King. His name was Enoch. He was one of the wisest souls I'd ever met, and he was an amazing 113 years old!

On the third day, they guided us to a great river. It stretched from the lush forest regions of the W-Quadrant to the chard chasms of Quadrant-4. We exchanged items with them; we gave them a computer-generated floating map of Ta-Amenta. They gave us food, water, and the directions to the next Isolate Klan city. We were then given the proper behavior codes to use for the next time we should meet an Isolate Klan group. We thanked our newly found *sister nation*, then slowly set out for our next encounter.

————

We heard them approaching from the east. It seemed they always came from that direction. We stood motionless and allowed them to overtake us - as if we really had a choice. We never knew how, but they always seemed to know we were coming. Over the past few days, we'd gotten used to the idea that they had a more efficient way of traveling through the Wasted Cities. Like the first three Klan societies, they continued to direct us to easier and shorter routes to Valhalla.

It wasn't until we were nearly half way through Quadrant-4 that we encountered the next Isolate Klan society. They moved like mist, coming from the east, keeping pace with Aten.

"Here they come," Piankhi announced.

King Enoch informed us of the area between countries. He told us that we would approach a region where the Isolate Klans recorded the deeds of nations. They made no attempt to conceal their arrival. They moved fast and chanted as the came. Pushing through the bush, they formed a powerful row of various hues.

Their King walked through the protective wall of men and women, just as Enoch did days earlier. He smiled as he approached.

"Greetings, Kashta. We've been expecting you. It seems you and your friends are learning to trust the forest, allowing it to get you to where you need to be." He was a tall man, light skinned, and shown the same kind of wisdom in his eyes and face that we saw on every other King we came into contact with.

Over the past few days, we'd learned to slowly bow our heads whenever a King approached. We kept our heads lowered until he finished speaking. "We know who you're looking for, and we know how to find her," he said, his voice as calm and emotionless as the Ntiu Tut back home.

His words caused my heart to skip. *How...how did he know,* "If you know our mission, Elder, I won't waste your time. Is she safe? How do we reach her?" I asked, finally able to look him in the face.

"She is alive, but she is not safe. She, like several of our brothers and sisters, are in the camps of the enemy. They are not far. As you should know by now, you are very close to the land of the *slavers*. Their main camp is in the third City, west of the artificial lake that sits at the base of the red mountain," he answered.

"Then may we make camp with you and yours, leaving tomorrow at sunrise?" I asked. The Ntiu Tut taught us that it is always proper to ask permission when seeking residence, no matter how short the stay.

Without saying a word, he nodded in the affirmative.

The next day we ate a delicious meal, thanked our hosts, then left for the artificial lake. Like sentries, every 200 het-meters an Isolate Klan warrior stood as a living sign, guiding our every step and keeping us on the right path. Less than 2 hours later, we approached the artificial lake from the east...

* * * * *

July 5 - 21rst Century

Nzinga, Nola, and Nefertari sat calmly in Raven's small flat. It sat snugly in the Richmond hills. The rent was too high, but Raven fell in love with its huge and spacious windows that overlooked the bay. They laughed loud and hard while listening to the latest Paul Mooney audio. They drank a bottle of the finest of West African wines and did their best to distract themselves from tonight's unfolding events.

Two weeks ago, several Blacks were shot and killed while waiting at the BART station in Downtown Oakland. This came after Oakland had declared itself as an 'African American city.' Tourism was high, the economy was on the upswing, and the cultural vibe of Oakland made it a powerful rival to its sister city across the bay. This did not go unnoticed. Jealous eyes spied an emerging international Black presence in the Golden state. And it was common knowledge that it was the loose-knit followers of the doctrines of Project Harmony who were responsible for the killings.

Several members of Project Harmony were professors at the university. They dominated the Anthropology Department and were making a smooth takeover of the Chemistry Department. In response to recent happenings, White domestic terrorism, the unprovoked attacks on Blacks, and the ongoing war with the police, the emerging military-wing comprised of the Double-Members of the African Directive decided to go on the offensive.

The three men parked the stolen car in the lot, that sat underneath the thicket of trees that grew along a small stream. They didn't talk; each knowing his role, there was no need for conversation. Two of them exited the vehicle, and slipped off into the darkness. They knew what they had to do. They studied their prey well. They knew their habits, their routes to their favorite coffee shops, and when and where their targets would be alone.

Kafra stayed close to the outer perimeter of the campus. He'd studied their security for months, and he knew how and when they patrolled the outer lots. Every hour, one or more security officers would make their rounds, buy coffee at the same soda shop, and rush through the parking areas. Tonight was no exception. Security officer Brad Sirling followed his same routine. He grabbed a sandwich from the coffee shop across the street from the social studies department, then rushed through the parking facilities. He was always a nervous wreck. "He probably wouldn't be a problem," Kafra whispered. He watched the young man go through his usual motions...not deviating once.

Skah and Amani stood huddled between the Social and Physical Science buildings. They hid in the shadows, watching for any signs of campus security. They were sweating. The palms of their hands were drenched.

"Here's where we part, my brotha," Skah whispered to Amani.

"I guess so, beloved." Amani turned right into the wide stairwell and began to slowly ascend the cement blocks. He was heading for the Anthropology Department.

Skah watched his friend disappear into the Social Science building. He then took several deep breaths. He nervously strutted across the neatly cut grass, then entered the Physical Science building. He wasted no time, pushing past several students on the way in.

Pulling the shiny black Glock from the small of his back, Skah held the weapon at his side. Opening the double doors to the Chemistry Department, Skah followed the trail of lights until they divided and went in separate directions. The list of professors was shown in a glass case that hung on a brightly colored mural.

"There he is," Skah said to himself. "Jacobson," he whispered. Dr. Jacobson was the director of the Chemistry Department and a member of Project Harmony. He openly suggested that Blacks be given a chemical serum of his own design that would painlessly sterilize them. He had his own web page with pictures of him and his colleagues performing abortions in Africa, distributed pamphlets about the views and aims of Project Harmony, and arrogantly proclaimed his constitutional rights to express his views.

Skah, having drew the 'lot' for this particular assignment, studied the man for three months. He knew when and where he ate. He knew where and when he walked to his small apartment, paid for by the depleting university funds, and he also knew when Dr. Jacobson stayed after hours to correct papers.

His unregistered gun at his side, Skah walked towards the office of his prey. The lights were still on, and he could see movement from behind the stained glass window that sat in the center of the expensive wood door. That's when he heard it, a shot from across the campus yards. *Damn,* he thought. *Amani should have used his silencer. I'll have to do this now.*

The movement inside the office stopped. Skah's heart started pounding; he didn't have much time... it was now or never.

Rushing towards the office door, Skah was startled when its hinges swung open, and there stood Dr. Arthur Jacobson. He was taller than what Skah had imagined, but something wasn't right about his skin. His glasses hung from his shirt pocket, and his reddish hair dangled in his face.

The two men stood motionless; it was like a scene out of a movie. Dr. Jacobson's eyes where stark white, and they were as wide as golf balls. Skah watched as the front of Dr. Jacobson's pants became soiled with urine.

"What... what do you want? I've got money, you can have it, just don't-"

The piercing whine of a miniature explosion drowned out the rest of Dr. Jacobson's request. In a deep splatter, he was hurled back against the stained glass of the wooden door. He clutched his chest, gasping for air. Skah aimed, then shot again. This time he struck the professor in the top of the head. It was over. A thick mist of purple painted the walls. Skah was in shock. He felt as if he was not inside his own body. He watched himself standing over the body of the former Dr. Jacobson. When he finally snapped to, he was sweating through his clothing. He leapt over the still warm body, and snatched as many files as he could. He didn't know what they were, but they belonged to his enemy. *Perhaps it contained information he could use,* he thought. Ignoring the taste of fear welling up in his throat, Skah dashed out of the office, down the hallway, and out of the Physical Science building. He thought he was going to be sick. The taste and scent of shock and fear reminded him of Alka-Seltzer.

Walking from the Physical Science building, Skah watched the university campus police run in and out of the Social Science Department. He maintained his distance, walking toward the stream that bordered and ran the length of the university campus. That was the plan: use the stream to get back to the car.

"Did you leave it?" a voice said from the shadows. Skah almost died from a heart attack right there. He swerved around and aimed at where the voice came from. It was an out of breath Amani.

"Why in the fuck are you hiding in the fucking shadows, are you trying to fucking kill me?" Skah was clutching his chest, breathing hard, and shaking his head.

Bending over, Amani tried to catch his breath. "I'm sorry, Skah-"

"I know, my brotha, it's just-" He didn't finish. Instead, he turned and vomited.

Grabbing his friend by the arm, Amani pulled him along the stream and toward the parking facilities. "Did you leave the card, Skah?" Amani asked, pulling his friend along.

"Of course I did, Black man. Did you?"

"Absolutely. I left it on top of the motherfucker's body," Amani answered. The two men continued to run over and through the stream, its cold water splashing up and around their ankles. From the distance, they saw a nervous Kafra sitting in the exact location they had picked last month. It was a perfect spot, just at the corner of the stoplight. When the two men pulled themselves from the muddy creek, no one noticed them jump inside the car. When the light turned green, the three of them drove off as if nothing happened.

———

Last night's events shocked the world. Two of America's most popular academics were slain in cold blood. Interviews with friends and family were shown against the backdrops of the victims lying in pools of blood. Project Harmony was never mentioned.

* * * * *

It was a fairly large camp; 60, maybe 70 men were permanently housed here. They were organized and well armed. It lay just beyond a small hilltop surrounded by lush forests in the south and protected by the artificial lake to the east. It's been here for some time now. It's once smooth white walls now shown signs of wear and tear. Everything was made of 'reinforced nylon plastic.' There were graves in a small clearing off to the west of the entrance. Several buildings lay in and around its perimeter. Neatly tucked behind the rectangular main structure was a small garden.

In two het-meter spreads, we slid on our bellies, wriggling through the thick leafy forest floor. We didn't make a sound. When we reached the edge of the embankment that overlooked their Base camp, I began scanning the area with Anpu's peepers.

"Let's keep it real, gentlemen, nothing fancy. I want to get as many brothas and sistahs out of this hellhole as possible. With or without Tefnut." Motioning to the others, I pointed to my wave-jumper. "Zero frequency," I said, pulling my Colbot-rifle over my shoulder.

Speaking in quiet whispers, I made clear what my intentions were. "Shango, you've got three minutes to locate the slave quarters. Start on the northwest side. Anpu, flow to the east. Oshun, you take the south. Enlil, you and Piankhi stay put. We'll need someone to watch our backs. I'll take out the munitions dump. Is everybody clear?"

No words were spoken. Heads nodded in agreement. Then, in a wisp of leaves and dirt, we were on the move. Looking back over my shoulder, I looked at Piankhi and Enlil. They lay on their bellies, motionless. I could tell that Piankhi wanted in. He's young; he'll learn.

It was nothing to slip past their hidden traps and snares. Moving against the wind, I found myself just het-meters away from a Cold Wind officer. He leaned up against a large tree, his gold 'kill pendants' reflecting the green of the canopy. Quietly, he sipped something from a thin metal flask. I kept my eyes on his waist as I approached him in the darkness. He wore his gun on his left hip. He kept his communicator on the ground. Bad mistake.

The metal flask made a dull thumping noise as it struck the matted vegetation on the forest floor. The muffled sounds of a man struggling for his life were the only indications of my presence. Turning towards Enlil and Piankhi, I raised my left fist. They returned the gesture.

The munitions dump consisted of several mobile cannons, surrounded by crates of small rockets, swords, and old style plasma rifles. Probably taken from the Wasted Cities they've looted. It was protected by a wooden fence and fitted with razor wire. A row of attack-jeeps lay just on the other side. I could hear them laughing from inside the main building. I impatiently waited for the others to gain their positions.

It didn't take long. Anpu was first to make contact, "Kashta, I'm in place. There are three attack-jeeps, four barrels of fuel-"

"Anpu, what's up?" I asked, nearly shouting into my wave-jumper. "Anpu!"

"It's okay, I've spotted where they keep the dead," he answered. "No sign of Tefnut," he added.

"Typical Cold Wind layout. Entrance on the north wall, slow traffic," Shango added.

"I've found the slave quarters. It's about 10 het-meters from the main structure, northwest," he added. Shango was one of the most efficient brothas in the Mesniu. I was glad he'd come along.

"I can't imagine how we've ever missed this place. It's a regrouping station for Aft-Patrols," Oshun announced.

"That means we move fast and dirty," I responded. "Aft-Patrols are known for their explosiveness. They're usually the most ruthless and 'cut-throat' of all Cold Wind Soldiers. If they feel threatened, they'll kill as many slaves as they can!"

And as if on cue, Enlil ended his silence, "If you're going to make a move, it had better be soon. I've just spotted a fairly large unit. They're about three nilometers north, and they're heading this way."

There are few things in the world that are as terrible, yet necessary, as battle. It happens in long drawn out spurts, in flashes of pain, anguish, and death. And so it was today, an intense, extended fight. From the four corners of the world, we rained death and destruction upon them. We attacked like the mighty ones from the south, like the olden Gods who tamed the regions of ancient Africa. There would be no stopping us. We are MESNIU.

Our movements were strong and swift. And though we came from different directions, we had one destination: the slave quarters.

It was a small building. A cement cut-out. It was no more than a granite box, yet it drove the passions of our ruthless attack.

We managed to catch the entire camp off guard. That's all we needed. I signaled for both Enlil and Piankhi to come out of hiding.

Super heated streams of Colbot knifed throughout the encampment. Our ancient war cries drowned out the sound of bursting bones, exploding concrete, and the screams of the dying.

The Cold Wind Soldiers weren't giving up without a fight. They struck from behind their plastic-nylon walls, behind gritting teeth, flaring nostrils, and advanced weaponry. I expected nothing less. Such is the nature of war.

Death was all around me. It didn't matter though. I had one thing on my mind: Tefnut. Stepping over the dead and the dying, I continued on my trek toward the slave quarters. Through the haze and smoke I saw it: a small dimly lit building sitting in a mossy field next to the main camp. My heart quickened because I understood that within its blood stained walls, was the most precious treasure in the universe. The closer I got, the more detached I became. Everything seemed to move in slow motion, and there was no sound. It was as if none of this was real.

I remained silent, shooting Cold Wind Soldiers as they ran towards me, their eyes filled with hate, their lives ending as a result of it. My degree of waking-trance was deep. I felt no pain, I felt no sorrow; only heat, only determination.

Looking south, I beheld the awesome might of Oshun. He was merciless, cold, death-dealing in his wake. Piankhi and Enlil joined me as I cut a path of destruction to the north. Like three great 'suns,' we burned our way to the ends of the encampment and beyond. Oshun was there to greet us. Anpu and Shango, having begun their deadly campaign from opposite sides of the camp, had made it easy for us. I was pleased.

I looked around and observed what we had done. It was always like this. Everything I knew was consumed by the timeless moment of battle. Every fiber of my being focused on the objective. The sounds of the world slowly returned. I heard the subtle crackle of flames. Then the random explosions of scattered fuel tanks and the thunderous sounds of falling debris.

"Anpu, secure the area. Shango, take the point. See if you can find us a ride home." Both men were supreme soldiers, they immediately assessed what needed to be done and simply executed.

"Alright, Enlil, Piankhi, cover me. Let's see who's inside." I slowly approached the scorched doors of the slave quarters. It was strangely quiet inside, perhaps too quiet. I placed my hands on the metal beam that held the doors secured. I stood there, frozen for what seemed like forever. It wasn't until I felt the piercing eyes of my fellow Warrior-Soldiers burning into the back of my head that I lifted my weapon and blew the titanium locks off.

At first, I couldn't make out any details. From within the darkness, only shapes and shadows moved about. Haze. Smoke and dust swirled in a mini tornado, then finally escaped from the dark cramped quarters.

"What do you see, Kashta?" Piankhi asked, kneeling behind me, his rifle raised and poised for action. Enlil said nothing. He simply stayed in the ready position.

I didn't answer. I raised my Colbot-rifle, turned it on its right side, and pulled the flat green lever on its outer casing. A loud click followed, and a brilliant greenish light lit up three fourths of the interior of the structure.

"Damn," Piankhi said, lowering his rifle to his side.

"Be careful, Kashta. There may be Cold Wind Soldiers inside." Enlil was right. It was an old trick, but I've lost many friends to it just the same. Searching left and right, I looked hard at the men and women standing and sitting in the human warehouse. They looked at me as if I were an illusion. They were shocked, afraid, delighted.

They stood in the middle of the building, watching me. A look of amazement shown on their faces. I tried to smile, give them a sense of reassurance. I reached out and touched them, on the shoulders, on their faces. I found close to 30 men, women, and children. They were haggard, malnourished, but I still hadn't found who I was looking for.

"Kashta!" was all I heard before I felt someone slam into my person. I didn't even have time to ready my weapon. It wasn't until I was on the ground before I realized who it was.

She found me!

There were no words spoken. We just lay on the ground; locked in an indescribable embrace. Tears rolled from my eyes, mixing with hers. This had to be the first time in years since I'd lost my Men-Ab (emotions stability). I didn't care. We pulled ourselves up from the dirty concrete floor and stared at each other.

"First things first," I said, breaking the silence. "That was stupid of you to try and find me. What the hell were you thinking?" I didn't know if I should put her over my knee or kiss her for a week.

"I can't believe you, Kashta. Is that all you have to say? I mean, really! I couldn't just... oh, just forget it," she said, storming out of the entrance of the dusty slave quarters.

"What?" I yelled. *Did I come on too strong? Should I have said 'thank you' first?* I asked myself. I never seem to get it right with her. I watched in silence as she hugged and laughed with the other brothas. "Where's my rifle?" I heard her ask them. I was lost in thought, so much so that it took me a minute before I realized I was being watched.

She stood next to four large sacks of corn. She was stunning; I mean, unusually beautiful. She was about five and a half feet tall. She had a mass of kinky dark brown hair covering her regal head. Her skin was flawless. Her full lips and high cheek bones were made even more beautiful by her sparkling slanted eyes. We stood in the slave quarters alone and looking each other over. The attraction was definitely mutual. Bending over and picking up what looked like a bag of books hidden behind a pile of stones, I couldn't help inhaling her shapely body. I just stood there, staring at her. Big mistake.

Tefnut had apparently been observing our symbolic dance. She walked in and stood between the two of us, her hands on her hips. "Are we leaving yet, or do you want to stay here?"

I was stuck. Couldn't speak. Nodding my head, I followed the two women outside the dilapidated building, and stood in front of it like a kid up to no good. The brothas noticed my awkwardness and began laughing.

"You need some help, Kash?" Anpu asked. More laughing.

Shango had secured an all terrain tractor and had attached a large feed trailer to it. The brothas and sistahs, young and old, were piled in the opened housing bay. Its reinforced steel alloy casing would provide plenty of protection. Shango was in the back with them, while Piankhi and Oshun were setting up to walk on either side of the huge trailer. Tefnut sat up front with Enlil. She kept her eyes forward, refusing to look at me.

CHAPTER 22

"We've reclaimed 23 adults and 10 children. They all appear to be strong and fit. Valhalla will definitely want to reclaim them."

"Well, they always do," Kash, Anpu returned. "And it won't take a rocket scientist to follow the deep tracks we're leaving behind. The ground is wet, and this blasted feed-trailer is slowing us way down."

I watched the men and women who sat piled in the back of the trailer's cargo area. Yesterday they were slaves. I couldn't help wondering how they felt, *what* they felt. They didn't speak to us. They sat huddled next to one another, talking softly amongst themselves. Their eyes were glazed over, probably been slaves for a long time now. And the babies...beautiful and tender, but old and wise at the same time. They reminded me of the children of New America.

She's doing it again. Staring at me. She watched me from the far side of the feed trailer. She wore a short blue garment. Barely a dress. Her womanly curves strained against its fabric. She was probably in her mid-twenties. Her body was well toned, and her skin had an almost golden hue. Her hands showed the wear and tear of a slave. I tore myself from her penetrating gaze and walked ahead, slipping in and out of the bush and occasionally placing canisters of fresh water in the cargo bin.

"I say you should just go over there and find out who she is," Anpu said smiling. As usual, he was busy trying to complicate my life.

"All in due time, Atef, all in due time." Anpu smiled and walked off. I watched her from out of the corner of my eye. She knew I was watching; a slight smile crept across her face.

———

On the fourth day, the inevitable happened. Like a whirlwind, they struck from the edge of the forest, vengeance in their eyes. Cold Wind. We scattered like mist, diving behind trees, behind rocks. The rescued ducked inside the safety of the feed-trailer. Reinforced metal walls protected them, as streams of crimson death streaked above their heads. In typical Valhallan fashion, the Cold Wind Soldiers attacked us from the north. "Keep going!" I shouted, waving for Enlil to continue driving. There was no need in both he and Tefnut staying behind, not with so many lives at stake.

Tefnut didn't respond, she just continued to shoot from the passenger side window. Her aim was as deadly as ever.

The engines whined and smoked as Enlil squeezed the accelerator. The loose gravel and muddy dirt whipped up into a brown froth. Huge rubber tires pulled and tugged at the earth. Within minutes, the rectangular vehicle, complete with feed-trailer, was sloshing through the vegetation of Quadrant-4. My brothas and I slipped into the south end of the forests. We've been through this before. One by one, we began to pick off our attackers, leaving a trail of blood in our wake.

"Follow that vehicle, soldier! We'll deal with the niggers!" I heard one of them shout.

"Get on the barker! I want two sonic-copters dispatched immediately," the one with the ponytail yelled.

This was heavy ground, and we couldn't call for backup. We're supposed to be on vacation. "Enlil, whatever you do, don't stop. Get the Lost-Found to safety at all costs," I roared into my wave-jumper. "Anpu, Oshun, let's finish this!"

Sonic-copters are the fastest gun ships around. They're maneuverable and heavily armed. They're small though, so all it takes is one good shot.

"Hey, nigger boy. Yeah... tonight's the night you gonna meet yo maker," a pot-bellied Cold Wind soldier yelled. He was a tracker. Enhanced olfactory, natural night-vision. Probably been in the bush for weeks.

I didn't say a word. Instead, I slipped into a waking-trance and followed the dictates of my spirit. As he jumped over a thick tangle of roots that lay at the base of a huge redwood, I executed a perfect

Serpent Kick, catching him in the throat. It wasn't pretty. A thick patch of blood erupted from his nose and mouth. Before he hit the ground, Shango shot him from ten het-meters away.

In one fluid motion, I waved my left hand in a downward motion. Shango, understanding this, dropped to the forest floor. I fired three blue beams of Colbot over his body. When the Cold Wind Soldier fell on top of him, he wasn't amused. I laughed my ass off.

Piankhi was hemmed down behind a thicket of trees. His youth and inexperience had finally managed to catch up with him. He fought back courageously from his hiding place, but they were moving in quick.

"Ah... Atefs... I think I'm going to need some help," he barked.

"Hang on, young Blood!" I shouted, running and firing at the same time. The Cold Wind soldiers scattered as I drew closer. That was all the time I needed, or so I thought.

He came out of nowhere; huge, strong, fierce, and powerful. At first I didn't recognize him. It's been a long time. His reflexes were as fast as my own. Moving in a blur, he managed to kick my Colbot-rifle from my hand and block my view of Piankhi in one swift motion. Pulling back, relying totally on instinct, my eyes adjusted to the dim light of the forest. It was my oldest living enemy. Balder...

* * * * *

September 7 - 21rst Century

It was six in the morning. Skah was sitting in a chair in the center of his tiny apartment, sweating profusely. He'd been up several days now, engaged in the most intensive meditative experience of his life. His heart and mind were attuned to the melodic frequencies of a MAAT HEKAU. For long moments in time and space, Skah was unaware of the limited environment around him. He joined with the infinite expansiveness of all creation. At first it was black, then grey, then bluish silver with white trim.

Sitting in a pool of sweat, Skah was enjoying a profound sense of peace. It was the first such experience in his revolutionary life. He didn't care that his clothes, drenched in perspiration, clung to his cold body. He didn't care that he had not eaten in three days. All the problems in the universe were small and trivial to him now. All of his petty wants and cravings, disagreements and disappointments, hang-ups and conditionings meant nothing to him now. Sometime during the last 72 hours, Skah had become aware of a greater reality.

He strained when he finally stood from his chair. His bones and muscles, having been locked in the same position for over three days, screamed in protest as he walked across the living room floor. His clothes hung off his body like wet rags. He was too excited to notice. This was a different kind of excitement, a calm, soothing type of joy. "Is this true happiness?" he asked himself. The answer came from within.

At first he wanted to call Nzinga, and tell her about his 'Insperience' (inner experience). With his newfound clarity, he wanted to do so many things all at once, tell so many people of his brief glimpse into the nature of all things. However, with this same new perspective came a sense of peace unlike anything he had ever known.

His heart had become as light as a feather. Images of his true nature, his true identity, flooded in his mind's eye. Standing and looking from the second story window, he began to reflect on his inward journey.

"We as human beings are dualistic in nature," he spoke aloud. "One part divine, one part...earth bound. I know this to be true because I have inperienced it." He started laughing. There was a kind of peace in this particular revelation. A peace that brought an answer to the most profound question in the universe: does a part of the human being survive death? The answer came from within.

Five days ago, he asked Nzinga not to call him for a week. He told her that he needed to go on a vacation, a vacation into the depths of his very being. This journey, he said, was to reacquaint himself with his spirit, his soul. She didn't like it, but she knew her man well. She understood that Skah had been going through some changes. And although he would not discuss them with her, she knew in her heart of hearts, that whatever he was going through, he had the strength to emerge whole, better than before.

All of these things Skah recalled as he calmly punched in Nzinga's electronic address through the HUSIA. Seconds later, He was typing a message asking her to call him when she got a chance. "The HUSIA," he whispered. This is a great tool. *Our people are truly talented,* he said to himself. That's when it hit him. If our people could be properly guided, guidance based on the tenants of our ancient African ancestors, we can be free almost overnight.

"Freedom comes through the submission to Amen (God). When we submit, a kind of peace, true freedom, and true happiness is obtained. When we as human beings exist in a state of calm, the answers to many of life's problems are gained," Skah proclaimed to his empty apartment. "Though I've only held this peace but for a moment in time," he spoke to himself, "it's been long enough to pierce the veil of Auset. Our people must learn to drink from the waters of Amenta-"

Skah hurriedly walked over to his bookshelf and pulled out several books written by a number of Black Authors. All of these books were great, he said to himself, but one in particular really explained the true meaning to the oldest story known to man. Finding the book in question, Skah skimmed over its contents. He found what he was looking for.

A few hours had passed before Skah's audio rang. He was sitting in the meditative position when he had to get up to go answer it. It was Nzinga. "I got your message, baby, are you alright?" she asked, the concern reflective in her voice.

"Never better," Skah returned. "I actually *insperienced* the duality of my being. And... more important than that, I've worked out a practical schematic on how we may approach the solution to the present condition of our world-community. And, Nzinga, check this out: I was there, I was actually there," he said excitedly.

"What do you mean you were there? Where were you?"

"I was at the Cross Roads of existence, baby. I was at the place where the dual nature of the human being can be found."

"Sweatheart, I think you need to get something to eat-"

"Ah, come on, Nz. I know it sounds strange, but I know what I'm talking about. It was the greatest thing I've ever been through," Skah returned. "I mean...I must have been in trance for hours, maybe days; I'm not sure. Anyway, I reached a point in which I split into two separate entities. One part divine, holding no boundaries, limitless in scope. The other half was connected to the 'phenomenal plane' in a big way. It was incredible, Nzinga. Absolutely beautiful."

"Well, what was it like - the duality part I mean?" Nzinga asked, her curiosity replacing her skepticism.

"It was totally quiet at first. There was no sound, total peace. Everything was BLACK, but it wasn't a scary thing, it was a beautiful, PERFECT BLACK," Skah answered. Clearing his throat, he continued, "Oh, yeah, although it was complete BLACK, you could still see, I mean see off into the darkness. The part that would be considered sky was Jet Black, while the part that could be considered ground was a Bluish Black. And it moved and swirled like water."

"You mean the ground was moving?"

"Call it what you want, baby. All I know is that it moved...kind of like it had waves rolling across the top or something. That's when it became apparent to me that what I was seeing *was* me! The PERFECT BLACK above, and the Bluish Black below."

"Did you look up and down? Is that how you determined that one area or region of yourself was above and below?" Nzinga was totally captivated by what Skah was describing to her. She knew he was serious, and she felt he really did experience *something*.

Skah didn't answer right away. He hesitated, pondering her question.

"Skah, are you alright?"

"I was thinking about the question you just asked, and, you know, you made me realize something. Technically speaking, there was no up or down. I guess I just interpreted it that way. Hmmnn," Skah said. "Alright now, you've helped me to realize something. The PERFECT BLACK was everywhere, and I got the impression that it originated behind me; don't ask why. The Bluish Black was contained within the PERFECT BLACK. That's how it was, my sistah. Thank you for your insightful question."

Nzinga was juiced now; she was beginning to feel as though she were a part of Skah's experience also. "Okay, now what about the duality part?"

"Oh, yes, the duality part. Now that was a trip, Nzinga. One part of me was the PERFECT BLACK, while a separate part of me was the Bluish Black, both at the same time. The PERFECT BLACK was calm and at peace. It, or I, just sat there in total bliss, watching, observing. It was the most beautiful moment in my life. I wanted to stay there, stay me," Skah answered. "Now the Bluish Black, well it was me also, but it wasn't peaceful at all. I mean it tugged and pulled and craved and just cried out for things, experiences, answers, everything. It was never satisfied. The PERFECT BLACK watched in peace as the Bluish Black begged and pleaded for things. It, or that part of me, was never at rest...never at peace. They were both me... both aspects at the same time. I prefer to be like the PERFECT BLACK. It was at peace, unchanging, forever blissful. And you know what else, Nzinga?"

"What?"

"The PERFECT BLACK has been with me all the time. I remembered it as soon as I became aware of it. It's the timeless part of us, the part that never changes, the part that never dies. It *is* all of us. It is our true selves"

———

Nzinga came rushing through the front door of the tiny apartment. She was both excited and worried at the same time. She tossed her small red leather purse on the couch and began calling for Skah. When he didn't answer, she got nervous. "Skah, where the hell are you?" she yelled, walking into the bedroom. She strolled over to the window; expecting to see Skah walking from the nearby corner store. Not seeing him, she turned to leave. "Ahhhhhh...you butthole!"

Skah was standing behind her. He had just gotten out of the shower. He was dripping wet and was wearing a purple tunic. He'd lost some weight since the last time she'd seen him, but other than that he looked great. There was a kind of peacefulness about him.

They embraced, kissed, then embraced again. "What's with all the paper and stuff?" Nzinga asked, pointing to the poster-sized pieces of paper thumb-tacked to the bedroom walls.

Three large sheets dominated Skah's bedroom wall. They were arranged so that they fit together to make one huge picture. It looked like a diagram of the human body, juxtaposed on a schematic of a city. "Oh, yes, this is what we need to do," Skah answered. "Using the story of Ausar as an example, I've being trying to come up with a present day solution to the ills that have been destroying our people. We can longer blame the white man, or anything else for that matter. It's time to take responsibility. 'As above, so below; as below, so above,' right?" he asked rhetorically.

"All that from a piece of paper?" Nzinga said teasingly.

"Very funny. Anyway, it's very simple. The answers to our problems have been here all along. It's like our ancestors knew we would be in this situation, so they basically left a road map for us to follow."

Nzinga was sitting on the bed. She calmly took her shoes off, then walked over to the bedroom wall where several images of ancient African Temples were hanging. She began tracing the pictures with her finger. "You know, most Black people will never give up their adoptive religions to replace them with real African Spirituality. They've been taught to both hate and fear all Black or African Spiritual systems," she said somberly, her eyes never leaving the canvases. "Hell, even Africans from Africa would rather be Christian, Jew, or Muslim," she added.

"You've got a point there, beloved," Skah returned, patting Nzinga on her round booty. "That's why we approach this situation the same way we did things in the African Directive. As you know, based on the teachings of the ancients, Ausar (God) was cut into fourteen pieces. Those pieces were then scattered all over the world. Everywhere a part of Ausar (God) landed, the people from that region or part of the world gathered around that piece and created a religion based on the information from that particular part. Sure, any knowledge from or about God is good, but if you don't have the complete picture, you'll only go so far-"

"Okay, I'm with you so far, but what does this have to-"

"Let me finish. Now, obviously what we have today, passing as religion, is not complete enough to rescue humankind from the shadow of the beast. If it were, we'd be in better shape than we are. Let's just admit that what we have just ain't working." Skah walked over to his filing cabinet and pulled out a thick yellow folder. He tossed it on the bed and continued with his revelation. "Nzinga, look at this," he said, pointing to the folder. "Black people already have what they need to free themselves overnight."

"What about the unity factor?" Nzinga interrupted.

"That's where the Story of Ausar comes in," he returned. "Ausar was able to unite all of the different regions of the country, and parenthetically his own body, into one united whole. Having done this, everything was possible for Ausar while he lived on earth as a man. Sound familiar? Anyway, we use this example to guide our people to the Promised Land."

Nzinga was starting to understand her wayward husband. She was used to his ranting. That's why they rented this apartment. They needed a place to retreat, a place to explore their spirituality uninterrupted. She started searching through the files inside the folder. "Skah," she said with a smile on her face. "I'm starting to understand. We unite the Black Body, Black people, into one body, one people," she said.

"Yes, yes, yes."

"How do you suppose we do that?"

"With these files. We connect ourselves to every type of Black man, woman, and child. That's how we do it, we connect ourselves, our body parts, then we gain access to all spheres of life. By combining the body, we gain unlimited access to ourselves. Remember, every sphere is a different region or part of the African community. Each sphere is specialized to do a certain work. That work can be in the entertainment field, the scientific field, the athletic field, the educational field, in government, anywhere," Skah answered.

"Alright, it's starting to make sense. We organize a particular sphere to do a certain work. The more 'spheres' we get to do what it is we need it to do, the greater the degree of influence!" Nzinga was just as excited as Skah.

"That's right. We gain absolute influence over the body, our people, and assign each part a certain responsibility. If that region or sphere fails to fulfill their prescribed responsibility, we eliminate that part permanently!"

Nzinga stopped what she was doing and looked up at Skah. "Don't talk like that, Skah. I hate it when you talk like that."

"Never allow your emotions to dictate your behavior, and never let your emotions hide the truth, Nzinga. We who were once hidden within the ranks of the African Directive have a particular agenda also." Skah turned and walked towards the window. He stood motionless, looking through the dusty glass and onto the streets below.

"What do you mean?"

"Why, it's quite simple, Nz. We are the ones who protect and serve the people. We are a new and special class of soldier. We're Warrior-Soldiers!" he answered. Staring out of the window for what seemed like an eternity, he then turned and looked into Nzinga's eyes. "We are like the ones who came from the south in the name of Ausar... under the command of RA. We are MESNIU..."

* * * * *

He recognized me instantly. His eyes narrowed. Then, raising his Plasma weapon, he began firing wildly. Instinctively, I dove behind the tree to where my Colbot-rifle had fallen. I grabbed my weapon as I landed in the soft mud. Balder and I are sworn enemies. He and I first met over six years ago. It was during a campaign on the Canary Islands. When New America discovered that the West Africans had found gold in its caves and hills, one of their crooked Corporations hired Valhallan assassins. One of them was Balder.

"You're getting slow in your old age, huh, cave man?" I said tauntingly. Not waiting for an answer, I immediately appeared on the other side of the thick tree trunk and returned fire. I was wrong. He was still fast.

"I see you, nigger... do you see me?" an old familiar voice hissed from the bush.

"Not yet, why don't you come out and play."

Every shadow was suspect. Every critter was fair game. Even in waking-trance, I couldn't hear him. He was a ghost.

"Kashta, Kashta. He's to your left!" Piankhi's warning came too late.

I fired wildly; shards of rock and rubble sprayed in every direction.

Balder appeared from behind several fallen trees, chucking hand held explosives. "Come on, spook, lets see what you got!" he shouted, disappearing into the bush.

I had managed to work my way over to Piankhi. His ankle was torn opened, but he'd survive. "Who is that guy, Kashta? He's as good as you are!"

"You don't want to know, young Blood," I returned, helping him to his feet.

"Where are the others, Kashta, why aren't they helping us?"

"That's because they're all dead, nigger." Balder was a large man. A full head taller than me. His body was like a wall of stone. Muscles rippled and flowed like steel cables as he moved in for the kill.

I moved and swirled to my left, and punched Balder as hard as I could. He dropped to one knee, but he was only stunned. "Piankhi, get out of here!" I shouted.

"Don't go far, coon. After I kill this ape, I'll be coming for you!" Balder hissed.

"It's going to take more than you to kill me, cave man!" I returned. "Where are the rest of your dogs, shaggy?" I taunted.

He said nothing as he wiped the spit from his cheek and rose to face me. We began to circle one another like gladiators. Total silence. Even the air stopped moving. *This is it*, I thought. It's going to be to the death.

"Come on, boy!" he yelled.

"Bring the noise," I returned.

I faked left, then stepped back and caught him with a solid punch to the shoulder. I was aiming for his throat. His speed and cunning matched my own. He dropped and executed a sweep kick and connected with my right ankle. It hurt like hell. Too much, I thought. Looking down at his boots, I saw the row of spikes jutting from its rubbery soles.

Showing rows of yellow teeth, he began to gloat, "I bet that hurt, huh nigger?" he said grinning.

My answer was swift and deadly. I rushed him, grabbing as much of his uniform as possible. We tussled and strained under the forest trees. Twisting his body back and to the right, he picked me up and tossed me like a rag-doll. I landed on my back and shoulder. The pain that shot through my spine felt like lightning. I strained to get to my feet.

When I managed to scramble to my knees, he was already on top of me! I had to duck and roll in order to avoid his spiked boots.

"Come on, I'd expected a lot more–"

I caught him in the groin. As he doubled over in pain, I grabbed a hand full of his long blond hair, and raised my elbow. I prepared to deliver the Death Blow. He wasn't through yet. He swept my legs out from under me, then pulled himself free in the process. He stumbled back, and lay up against a thick Redwood. We both glared at each other, breathing heavily.

As we prepared ourselves for mortal combat, several warriors from the first Isolate Klan society materialized from out of the forest. Like phantoms, they were everywhere at once. Piankhi, Anpu, Shango, and Oshun stood with them. They even had Cold Wind Soldiers with them.

Then, from behind a wall of brave Isolate Klan warriors, Enoch, their King, walked towards me. He looked sad and disappointed. "Take him and his kind to the edge of the artificial lake and let them go," he said, pointing to Balder and the rest of the Cold Wind Soldiers. "Hello again, Kashta."

"Hetepu (peace) Elder," I said, lowering my head in the process.

He turned, then raised his curved staff. "We will take Kashta's men to the beginnings of their City. There, we will give them food, water, and our prayers. After which, we will send them home. Those who wish to go with them, and perhaps live amongst them, may do so. But remember, you will always have a home with us."

CHAPTER 23

We were almost home. The sky had changed from that perpetual sooty haze that blankets Valhalla and New America, to a crispy blue sea sprinkled with white ash. Most of the Isolates choose not to come with us. They remained behind, smiling as we stood there in shock. We'd thought for sure that they would be eager to return home with us.

We took turns driving what turned out to be a Forest Cutter. It was a type I'd never seen before. It was shaped like a wedge turned on its side and was held up by three enormous treads. Its steering system was a sight to behold. It consisted of two triangular accelerators that grew out of a steel dash. They were no more than foot-long joysticks. Speed was controlled by pressure, which was generated by rubber tubes that lined the inner housings on each grip. The harder you squeezed, the faster the thing went. Needless to say, when it was my turn to drive Tefnut got out and walked. Later that day, I teased her about how she lost her Men Ab and about how she should really work on her meditations. It took Anpu and Enlil to keep her from shooting me.

"Let's stop here," I said, holding up a raised fist. "Oshun, have you made contact with the hospital of Kawa?"

"Yes, I have. They're expecting us."

Normally we would have simply checked in through customs, gotten a few shots, probably tested for infections, and treated with homeopathic agents. Not this time. We've got 33 people who need to be looked at. One of whom is the beautiful sister who caught my eye back in Quadrant-4. Her name was Kali.

The hospital of Kawa is where we take all non-native Ta-Amentans. That includes Alkebulanians (Africans), New Americans, or the *Lost-Found* we snatch from slavery. It's mandatory. Everyone has to be checked out; they may need treatment...or worse.

We stopped next to a massive heap of cement that grew from a thick wall of red clay. It led from a series of crumbling buildings and tapered off into a shallow stream. I dropped my Colbot-rifle and walked over to the now smoking vehicle. Reaching into its cargo bay, I took out the last canister of water and passed it around. Children first. Then I gave it to the adults. This was to prevent anyone from drinking the water from the stream that cut a shallow groove in the soft mud before us. Oshun, Piankhi, and several of the men who were slaves only days ago bravely stood watch near and around the perimeter of our new camp. Anpu and I decided to explore the cluster of buildings that stood just beyond the small hillside. We cautiously walked through them, exploring each of their tiny rooms. They were clear.

As night fell, we all sat around a small fire. The brothas and sistahs were finally beginning to warm up to us. Enlil immediately seized the opportunity and began asking questions about their culture, their lives. Kali, being as bold as she was beautiful, spoke first. When she stood, I caught Tefnut rolling her eyes.

———

It's strange. I've been doing this for all of my adult life, rescuing our people from bondage, spiriting them away, and carrying them to the safe bosom of Ta-Amenta. Yet, I've never really spoke to them before. I just did my job. Cold, calculating, death-dealing if need be - but for what, for who? The Ntiu Tut ordered us not to speak to them, "Just bring them home, let us tend to them," they would always say. I wasn't prepared for this, none of us were. We'd never had this much time with them before.

They called themselves by many names. Some said they were Black, others called themselves Christians, a few called themselves Muslims, and some even called themselves African Americans. They had just as many names as they had hues of skin. We learned that most were descendants of African Americans who were captured during and after the Great Ethnic Clashes of 2017. We learned how they were forced to work in the Wasted Cities, how they organized their slave societies, and about how they were bred as animals.

Anpu, Oshun, and Piankhi stood watch. Tefnut and Enlil, being experts in communications, documented the origins, structures, and overall syntax of their language. I was more interested in their 'Belief System.'

It was an incredible tale, all of which was contained in the sack of books Kali had taken from the slave quarters. It told of how a group of self awakened Gods rose to challenge the ruling powers in the land of Eagles and Griffins. It was all written in old American English and was difficult to read, but I felt compelled to continue.

Most of the 'Scriptures' said that these Gods came before the creation of the Nation States. It told of how they guided a New Society of men and women and taught them the virtues of life and death. Through persuasiveness and determination, they apparently freed the Blacks from the yoke of domination by restoring their true culture and identity.

When it was my turn to ride with the Lost-Found, I eagerly sat amongst them. Kali, having found a bridge to communicate with me, used it to her advantage - and to Tefnut's dismay. Pulling a large package from a brown leathery sack, she handed me a thick purple book. Like a child riding a Menmen for the very first time, I happily took it and began leafing through its yellowed pages. Having scanned through most of the dusty books and scrolls earlier, I thought I was over my initial shock of the similarities between the religion of Kali's people and the actual history of Ta-Amenta.

We were about three hours north of Ta-Amentan borders when I finally picked up on some of the titles of their Gods. They were names, slightly altered, but recognizable all the same. "Amazing!" I yelled, "They deified them, made them their Gods," I said to Kali. She just looked at me and frowned. It all made sense. Kali is a descendant of the Black people who were captured around 2020. That was right before our people petitioned for a territory within the boundaries of Old America. The Ethnic Clashes were in full bloom, American diversity was a total failure, and Black people were struggling to recapture their culture... their humanity.

"Have you read this, Enlil? I mean really read it? It's incredible," I asked. Enlil said nothing. He just continued to write in his journal. I rambled on, "According to their religion, a powerful group of Black men and women rose up and challenged the Eagles and the Griffins in the twenty-first century. One of them was named Skah. And that's where their knowledge of those people stopped. That's all they have. And over the years, they've passed these stories from generation to generation. The history of these people slowly giving way to myth... to folklore. Eventually, these revolutionaries were deified, worshiped as Gods by Kali's people. But to us, they were not Gods. They were the men and women who founded our country."

* * * * *

April 11 - 21rst Century

Skah slowly stepped towards the podium. Surveying the immense crowd, he arrested the butterflies that danced in his gut. Taking a panoramic view of the Oakland sports complex, he figured that there must have been twenty thousand people in attendance. He smiled as the mostly Black crowd cheered and clapped as he waved to them. Clearing his throat, he turned and smiled at Nzinga. She sat nervously behind him, in the second row towards the center of the rostrum.

This was his ninth speech this year. He was exhausted, but his message on how and why Black people should unify was finally beginning to crack the hypnotic hold which seemingly held Black people in a perpetual state of inactivity. He didn't browbeat the people into doing what he thought was right, he simply offered the people the same ancient formulas given to the Blacks of the Hapi (Nile) Valley.

"Hetepu (peace) brothas and sistahs. I hope this glorious day finds you in good spirits." The huge crowd cheered louder, clapping in the process. "I'm not here to waste your time, beloved, so I'll just get right to the point. Slavery...was a good thing." The crowd started mumbling. "That's right, that's what I said. Slavery was a good thing," Skah repeated. "Now, before you allow your emotions to get the best of you, causing you to start tearing up the stadium and whatnot, just open your mind and remember that the Creator has a Master Plan. All we need to do is get in step with that plan, and we sail into victory." The audience clapped and cheered, their arms waving.

"In order to understand the concept of our enslavement as having been a good thing, or, at the very least, a necessity, you must understand the Master Plan. In order to understand the Master Plan, you must be able to clear your mind of all thought. With that clarity comes a peace the likes of which cannot be equaled. Through peace comes the voice of God. Only when you have quieted the distractions that this world puts on us can you hear the melodic song of the creator of the heavens and the earth. "

The crowd erupted in a series of: *that's right*, and *hellos*, and *amens*; the usual African American acknowledgments. Skah cleared his throat again, "God speaks to all of us, beloved brothas and sistahs. And it is through God's infinite wisdom, and under God's right-guidance, brothas and sistahs, that we learn the wonders of the times. I'm talking about the 'Nature of Cycles.' You see, beloved, in the cosmic scheme of things, there are great cycles that exist in the universe. These cycles move as waves while maintaining a Grand System of checks-and-balances. I'm not talking about that stuff going on in Washington D.C., either," Skah added. More roaring laughter.

"I know, I know," Skah acknowledged, "what does that have to do with slavery being a good thing...? Well, when you learn to reject what this world has to offer in terms of what makes a person happy, then your journey truly begins." Skah walked over to the podium, took a sip of water, then turned and winked at Nzinga. She smiled back at him.

"Some of you may be asking yourself, *what does this have to do with the cycles of the universe?* Well, I'll tell you," Skah answered himself. "Why are we as a race the only group of people in search of ourselves? In a time when other populations are sacrificing their cultures and their very identities to be included in the mad-dream of the children of Gog and MaGog, you continue to rebel." The crowd listened intently. "I mean, think about it: we are the only group of people who came to the shores of this country now called America that had its language, customs, belief systems, identities, and everything that made it unique systematically destroyed. Why... why do you think that happened? Because the CREATOR has a Master Plan," Skah said, answering his own question. "The Creator knew that after the wicked Masters of this world succeeded in crushing the descendants of the original people - us - that this would create in them - you - a longing for their former culture, their true identity. This longing was set to a cosmic Time Table," Skah said jokingly. "This table, or cycle, was set to go off in roughly 400 years." The audience started laughing and clapping. Skah laughed right along with them.

"This was a strategic move because Amen, or God to some of you, knew that the lure of this world would seduce the other people of the earth, and that they would volunteer their cultures and their souls to SET, the ruler of this world. After the rest of the world would eventually submit to the desires and imagery of SET, that special Time Table I spoke of earlier - and I don't mean a literal, mechanical device implanted in your head or chest... okay, brothas and sistahs," Skah added. The crowd laughed. They started clapping and stomping their feet.

"Anyway... this device, or better yet... this feeling in each of us as individuals and as a race of people, would ignite. This ignition would cause HERU - us - to search for our father, AUSAR. Now stay with me, people, because this is going to get crystal clear in a moment," Skah said, turning and walking to the other side of the stage.

"Let me make it plain, brothers and sisters," Skah said, pacing back and forth. "If you, the original people, had come to the shores of America in one piece, the salvation of the world would be impossible. I'll say it again... if you had come to America in one piece - that is, with your culture, language, beliefs, and identities whole - there would be no avenue for a Second Coming. Why do I say this?" Skah asked rhetorically, "Because you would have succumbed to the enemy just like everyone else. Yes, you would," Skah said again, responding to shouts in the audience. "Yes, you," he said pointing. "You would have done the same thing every other people have done... you would have bought into the twisted dream of this world, given up your own culture, and cashed in your very souls for the fast-food mentality of SET." Soft murmurs went throughout the crowded arena.

"So... my Black brothas and sistahs, the Master Plan was for you to be used as a living Trust Fund for God." The audience began to clap and nod in agreement. "Oh, yes, Black man and woman, the Creator of the heavens and the earth hid itself in you, the least worthy of all human beings, so that it, God, would rise again in a new day and in a new time. The Second Coming is based on that special Time Table... that feeling or longing to be your true self. It was placed in you in the beginning of time." Skah walked back and forth across the stage; he was sweating, but he felt good.

"You see, brothas and sistahs? You see how the cycles work?" Skah asked. "The same battles that were fought by our people thousands of years ago are being played out again today. You had to be destroyed so that you could be Born Again, in this day, and in this time. And without that longing to be your true self, you would have done the same thing the Japanese did, or the Chinese, the Koreans, the Mexicans, the Arabs - it doesn't matter, they all sold out," the crowd was on their feet, "they all submitted to the wrong master. But not you, you refused to submit to mammon. You longed to share in the Dream of the Creator of the Heavens and the Earth..."

WASHINGTON

Deep within the catacombs of an undisclosed underground facility, nestled in one of its many secret rooms, eight men sat in a dimly lit chamber. Its shiny black walls held three large flat-screens. On each screen shown images of Skah during today's rally. Amidst the cigar smoke and shadows, one of them called from the darkness.

"This Skah person, who is he?"

"I'll tell you who he is," another answered. "He's the most dangerous threat to our food supply in over 100 years."

* * * * *

We stood there, on the marbled floors which led to the entrance grid to the Third Border Station. The Lost-Found were just as amazed at my fellow Ta-Amentans, as my countrymen were at them. Kali walked beside me, keeping close, even grabbing onto my arm on occasion. The sleek black stealth vehicles that zoomed past frightened her.

"Kashta, your country is just as strange and wonderful as Valhalla. We've always believed in the *Land of the Blacks,* where our people lived in peace and prosperity. Some of our men have set out to find this place. They never returned. We just assumed that they died looking for a dream, a myth." Kali's eyes were watering.

"We're as real as the Valhallans, Kali. And your brothas and sistahs who spoke of us, they were right. Ours is a country devoted to achieving peace of mind, body, and spirit. We, like many other nations, aren't perfect, but this is our home. We love Ta-Amenta; we'd die for Ta-Amenta."

We walked through the Photo-Sonic Light Chambers and were bathed by low doses of highly concentrated pulses of 'Solar Melanin.' It's blue-black rays destroy most viruses, bacterium, and chemical agents. It also reveals any abnormalities found in our systems. The Mafdet guided us throughout the Border Station. It's their job to do so. They, like the K'huti, are a specialized division of Mesniu. They are charged with guarding and maintaining the borders surrounding Ta-Amenta. I recognized many of them. Some of them knew me, too. That didn't matter though, because I had to go through the same 're-entry' procedures as everyone else.

When I finally exited the last of the PSL Chambers, I was led to the usual waiting area. It's a large cafeteria, surrounded by huge tele-monitors that grow from stainless walls of flexi-glass. Rows of long rectangular windows give a most excellent view of the borders between New America and Ta-Amenta.

Kali was sitting by herself. She had found herself a booth and was looking quite ill at ease. She was drinking what appeared to be celery juice and had been crying. She managed a smiled as I approached. This did not go unnoticed. I could feel Tefnut's eye's burning a hole in the back of my head. I didn't care. I felt drawn to Kali.

"Hello, Kali," I said, sitting on the opposite side of the small table.

"Hello, Kashta," she returned.

I got the strangest feeling. *Had I done this before?* "It won't be long now. We'll be out of this place in an hour or so," I said.

"No... you will, Kashta. But where will my people and I go? This may be a Black country, but I've seen places like this before, in Valhalla," she returned. "I'm sure your administrators are going to want to talk to us, look deep into our minds," she added.

This was the first time I'd noticed how strong her accent was. It sounded like a cross between the Timeless Dialect and New American Black English

"Wait, Kali. Yes, you will have to go through more tests. But it's not what you think. It'll be in the hospital of Kawa. Kawa is the size of a small city. After your stay there, you'll be eligible to enter Ta-Amentan society-"

"So what you are saying is that we get put with the rest of the animals, the poor unfortunate Blacks who didn't have the privilege of having been born in Ta-Amenta."

Damn, she had a point. I'd never looked at it like that before. We Mesniu spend our lives rescuing Blacks from the horrors of slavery, but after we bring them here, we forget all about them. We go on about our merry lives. "Your right, Kali. I don't know what to say. I've never really thought about what happens to the Lost-Found after we bring them here." I sat there, my hands at my side. I had no words to comfort her.

Her eyes began to water. She turned and watched the NARS streak off into the northern skies.

"Will you come and see me, Kashta? I've loved you since the first moment I saw you," she said, the strength returning to her voice.

"You love me-"

"I've dreamt of you since I was a child, Kashta. I knew there would be a day when you would come for me," she returned. Her eyes were strong and determined. She reached for my hand, then continued, "I feel you, Kashta. Do you feel me?"

The words she used were hypnotic. They reminded me of the way the female Ntui Tut spoke. "I feel you, Kali. Since the first day I saw you. I'll come and visit you. I promise. But...my heart-"

"I know, Kashta. Don't say it. Just promise me you'll come and see me."

CHAPTER 24

I've been up all night. Tossing and turning; impatiently waiting for the blue yellow rays of Aten to pierce the darkness. When it finally did, I lay on my sleeper, quietly watching as soft patterns of light slowly danced across the ceiling. My muscles ached, probably because I hadn't given myself time to recover. I mean, I've been going nonstop for the past month.

I strained against gravity and walked into the dining plane to pour myself a catch of water. My entire body shivered as I stumbled across the dimly lit room. When I was finally able to seat myself, I sipped calmly; methodically recalling the conversation I had with Kali the night before. It's amazing. I was so *full* of myself, my country, so ethnocentric, that is, that I'd never really put much thought into what happens to the Lost-Found.

"Damn, she had a point," I whispered. "What happens to them? Where do they go, where do they live?" I asked myself. I couldn't shake the mental image of thousands of black men and women wasting away in sanitized hospitals. *That would make us no better than the Valhallans. Maybe they were better off without us. Who says we have the right to bring them here?*

I somberly walked over to my favorite window. It was a huge rectangular stretch, composed of the clearest silver grade glass. It faced the south. I opened it, then slid it into its separate housing shelf. Taking in the sweet morning air, my body slowly began to rejuvenate. I watched contently as the zooming Menmens raced back and forth throughout the city. In the horizon, the glare reflecting off the Pyramids made them look like stars that had fallen from heaven. *Maybe I should go and visit Kali.*

I slipped off my wears and programmed a steamy cascade in which to bathe. As soon as I stepped under it's perfectly heated falls, my multi-viewer buzzed and quaked. "This had better be important," I mumbled.

My patience was gone. The noise from the aggressive manner in which I entered my code echoed throughout my empty het (house). My flat-screen flashed several times, then shimmered into a crystal clear image.

"Hetepu, Tefnut. What's up?" I asked, looking past her cold and unresponsive glare.

Without altering her expression the slightest bit, she simply asked in her formal, this-is-all-about-business tone, "Are you watching the American Network? If you're not, you'd better switch it on. Oh yeah, the Ntiu Tut want all Mesniu, you included, at the Ka-Ba-Ra Chamber in three hours."

"What do you mean, *me included?*" I asked. Too late, she had managed to terminate her transmission before I finished my question.

I closed-out the HUSIA port on my multi-viewer and launched straight into the commercial channels. The American Network is a huge conglomerate satellite driven monster. It's the most powerful cable entity in New America. I heard the familiar rush of energy as I broke lines and penetrated into one of our sister data streams.

My mouth dropped as I watched a skinny Asian lady discuss the ramifications of the Ta-Amentan invasion of Valhalla! Images of K'HUTI and other Mesniu factions were shown against a backdrop of burning buildings.

"This is Wilma Lee, reporting live from Southern Valhalla. It appears that late Sunday evening several Ta-Amentan soldiers crossed over into the southern Valhallan territories, killing several in the process. We now turn you over live, to a news briefing being held at the Valhallan Capital." As she turned and stepped off camera, a semi-transparent frame quickly grew into a large flat-screen. Sitting in a row of Valhallan Military personnel sat Balder and several other Cold Wind Soldiers. Three official-looking men, one of whom I'm sure I'd seen before, were talking to the New American press.

"We do not understand why these people have decided to transgress against our beloved home, but rest assured we Valhallans will not take this lightly," the one in the middle said. He wore a dark suit, red tie, and a large blond braid hung across his shoulder.

"We are prepared to go to war. We stand before you and the rest of the world and suggest that this was a failed attempt at invasion! We further submit that Ta-Amentan authorities have purposely violated the Intra-Continental Treaty and are now, at this very moment, planning an attack on our Nation." This time, it was the familiar looking official who spoke. I couldn't take my eyes off of him.

More images of past battles were flashed across the screen. Then came the twist, as several pictures of dead white children were displayed against a backdrop of burning houses. A yellow caption underneath them read: killed by Ta-Amentan troops.

As the gruesome images faded, they were replaced by the three Valhallan spokesmen. They stood innocently around a holo-map of a series of Wasted Cities. That's when it came to me.

"That's the asshole from last moon, the one calling the shots in front of the Valhallan Embassy!" I jumped from my seat, heart pounding. "This isn't good; I mean the way the New American Network operates, every country in the free world will be convinced that we initiated an attack against Valhalla," I snapped.

I terminated the transmission. The soft sound of my cascade hummed in the background.

As my Men-Ab (stability) returned and I began to fully comprehend the sheer magnitude of what was happening, an even more frightening thought entered my mind.

How do I tell Warrior-King Senwosret?

* * * * *

January 16 - 21rst Century

The government of the United States had declared war on Black organizations. Chocolate cities went without electricity for weeks at a time. Food and water were luxuries, given to the frighten families who continued to cooperate with the Beast. Most refused to surrender over their sons and daughters. Throughout the community, young boys and girls dreamt of the day in which they would pass their Rites of Passage and become members of the Mesniu. They wanted to become scientists. Others looked forward to becoming artists and inventors. "All for the glory of Kush," they would say.

The highly aggressive Mesniu were the most organized and dangerous Africans in the diasporas. They were the elite; composed of the most militant men and women who had earned Double-Membership from various organizations from years past. They were secretly funded by 'well to do Blacks' and the ultra successful HUSIA endeavor. They were economically independent, respected throughout the third world, and were preparing to go to war with the newly emerging World Government.

―――――――

A borderless, faceless power moved from the shadows and stepped into the light. Project Harmony. It had become the most powerful and influential organization in the world. The Keep, born of unnatural affection, foresaw the coming of the son of man. They recruited from the richest families, and from the most prestigious universities. The minions of The Keep sowed their seeds of control through the polished policies of Project Harmony. World citizenship, unlimited trade, and free health-care, was the hook. Cameras on every street corner, state run religions, and the complete control of the music industry, was the trade. The destruction of the Black Race was the sacrifice. It was all a ritual. An arcane spell created to prolong the rule of false gods and beasts in human form.

―――――――

The armies of The Keep were legion. The showdown was at hand. Gog and MaGog had observed the rise of a new consciousness in the masses of Black people. It frightened them. For it had been prophesied that an angry Black one would rule the land between the two waters. This they could not allow. Their plans were intricate. Their control pervasive. The army of La Raza, controlled and directed by The Keep, had garnered tremendous support among the young Latino population. They had no idea whom or what they served. They flooded the streets by the millions, fighting for rights that served another purpose.

"The rise of a Black messiah will be crushed. We will use the Mexicans to win our battles on the streets, and we will manufacture a savior to placate the frightened masses who sit huddled in their homes," the shadowy figure barked. The President said nothing. He hated The Keep. They made his skin crawl. "Even now, one of our operatives is preparing to initiate our final solution. Observe," the raspy voice demanded, pointing at the huge flat screen that dominated the Oval Office.

George Cranberry, the first foreign-born citizen with a serious shot at being President of the United States, stepped onto the world stage. Like a clean cut Jesus, he appeared out of nowhere - or so it seemed. He was tall, well spoken, intelligent, and good looking. He was born and bred on the doctrines and philosophies of Project Harmony. He had money, power, and all the connections needed to facilitate a revamping of the American social fabric. His blond hair and blue eyes made him an instant smash hit to a rapidly shrinking white American public.

The Newly created Multi-Media cable station 'American Network' was the first to broadcast George Cranberry's debut speech. Millions of frightened citizens watched in quiet desperation as the tall, evenly tanned man walked to the podium in front of the White House. Clearing his throat, then tapping his mobile-comp, George Cranberry said exactly what he was trained to say.

"I stand here before you, my fellow Americans, with an awful truth. This truth may be hard for some of you to come to grips with, but eventually, you shall. I have studied the problems in America for over twenty years. I have compared our problems here in this great land with the issues and dilemmas of other people in other lands. What I have found both saddens me and liberates me at the same time." He was a good speaker. He was clean, and his words were well chosen. He sounded like a doctor, or better yet, like a barber who had just given somebody a fucked-up hair cut. He continued on by saying, "This problem I submit to you lies at the center of what keeps this great Nation from moving forward with the rest of the great nations of the world."

The camera moved in closer to his face. The tiny cracks around his blue eyes and thin lips gave him an almost reptilian appearance. He held up a computer-generated chart, showing the three primary races of man. In the center, shown with a large red circle around it, was the so-called 'Negroid' division of the human family. "Yes, ladies and gentlemen, it both saddens and hurts me to say that the problem with our country is the teeming masses of breeding Negroes, living in and around our magnificent cities." He shook his head, as if what he just said caused him pain.

"In fact, the latest demographic polls suggest that, based on the unusual reproductive capabilities of these people, our estimates show that in the next fifty to sixty years Blacks will out number White people in this country. Now, that in itself is not the problem. The problem lies in the fact that these people just aren't capable of leading this great nation. Now, before you get upset, I'd like to take the time to admit that there has been gross discrimination in the past against Negroes. There's no doubt about that. But let's forget about the past. There's nothing we can do about that. Hey, we apologize," he added. "Now I think it's time we seriously consider what the discrimination has done," he continued.

Tapping the small rectangular computer, a series of charts and graphs lit up on the huge tele-monitors behind him. They all showed the same thing, "Now look at this, ladies and gentlemen, Blacks are scientifically shown to be less intelligent, motivated, and capable of competing with the other racial and ethnic types on an even playing field. That's the result of discrimination and racism on the part of Whites; I'll be the first to admit that," he said in a mock tone. "But the bottom line is this... as a result of past wrongs committed against these people, they, and to a certain extent, other non-white populations, should be deemed inferior by virtue of past circumstances, but not by 'genetic' heritage. It's not their fault, it's not our fault, it's not anybody's fault. It's just the roll of the dice."

In every household in America with a tele-monitor, the people were mesmerized. They sat glued to their shiny flat screens. The computerized, automated polls showed that the vast majority of the viewing audience approved of George Cranberry and believed in what he was saying. The numbers were soaring.

Clearing the tele-monitors, then straightening his tie, George Cranberry, in his most eloquent voice, offered his solution to the American Race Problem, "I have proposed to the various governmental institutions, agencies, educational faculties, and private foundations a most humane way in which we as civilized people can maintain and remedy this problem once and for all," he said, slamming his fist onto the wooden podium.

"Through a combination of privately funded grants and government sponsored initiatives, I am prepared to launch the Right Way Directive. This will be a Five Year Program to safely and humanly sterilize all African and/or Black populations in the United States." The polls began to drop for about a second, then they soared even higher than they had previously been. George Cranberry continued, "Of course, this will be on a voluntary basis, but just think of it: millions of responsible Americans fulfilling their duty to themselves, their race, and their country. Oh, it just warms my heart to think of it."

"We have already gotten this Initiative on several ballots across the country. California, Utah, Texas, Mississippi, and many others have accepted this great plan of ours. And more states are joining the ranks of the sane everyday. Let's keep up the good work, America. And remember: by helping our less fortunate Americans, we help ourselves-"

———

NEW YORK

Sitting in a brightly lit room, tucked under the waving flags of a hundred nations, several men sat in front of three large flat screen tele-monitors. They were linked by satellite with their shadowy constituents, who sat deep within the stygian halls of places unknown.

"It seems that you have chosen the right man for the job," a voice said from the New York circuit.

"Yes, sir, we did indeed. Now let's see what happens after a few more months of manipulating public opinion. It'll only be a matter time before that maggot, Skah, resurfaces with a response. By then, it'll be too late," the thinly built man from Washington responded.

———

In an ocean of White hostility, Skah still had to deal with certain members in the African community. Those who had already been bought and sold were easy. They were either killed, shot down in the streets, or made deals. Names were dropped. Addresses were given, and resources were turned over. Then there were the intellectuals. The Africentric scholars who had influenced Skah's development on every level were upset. Many felt that Skah was taking credit for teachings he did not create.

In the new headquarters of the Mesniu, the members sat impatiently as several Africentric scholars yelled in protest. The small walls of the red brick building vibrated as each Black scholar took turns protesting Skah's supposed arrogance.

"How dare you suggest that you are responsible for this body of work?" Minister Tut shouted. "I remember when you were just a snot-nosed boy who sat at my feet! Now you're talking about the things I taught you as if you're the teacher!" he added. Huffing and puffing, he angrily took his seat.

"That's right!" Dr. Jackson added. "All of the political and economic doctrines you people use, we taught it to you."

"And don't forget the books we've written," Professor Africa said sternly. "All of our books are sitting back there on your shelves. You've taken what we've written-"

"And took it to the next level!" Nzinga interrupted. "Look, we love you brothers and sisters. We will be eternally grateful for all of your hard work. But is not the student supposed to stand on the shoulders of the teacher? Is not the student supposed to see further as a result of that position?" she asked, holding back her scorpion's sting.

"Besides, beloved scholars, none of you have been able to do what we have done. Don't look at Skah as if he deliberately tried to steal your thunder. He sacrificed himself for you. We will never allow the world to forget from whom and where we've learned the things we now bring to the masses. But none of you ever attempted to put the body of Ausar back together," Kafra said. He and Charles X were sitting next to Skah. Skah said nothing.

"What do you mean he sacrificed himself for us? Just what the hell are you people tying to say?" Sister Dr. Melanin asked, her stack of books falling as she stood.

"Listen," Skah interrupted, "I know from whom and where I received the teachings. My mother... my father, and all of you. There is no doubt about that," Skah added, then clearing his throat, "But I felt that by going on point, that would force the enemy's hand. It's time to resurrect Ausar! No more bullshit! We can't just keep giving speeches, taking the peoples money, writing books, and shit like that. Just as you have taught all of us, Minister Tut, I have journeyed to the great waters. I understand that there will never be a perfect time to act, to move. We can't sit around watching the clouds and waiting for some sort of magical sign. Now is the time!"

Professor Ra was not amused, "Who are you to decide on the lives of the people? Who are you-"

"I'm the one who's going to take the heat!" Skah returned sharply. "I'm the one who was labeled a sworn enemy of the United States. When they come for me, I'll be ready. Will you?"

"We'll all be ready, Skah. For you and everybody else," Amani interjected. "And all of you will take your place among the people as scholars, as teachers. We are Mesniu. We are the Warrior-Soldiers in this Great War. We have been charged with the resurrection of Ausar! When they come for us, you must continue to teach the people. But be warned, you must teach them the Spiritual Cultivation System as taught by our ancestors. Nothing else will do. If you transgress, we will come for you," Amani added, staring the elders down.

"What is this... this... cultivation system you people keep speaking about?" Professor Ra asked, his demeanor changing, calming.

"The African Diaspora is being taught to view itself as Ausar. And so it becomes the responsibility of the community to follow in the footsteps of Auset. We will reassemble the body of Ausar...the Black community. Just as our ancient story goes, the scattered remains will be pieced together. Then each segment of the community will be assigned a responsibility," Skah returned.

The Elders sat stoically, their eyes intense, their imaginations captivated. Nzinga continued, "The Entertainment and Sports world has been assigned the awesome task of providing the economics to and for the community. It's the only avenue towards true economic independence. Billions of dollars have been amassed by Black folks over the years, and with the loss of the natural resources on the African Continent, any and all funds are being drawn from the entertainment and athletic spheres. Within five years of this newfound co-operation, the African American population will be richer for it."

"The Scientific community, having been funded and financed by a highly conscious Black sports and entertainment engine, has been assigned the task of developing new and improved ways for bettering the standards of living for the human family in general, and Black people in particular. They are expected to continue the traditions of Black scholars from the beginning of time. Scientific innovations and brand new technologies will be developed for the community. All manner of scientific discoveries are being made by Black folks as we speak. Along with these re-discoveries come patents," Nefertari chimed in.

Charles-X was not to be left out, "The Educational sphere has been assigned the responsibility for perpetuating Black Culture. That's why the world government... this Project Harmony shit, is pumping out all this new crap. Diseases, manufactured wars... anyway, unlike what happened in the late twentieth-century, with none of the 'Black dollars' circulating in the community, Africentric schools are being raised with 'Black money.' The schools are based on an ancient Spiritual model of strength, self-discipline, inner growth, and respect and knowledge of self."

"And for those who served in the armed forces... who were discharged for one reason or another... these brothers and sisters may not have had a home in America's armies, but they have become welcomed soldiers in our community. Their expertise is what made Mesniu what it is. They safeguard our community! Who do you think... no, scratch that... how do you think we've been able to keep La Raza and MS-13 off our ass?" Amani interrupted.

———

'Ausar lives again' became the new battle cry. As the consciousness of black people changed, so did the language. However the struggle to build a powerful and vigorous Nation of Black people from within the belly of the beast did not go unchallenged. The Owners, the real power players, the true shot-callers, brought their *chippers* online. Media messiahs, agenda setters, movie directors, radio personalities, educators, and the world-information machine, began to manufacture a climate of fear. This, with the Government sponsored RWD, would usher in a dark era in American history. These were the times of the Race Wars...

* * * * *

It never fails; I mean, about walking up to the Ka-Ba-Ra Chamber. Its broad sweeping angles, its beautifully sculptured corners, its overall size; this place always gives me a sense of awe. And then there's the gathering. The men and women sworn to give their lives in service of Ta-Amenta. To independence. I'm a part of that team. We are known throughout the world as Warrior-Soldiers. I'm one of the best. I'm K'HUTI.

I respectfully greeted the numerous Mesniu who stood in and around its huge double doors. In typical Black fashion, the brothas and sistahs were highly animated in their conversations and perfectly sharp in their blue and black unifs. When the Great Chime rang in its sequence of thunderous melodic tones, we were rushed into the building by Mafdet warriors; the look of death shown in their eyes.

We piled into the Great Conference Room. Its seats were arranged such that they surrounded the immense center stage, creating the illusion of a half moon laying in the center of a lake. On the stage itself stood the Ntiu Tut. They sat in what seemed like suspended animation, their faces set in black, brown, red, and yellow stone. As usual, I found a seat in the third row. I hated sitting in the back; it always felt like I was missing something. In the southern corner of the Great Conference Room stood The Grand Recorder. He or she - we never knew, they always wore full Ceremonial Regalia - stood in front of the 'electronic columns.' Turning, then walking in slow deliberate rhythms, the Grand Recorder activated several silvery flat organic terminals. Then the large flexible screens began to flicker, casting a light blue glow on and around the Ceremonial Tehuti Raiment the Grand Recorder wore.

As if on cue, the Mesniu became quiet. The Grand Recorder stepped away from the electronic columns as the center of the stage illuminated, showing three rows of seated Ntiu Tut.

In slow deliberate movements, Shekem't Ti approached the front of the stage, stopping at its smooth cut edge. She smiled, surveying the crowd, and displayed a peaceful charm and grace. She clapped her hands three times, driving away the negative energies. She then cleared her throat and spoke.

"Hetepu, men and women of the Mesniu. I'm quite sure most of you know why we have summoned you all here today. Well, it looks like once again war threatens the sanctity of our beloved Ta-Amenta. It seems that despite all we have been through, we still have not learned that most valuable of lessons." Shekhem't Ti sounded more disappointed than anything else. She just stood there, staring at us.

Shekhem Muntu was next to stand. He patted Shekhem't Ti on the shoulder, then walked over towards the Grand Recorder, posting up next to him - or maybe her; we never knew. They both stood motionless, surveying the crowd. I stopped paying attention. I was more interested in finding Tefnut.

"It seems that the Valhallans are in need of a battle. Our sources tell us that due to transgressions on our part, the Valhallans have been ordered by the ones whom they serve, to destroy the glory of Ta-Amenta. This we can never allow; not now, not when we are so close to fulfilling our Great destiny as a people." Shekhem Muntu ended his conversation with us on that note. He was good for that, a master of suspense.

"There's Warrior-King Senwosret," I whispered. The Warrior-King was in the front row with the other Supreme M'sha (soldiers of all kinds). I wonder if... too late, He knows I'm here. As long as I live, I'll never know how he does that. It's like he can read our minds, feel our presence. He's always a step ahead of us. My heart stopped as he turned and made eye contact with my person. He nodded his head, a slight smile shown on his face.

Shekhem Tao stood and joined Shekhem Muntu and the Grand Recorder. He is one of the oldest of the Ntiu Tut. It is said that he once transcended his mortal form and held council with the ALL IN ALL. "We have been forbidden by Divine Law to interfere with the workings of the Mesniu. It is ordained that each of you must grow Spiritually without our direct help. All beings must do so. Tell me, Supreme M'sha, have the Mesniu forgotten their true purpose... their ultimate destiny? I think they have. They... you, only believe in bloodshed. You have become the aggressors. You fight for sport, for lust, for greed. Because you are short sighted, our original purpose has been lost. We travel in circles, Sebek laughs." Turning, Shekhem Tao walked back towards the rest of the Ntiu Tut. "I am tired, I don't want to look at any of you any longer," he said, taking his seat. Seconds later, he was in deep trance.

Shekhem't Ari't was next. She is known as the fiery one. The entire Mesniu braced itself for a real tongue lashing. "Yes, it seems my dear brother is correct. The Mesniu are out of control. They no longer remember their sacred code of honor. Even now, we give them the answers, and still they sit there. The light shines in the darkness, but the darkness comprehends it not." She joined Shekhem't Ti at the edge of the sparkling stage. Like two beautiful Black Doves, they looked into our hearts, our minds.

Was all of this the result of our having gone into Quadrant-4? We broke no Divine Laws. We went in the name of love, of MAAT. This 'meeting' was getting stranger by the moment. The Ntiu Tut, huddled in thought, in meditation, spoke in hidden inclinations and secret codes.

CHAPTER 25

I sat alone. Lost in thought in one of the Round Rooms in the east wing of the Ka-Ba-Ra Chamber. *How many Round Rooms were there?* I couldn't help wondering. I fell in and out of trance. My body swayed rhythmically to the thunderous claps of my heart. Cold Wind was getting closer. I could almost feel them... hundreds of Valhallan troops marching just north of the Aztlann borders. And to make matters worse, the Americans have joined them. They were preparing to march on my beloved country. Our little excursion into Quadrant-4 was exactly what the Valhallans needed... an excuse to supersede the North American Intracontinental Treaties... to make war. The Ntiu Tut warned us about this. But I didn't listen. Now we as a people stand at the gates of destiny. Will *RA* shine once more upon our faces?

––––––––––

The sky was black. Streams of smoke and ash rose in thick columns - painting tired clouds in a glistening film of soot. Beneath a jagged skyline, the bodies of the dead lay in twisted heaps. The fighting began almost three nights ago. Such is always the case. By the time the general public finds out about a so-called impending war, we're already counting the dead.

Like shadows, we silently 'fell' just south of an abandoned city. Resembling giant black reptiles, the NARs shiny dragon-like wings folded, then slid into their housing. Shimmering, their special Melanin polymer surfaces absorbed the ambient light, hiding them. We've managed to slip in undetected. At least for now.

We're professionals. Before the dust on the trees disturbed by our landing reaches the ground, we're out of the NARs, and sizing up our environment. There were no sounds. I'm on point as usual; Delta formation, five het-meter spread. We stay close and huddle near the abandoned storefronts. We move in and out of the dim, like ghosts. In many ways, that's just what we are.

Upon reaching the edge of a large avenue, I motioned to the ground. My Pod froze. Pointing, I drew their attention to the half hidden figures crouching near a row of buildings that stood across a sea of cracked tar.

We stood there, watching, waiting. The natural light that shown on their grayish forms gave no indication of identity. At first, I thought maybe they were Isolate Klansmen.

"They spotted us," I relayed to my Pod. One of them raised the Mesniu sign for unity. An upheld fist. We returned the gesture, our daath-Geb reflecting the dull grey-white flecks from the walls of the Wasted City.

"They must be the *First*, Kashta," Tefnut said. She had managed to get herself assigned with me.

"Let's join Pods," I snapped. "Be careful, though. We may not be able to see them, but I'd bet the stars that Cold Wind is all around us," I added. About halfway between the location of the first Pod and the safety of the huge leaning tower we were hiding under, I waved my team on, urging them to hurry. "Let's go! We don't have all night!"

Rushing past the crag, we found ourselves in the presence of a Pod of beleaguered war-torn Mesniu.

"Where's the rest of your team?" Ra'mesh asked, tossing a slim of med-packs.

"They've gone on with the ancestors," a familiar voice rumbled. I immediately recognized its owner. His ren (name) was Asa. Been around for a long time, a serious Warrior-Soldier. In fact, I served under his command in North Africa three years ago. "The second Pod are held up about two het-meters north," he added.

"What are we up against?"

"Two, maybe three full Valhallan units... backed by New Americans."

"What are they carrying?"

"Attack-jeeps, Mercury cannons, you know, the usual... got a film crew too."

"Filming what?"

"Don't know, don't care, Kashta." Asa waved his hand, motioning to a frail-looking officer standing at the far end of the charred alley. The young woman came running, her daath-Geb mask pulled back and away from her face.

She stopped beside Asa, then handed him a thin stack of blue sheets. Reconpeep-slides. Asa shuffled through them, then handed them to me.

I thumbed through them. "Okay... so the Valhallans are bringing the muscle. The Americans are bringing the tech... hmnn... been here for a while." The shiny blue pages held images of half-built structures. Attack-jeeps were on some of the pages. Gunships were on others.

"How did we miss this?" Tefnut asked.

"Wait, it gets better." Asa reached into a tiny flex-pouch underneath the tattered left breastplate of his daath-Geb. He then pulled out a large transparent grey and blue schematic. Taking it, I began to examine its shiny surface.

The schematic showed rows of Valhallan troops. They looked like ants marching over brown and green waves. "Okay... so we're going to need back-up. This is definitely Heavy Ground."

"What else do you see?" Asa asked, sounding more like a Ntiu Tut than a Warrior-Soldier. "Look at the top of the schematic. The northern parts." He pointed to an area just below the thick yellowish border of the large photograph. At first, I didn't see what he was referring to. My eyes continued to scan the diagram.

"Hmnn... they've managed to construct a storage facility this far south... wow... confidence is high."

Anpu held the schematic over his head, rotating it slowly. "That's a storage facility. But something's not right," he added.

Tefnut and Ra'mesh examined the rectangular map, spreading it to its limits. "Look at how far the Cold Wind unit is from the storage facility," Ra'mesh said, looking at Asa.

I stood next to Tefnut. I stared at the huge blocky building. I looked at its dimensions, its entrance, the material it was constructed from. "This is a 'front'. They're not invading at all. That entire complex is probably loaded down with food... nothing more."

Asa smiled. Winking his eye, he took the schematic from me and held it so that everyone could see it.

"That's correct, Kashta, it's not a real invasion. It's basically a decoy. They want us to watch this so-called unit, while they're fighters keep going south, into the Ta-Amentan/Aztlann border. They'll justify their military 'build-up,' if you will, by mentioning the so-called Ta-Amentan invasion. It's all a game," he ended, handing the schematic back to me.

"Alright. The Valhallans have seeded the world into thinking that they are building-up their forces in response to the Ta-Amentan invasion. While the world watches and waits, they secretly slip through the southern parts of sector 12; the border regions," I repeated.

"That's correct. We engaged the northern unit yesterday. They were heavily armed, but they were basically on a suicide run. They probably didn't know it, though. Anyway, that's when we noticed the New American cameramen filming us. It was all a setup." Asa was straight and to the point. "Tomorrow, we send half of the Mesniu to observe and report... just to keep an eye out. The rest of us will locate, assess, and eliminate our prime target." Having said that, Asa turned and walked towards the rear of the alley we had been using as cover.

"How close?" I yelled after him.

Without turning, he answered, "About two hours away... south." Then he disappeared within the dust and mist of the concrete enclosure.

———————

Two hours melted into seven. Aten stood scorching, hanging in mid-air like a gigantic yellow eye. Moving through the dense underbrush, we sweated in our daath-Geb. Its temperature regulating systems strained to make its internal environment bearable for us. Our Colbot-rifles held low, our wave-jumpers surfed the Zero-frequency; our faces, hidden behind its leathery plates. *Just another day on the job.*

In three sweeping rows, we ran, walked, and leapt over and across the damp leafy forest floor. For the first time in many months, I was not in command. I was under the direction of a senior officer, Asa. He was about five het-meters ahead of me, strong, determined, experienced. He was what I would someday become.

"Alright, people, we've found what we've been looking for. Remember, let's keep the MAAT (stay calm)." Asa's voice sounded like a quiet storm sweeping across our wave-jumpers. "West Pod, move right and south. East Pod, move left and south. Go," he snapped.

I was on the East team. Ra'mesh, RaSol, and Sumanguru, were with me. We moved in lightning quick flashes - darting in and out of the bush like blue-black angels of death. The West team was no less dangerous. Tefnut, Anlamani, and Sefuwa, to name a few, moved away; disappearing into the green, looking very much like a mirror image of ourselves. Asa's Pod remained in place - their daath-Geb shimmering in and out of focus.

"When you reach the edge of the clearing, remain in place. We'll plan-up together; over the Zero-frequency," Asa instructed.

Ten het-meters before we reached what appeared to be an embankment, we dropped to our bellies and crawled the rest of the way. That's when we found them.

They were located in a fairly large man-made gorge. It was shaped like a huge rectangle. Three hundred het-meters across by six hundred het-meter long. Its floor was covered in bright yellow-red dirt, and its dried mud walls were surrounded by trees and thick vegetation. Fifty Cold Wind Soldiers worked feverishly under the hot sun. Like a colony of albino ants, they had managed to partially construct a Terrestrial Holo Dish. It sat comfortably on a sandy hill. Its three large support beams stretched from its base and bit greedily into the soft earth.

I examined the strange tower closely. Its tangled, glistening, and metallic columns gave it a kind of organic look. The Valhallans were master craftsmen. This thing would allow them to 'take' a picture of the entire border regions. Our defenses would be wide open. Two small jeeps slid back and forth across the sand. They pulled logs up and away from the THD. The men said nothing as they worked. They just followed the dictates of their commanding officer.

He stood over them like a blond 'watch dog.' He was heavily armed. Carrying his standard issued Valhallan Mercury-cannon, his movements were determined and powerful.

"South Pod, cover the mouth of the depression, make sure no one gets in or out. By last count, they shouldn't get another delivery for about an hour." Asa had it all figured out. He was one of the best K'huti I'd ever seen. "West Pod, you flush them away from the mouth, herd them towards the north, towards us," he added. "We'll do the rest."

"How much time have we got?" I asked.

Laughter.

"As usual, Kashta battles Chronos. Good question, little brotha. Anyway, we've got less than 45 minutes before the New American film crew gets here. I expect to be done in 20."

I looked at my companions. They returned my glances. I couldn't see their faces, but I often looked at the people closest to me before battle. They could very well be the last brothas and sistas I'd see in this plane of existence. Turning, I prepared to serve my people. That's when my mind began to drift. I couldn't help thinking about what the Ntiu Tut had said at the briefing a few days ago. How we had forgotten our true purpose... our destiny.

I thought about Asa. He was a master at this game. It's what he's done all his life. He was a Warrior-Soldier, pure and simple. Was that my destiny, to be a killer for the rest of my days? I wondered what Tefnut was doing.

I squeezed my palms, causing my daath-Geb to discharge all accumulated wastes. I slowly pulled my Colbot-rifle from its housing and waited for Asa's command.

Just when I thought we would never attack... we did. It started in a blaze of crimson fire and quickly melted into blue streaks of death. The cries of startled men soon followed. The West Pod had done its job. The Cold Wind unit was caught off guard. They tried to escape by retreating deeper into the artificial depression... towards us.

"We're under attack!" they shouted, running in every direction.

"Fall back, fall back!" they screamed. The twenty or so men working on the THD dropped their clamps, their lasers, and their polymer mesh screens, then raced for their weapons.

"Steady now, people... steady..." Asa's voice was as calm as ever. It hardly made a ripple over the wave-jumper's static detector. We calmed ourselves in the shadowy underbrush. Our actions hanging on Asa's every word. Our bodies were tense. Our muscles ached to explode. We watched and waited as the Cold Wind unit frantically stumbled over and on top of each other.

In the distance, we watched as the West Pod jumped and danced over the bodies of the fallen. There it was again, the rhythm of battle. It just happens. It was like a soft, deep wave. It made everything move in slow motion and caused all sound to disintegrate. The Mesniu called it *The Song of Heru K'huti*. The Ntiu Tut called it *The Wave of Death*.

CHAPTER 26

It was like a moment looped in time. The screams, burning foliage, and the vapor-like haze of heat radiating from the ground gave everything a surreal quality. I was frozen, caught in the grip of an awful beauty. That's when my spirit took over. Without my conscious consent, I turned towards the grass green tent that served as their command station. My heart dropped as I watched their commanding officer rush from its slit of an entrance. His rifle in hand, his blood stained sword hung at his side, and his long blond hair was pulled back in a thick yellow braid.

"Balder..."

My trance was broken. And just in time. Asa's voice thundered across my wave-jumper. The six of us leapt to our feet, then managed to stumble down the shallow embankment. In controlled bursts of blue light, we covered one another during our descent.

"What the hell is going on? How did these monkeys know we were here?" one of them shouted. He dropped his portable-comp, and sprang for his weapon.

"Kashta, cut their throat!" Asa shouted, pointing to a short, lightly built man who appeared to be their com-officer. *I wanted Balder.*

"What about their commander-"

"Forget him, just do as I say," Asa snapped.

Then in an obscene display of power and speed, Balder struck down two K'huti. Just like that, no words, only death. My blood started to boil.

"How much time?" Anpu shouted, crouched behind a huge tree.

"Less than 15 minutes, people! Let's end this," Asa roared.

We pressed on, shooting, yelling, and avoiding the red flashes of death that spilled snakelike from their rifles.

"Ra'mesh, Amaadi, Osei, plant the Sparks, let's shut their eyes," I said, pointing at the THD. In quick frantic bursts, the three men danced their way towards the Holo-Dish. In frantic clips, they began securing the explosives. Disobeying orders, I continued to track Balder. He'd managed to slip off into the bush.

"Kashta, where the hell are you going? I thought I told you-"

I turned in time to see Asa shot... point-blank! Square in the chest. And though his daath-Geb took most of the heat and force, he was blown from his feet like an ebony rag-doll.

"Asa!" Tefnut raced passed me. Avoiding the crimson rain, she stepped and wriggled her way to our fallen commander. Ignoring her own safety, she kneeled beside Asa's limp body and held his head gently in her arms.

"How is he?"

"He's okay, no thanks to you. What's wrong with you, Kashta? It's like I don't even know you anymore!"

I pretended not to hear her. *Hell, maybe she was right.*

"I've got something to do, Tefnut. Just keep him safe." I ran passed her and joined Anpu behind a row of large trees. I pulled my daath-mask over and away from my face. The smell of scorched flesh assaulted my nostrils.

"How many are left?"

"Counting us, seven," Anpu returned. "Over there," he said pointing. Ra'mesh and Amaadi were crawling away from the half finished THD. They'd successfully managed to plant the *Sparks*. Osei wasn't so lucky. His limp body lay in the dirt and sand, half buried under its cold metal leg. "Look," Anpu said again, directing my attention towards the north end of the small enclosure. Tefnut had actually dragged Asa's racked body just beyond the green thicket near the edge of the artificial forest. They were still easy targets, though.

"When those explosives go off, it'll only be a matter of time before the whole world closes in on this place."

"So what's your point, Kashta?" Anpu demanded.

"My point... my point is I've got business to take care of. Long over due business. If I'm not back in 10 minutes, get the hell out of here!"

"Not good... not good. This is not the time for revenge, Kashta. What about everything we've been taught? Everything we stand for?"

"I'm serious, Anpu... just make sure the rest of the team makes it out of here!"

For the first time since I've joined the Mesniu, I was willfully disobeying a direct order. There was no turning back now.

The Cold Wind Soldiers were starting to regroup. They had managed to find cover on the northeast end of the small gully. Surrounded by a thick patch of trees and protected by a medium sized wall of boulders, they began to fortify their attack. Thanks to me, they still had contact with their northern unit.

"Kashta!" Asa bellowed. "Whatever it is you're going through, I suggest you let it pass. Get the rest of the Pod and pull out!"

I ignored him.

Kneeling down next to Anpu, I finally admitted what my intentions were, "I'm going after Balder."

"No shit, Kashta! You're risking everything. And just to get back at someone who means nothing... less than nothing-" shaking his head, he pointed to a section of the gorge where the Cold Wind unit were held up. "Over there," he said pointing, "Balder."

He was yelling at some of his soldiers. They kept looking at the Holo-Dish, and then back at him.

"The Birth NAR will be here in seven minutes; let's get the hell out of here! Now, K'huti!" Asa was in pain.

Patting Anpu on the shoulder, I eased my way past him and disappeared into the maley. I stayed close to the edge of the greenery... and effortlessly slipped into waking-trance. It was a mess, blue and red flashes crisscrossed back and forth across the gully floor. The bodies of the dead lay in and around the small enclosure. Osei, Mafdet, RaSol, all good Warrior-Soldiers, would never know another sunrise. Their 'preprogrammed' daath-Geb was already causing their limp bodies to mummify rapidly.

I continued to stalk my prey. I watched him from the green, my heart beating in slow deliberate rhythms. My breathing was deep, my consciousness focused. *Was I being driven by hate?* I asked myself. *Had I lost my 'Men Ab em Aungkh em Maat' to such a degree that I no longer knew right from wrong?* For a brief moment, I hesitated, not knowing if I should continue. I stood less than five het-meters away from one of my most hated enemies. Watching him from underneath the forest canopy, my mind flashed back to what the Ntiu Tut had said days earlier. They said the Mesniu had forgotten our destiny. They said we no longer followed the path of MAAT. *Perhaps they were right.*

Over the years, we Mesniu had become accustomed to war. We actually looked forward to it. The Valhallans were our sworn enemies, and we hated them. Finding new ways to protect Ta-Amentan interests became our sole purpose. We'd forgotten our history, why K'huti had been created back in the days before the formation of the Nation-States. In the beginning, the Mesniu were rarely aggressive. The founders followed the ways of MAAT more closely than we do today. They did not find pleasure in battle as we do now. Hate did not drive them. Hate did not govern their behavior.

I am K'huti. We operate under a different set of rules. We move in extreme circumstances. It was no use; no matter how hard I tried, I couldn't forget my oath, my responsibilities to my people. I pulled my daath-mask up and over my face and head. I dropped to one knee, my right hand covering my heart, my left hand raised toward the heavens. "I did not forget why the Mesniu, and therefore the K'huti, were created. It was not for war. It was not to inflict unjust pain and suffering on our enemies. No, that is the way of the Valhallans, of the New Americans," I yelled to the heavens... to the stars.

The Mesniu were created in the tradition of Heru K'huti. We strike only when threatened. We make war only after all other options have been exhausted. And the K'huti, the best of the best of the Mesniu, move in the memory of Auset. We have been charged with the responsibility of rescuing our brothas and sistas who have been made into slaves. We strike under the cover of darkness. We move in the shadows.

"Perhaps the Ntiu Tut were right. Maybe we did forget our destiny," I whispered. Everything stopped. Looking towards the heavens, I glimpse eternal Ra. Smiling, I said into my wave-jumper; to Tefnut, "On this day, I remember. We Mesniu must never stop. We must forever push forward. Our destiny is to remove every Black man and woman from the ignorance of themselves. In the tradition of Auset, we must restore the body together. We must resurrect Ausar. That's why there have been so many excursions into Quadrant-4, not to do battle with Cold Wind. No. That is and was a colossal waste of time-"

"Kashta, what are you doing?" Tefnut barked. "What's wrong with-"

"Don't you see, Tefnut? It was the Isolate Klans we should have been after. That's what the Ntiu Tut meant when they said we'd forgotten our true destiny. Our purpose is not to continue fighting the Valhallans...or the Americans until the end of time. Our purpose is to find and rescue our people who are spiritually and mentally dead. Yes, we are K'huti. We honor the Laws of Maat. And as long as those Laws are trampled on, Maat, harmony, peace are all unreachable."

And so it was... on the blood stained dirt of the battle fields where I discovered the true purpose of the Mesniu; where I came to my senses. Lifting my wave-jumper to my dry mouth, I spoke to my commanding officer. "Asa, this is Kashta. I'm pulling out, sir."

There was silence at first, then a deep calm voice lifted from the tiny melcrom speakers, "I thought we'd lost you, Kashta. What's your location?" he returned.

"I'm on the northeast embankment, just behind the Cold Wind unit," I returned, watching the frantic white soldiers shoot wildly into the western edges of the manmade forest. "How much time have I got?"

"Less than five minutes. You'd better double-time it. The Birth NAR will be here in two."

Damn it, Chronos. I only had one way back. I'd have to cut straight across the floor of the huge gorge. I'd be an easy target. "Asa, are Tefnut and Anpu with you?"

"Tu (yes). What's up?"

"I'm going to make this a straight dash, right across the gully floor-"

"That's not a bad idea, Kashta." It was Anpu. "Use the THD as a shield, we'll cover you from here."

"Be careful, Kashta," Tefnut added.

Pulling myself up and through the thick vegetation, I waited at the edge of the forest. Preparing to step onto the sandy bottom, I was amazed to see three Cold Wind Soldiers race towards the THD.

"They're going for the Sparks, Kashta!" Anpu snapped. In the distance, I watched him and Tefnut emerge from the protection of the trees. By the time the three Cold Wind Soldiers reached the base of the Holo-Dish, they were exchanging heavy fire. I had to do something.

I stepped from the shadows, determined and focused. So did Balder.

"I told you I'd kill you, nigger." He pulled his diamond wedge blade from its side holster and rushed me. Using my now empty rifle as a weapon, I swung it wildly at Balder, striking him on the arm.

Yelling, he dropped his blade. "Come on!" He was furious. He hated me as much as I hated him.

"Kashta, we don't have time for this, let's get the hell out of here!"

I couldn't. In one swift motion, Balder rushed me. We collided like two great forces. The immovable object meets the irresistible force. Thousands of years of hate locked arms and strained for an advantage.

"You're a dead nigger!" Balder was full of rage. He was the type who used his emotions to power his actions.

Freeing my right arm from his vise-like grip, I doubled over and shoved my elbow into his abdomen.

The air rushed from his body. Yelling and coughing, he was quick to recover. "Is that the best you can do, nigger?" He was strong, and probably as fast me. Moving with dizzying speed, he completed a left spin kick and caught me flush on the right side of my head.

I slammed into the hard trunk of an old tree. I felt everything. My daath-Geb was 'soft', my face-plate hung limp around my neck. I didn't have time to adjust. When my vision finally cleared, he'd managed to get both hands around my neck. "Die, you sack of mud!" he yelled, foam spilling from his mouth.

I gave him two quick and powerful blows to the heart. Coughing, he released my neck and stumbled backwards. I pushed off the base of the tree and slammed into him. We both fell over, rolling in the dirt like animals. Punching and scratching, snorting and huffing, we broke away from each other. Our hate was real, it was tangible, and it would not be denied.

"Let's get this over with, caveman," I taunted. He spit in my face.

Yelling, he gritted his teeth and charged. We locked arms for a second time. For what seemed like days, we struggled for supremacy. This was not simply a fight between two men. It was much larger than that. It was the clash of ideologies, of distinct cultures. We were a drop of water in an ocean of time. We continued the battle that had raged since The Days Of Heru. Balder was a vicious fighter. His every move was intended to inflict maximum damage, pain, and suffering.

I was running out of time. My private war had to end here... now. I observed my person. My breathing was on time. Deep, not shallow. I sang The Chant of Death as I lowered my right shoulder, then twisted and lowered my body under Balder's. Holding onto his left arm, I swung him around so that our backs met. Without letting him recover, and ignoring his curses, I reached up and back, grabbing his head and neck in a reverse sun-lock. Instinctively, he started tearing and scratching at my hands and arms. I anchored my palms under and around his chin and throat. I pulled with all my strength. Straining, I lifted his struggling body from the ground. Then, in one supreme effort, with both hands locked around his neck, I violently flexed and jerked forward.

The dull sound of snapping bone and tearing gristle invaded my ears. Balder's body shivered and jigged, then finally went limp. I lowered him to the rocky earth. I rolled him over. A pool of deep red blood gushed from his mouth. His eyes remained opened. Even in death, he held a look of hatred on his face. I stood over Balder's ragged form. I expected sorrow, relief. I felt nothing.

"Kashta, let's go!" Tefnut snapped. She stood at the base of the Birth NAR. Anpu and Sumanguru were frantically carrying Asa to the ship, as several Mesniu stood alongside its black sleek body.

Rising up and away from the smoldering cut-out of a valley, we shielded our eyes as the light from the Sparks destroyed the Valhallan THD.

"Are you alright, Kashta?" Tefnut asked, holding my bandaged hand.

"Tu. How are you?" I returned. This was the most we've said to each other since returning from Q-4.

"I'm good," she said, sitting next to me.

"Listen, Tefnut. I'm sorry for how I've behaved. Listen, I-"

"I see you two have made up." Anpu said. I hadn't noticed before, but he'd been shot several times. His daath-Geb was torn to shreds. He placed it across a nearby seat on the NAR, then plopped down. He then tore a piece of it off and ate it. He was one of the only people I knew who actually liked the stuff.

"Great timing, Anpu," I said.

"Oh… sorry about that," he returned, a sly smile on his face. "Hey, Sumangura, what you got there?" Anpu bounced from his seat and joined the remaining team who sat huddled around Asa.

"Tefnut, listen. I haven't been true to myself, or you. I've been afraid. Mostly about how I've felt about…"

"Alright, young lady, you're next." it was a Med-Officer. Tehuti Klan. His blue ibis shaped badge beamed from his chest. Letting out a sigh, Tefnut kissed me on the cheek, then followed the slender man to the rear of the NAR.

CHAPTER 27

I've been indoors for what seemed like years. Lounging around my het, eating too much, and watching the American Networks. It's strange. They have yet to mention last month's operation. *That figures, typical American cover-up.* Sluggishly, I pulled myself from my cushion and walked to my food-space. Finding a bag of herbal tea, I placed it in a ceramic catch of water and began to heat it. Its sweet melodic fragrance gently lifted my ailing spirit.

It was still dark; Aten had yet to pierce the dawn. "Now would be a perfect time for meditation," I proclaimed to my spirit. I found and then placed a round chair on my outdoor patio. I seated myself in the proper position and began to take deep rhythmic breaths. It wasn't long before I felt my true-self separate from my physical person. The pain and grief that so afflicted me for the past few weeks slowly drifted away. I chanted a 'Healing Mantra.' Its life giving vibrations mended and repaired my person.

Aten had risen partway between the horizon and its zenith. In a blue-yellow concert, its life-giving rays struck and bounced along the surface of the earth. It's a new day. I am born again. When I engage my person in intensive meditative sessions, I lose sight of my immediate environment. Today is no exception. My tea had overcooked; the water evaporated. "Oh, well," I said to myself, "life continues."

Stretching, I picked up my round chair and returned to the comfort of my het. I was starting to feel pretty good. This was going to be a great day, a day of judgment and change. My morning rituals complete, I finally noticed that there were several messages blinking across my multi-viewer. Two were from my parents. There was a message from Anpu. Several from Tefnut, and one from the Ka-Ba-Ra Chamber. Using my finger, I physically pointed to the message from the Ka-Ba-Ra Chamber. The silvery rectangular box that held the message began to flash. Seconds later, it grew, filling the entire screen.

It was from Warrior-King, Senwosret. *And it wasn't bad news*. He basically wanted me to enjoy myself today. When the message ended, its box shrank, retaining its original size and shape. With a sigh of relief, I leaned back in my chair. Thinking about the wonderful day ahead, I couldn't help but smile. I then touched the message box from my parents. It shimmered, then flexed to full screen size.

It was from my father. In his usual 'short and to the point' approach, he was glad that I had made it home okay and that he and mom would see me later.

"Cool."

It was getting late. *I had better get started*, I thought. Pushing away from my still warm multi-viewer, I waved the power off and got up for a cascade (shower).

The streets were particularly crowded. Bright-eyed Ta-Amentans were busily going in and out of the various markets; no doubt engaged in last minute shopping for their loved ones. On my way to the Central Menmen Station, I noticed the Sacred Incense burning at almost every Temple.

The Menmens were running every fifteen minutes today. They normally run every hour. Today was a special day though. It is the day in which we Ta-Amentans regard as a very significant time in the lives of our younger citizens. In the tradition of our people, it is known as the 'Wehemi Mesu,' or the 'Time of Rebirth.' It is the graduation, or 'Rites of Passage' from one stage of existence into the next. It is a most important time in a young person's life. It is when they leave the dominion of childhood and join the ranks of those striving to qualify to become adults.

The Menmen was crowded. I stood in the center aisle, allowing the elders to seat themselves. Upon approaching Napata, I noticed how quiet it was. There were no vehicles streaming in and out of its normally busy streets. There were no Menmens streaking to and from the main centers. All was still, as it should be on this day.

Just beyond the great economic capital of Napata, is the Ka-Ba-Ra Chamber. Its huge gleaming presence looked strangely peaceful. On any other day, I would stop at the next station, joining my fellow Mesniu to walk within its Sacred Chambers and Secret Rooms.

We continued on, heading west at a fantastic speed. We soon came upon the Sacred Space of Sekert. It is here where our great Temple Cities are built. Gigantic gleaming pyramids, lofty towers, and the statues of the Honored Ancestors are placed in geometric perfection throughout this most majestic landscape. Today however, there is but one city that we long for. On.

It is here, in the fabulous city of On, where we conduct our most sacred rituals. We embalm and mummify the bodies of the Ntiu Tut, our Kings, and our beloved Queens. It is here where we lay to rest all of the men and women who have devoted their lives to making Ta-Amenta a heaven on earth. And it is here where we proudly acknowledge the completion of one phase of life by our younger people and welcome them into another. On. The city of light. It is here where we are all reborn.

Upon approaching our greatest of cities, we turn our heads in unison, watching as Menmens from all corners of Ta-Amenta converged on the Great temple of Ipet Iset. This is the temple used by Ntiu Tut to ceremonially bring the graduates of the Wehemi Mesu into adulthood.

Ipet Iset is a magnificent structure. It is built of stone, gold, and platinum. Polished to perfection. It is said that on a clear afternoon one can see its shinning walls from the eastern shores of Ta-Amenta. It has two great doors. One for going in... the other for leaving. For starting a new life. The interior resembles an immense auditorium. It has a center stage made of pure silver. On either side of the circular stage sit two aisles of platinum. The left aisle leads from the chamber of youth. That's where the graduating brothas and sistahs wait nervously. To the right of the stage is the great chamber of rebirth. After meeting with the Regional Instructor at the center of the stage and having received his or her 'third eye,' the person exits through the right corridor and enters the chamber of rebirth.

In the chamber of rebirth, there is a platinum pool of the purest of water. The new adult must walk through unaided. Upon reaching the other side of the pool, they are given their Incarnation Objective. Having received it, they qualify to continue their studies, and move on to adulthood.

It was this way before I was born. And it shall remain so long after my body has returned to dust. So be it.

We have reached the last Menmen Station. It directly faces the Temple of Ipet Iset. As its metal doors swung open, we were greeted by the beautiful light of the golden rays of Aten. In fantastic spirits, we exit the mechanical world of the Menmen, and step into the natural world of Ta-Amentan time and space. We greet one another with pride and good wishes. We have come a long way. On days like this, we recognize the sacrifice of our ancestors by keeping their spirits alive through our culture and traditions, passing them onto our youth. It is our belief, that as long as we continue the dreams of our ancestors, then we as a people will never die.

In rows of 20 persons, we walked the mighty aisles leading up to Ipet Iset. Family members greet one another along the way. Hugs and kisses, tears of joy, and shouts of praise sound off all around me. My own heart quickens because soon I will bear witness to the continuation of my beloved countrymen.

"Kashta," I heard in that familiar and melodic voice. Turning, my heart rejoiced to see Tefnut. She was dressed in traditional ceremonial attire. Blue and white. She was stunning. It's been a long time since I've seen her dressed thusly. I'd forgotten how beautiful she is. "You look good," she said.

"Hetepu, my sister," I returned. "You look like Auset." I couldn't take my eyes off her. I felt the only thing to do was to embrace her. So I did. Holding her in my arms the way I did brought images and feelings that were both old and new at the same time. It felt as if we'd been here before... like two old spirits greeting each other after a long, long night....

www.ingramcontent.com/pod-product-compliance
Lightning Source LLC
Chambersburg PA
CBHW050503260626
47157CB00004B/1169